Zulie had told Zag: she was going to spell the whites, badmouth them, bring trouble to Sabrehill.

Something bad, very bad, was going to happen.

There was Mr Ash, the white man in whose bed she now lay and whose hand now strayed to her breast. The very moment she had first seen him, she had known that he was more of the trouble she had asked for, trouble for Sabrehill. Miss Lucy was obviously entranced by Mr Ash, whether she knew it or not; but she, Zulie, would take him from Miss Lucy, and how the white bitch would suffer! Scorned for a black conjurewoman!

Mr Ash would buy his Zulie, steal her, do anything he had to do to get her away from Miss Lucy and take her to Charleston. And *he*, not she, would be the slave.

By the same author

Sabrehill
Rebels of Sabrehill
Storm over Sabrehill
Hellcat of Sabrehill

RAYMOND GILES

Slaves of Sabrehill

PANTHER
Granada Publishing

Panther Books
Granada Publishing Ltd
8 Grafton Street, London W1X 3LA

First published in Great Britain by
Panther Books 1984
Reprinted 1985

Copyright © Fawcett Publications, Inc. 1975

ISBN 0-586-06127-4

Printed and bound in Great Britain by
Collins, Glasgow

Set in Times

Once again –
for Maggie

Part One

1

No one saw them coming.

They drifted past Sabrehill and the Devereau plantation in the waning light, but they were as elusive as shadows. If a patrol had spotted them – two mulattoes, apparently, and a full-blooded black, armed and without identification or passes – there would have been trouble, and men would have died then and there. But no one saw them, not even the hands leaving the fields. They might as well have been invisible.

By the time they reached the Buckridge plantation, it was dark, but nevertheless they waited in a small, thickly wooded grove, patient and still unseen. Only much later, when the lights began to go out here and there around the mansion, did they at last leave the grove.

Quinn led the way – a file of three riders moving unhurriedly through the stifling night. Under his mask, sweat poured down through his thick beard. His nerves were drawn tight, but there was no fear. With every sense concentrated on the raid, there was no room left in him for fear.

They were seen at last. A few house servants, on their way to their own quarters, moved fearfully, silently, off into the darkness. Perhaps the masks were seen in the night, perhaps not. No alarm was sounded.

The three riders walked their horses right up to the house. They dismounted and hitched to a post. They stepped up to the door as boldly as if they were invited guests.

Quinn drew one of his two flintlock pistols. The door was closed but, he found, not yet locked. Flinging it open, he stepped swiftly into the big central hallway. The raid had begun.

A single dim light burned in the hallway. That was good; it left the area shadowed, and the stain on Quinn's and Harpe's hands and foreheads was less apt to be seen for what it was. Quinn hoped that they might seem as black as Xenos, the third man in their party.

There was no sign that they had been heard. Harpe laughed. 'Nobody home?'

'There'd better be,' Quinn said. 'We need a hostage.'

That was how Quinn liked to work: get in, grab a hostage, and get out fast. Take a woman, preferably, and release her – raped, beaten, terrorized – a day or two later. The terror was as important to Quinn's future plans as any silver or gold he might steal.

He turned at the sound of footsteps. It was an elderly black female house servant coming down the stairs, and she was nearly with them before she realized they were there. The instant she saw them, she screamed. She turned and tried to run back up the stairs, but Xenos charged after her and dragged her down again. He jammed a pistol against her breast and said, 'Woman, no more!'

But a mere nigger, Quinn thought, didn't make much of a hostage.

They were in luck. The next person to appear was another woman, a white woman this time, quite likely the mistress of the house. She came out of one of the side rooms, and Harpe immediately grabbed her. She was a handsome bitch, Quinn noted with pleasure, and would do very well for his purposes. Her eyes rolled with fear, and she whimpered, but she didn't scream.

'Who's all in dis heah house?' he asked, waving his pistol in her face. He made his voice as thick with field accent as he could manage.

'Please . . .'

'Who all heah?'

'My husband. My son Royal. Abbie, my daughter.'

'Wheah deh?'

Before the woman could answer, a man of about fifty years and a youth in his early twenties entered the hallway from another side room. At the sight of the masks and guns, they froze. For an instant, Quinn thought the younger man was going to run, and he leveled his pistol to shoot him down, but the moment passed. The older man, his face as gray as his mustache, began to sputter some inane objection but immediately fell silent as Quinn brought his pistol to bear on him.

'Duh gal and dese heah, dat all?'

'Yes,' the woman said. 'Please, please don't – '

'Wheah duh gal?'

'In her room, but – '

'Don't you touch her, God damn you!' Buckridge roared. 'Don't you dare touch her!'

Stepping forward, Quinn swung his pistol hard, laying the heavy barrel alongside the man's head. There was a sharp popping sound. Buckridge fell back against the wall, his eyes slowly rolling up in his head and then closing, and blood began to pour out of his hair. By some miracle he managed to stay on his feet. While the two women sobbed, Quinn swung the pistol toward young Royal just long enough to let him know what would happen if he moved.

The girl. In her room, the woman had said.

Quinn ran up the stairs. He had just reached the upper hallway when the girl stepped out of her room. She cried out just once as they stood there, almost touching, staring at each other in the dim light from the bedroom. For almost half a minute they stared.

And then, somehow, Quinn knew. Whatever came next, it could not end well for this girl.

She, and not the older woman, would be their hostage,

of course. There was no question, this girl had to be, she was so perfect for the role, so doomed to it. She was no more than sixteen, and small for her age and delicate and lovely. She wore only a thin cotton nightgown and slippers, and there was already terror in her wide, dark-brown eyes. Terror and doom.

She was a victim, and meant to be a victim, and they both knew it. Quinn felt a sudden wave of pity for the girl. It was a feeling he often had for those he was going to hurt – and it saved no one.

He almost said, *I'm sorry*.

But she would never know that. Seizing her around the waist, Quinn half-carried and half-dragged her down the stairs. In the lower hallway, he backed into a corner, holding the girl in front of him, her back to his chest. With both his hand and his chest he felt her heart pounding as he put the muzzle of his pistol to her temple.

'You move,' he said, 'I gon'kill dis heah gal.'

The rest was easy.

As always, Quinn had approached the raid with a certain sense of fatality. Either he would collect a bullet, or he wouldn't. Either he would wind up at the end of a rope, or he would escape. Now, however, he felt completely in control. It was impossible to do much in the way of planning a raid such as this, but now he felt that whatever might happen, he would be able to improvise brilliantly.

The other members of the family and the house servant huddled together in a far corner of the hallway, their eyes always on Quinn and the girl. Harpe and Xenos, meanwhile, looted the house, ripping, tearing, and smashing as they went. It took only minutes to locate the silver, the few gold pieces, and what money and gem stones were kept in the house.

Xenos came down the stairs with a loaded sack.

'Got it all, Mr Quinn,' he said.

12

That was a mistake. Quinn nearly shot him on the spot.

Instead, he said, 'Good. Now, burn down this heah place.' Mrs. Buckridge wailed, and Quinn repeated: 'Burn it!'

Harpe and Xenos had already smashed out most of the windows. Now they went from one to another setting curtains and drapes on fire. The place would soon be an inferno.

As long as he held a gun to the girl's head, Quinn was certain that the rest of the family would not dare any kind of defiance. He proved to be right. They docilely obeyed as he ordered them to leave the burning mansion and lead the way to the stables. A number of blacks were now lurking in the shadows, and Quinn knew that the overseer had to be somewhere nearby, but Buckridge shouted that no one was to fire a shot, no one was to do a thing.

Quinn kept the gun on the terrified girl. Harpe and Xenos followed them, carrying the loot and leading the horses.

They took two Buckridge horses, one to pack the loot, the other for the girl. But for their departure from the plantation, Quinn lifted the girl into his own saddle.

'You don' follow, patrol don' follow, one whole day,' he ordered. 'Den we let her go. Oderwise, she die!'

Then, calmly, unhurriedly, the raiders and their hostage rode off into the night.

2

Fire!

The moment the alarm began, a repeated hysterical strident ringing, Zagreus was out of his bed. He fought sleep as if it were a blanket thrown over his head, fought it off and reached for his clothes.

Fire!

The alarm never ceased, never slowed. Fire was the most dreaded destroyer of the countryside, feared every bit as much as insurrectionists and land pirates. And the most dreaded sound was that of the alarm.

Still fastening his clothes, Zag hurried down the stairs from his room over the coach house. Outside, standing in the east service lane, he could see no red glow anywhere in the sky. Perhaps, just perhaps, the fire was not at Sabrehill. Zag ran along the lane toward the big-house courtyard.

Others, as fast as he, were already gathering – carpenter, blacksmith, gardener, all those who lived closest to the big house. Jebediah Hayes, the black overseer, continued to pound the alarm, a triangle of metal that hung at one side of the courtyard. Looking around, Zag saw Miss Lucy, the mistress of Sabrehill, emerging from the big house. Even in the dark of night he could see that she was frightened. 'Jebediah,' she said, 'what is it? What's burning?'

'Not here, Miss Lucy – '

'Oh, thank God!'

'It's at the Buckridge plantation – they just sent a rider by. But it's worse than that, Miss Lucy. They were raided, most likely by renegades. And the raiders not only started the fire, they carried Miss Abigail off.'

Miss Lucy's hands went to her face, and the fright in her

eyes became even greater. She knew what could happen to a white woman, indeed to any woman, at the hands of renegades.

'Jebediah, we've got to help!'

'Of course, ma'am.'

'Do anything you can, anything at all!'

Irish, the house boy, came running across the courtyard. Jeb handed him the hammer and told him to keep on pounding the alarm. 'I want every hand on this plantation awake whether he means to help or not. Zag, the alarm in the quarters isn't ringing yet – get someone on it. You other men, you women – you know what to do?'

They knew. The fire drill had been pounded into them since childhood, pounded into them so that they would never forget. They had been told repeatedly that one day their lives and the lives of others might depend on it.

Wagons had to be rolled out. Teams had to be hitched. Buckets and barrels had to be collected and loaded and then taken on the long, fast drive past thousands of Sabrehill and Devereau acres until at last they reached the Buckridge plantation.

Men had to be transported to the fire. There would not be enough transportation for all, and wagons would be raced back and forth through the night, picking up those hands who walked part of the distance. There would be no time for passes tonight and no thought of patrols. A plantation mansion was burning.

Zag got the alarm in the field quarters going. With others of foreman, or driver, rank, he went from cabin to cabin, making sure that every three-quarter and full hand was up. He knew, of course, that in spite of all the teaching and warnings and drills, not all of the hands would be of help. Some would slack off. Others might dare actively to sabotage efforts to fight the fire. There was many a hand on Sabrehill and the other plantations of the region who would dearly love to see a white master's house burn – any white master's house.

With the hands up and out of the cabins, Zag hitched teams and loaded wagons, assisted mainly by his two younger brothers. Though he had already put in a hard day's work, he never paused, never rested, and before long he was bathed in sweat. Jeb Hayes, the overseer, went on ahead to the fire, and Zag took over the job of dispatching the wagons. Then finally, the last wagon was ready and Zag himself drove it toward the Buckridge plantation.

'Oo, ain't that pretty,' said a voice in the wagon behind him when a pink glow showed in the night sky. It was Paris, the younger of Zag's brothers.

'Mm-mm!' said the other brother, Orion. 'Look like we too late, Zag. Might just well let'r burn now. But Paris sure right. Mighty pretty fire.'

'You don't let no white folks hear you talking like that,' Zag said. 'Nigger starts talking that way about fire, he gonna get whipped or even hung.'

'You help put out fire, Zag?' Paris asked.

'You damn right I going help.'

Orion laughed. 'You see that? Old Zag, he in charge of stable and coach house now, he talk more like a big-house nigger all the time.'

'Talk like one, smell like one,' Paris agreed.

'All I say is, don't let white folks hear you talk like that.' Zag insisted. 'I don't want nothing bad happening to you.'

'Sound like Momma Lucinda,' Orion mocked, referring to the big-house cook. ' "Now, don't you say that! Don't you talk like that, you hear me!" '

'Momma Zagreus,' Paris agreed. 'Just don't ask me help you with no fire, Momma Zag.'

'Honey boy,' Zag said cheerfully, 'I'm going work your tail off.'

Hands from at least two other nearby plantations were

16

already there when Zag and his brothers arrived. Mr Paul Devereau, in shirt sleeves, was driving a wagon full of hands around to the river side of the blazing mansion. Major Kimbrough and young Quentin Kimbrough were directing the lines of bucket brigades and not hesitating to swing buckets themselves. There were times when even soft-palmed gentlemen planters ceased to sneer at physical toil.

'Zag!' Jeb yelled across the firelit Buckridge courtyard. 'Get that wagon down to the river. When you've unloaded, send Paris in the wagon back along the road to pick up hands. You and Orion help with the water.'

Rounding the house, Zag saw the Buckridge family. Mr Royal was driving kegs of water up from the river in a wagon. Mr Owen Buckridge appeared to be trying to organize another bucket brigade. Shaking his fists, sobbing, running about, he looked like a broken, ineffectual man, trapped in a nightmare. Miss Lucy, driven by Irish, had already arrived from Sabrehill, and Mrs Buckridge – Miss Callie – had collapsed into her arms.

Zag drove down to the landing. There Sabrehill's chief driver, a bald, rock-hard old warrior named Cheney, helped them unload, and Paris drove the wagon off. Cheney was filling kegs with river water and easily lifting the eighty pounds or more to a wagon bed, and Zag tried to find out if he could do as well. Orion joined one of the lines swinging buckets.

'Move that water!'

'Move those lines!'

'More water in the courtyard!'

'The office is burning! Where's that water?'

'More water over here!'

'Move it, damn you, move it!'

After the first swift couple of hours, the night seemed endless, and Zag thought his back was going to break. There were no rest periods. The hands worked until they

17

dropped, and then they were quickly urged back to work again. Zag saw several drivers going up and down the bucket lines wielding whips.

'More water! Get that water moving!'

'Water for the kitchen! Kitchen's going!'

Though the mansion stood close to the river, an inexhaustible supply of water, it soon became clear that little other than the foundation could be saved. Nevertheless, the fire had to be stopped for the sake of the surrounding outbuildings. Showers of sparks were raining down on barns, stables, mechanics' shops, storehouses, house servants' quarters, and a dozen other buildings. Several of them had caught fire already.

When Zag could no longer lift kegs, he carried buckets. Cheney had started with the kegs before him and had outlasted him, but even he had to change to the buckets after a time.

'Tell you what, Zag,' he said, 'you see that short line up there, swinging the buckets, got to have water brought to 'em? I take more water to 'em than you do – more and faster!'

It was a challenge Zag badly needed. It somehow lightened the task and speeded the work, and he had about decided that after tonight he was going to be a cripple for life. And so the two men drove themselves, drove themselves and each other, up from the landing toward the house, and back again, time after time, aching, groaning, laughing, sobbing, but never stopping.

Until Zag dropped.

For a time, perhaps only a moment or two, he was unconscious. Then he realized what had happened, and he began to laugh, softly and hysterically. He was angry with himself for having lost the game, and yet relieved – relieved that for the moment, at least, the game was over.

His laughter turned to a short, hard scream as a whip streaked like fire across his shoulders.

'Damn you, boy,' someone roared. 'God damn you!'

The whip cut across his shoulders again.

His first thought was that Cheney was whipping him for falling down on the job. But that didn't make sense. Cheney could be mean, but not like that. And the chief driver hadn't even been carrying a whip.

As Zag struggled to his knees, the whip came down a third time.

'Get to your feet, nigger, you hear me, damn you?'

No, that wasn't Cheney. Cheney, rushing on with his buckets, was nowhere in sight. The black man now raising the whip for the fourth time was no one Zag had ever seen before. He was probably one of the Buckridge drivers.

'Get to your feet, I said!'

A tide of anger brought fresh strength to Zag. He had been working for hours to help save the fire-gutted Buckridge mansion and its outbuildings, he had worked himself to exhaustion, he had worked until he had passed out. And now this Buckridge bastard was putting the whip to him.

'Nigger,' he said, climbing to his feet, 'I think I'm just going to kill you.'

Not in all of his years in the fields had Zag ever said such a thing to a driver. Behind his back, yes, but not to his face. You simply did not do that, because the driver was the strong punishing arm of the overseer and the master – of the white people. And you did not defy the white people, you did not threaten them. To do so meant the whipping post, mutilation, possibly death.

That Zag should take such a risk, then, suggested that he really was angry enough, or insane enough, to kill.

He took one step, and the driver's eyes widened with fear. He took another, and he heard the hiss of the whip through the air. It took him low across the forehead, and suddenly he could no longer see.

If he had not been out of control before, he was now:

19

the pain and the blindness maddened him. With a cry of rage he threw himself in the direction he had last seen the driver. His hands tore at a shirt, clawed at flesh. The driver slipped away, and the whip kept falling. Zag swung a fist backhand and hit someone, hit something. The driver was calling a name, calling for help. Zag hurled himself at the voice and found a throat.

And then, as quickly as it had begun, it was over.

Someone had torn him away from the driver, and his sight was clearing, though blood streamed down his face. 'I kill him,' the driver was screaming, 'I kill him!'

But Jeb Hayes, Sabrehill's black overseer, was holding the man back – holding him easily by gripping his whip arm in one big fist.

'No,' he said quietly, 'you are not going to kill him. And you are not going to whip him anymore. Do you hear me?'

'I kill – '

Zag saw Jeb's grip tighten on the driver's arm, and the driver gasped with pain.

'No,' Jeb said. 'You'll kill nobody. And you will not whip any Sabrehill people, you understand? If you're going to whip, you whip your own. But not Sabrehill people.'

Now the driver had a new object of fright. He didn't like the once-handsome whip-blazed face that looked down at him. He didn't like the smile on that face or the soft voice or the grip of his arm. Zag didn't blame him. He wouldn't have liked them either.

'God damn you, nigger,' the driver whined, 'goddamn stinking nigger.'

Jeb laughed softly. 'Now, is that any way for one black man to talk to another?'

'Going call Mr Dwyer, going call Mr Buckridge, get them after you, Mr Dwyer going – '

'You just remember, keep your whip off of my people.'

'Going call Mr Dwyer – '

'You don't have to,' a white man said. 'Mr Dwyer is here. What the hell is going on? Nigger, let go of my boy's arm.'

Jeb's fingers slowly loosened on the driver's arm and slipped away. This white man, Mr Dwyer, was almost certainly the overseer of the Buckridge plantation. He was a wiry man with long brown hair and a short beard. The eyes behind the steel-rimmed glasses were hard and angry.

'Your *boy* Mr Dwyer, sir,' Jeb said quietly, 'was whipping my man.'

'Then he musta had it coming. *Your* man, you said?'

'I'm the overseer at Sabre – '

'I know who you are. As far as I'm concerned, you're just another nigger, and you'd damn well better get *your* hands working, or I'll beat their lazy asses and yours, too.'

Zag saw something flicker in Jeb's eyes, something that could be dangerous – to all of them.

'You right, master, sir,' he said, a mocking hint of field accent in his voice, 'you sho' right. Sabrehill got a lot o' lazy nigger, sir. Now, s'pose I just send all the lazy ones home, and you see how many you got left to fight the fire, master, sir.'

'God damn, nigger, are you getting snotty with me? I always heard you was snotty!' Red-faced, Mr Dwyer stepped toward Jeb, raising a fist as if to strike. 'I don't take no nigger shit – '

Jeb didn't seem to hear him. He turned to Zag. 'Zag, what happened? Why did this boy whip you?'

'I passed out, Mr Jeb. I done work so long and hard, I just plain passed out. Then I was starting to rouse out of it, and that there – '

'That ain't true!' the driver interrupted. 'He was just lying there on the ground laughing. We all, we working our asses off, trying to save the big house and the kitchen and all, and this here nigger is laughing his goddamn head off!'

'Not laughing at *you!*' Zag protested. 'Laughing 'cause I hurt so much. Don't laugh, you got to cry! But I work hard

21

as anybody! Don't spend my time with a goddamn whip in my hand. *I work!*'

Cheney had arrived back from the house. 'This is sure the gospel truth, Jeb,' he said. 'Mr Dwyer, sir, I never in my born days see no darky work harder'n this here boy. Now, me, I been working with him all night, side by side we been – '

'*All right, God damn it, who do I have to kill?*'

The voice was vicious, ugly, like a rusty knife. Zag, and the others, turned toward it. A half-dozen paces away stood Mr Owen Buckridge, aiming a pistol at them. His eyes, catching the light of flames, were mad.

'Who do I have to kill, I say?'

'Mr Buckridge,' Mr Dwyer said nervously, 'we just had a little trouble – '

'Goddamn fire is burning down my house, and a bunch of niggers stand around and jabber!'

'I'm just getting them back to work – '

'What's the matter with you, Mr Dwyer? You don't know how to work hands? You want my house to burn down?'

'Mr Buckridge – '

'Just tell me, God damn it, *who do I have to kill?*'

'Get the hell back to work, you damn niggers,' Mr Dwyer said nervously. 'Get your black asses moving. But remember, we all are going to settle this later. *Move*, now!'

The group dispersed. As Zag looked back over his shoulder, Mr Buckridge turned away and wept.

'All right, what happened?'

'It was just like I said, Jeb. I just plain passed out. And the next thing I know, that damn driver is whipping hell out of me. Don't know why he had to do that.'

'Because a house was burning, and he was scared. Scared that it might seem that he wasn't driving hard

22

enough to stop the fire. Scared of his overseer and scared of his master. Don't blame him too much, Zagreus.'

'Don't blame him, shit!'

The wagon, loaded with hands, swayed and bumped along the road back to Sabrehill. Jeb drove, and Zag sat on the seat beside him. Dawn had come and gone – it was well past 'day clean' – and this was the first chance they had had to discuss the whipping incident.

'Guess I got me a peck of trouble, don't I?' Zag said.

'Could be you got some. Is it true that you said you'd kill that driver?'

So Jeb had been asking some questions. 'He said he'd kill me, too,' Zag said nervously.

'Yes, but you threatened him first, the way I heard it.'

'Only after he whipped me. Jebediah, I was doing my very best.'

'I believe you.' Jeb was silent for a moment, thoughtful. 'Zagreus, don't you go talking about this to a lot of people. Let it die down. When we get back to Sabrehill, you get yourself a good rest, and then we'll go see Miss Lucy. She may talk soft, but when she gets her back up, taking care of her own, she can be tougher than a goddamn swamp 'gator as I have cause to know. I don't think you have too much reason to worry.'

Zag immediately felt a degree of relief. If Jebediah Hayes said it, it must be true.

It was hard for Zag, at twenty-seven, to remember that Jeb was four years younger than himself. It wasn't simply that Jeb was physically so big and looked considerably older than his years. It was the dignity with which he carried himself, and his obvious intelligence. Since he had become Miss Lucy's right-hand man, people just naturally found themselves addressing him from time to time as *Mister* Jeb, even if he was black. Even those hands who didn't like him – and there were those who called him a 'white man's nigger' – were forced to defer to his dignity.

23

Zag was one of those who did like him, liked him very much. He felt a great deal of admiration for Jeb and in recent months had taken him as a kind of model. Jeb could read and write, it was said, and he could talk big-house talk as well as any white man. It was rumored that he had been brought up in a plantation mansion, but Zag knew for a fact that he had been a field hand and a rebel. And no master, no overseer, had ever been quite able to break him. His back was a mass of scars, he had a whip blaze slanting across his face, and he walked with a limp – but he remained forever 'that damned snotty Sabrehill nigger!'

And somehow he had become overseer of one of the finest plantations in South Carolina.

Well, Zag had thought, if Jeb could do it, so could he.

Not become overseer – no, Jeb had arrived there first, and besides that was too bold a dream. But he could rise in position and status. He could be something more than a good field hand and an accomplished stud.

There were those at Sabrehill who derived their superior status from being troublemakers and rebels, and their number had increased in recent years, but Zag liked Jeb and Miss Lucy too much to join them. There were others who went in the opposite direction and became drivers, or gang foremen, but Zag had no taste for the authority of the whip. He much preferred the authority of special knowledge and skills. That was to be his way to rise.

From childhood Zag had loved animals, and horses most especially. Long before he was old enough to be of help, he had hung around them, much to the annoyance of Old Walter, who was in charge of the stable and the coach house. Even after he began working full days in the fields, Zag spent late evening hours and weekends with his beloved horses, grooming them, cleaning harness, fastening onto all of Old Walter's lore. Old Walter had his own assistants, and Zag had other rivals, but they all died or lost interest or otherwise faded away. Only Zag had remained faithful.

He had remained faithful, that is, until a few years ago when his woman died in childbirth. That had taken the heart out of Zag. It had seemed to him that there was no longer anything worth working for, nothing worth rebelling against, and no consolation in his horses. Thereafter he had simply done enough work in the fields to avoid the whips – most of the time – and taken his consolation from women and whatever liquor he could get his hands on.

Jeb's example, and Zag's admiration for him, had changed all that. Soon after Jeb had taken over the management of Sabrehill, Zag had returned to the stables. Working as hard as he ever had in his life, he had resurrected his old skills and knowledge. And when, a few months ago, Old Walter had announced his retirement – had said that he was sick to death of goddamn mules and horses and intended never to do another lick of work for the rest of his life – Zag had immediately gone to Jeb and asked for the job. And got it.

Now he continued to work hard. He strove to drop his field accent and to talk better big-house language – to talk like Jeb – because he knew it was shrewd to do so. It made communication easier, and it was a symbol of his new status. He had learned a little reading and writing as a child from Miss Lucy's tutor – though it was unlawful to teach a slave – and now he hoped to improve and enlarge upon that knowledge. Such skills were useful, and, again, they signified status. Like Jeb, he would have pride. He would have dignity. Someday he might even marry again and raise a family. A man had to take what was at hand and see what he could do with it. He would, by God, make himself a life.

At last the long weary trip back to Sabrehill was over. As the wagon pulled into the east service lane, the hands it was carrying dropped off of the back and walked heavy-footed toward the field quarters. Jeb pulled up by a wagon shed, and Zag climbed down from the seat to unhitch.

He and Jeb did it together. When he was about to clean the harness and hang it up, Jeb said, 'Don't bother. I'll get someone else to do it. Everybody who worked last night – who really put his back into it – he gets the day off.'

'But how you know who all did?' Zag asked, pleased.

Jeb smiled. 'Don't you worry. I know. You go find yourself some breakfast and a rest.'

That was about all Zag wanted at the moment. That and maybe a woman. Yes, definitely he would like a woman. For some reason hard physical work brought on the need.

But the first thing he did was head for a nearby well where he and several others took turns pouring buckets of water over each other. Then, feeling halfway free of soot and grime, he headed for the big-house kitchen.

The sun was well up by that time, the day was bright and hot, and the buildings along the east and west service lanes were almost blindingly white. The cupola that crowned the two-and-a-half story mansion glittered in the sun. Sheep were grazing lazily on the grass in the middle of the circular courtyard that lay here on the north side of the mansion. The plantation office and the kitchen winged off from the mansion, northeast and northwest respectively, each connected to the main building by a portico. Noting that Miss Lucy was in the office, Zag crossed the courtyard to the kitchen.

Momma Lucinda, the cook, saw him coming, and she frowned as he got closer. She was a strong, handsome woman of about forty, and the way Zag felt now, he couldn't help noticing that she had a good body.

'You got a stripe on your head,' she said. She announced the fact as if he might not know it and ought to be told.

'That's right, Momma Lucinda.'

'Then it's true what I heard, that you tangled with a Buckridge driver name of Nemo?'

'Don't know his name.'

Momma Lucinda shook her head. 'Zagreus, you're a good boy. How come you got to get yourself in trouble?'

'Ain't in no trouble, Momma,' Zag said uneasily. 'Got Jeb on my side, and if I got him I got Miss Lucy, and if I got Miss Lucy I ain't in no trouble. Ain't that right?'

'You just stay out of it.'

'Got something for me to eat, Momma?'

She served him a plate of last night's stew and a big mug of milk. He sampled them and found them delicious.

'Is it true what they say,' Momma Lucinda asked, 'that they done carried poor Miss Abigail off?'

'Reckon it is, Momma. Reckon they won't be seeing her no more.'

'Now, don't you say that! Just don't you talk like that!'

Zag laughed. Orion was right: Momma Lucinda was a great one for telling people not to say and not to do.

He ate sitting on the west steps of the kitchen, where he would not be seen by any guests coming up the long oak-lined avenue that led from the road to the courtyard. When he was finished, he made a trip to a 'necessary house,' and then at last returned to his room over the coach house.

He was proud of the room. Formerly one of several used to store old harnesses and other gear, he had cleaned it out and plastered and painted the interior walls himself. It had two large, glazed windows, and with the carpenter's help – and Miss Lucy's blessing – he had built his own bed, as large and comfortable as any he had ever known, and Miss Lucy had provided his other furnishings: cabinet, table, chairs, even a couple of pictures to hang on the wall. The place was hotter than hell in the summer, of course, but, outside of the big house, what quarters were not? Come fall, he would devise himself a fireplace to keep the room snug in the winter.

His sister, Erzulie, he saw as he climbed the stairs, was

waiting for him. She glanced at him, then looked again, harder, and pain grew in her eyes.

'They cut your face,' she said.

'It's all right, Zulie. It ain't bleeding no more.'

'I hear how they whip you. Don't hear they cut your face.' Zag stood still while Zulie inspected the cut, touching it with gentle fingers. 'How many stripes they give you, Zag?'

'I don't know. Didn't count.'

She began unfastening his shirt. 'Take off your clothes. I got medicine in case you need it.'

'Voodoo medicine?'

'Medicine.'

Zag shed clothes and boots, glad to be rid of them. A faint breeze swept through the open windows somewhat relieving the heat. He wanted only to be alone, to lie down and sleep, but first he had to yield to his sister's ministrations.

'Six stripes,' she said, inspecting him. 'Six good ones, anyway. Maybe a couple not so good. I see you working your butt off for them Buckridges, and they stripe you. Put a scar on your face.'

'Don't matter, Zulie.' Now, several hours later, having calmed down, Zag really did feel that the incident was minor, as long as it did not lead to further trouble. Basically, he was an easygoing person with no inclination to harbor grudges. He wondered if his new scar might not look rather impressive; he had always thought that Jeb's did something for him.

'Gonna put some medicines on you right quick,' Zulie said, 'then I got to get back to work.'

'How come you got to work?' Zag asked, surprised. 'You was there at the fire last night.'

'Well, Zag, honey, you know your little sister here ain't very strong. And I'm just as clumsy as I can be! And there I was in that line, passing buckets of water along, and somehow I got to dropping more buckets than I passed. I swear to you, Zag, honey, I tried, I really did try, but I guess I just dropped more buckets of water than anybody last night! And finally that Mr Dwyer, he was jumping up and down, and he was screaming at me, and he kicked my little old ass back here to Sabrehill and gave it a nice night's sleep.'

Zag laughed. It was quite untrue that his sister was either weak or clumsy. Less than a year younger than he, she was almost as tall and almost as broad in the shoulders. The only fat on her body was in her generous, pointed breasts, carried high on a deep chest, and her long, shapely legs could carry her at a run from daybreak to dusk. Furthermore, she moved with the grace of a cat, and she had a punch that could floor any man.

She was also, Zag thought, very beautiful. Her head seemed small for her big, strong body, and it gave her a doll-like quality in spite of her size. Full-lipped, with long arching brows over large eyes, her features were delicately, exquisitely sculpted. Her hair was a tight black skull cap, and she usually covered it with a colorful handkerchief, which served to intensify her beauty.

Zag loved her, though love was a word he rarely used. Since the death of Cissie, his wife, she and his two brothers were the only people in the world he did truly love. And he had complete faith that they loved him in return. They held differing views, they often quarreled, they mocked and teased each other. Yet they remained a family – ready, if need be, to die for each other.

But he and Zulie had always been especially close. As babies, they had slept in the same crib. They had played naked in the dust together, put on their first shirts together, grown up together. Like many another close brother and sister, they had discovered and explored their sexuality together, and briefly, more than a dozen years ago, they had been lovers – each the other's never-to-be-forgotten first. Zag looked back on the affair with amusement – it had been as much comedy as passion and vastly entertaining. Their mother, who had been quite aware of what was going on, had soon separated them, instructed them, and sent them on their ways to whatever loves might await them. Only a few times after that had they lapsed back to their childhood 'game,' but the bond between them remained.

And so Zag put up with Zulie's mothering. He let her apply her magical ointments and mutter her little incantations even though he thought he didn't really need them. At least these ointments didn't smell bad, as some of them did. In fact, in their light, spicy way they were very nice.

'There,' Zulie said when she was finished, 'now the stripes go away, and you don't fever, and maybe the mark on your face don't get so bad.'

'I thank you, Zulie.'

Groaning, Zag stretched himself out naked on his bed. Fortunately the stripes on his back were not so bad that he could not lie on it. He was damp with sweat, but the breeze felt good, and now at last he would get some sleep.

But Zulie was not ready to let him sleep. She looked down on him fondly and admiringly for a minute. Then she sat down on the bed and stretched out beside him, propped up on an elbow. Zag wished she would go away. Not only did he want to sleep, but with his need, it was disturbing to have her so close.

Zulie put fingertips lightly on his chest. 'Zag, honey,' she said, 'I'm going to do something for you.'

Zag closed his eyes. 'What's that?'

'Going make old Buckridge pay back for that scar on your face. Buckridge and Dwyer and Nemo and all them over there.'

'Aw, Zulie, you ain't going do nothing – '

'Going fix them all.'

'You just let Jebediah and Miss Lucy take care of

30

everything. They fix everything, won't be no more trouble –'

'They ain't going see that Miss Abigail no more. That's the first thing – '

'What do you mean?' Zag opened his eyes. 'Guess they ain't going see her, but what that got to do with you?'

'Going make sure. Going put a spell on her.'

'Now, you shut up that talk!' Alarmed, Zag sat up on the bed. 'You ain't going put no voodoo badmouth on nobody! No voodoo, no obeah, no nothing like that!'

Zulie's eyes hardened defiantly. 'Maybe I already done it.'

'Then you take it off.'

'Maybe I can't.'

'You do it! Zulie, ain't no harm in a little witch medicine, little voodoo love charm, nobody mind that. But you go putting voodoo badmouth on white folks, you going get yourself killed!'

'Ain't neither – '

'Momma Lucinda told me about witches that got burned when she was a little girl, one right in Charleston. She told me about witches got hung!'

'Who going know – '

'Zulie, remember what our momma told us about badmouth? If you don't take care, if you use it wrong, it comes back like light from a mirror. Turns on you. Does worse to you than to your enemy. And that Miss Abigail ain't no enemy at all. What she do to you?'

'She's white,' Zulie said sullenly.

Zag shook his head with disgust. 'She ain't no more'n a child. Now, Zulie, you take that spell off.'

'Put plenty of spells here at Sabrehill that didn't come back at me. Put one on that Mr Turnage, remember that? That didn't come back at me.'

'Zulie, you got to take that spell off!'

Zulie's shoulders slumped. 'Didn't put it on yet.'

31

'And you ain't going to. You got to promise me.'
Zulie did not answer.
'Promise!'
'. . . Promise.'
Zag sighed with relief and fell back on the bed. He wasn't certain how much he believed in Zulie's powers. As a child, he had believed absolutely in their mother's – Momma Erzulie's – voodoo powers, and it did seem that Zulie's medicines often helped to heal. Certainly, she had a large following on the plantation, though was not without rivals. But her curses? Zag was at one and the same time afraid of them and afraid to believe in them. But most of all he was afraid that they would bring her harm from the white people of the countryside.

'Zag,' Zulie said after a minute, 'you mad at me?'
'Course I ain't mad at you.'
'Only wanted to do it for you.'
'I know that. Only you remember your promise.'
There was another minute or two of silence. The breeze through the hot room was delightful. Zag closed his eyes and at once began to drift off into sleep.

And then Zulie got her revenge.
One moment she was lying on the bed beside Zag. He felt her weight shift. Then, as he opened his eyes, she was over him, grinning down at him from arm's length. Her thighs gripped his, and her long fingers attacked his ribs.

'Don't want no help from Zulie, huh? Don't allow no badmouth!'
Zag burst with painful laughter and, all male, reacted instantly to her closeness. 'Zulie, you stop that!'
'Make Zulie promise no spell – '
'You stop!'
But she didn't stop. As he tried to thrust her aside, she gripped his wrists with amazing strength, and when he tried to buck her off, her legs encircled his.

'Don't want to stop. Why you want me to stop, Zag?'

32

'Damn you, woman!'

'Don't you like your Zulie?'

He at last freed one wrist. When he returned the tickling, Zulie shrieked and kicked free of him and rolled away, laughing, to one side.

'Oh, Zag, honey!'

Zag looked down at his maddeningly independent flesh and groaned. 'Now look what you done.'

Zulie continued to howl. 'Yeah, would you look at that!'

'Zulie, you are a mean woman.'

'Mean! Why Zag, honey, ain't I always nice to you? Your Zulie love you, you know that.' She reached out to fondle him, and he batted her hand away. 'What's the matter, Zaggie, you don't like your Zulie no more?'

'Go away, woman, just go away.'

'Poor Zag.'

Zulie controlled her laughter. Sitting up on the bed, she stroked Zag's forehead for a moment.

'I'm sorry, Zag.'

Zag didn't answer.

'Sure you don't want a little pleasure with Zulie'

'We're too old for that. That's for pickaninnies.'

'Didn't say that the last time.'

'Last time was long ago.'

Zulie got up from the bed. 'Tell you what. To show you I ain't really a mean woman, I'm going to do something for you.'

Zag groaned. 'Just haul your ass away from here, will you Zulie?' The way he felt now, he wasn't sure he would ever sleep again.

'Now, don't you be mad with Zulie. 'Cause she's going send you something nice and sweet, make you feel happy again. You just wait. Bye-bye, now!'

Zag closed his eyes again and tried to relax – though it seemed quite impossible under the circumstances. He heard Zulie going down the stairs, and he assumed that she was going to send him one of his girls. Good enough. He would be grateful. But while she liked to believe that it was her voodoo powers that made her successful in this procuring, Zag was inclined to think that his own attractiveness might have something to do with it.

It was, of course, fitting that he should be attractive to women. He was the son of Momma Erzulie – priestess, witch, *mamaloi* – who was named for one of the *loa*: for Erzulie, the goddess of love. His momma, on telling him he must stop his games with Zulie, had promised him great success with women, and he had had it.

But his successes seemed hollow now. Wistfully, he remembered how, as a boy, he had pursued girls with a great and infectious enthusiasm that had brought him many a conquest; how in turn he had delighted in being conquered.

And then one day he discovered Cissie.

She had been at Sabrehill all the time, of course. But, like Zag, she had been growing, ripening, for that particular day. And when it came, the games were over for both of them.

It was simple as that. Zag, who had been living in a barrack with other young unmarried men, found an empty cabin, small and ramshackle but salvageable, and they moved into it together. A field hand who called himself a preacher offered to say a blessing for them, and they accepted. They were man and wife.

The months that followed were the happiest of Zag's life. He and Cissie worked together in the fields. Their only worry was that Mr Turnage, then the overseer, might molest Cissie, and they did their best to avoid that. Zag redoubled his efforts to win a place in the stable and get out of the fields, taking Cissie, he hoped, with him. They repaired their cabin. They started their own garden. And they made love constantly.

Until that evil day when Cissie died in childbirth.

Zulie's magic could not save her. Mother and child both died, and Zag felt as lost as if he had gone with them. Finding that he could no longer live in the cabin – the memories there were at once too sweet and too agonizing – he burned it and everything in it. He was not whipped for the deed – Miss Lucy herself prevented Mr Turnage from doing that – but he would not have cared if he had been. Nothing mattered anymore.

And yet resurrection of a sort at last occurred. Jeb Hayes came to Sabrehill, and a few months later the two of them became friends. And from his own ashes and dried bones, Zag began to put himself together again.

But one thing could not be resurrected, and that was sex as it had been – sex, love, pleasure. As a boy he had found it exciting, playful, adventurous, an unlimited joy. But with Cissie he had gone beyond that, on to something that had bound them together and made them one, on to a shared ecstasy he had never before imagined. And having had that, it was impossible to go back. It was impossible to return to his former state of innocence. Oh, the impulse and the compulsion were still there, the want and the need, but when, months after Cissie's death, he at last yielded to them, the old joy was gone. There was pleasure, yes, and consolation, of a sort, and relief. But not joy.

And he didn't think he would ever find the joy again. No, that was finished for him, as finished as his own boyhood.

But pleasure was something, at least, and not to be scorned, and he could give as fully as he received. So he took what came his way, without often seeking it. His apparent indifference actually seemed to draw women to him.

'Zagreus?' a female voice called from down below. 'Zag, can I come up?'

He recognized the voice. It belonged to Vidette, a young, plumply pretty kitchen wench, who had worked hard at the Buckridge fire. She and Zag had had some good times together, and he was very fond of her.

'Come up if you want, honey.' It was his strict rule that his women should always ask first.

He heard footsteps on the stairs, and Vidette's head and shoulders came up through the open trapdoor.

'Zulie told me you so tired you can't sleep. Said whyn't I come over and see you a while – '

She broke off as she crossed the room and saw him lying naked on his bed, all too splendidly ready for her. Her eyes widened. She crossed her arms over her chest.

''Pears to me you taking one hell of a lot for granted!'

'Aw, hell, Vidette, I didn't tell Zulie to send you, not you nor any other. It was her own damn fool idea. Now, why don't you go away and let a man try to get some sleep.'

Vidette continued to stare at him for a minute, considering. Then she grinned.

'Oh, well,' she said, 'I just helped put out one fire. Reckon I can put out another.'

With a flourish, she tossed off her dress.

They watched the burning from a distance, flames that showed nothing but their own crimson and gold streaks and made the night seem all the blacker. After a time, they turned and rode away, not even shadows now, but part of the night. There was no longer need for masks. In that darkness, not even the girl, riding close by, could see them.

Now and then Quinn heard a whimper, a sob – the girl, but she never said a word.

He could not get over his persistent sense of her doom. Certainly it was not part of the plan that she should die. They would keep her a few hours, perhaps until just before dawn. Then they would do what had to be done and let her go.

Quinn knew it was not going to work out that way. He had known from the moment he had first seen her.

They traveled quickly yet carefully and unhurriedly, staying mostly in wooded land and resting the horses frequently. They took turns scouting in the night ahead. The girl in her thin nightgown was tied to her horse, and her horse was always tied to another, but they took no chances with her.

Near dawn, when Xenos was scouting ahead, Harpe rode close to Quinn and whispered. 'Do it now?'

Now was the agreed-upon time, but Quinn answered, 'No.' He hardly knew why he said it. Perhaps to delay the girl's death, if that was to be her fate. Perhaps to insure it.

'Why not? Sun up soon.'

'We told those people we'd hold her a whole day. Let's do it that way, or even a little longer. The longer they don't see her, the more protection she is for us.'

'But we can't wear masks all day long. And if she sees our faces in daylight, she's bound to recognize that we ain't what we're supposed to be.'

'I think you're wrong. A man's only got to look a little mulatto to be taken for a nigger, and it's up to him to prove he isn't. On the other hand, if he claims to be a nigger, or doesn't deny that he is one, sure as hell nobody is going to say he's white.'

Quinn was not nearly as sure of himself as he tried to sound. For one thing, he knew perfectly well that stained hair and skin might be recognized as such, and the stains would announce that they were white, not black. And for another, while he was certain that Harpe, with his blond hair and mustache darkened, could be taken for a mulatto, he was not at all sure that he himself could. How many bluc-cycd mulattoes did you scc?

In any case, Quinn intended to take the chance.

37

'Well,' Harpe whispered, laughing softly, 'if you think it's a good idea . . .'

'I do. Let's just see what happens.'

'You're the boss, like they say up north. I don't give a damn one way or another.'

It might well depend on the girl, then, whether she lived or died. Though Quinn had not yet definitely decided that they would kill her if she recognized them as white, they certainly preferred that she didn't carry that information away with her. No, much better for their safety and their future plans if she were dead.

And so Quinn watched her carefully as dawn pinked the east . . . watched the small miserable figure in the cotton gown, her slippers long gone . . . watched to see if she might notice . . . might understand . . .

3

'Zagreus! Hey, there, Zagreus!'

It was Jeb's voice, dragging Zag from some swiftly fading dream of Cissie. He reached for the dream, but it escaped him, and, awakening slowly, he rolled over and reached for Cissie herself. His arm went around her and pulled her close against him – even as he realized that she was not Cissie at all but Vidette.

'Zagreus? You up there?'

'Yeah . . . yeah . . . up here.' Jeb probably knew perfectly well that Zag was in his room – and also that he was not alone.

'Sorry to wake you up, Zag.'

''S all right.' From the cast of the light, it seemed to be late afternoon. Zag was confused. What was he doing in bed with Vidette? It must be Sunday afternoon – but it couldn't be, could it?

'Miss Lucy wants to see you. You get dressed and go to the office as soon as you can.'

Jeb's words brought it all back to Zag – the fire, the whipping, the fight – and his stomach gave a sick lurch. He told himself once again that with Miss Lucy on his side – and surely she would be – he had nothing to fear. But the trouble was that some white folks could be so unreasonable. It was as if they couldn't tell one black from another. Mr Buckridge had lost his big house and his daughter to black raiders, and for that he would want to 'get' somebody as soon as possible. He would be longing for his first taste of vengeance against black people – any black people – and there were plenty of white people who would be willing to help him get it.

And, by his fight with the Buckridge driver, Zag had made himself a readily available potential victim.

He remembered an incident he had heard of some years previously. At the time of the incident, it seemed, there was a great deal of fear of a slave insurrection, and the militia was very much on the alert. And then one night a drunken militiaman blew a trumpet as a joke, and those whites who heard the call assumed it was the signal for an uprising. An old slave with a trumpet was soon located. And on that flimsy basis alone – possession of a trumpet – and though the trumpet was covered with cobwebs and obviously had not been touched in years – a Court Magistrate and Freeholders found the slave guilty and sentenced him to die. The slave was hung the next day.

Zag was quite aware that the same thing or worse could happen to him.

'Zag, do you hear me?'

'Yeah. Hear you. Tell Miss Lucy I be there soon.'

Downstairs Jeb's boots scuffed away from the coach house. Zag pulled himself up onto his elbows and looked at Vidette. She appeared to be sound asleep. The breeze had died down, the room was stifling, and he was bathed in sweat.

Miss Lucy wasn't going to let it happen to him, he told himself, still groggy with sleep, as he got to his feet. She wasn't going to let it happen.

He splashed water on his face and used wet rags to bathe his body. Two fresh buckets of water, still cold from the well, had appeared under his table, and it could only be that Zulie had brought them while he and Vidette were asleep. He smiled. It was the kind of thoughtfulness he could always expect from Zulie.

While he was putting on old but fresh clothes, Vidette stirred and blinked her eyes. Her hands behind her neck, she arched her back and stretched luxuriously. She smiled up at him.

'That was nice,' she said dreamily.

'What was nice?'

'You know, all of it.' The smile turned to a frown. 'What you doing, your clothes on that way?'

'Got to see Miss Lucy. She sent for me.'

The frown went away, and the smile came back. It was a nice smile, Zag thought; so pretty and pleased and satisfied.

'Oh,' she said, 'well, I be here when you come back.'

Zag laughed and sat down on the side of the bed. 'No, you won't,' he said. 'When I get back here from Miss Lucy, I want you gone.'

'Old mean man. I ain't used up yet. Sleep all day, how'm I gonna sleep tonight, you make me go away, and I ain't used up?'

She had a point, but he said, 'Find yourself another. You got plenty.'

'Don't want another. Want Zag.'

He leaned down and gave her a brief kiss. 'Vidette, that's nice of you. But I don't know what Miss Lucy'll want or when I'll be back or – '

'Tell you what. I go away now and come back tonight, when you done what you got to do. Then we get all used up and sleep re-e-eal good.'

Zag considered. Since he had started with women again, long months after Cissie's death, he had gone quickly from one to another, careful to allow none to have any special claim on him. And the very fact that he was so fond of Vidette was one good reason to stop having his pleasure with her quite so often. Furthermore, she was showing signs of wanting to settle down, signs that made him nervous. No, it would be best if he didn't let her come back tonight.

Still . . .

She slid an arm over his shoulders. 'Aw, come on, Zag.'

He kissed her again.

41

'Tonight, Zag?'
'All right. Tonight.'

She was a tall woman, though she did not look so tall now, while sitting at her desk. She was dressed, as always, in black. About thirty years old, she was fair of complexion, and her eyes, large and very blue, seemed to Zag to look right into him, so that it became very difficult to say anything that was not true. She was handsome, he supposed, or even beautiful, except for one thing. On the right side of her face she carried a long straight scar from her temple through her cheek to her jawbone. Her beauty was marred forever.

'And now, Zagreus,' she said in her low, slightly husky voice, 'I want you to tell me exactly what happened.'

Feeling rather like a small boy, he told her. Cheney stood nearby, smiling slightly, looking rested. Jeb moved restlessly about the office in a way that showed that he still had had no sleep. Finally, at Miss Lucy's signal, he sat quietly down on a chair. Only a very few people ever sat with Miss Lucy except when told to – Momma Lucinda, Leila the housekeeper, and sometimes Jeb. Zag didn't know why that was so, but it was.

'Now, you may have told me all that happened,' she said when he was finished, 'but you haven't told me all that was said. Is it true that you threatened to kill the driver?'

'I don't know exactly what I said, Miss Lucy. Might have said that, 'cause I was hurting so. But couldn't have done nothing much, 'cause right after that was when I couldn't see, from the hurt and the blood in my eyes and all. All I know is how he was whipping me and yelling how *he* was going to kill *me*.'

Miss Lucy looked at Jeb, and Jeb returned the look. There seemed to be some kind of understanding between them.

42

She turned to Zag again. 'Zagreus, I don't have to tell you that something like this can lead to further trouble, but I think we'll be all right. Now, I want you to eat an early supper and put on your best clothes. You will drive Mr Jeb and Cheney and me to Kimbrough Hall this evening. We'll meet a number of people there, and I shall probably ask you to tell them exactly what you have told me.'

'Yes, ma'am.'

'And no matter what you hear said there, Zagreus, remember – you are not a Buckridge hand or a Kimbrough hand. You belong at Sabrehill, and we shall protect you. Try not to worry.'

It was all very well for Miss Lucy to tell him that, but *how* was he to try not to worry? He knew perfectly well that if he and Miss Lucy and the others were to go to Kimbrough Hall, it was because he was on trial. It might not be a legal slave court, but great planters like Buckridge and Kimbrough were inclined to place themselves above the law and do as they pleased. If it became necessary, they would politely apologize to the proper magistrates later.

There were a number of carriages in the Kimbrough Hall courtyard when they arrived that evening. Ordinarily, the big planters liked to go to Charleston or The Piedmont or even up north for the worst heat of summer, but fear of rebels and raiders was keeping many of them at home that year. Looking surprised that Miss Lucy should have not one or two but three of her people with her, Mrs Kimbrough greeted the mistress of Sabrehill and said that the meeting was being held in the main parlor, as the plantation office was too small. She took Miss Lucy into the house, and Zag, Jeb, and Cheney were left to sit on the steps outside and talk to the drivers of the other carriages.

It was a half-hour before a house boy appeared, to say

that Cheney was wanted in the parlor. Five minutes later the same boy said that Jebediah was wanted, and Zag was left to sweat alone for another five minutes.

Then it was his turn to enter the Kimbrough parlor.

He recognized most of the people who were there. There were the Kimbrough men, father and son, of course. There was Mr Buckridge, looking older, grayer, and sicker than Zag could have believed. Dr Paulson, who occasionally visited Sabrehill, was there, and so was Paul Devereau, the planter-lawyer friend of Miss Lucy. There were a couple of others whom Zag did not know. Jeb and Cheney stood on one side of the room, and Mr Dwyer and Nemo on the other. Miss Lucy was the only woman present, and Zag nervously edged his way toward her.

She smiled up at him. 'All right, Zagreus,' she said, 'you know what we're here for. I want you to tell these gentlemen exactly what you told me.'

Every eye was on Zag, making him feel naked and vulnerable. He wasn't used to this sort of thing. His voice shook, shaming him, and his knees nearly turned to water. Yet somehow he managed to tell the story, speaking clearly and using his best language.

All the time he was speaking, Mr Buckridge's gaze was on him, baleful and unwavering. After a brief silence when Zag finished, Buckridge was the first to speak: 'I didn't hear him say a damn thing about threatening to kill my driver.'

'Oh, but I'm sure he did threaten to kill him,' Miss Lucy said quickly, and both Zag and Buckridge looked at her with some surprise. 'After all, if anyone inflicted you or me with unexpected and unreasonable pain, might not we react in the same way? I'm sure I would. And you, Mr Buckridge, you did! When you saw your people and mine engaged in a trivial quarrel while your house was burning, I'm told that you brandished a pistol and asked who you had to kill to get the people back to work again.' Miss

Lucy's voice hardened ever so slightly. 'Now, would you actually have killed my valuable property, Mr Buckridge?'

Buckridge looked uncomfortable. 'My house was burning. My daughter had been taken – '

'Exactly. You didn't really want to kill anyone. You merely wanted our people to behave in a manner appropriate to the circumstances, and you spoke very strongly and threateningly – and quite properly so – to effect that end. Which is exactly what Zagreus must have done.'

'Miss Lucy,' Major Kimbrough said dryly, 'your observations are interesting, but they evade the point.'

'Oh?' Miss Lucy sounded very innocent.

'We all know that discipline at Sabrehill has never been what it should have been, and it can hardly be that now, with just a widow lady running the place – '

'Hear-hear,' said Dr Paulson.

'And now we see the result of it,' the major went on. 'Now we have a perfect example of how an undisciplined black can rise up and make trouble for his master.'

'You refer to Nemo?' Miss Lucy asked, still innocent.

The major looked surprised. 'No. I mean your Zagreus.'

'Oh. I was not aware that my Zagreus had made me any trouble at all. But do go on.'

'Miss Lucy,' Buckridge cut in, 'how can you say that? Your Zagreus attacked a driver and threatened to kill him.'

'No.' Miss Lucy's voice hardened again.

'He most certainly did attack – '

'No, Mr Buckridge, he did not attack a driver. With all due respect, sir, what my Zagreus did was rise up and attempt to protect himself – *my property, sir* – from a stranger with a whip. You seem to forget, sir, that your Nemo is no driver to my Zagreus, he is merely another – '

'Aw, now, Miss Lucy,' one of the other planters interrupted, 'You're just playing around with words, and we all know it. Your Zagreus knows that the hand that holds the whip is the driver's hand, and both Zagreus and Nemo were at the Buckridge plantation to do a job. Maybe Nemo was mistaken about your boy, or maybe not. But your boy was sure as hell wrong to raise his hand against a driver.'

'That's the truth of it,' said another planter, 'and with all due respect to you, Miss Lucy, if you can't discipline your people we've got to do it for you. And I move we take a vote on whipping this nigger right here and now. Get it all done and over with.'

A murmur of assent went through the room, and Zag felt thoroughly sick. He was going to be whipped, whipped badly, and he knew it, and there wasn't a thing in the world that Miss Lucy could do about it. She was, after all, just one woman in a world that was run by men.

'A moment, gentlemen, a moment,' Paul Devereau said, standing up from his chair. He was a white-maned, solidly built man in his early thirties with a knack for dominating a crowd, and he looked about the room from intelligent, deep-set eyes. 'I know there is not a man here,' he went on resonantly, 'who wants to be anything but utterly fair to Miss Lucy. Now, a case for the prosecution has been made, so to speak, and if Miss Lucy wishes to defend her boy, as is her right, surely she must have that opportunity. Shall we not be certain we have heard her out before we act.'

'Of course,' Major Kimbrough agreed. 'Miss Lucy, if there is anything further you would care to say . . .'

'Only a very little . . .' Miss Lucy was silent for a moment, and her eyes seemed to be fixed on some distant horizon that only she saw. The others in the room looked at her all the more intently.

'I reflect on the harsh ironies of this life,' she went on softly, and the others had to strain to hear her. 'A neighbor's house burns, and we all struggle together to save it – and that leads us to this evening of contention and debate. A fine boy like Nemo here, dedicated to his master, strives to help save the house – and that leads him to whip a neighbor's boy who lies upon the grass. And why does the neighbor's boy lie upon the grass? Because he has driven himself to unconsciousness, serving the same cause. Because he has served that cause so well, he is whipped – and because he defends his mistress's property, he is threatened and whipped again. Ironies heaped upon ironies, gentlemen, harsh and unjust.'

'Now, see here, Miss Lucy,' Buckridge began, 'you can't – '

'Owen,' Paul Devereau said, 'I do want to hear this. It's really quite good.'

'Yeah,' Dr Paulson said, grinning. 'Sounds like her pa.' 'Do go on!'

'Gentlemen,' Miss Lucy continued, 'since I was a little girl, I have known the Sabres and their neighbors to live in peace with each other, always cooperating, each doing everything he could to help the other. We have fought fires together. We have helped each other pick crops before they spoiled. We have lent carpenters and blacksmiths and other mechanics back and forth to get necessary work done. We all stood together during the Panic of 1819. And we have always respected each other and each other's property. Now, just because in trying to do his duty Nemo gave Zagreus a half-dozen undeserved stripes, I am certainly *not* going to demand that Nemo be whipped –'

Buckridge looked surprised. 'You're damned right you're not!'

'But of course not. Because if it had been *my* house that burned, and *my* boy who whipped yours – your poor boy who worked so hard for me that he fell to the earth unconscious – I could never allow you to whip my boy in return, dear Mr Buckridge. I could not then, and I cannot now.'

'Now, wait a minute – '

'She's got a point,' said Paul Devereau quickly.

'We must not penalize ourselves or our people for small mistakes made in the name of friendship,' Miss Lucy said. 'It's as simple as that.'

'Personally, I've been afraid we might make a mountain out of a molehill,' Dr Paulson said, 'but I thought we should hear all the facts.'

'Oh, I quite agree,' Paul Devereau said. 'Let's not blow this whole matter up out of proportion. Don't you agree, Major?'

'Well, I don't think anyone wants to do that . . .'

Unused to the big house language – what in the world was a 'harsh irony'? – Zag had found the discussion difficult to follow, but he felt a shift of mood within the room. Mr Buckridge looked disheartened but not angry, and at his nod Mr Dwyer and Nemo departed. The two planters whose names Zag did not know were beginning to look bored. Mr Devereau looked pleased, and Dr Paulson was laughing about something with Miss Lucy. Mr Buckridge said, 'You know, we have other matters to discuss,' and Miss Lucy turned in her chair to say, 'You all may go outside now. And Zagreus,' she added in a lower voice, 'take care – no trouble.'

The warning was unnecessary. Zag planned to stay close to Jeb and as far from Mr Dwyer and Nemo as possible. He walked toward the door.

And suddenly, with a vast surge of relief, he knew that he was not going to be punished for his fight with Nemo after all. Thanks to Miss Lucy, the danger was past.

For this time.

And now it's my turn, Lucy thought, with a smile to herself. Now that they've failed to give Zagreus a whipping, they'll try to give one to me. But they won't find it easy.

'All right,' Mr Buckridge said, taking the floor, 'I agree

that we should not build up this one single incident all out of proportion. But you all know that we haven't really gotten to the root of the matter. You all know that last night, at a very important time, discipline broke down in a very important way. Yes, true, it was a small incident. But it's symptomatic, you might say.

'Now, I hope you all will listen to me, because after last night I think I have the right to say this. Just since last winter we've had three of these raids in this district. There have been others in the last year or so in outlying districts. The militia and the patrols haven't done a damn thing about them, and all of them, or most, have been made by blacks, just like at my place.'

'Thought you weren't sure about one of them at your place,' Dr Paulson said.

'There was something funny about the way one of them looked, and another one called him *Mister* something-or-other, the way a black would talk to a white man. But at least two of them were blacks, and that's the point. It's free Negroes and runaways that are causing all this trouble, and what do our people think when they see 'em getting away with it? They think, Why by God, why can't I do that too? Why do *I* have to work for a living? Why can't *I* just go out and take what I want and loot and kill and carry off white women? Why not?'

Buckridge spoke as if addressing the entire room, but Lucy had no doubt that he was aiming his words at her. Neither did she doubt that this whole matter had been discussed before her arrival. Mr Buckridge was spokesman for the group.

'And that's why it's so goddamn important – excuse me, Miss Lucy – so important that we all maintain discipline among our people. I mean, they have got to know, by God, that we are the *white* people and they, by God, have got to stay in their proper place! Now, is there anybody here who disagrees with that?'

49

Buckridge looked around the room as if daring anyone to disagree. 'No, Owen,' Major Kimbrough said slowly, 'I think all of us here would go along with that.' Others nodded and murmured assent. Lucy thought she might qualify any agreement a great deal, but there was utterly no point in saying so: she was not here to antagonize these men. She kept her face impassive.

'Now, how do you keep discipline?' Buckridge went on. 'Well, I think we all know, but I can only speak for the way I do it, and I want to stress that I have never been a cruel or unreasonable master. I don't believe in cropping ears or cutting off fingers, though some very respectable opinion –' he nodded toward the planters McClintock and Pettigrew – 'some right here may disagree with me. I only brand in extreme cases. I don't believe in putting a proven hand to the post every time he makes a mistake. And furthermore, I feed my people as well as anyone else around here does, and they have plenty enough good clothes and sound roofs over their heads. I don't give a damn about any law that says they must always wear coarse clothes unless they're in livery. You all saw my Nemo – when he goes calling, he looks just as fine as any of Miss Lucy's people. Anyway, most laws, as we all know, are meant for the goddamn sandhillers and not for the quality.

'So I say I treat my people damn well, and even with the cotton and rice market down, I don't try to do it on any twenty dollars per hand a year.

'But – Miss Lucy – gentlemen – I demand something in return! I demand loyalty and hard work and discipline! Am I wrong?'

There was another round of agreement. Paul Devereau looked at Lucy and said, 'I don't think any of us would differ on that, would we?' Lucy merely cocked an eyebrow. Her turn would come.

'Now, the law,' Buckridge continued, 'just says a plantation must have on it a white person responsible for the slave population. But *I* say you have got to have more than that. I say you must have a white *man* with a strong sense of discipline. You must have a white man who knows how to whip a nigger into shape and keep him that way. I'm that kind of man, and so is my son, and on my place there's not only us. There's the *white* overseer and his son too. And I've got some rice tracts downriver, and *they* have overseers. I tell you, I just don't let a gang of hands work way off on their own with nothing more than a pass. A Negro hand on his own is a menace to himself and to everyone else. Now, wouldn't you say that was true, Miss Lucy?'

'I would say,' Lucy answered carefully, 'that experience has taught us that it depends on the hand.'

'Owen's right, with a very few exceptions, Miss Lucy,' Major Kimbrough said, shaking his head.

'Damn few,' Buckridge insisted. 'That's why you have to keep watch on them all the time. And why if your Zagreus was mine, I'd whip hell out of him. And why I have every hand locked up at night and have my overseer do a head count every morning. I understand that Sabrehill never did that, Miss Lucy, and you know you've had quite a few runaways.'

'That's true,' Lucy admitted. 'But I'm afraid that that was the result of a period of overdiscipline – the kind of cruelty that you and I both deplore, Mr Buckridge. The situation has been corrected, and I think you'll find our people becoming happier to remain at home.'

'Miss Lucy, no offense, but maybe, just maybe, they're happier to stay home now because of the lack of discipline.'

'There is no lack of reasonable discipline at Sabrehill, Mr Buckridge.'

'Now, Miss Lucy,' Major Kimbrough said, 'I hate to contradict a lady, and I think you really mean what you're saying. But there's just got to be a lack of discipline. You're all alone there at Sabrehill, the only white person on the place, and you weren't brought up to run a plantation. No *lady* possibly could run one. So what have you got – '

'What you have got,' Buckridge said, 'you've got a big plantation run by a black man. And we all know what that means.'

'I'm afraid I've got to go along with them on this, Miss Lucy,' Dr Paulson said, 'These free black farmers and planters with their own slaves, they let their people run free.'

'That's right,' Buckridge put in, 'they let them run *free*, is the right word. There's no discipline on most black farms at all. And that sets a bad example for the people on *our* places! And, Miss Lucy, that is exactly the situation at Sabrehill. Here we have one of the finest plantations in South Carolina being run by a *black* man, the people never locked up, no discipline – '

'Owen,' Paul Devereau said, 'if you know anything at all about Jebediah Hayes, you know his is by no standard an ordinary man.'

'We know that, Paul,' the major said wearily. 'I've talked to Jebediah, and he's surprisingly bright. However –'

'He's more than that,' Lucy said. 'He's a capable, perceptive, well-educated – '

'Educating slaves is against the law,' McClintock said, 'as it damned well should be. You don't *educate* a nigger, you *train* him.'

'Miss Lucy,' the major said, 'even if we did agree that the discipline at Sabrehill is just fine, and even if we did agree that your Jebediah is the best possible overseer, there is still something else.'

'And what is that?'

'It just ain't right,' McClintock said, 'for a white lady without a husband, even a widow lady like you, to be living all alone on a big plantation with nobody else but her black people and . . . and that big nigger buck.'

The room was suddenly quiet.

Yes, Lucy thought, there was that too: the matter of propriety and the protection of gentle womanhood. She had encountered it often before: the idea that when a woman without a husband reached a certain age – even a lady – she might become susceptible to the barnyard attractions of the blacks. After all, didn't these cavaliers frequently have their black girls before marriage and not infrequently after? And might not a white woman find the bucks as attractive as they did their wenches? Of course, a lady was supposed to keep her sensual feelings as tepid as weak tea, but what if one day she found the kettle brought to a boil by a handsome young black? What if one day a respectable spinster or widow lady or even a lonely wife were to look at a potent young stud and think, *My God, what have I been missing?*

Well, Lucy thought with a touch of anger, maybe these fine chivalrous gentlemen had a point. Yes, a lady just might do that!

But she kept her face carefully blank.

Buckridge looked frustrated: 'Please don't misunderstand, Miss Lucy. We're speaking to you as your friends. Why, you're almost like a daughter to some of us here, and we know you would never be anything but a perfect lady.'

'And I am sure,' the major said, 'that your Jebediah is personally loyal to you and would never harm you.'

'But suppose that raiders come to Sabrehill, Miss Lucy. Who would protect you? You know you can't count on any black. You've simply got to get yourself at least one white man, so you'll be protected!'

To remind Buckridge that he and all of the other white men on his own plantation had been unable to protect his daughter would have been cruel, but Lucy had to bite her tongue.

53

'What would you suggest I do to remedy the situation? she asked. 'Find myself a husband?'

Major Kimbrough glanced at Paul Devereau, the one bachelor in the room. 'That would be ideal. I'm sure he would eventually prevail on you to hire a white overseer, but even if he did not, Sabrehill would once again have a white masculine authority.'

'Unfortunately I haven't had a plethora of suitors knocking at my door of late. Do you have an alternative suggestion?'

'Hire a white overseer, preferably a married one with a couple of near-grown sons. Sabrehill really needs more than one white man on it. Three would not be too many.'

Lucy pretended to consider the idea. 'And what would I do with Jebediah? He's performed so marvelously it seems wrong to demote the poor boy to assistant overseer.'

'He shouldn't be assistant overseer anyway,' Buckridge said. 'That's another white job. Miss Lucy, you've been telling Mrs Buckridge how you plan to start entertaining again one of these days, and I recall how Jebediah was a mighty fine butler at one time. Now, you're going to need a butler – '

'Well, now, that's an interesting idea, Mr Buckridge,' Lucy said with a smile. 'Do you know, I think all of this is going to work itself out quite well.'

'Why, of course it is, Miss Lucy,' the major said, 'and please believe me when I say that we're only trying to be of help.'

'I know that, Major, and I do appreciate it.'

'After all, it's not as if you had any men folk of your own who could help you.'

Lucy looked uncomprehendingly at the major for a moment, carefully timing her reply to give it the most force. She smiled slowly.

'Oh, but you're mistaken, Major,' she said. I most certainly do!'

This was the moment she had been waiting for: let them air their complaints, let them make their suggestions, and only then give them what they wanted – or pretend to do so.

She watched their reactions: mere interest on the part of Pettigrew and McClintock, surprise on the part of Buckridge and the major, something like dismay on the part of Paul Devereau. No, she thought, Paul would not like the idea of having male relatives who might be helpful to her. If anyone was to be helpful, it must be Paul himself.

'I don't understand,' the major said. 'If you have male relatives who can help you, why aren't they here?'

'Just who do you have in mind, Miss Lucy?' Paul Devereau asked.

Lucy didn't answer directly. 'Now, you all must know that I have my uncles and aunts and cousins the same as anybody else. Oh, most of them aren't very close, but still they are relatives. Paul, do you remember my cousin Ash, from Virginia? He visited down here years ago.'

Paul frowned as if searching his memory. He nodded.

'Mr Asher McCloud,' Lucy went on, 'my third cousin. I don't think I was more than fifteen years old when I last saw him, but, Paul, I remember that you boys went hunting together.'

'Yes,' Paul said. 'Yes, I remember Mr McCloud quite well.'

'Handsomest boy I ever knew. Well, Ash and I exchanged some letters during the winter, and last spring I invited him to come to Sabrehill for a nice long visit. And only a short time ago I received his reply saying he would be more than happy to accept.'

'Well, this makes considerable difference,' the major said.

'Yes,' Paul Devereau said, 'it certainly does.'

'You're considering having your cousin take over the management of Sabrehill?' Buckridge asked.

'I would be very foolish not to leave open any helpful possibility,' Lucy answered carefully, 'even the possibility of combining the Sabre and the McCloud interests.'

That came close to being a lie. It was true, of course, that she would not dismiss any possibility thoughtlessly, but she certainly had no inclination toward putting Sabrehill – or herself – into McCloud's hands.

Buckridge looked pleased. 'That sounds almost as if Mr McCloud isn't married, Miss Lucy, if you'll pardon the presumption.'

'He is not.' Lucy smiled. She saw that Paul was keeping his face carefully guarded.

'When is Mr McCloud due to arrive at Sabrehill?' he asked.

She shrugged as if the question was of no importance. 'His own interests are keeping him busy at present, but he should be here by late summer or early fall.'

She saw at once that they didn't like that. The major's face hardened, and Buckridge's grew worried again.

'In other words,' Pettigrew said, 'Sabrehill isn't going to have a white man on it for quite some time yet. Maybe a couple of months or more.'

She had been sweet and ladylike quite long enough. She liked the major and Mr Buckridge and even, in a way, Paul Devereau, but she refused to be bullied. It was time, she decided, to exhibit some strength.

'All right,' she said, hardening her voice, 'let's have it out.'

'Miss Lucy, you have got to understand – '

'Mr Buckridge, I do understand. Gentlemen, I understand quite well why you invited me here this evening. The matter of Zagreus and Nemo, important though it was in your eyes, was essentially a pretext. For months now you have been talking about "that damned scar-faced Sabrehill woman – " '

'Miss Lucy!'

'Major, let me continue. For months, gentlemen, you have been prattling about the inability of any *lady* to run a plantation. Frankly, there was a time when I would have agreed with you, but with the help of my overseer, I seem to be doing quite well.'

'Miss Lucy, it's a matter of discipline – '

'Mr Buckridge, you keep saying that word as if it had some special magic in it. The fact is that my people are no more lacking in sound discipline than are yours.'

'Now, we've heard of some mightly restless blacks at Sabrehill.'

'If some of my people are restless, that's true of every large plantation in the South, yours no less than mine. And the way we've been treating blacks in recent years, it's no wonder.'

'Now, Miss Lucy,' McClintock said, 'if there's anything we know, it's how to treat blacks.'

'No, I really don't think we do. I really don't think that many of us in our whole lives have applied much intelligence to the problem. But let that go, if you wish – you're all geniuses at handling blacks, and I am not, and there should be a white man at Sabrehill.'

'That's exactly right,' Dr Paulson said, 'There really should be.'

'Very well, I have told you that there is *going* to be a white man at Sabrehill.'

'But not for months,' Pettigrew said. 'And how long will he stay?'

'I really don't know. Perhaps for a very long time, perhaps not. But in any case, I am not going to be pushed into anything as stupid as a marriage of convenience, or into giving up an excellent black overseer for a white one who may turn out badly. We've had a bad overseer at Sabrehill, and I say, "No, thank you." ' She looked around the room. 'Now, do you all understand me?'

'Gentlemen,' Paul Devereau said, 'let us be reasonable. Miss Lucy has agreed – '

'If so,' Lucy said, rising to her feet, 'I think I had better leave now. Because, gentlemen, my patience is wearing thin!'

So they had thought they would dominate her, had they? Thought that if that scar-faced woman at Sabrehill could not keep 'discipline' among her people, they would have to do it for her. Whip one of *her* hands, would they, and then insist that a *man* take over the management of Sabrehill? Well, they hadn't succeeded, and if Lucy had anything to say about it, they never would.

She had departed from the Kimbrough parlor with an irritated frown on her face, but she had had to clinch her jaw to keep from smiling. Now, in the darkness of the calash, she allowed herself a rare broad grin. Zagreus was driving, and he and Cheney were humming a tune often heard among the field hands. Beside her, Jeb chuckled as if he sensed how good she felt.

'As I expected,' she said, 'they brought up the matter of there being no white man at Sabrehill.'

'A scandal and a disgrace,' Jeb said, 'yes, indeed. And how did they react when you told them about your cousin?'

'They didn't like the idea that it would be some time before he arrived here, so I showed them a bit of anger. I'm sure they expected to walk all over me. I had to show them that even if I made a concession, they simply couldn't do that. I hope they'll leave me alone now until my cousin arrives.'

'Even if they do, what happens after he leaves?'

'Oh, Jebediah, there'll be another interval with my neighbors becoming increasingly aggravated, scandalized, and provoked – until another cousin or uncle or whatever I can get arrives. Then they'll all simmer down again for a few weeks or months, until I'm *again* the lonely woman at Sabrehill. And eventually *another* cousin will appear. Who knows? If Ash is still as pleasant as he was as a boy, maybe I'll invite him back for future visits. It can go on forever . . . or at least until my neighbors are tired of the silly game.'

Jeb laughed quietly in the dark.

'You know, Miss Lucy,' he said, 'it is possible that one day you'll meet a man you'll want to take over Sabrehill.'

'You mean . . . marry?'

'It could happen. Maybe one of those cousins you've mentioned.'

'Ash, you mean? Hardly likely.'

But was it? There had been a time in her life when she had prayed that never again would a man come near her. But, to her considerable surprise, that had passed, and she had found herself lonely. And of all those whom she might have asked to Sabrehill, why had she thought of Ash? Because she remembered him as tall and strong and darkly handsome. Because for all of a spring, and for weeks after he had left, he had been a fifteen-year-old girl's ideal. But that was so long ago, she could hardly take it seriously now.

'You forget two important things, Jebediah,' she said. 'One is that I carry a scar that would offend any man.'

'Not true, Miss Lucy – '

'And the other is – God help me – most men bore me. They have no intelligence, no conversation. They learn their Latin and Greek and go off to college, and return more empty-headed than they went. I am not indifferent to a well-turned leg, my friend, believe me – do I shock you? – but it does seem to me that marital bliss should consist of something more.'

'Oh, Miss Lucy-child, we shall never make a fine Carolina lady out of you!'

It warmed her when he called her Lucy-child, as only

59

the oldest people of Sabrehill or the very closest of her household ever dared to do. Jebediah Hayes had been brought up as a favored houseboy on the Pinkham plantation, and as such he had been both tutored and self-taught. That made him dangerous in the eyes of most white people, of course, but Lucy had been delighted to find that here, at last, was a man she could talk to, a mind on her own intellectual level. She remembered when he had first arrived at Sabrehill, rebellious, arrogant, half-mad –

But she dared not think of that.

'My father always claimed that he didn't raise me to be a lady,' she said.

'Then, to be what?'

'A farm girl. A woman, and a wife – ' She broke off. She had not meant to say that. The creak of harness and the clatter of hooves filled the silence until Jeb spoke again.

'And so you shall be,' he said gently. 'And then you'll want a white overseer so that you and your husband can go to Charleston together. You can't leave Sabrehill with just a black man in charge, you know, and you'll want to go to the balls and the Jockey Club races and the grand parties – '

'Jebediah Hayes, are you trying to get away from me?' She tried to say the words teasingly, but there was worry behind them.

'Now, why would I want to do that?' he teased back. 'Why in the world? Anyway, it would take an act of the state legislature to free me now, and the legislature has a way of ignoring such petitions.'

'Oh, we both know there are ways around that.' There were always such strategies as selling a slave to an out-of-state abolitionist. 'But seriously, Jebediah, you know how much I still need you.'

'Then I'll stay.'

The idea that Jebediah might wish to leave her now was frightening. She thought back to that hour when she had found herself the only white person at Sabrehill, a white woman alone on a vast plantation with hundreds of blacks' lives depending on her. A long savage history of personal tragedy had led to that hour, a history of lust, hatred, and vengeance that even today she could not bear to look back on. Better to pretend that it had never happened; better to pretend that the past did not exist.

Oh, one day she would face it all, of course; she would have to. And there were always a few of the brighter incidents of childhood and youth to remember. But for now it was best to pretend that history had begun in that hour of an autumn morning, not long ago, when she had stood in the wide cupola atop the Sabrehill mansion and looked out over her little kingdom. 'I don't know what to do!' she had cried out in panic. 'Jebediah, I don't know what to do!' But Jebediah Hayes, her friend and overseer, had soothed her fears: 'Don't be frightened, Miss Lucy-child. We'll take care of it, you and I. Don't be frightened.'

And, as he had promised, they had indeed taken care of Sabrehill and its people; she thought they had done a good job. The work had been painfully hard, because they were both limited in their knowledge of plantation operation, but they had brought all their wits and energy to the task. Lucy had poured over the plantation journals and record books, learning all that had to be done. Jeb, in the fields and in the quarters, had worked as hard as any hand. With a minimum of aid or advice from their neighbors, they had kept Sabrehill operating and prospering, and the year ahead looked good. But Lucy was still far from ready to direct the plantation without Jeb's help.

Zagreus interrupted her thoughts. 'Miss Lucy, Ma'am, something on the road ahead. Something up by the crossroads.'

Lucy leaned forward in the carriage and peered between Zagreus and Cheney. Yes, there was something at the crossroads: torchlight that made the night seem darker, and men afoot and on horseback milling about. And as they moved closer, there were shouts and something that could have been a cry of pain.

'Slow down, Zagreus,' Jeb said. 'Let's just take it slow.'

The figures became more distinct in the flickering torchlight, and the painful cries were repeated. Lucy clutched Jeb's arm.

'Jebediah, what is it? What are they doing?'

'I don't know. Maybe it's a patrol.'

But they soon saw that it was not. The patrol never wore masks or hoods.

'Jesus,' Cheney said. 'Miss Lucy, let's get out of this here place.'

'Shut up,' Jeb said quietly, 'just keep your mouth shut. They've seen us, and we can't turn and outrun them. Zagreus, just keep on going, slowly.'

Three horsemen, two hooded and one masked with a scarf, were riding toward them. The nearest held up a hand. 'You, there,' he shouted, 'you, nigger! You stop right there!'

At Jeb's touch, Zag reined up the horses.

'What you niggers doing on the road at night?' the horseman demanded, riding closer. 'You got you a pass?'

The accent was sandhiller-white, and Lucy now knew almost certainly what was happening on the road ahead. Apprehension turned to sickness, a kind of nausea. She could only hope that it would not be too bad – not castration, say, or some other mutilation.

She leaned forward so that she could be seen. 'They don't need passes,' she said in a hard voice, hiding her sickness. 'They're with me. Now, get out of our way.'

'I'm sorry, ma'am. I didn't see there was a white – '

'I said, get out of our way, boy, you hear me?' Lucy

62

snatched the whip from its socket. She had a certain pity for white trash, but sometimes there was only one way to handle them. 'You move those horses!'

'Ma'am, we can't let you go up there, a nice white lady –'

'*Move!*'

She struck out with the whip, and the horsemen twisted their mounts away.

'All right, God damn it, just don't say you wasn't warned – '

'Zagreus, drive on.'

The horsemen stayed with them, almost like an escort. There was little chance, Lucy knew, that she could stop what was happening, but she had to try. Ahead, there was the crack of a whip and another scream.

There had to be at least a dozen more of them, she saw, as they reached the crossroads, all of them hooded or otherwise masked. They looked like spectres from Hell in the torchlight. The whip kept cracking like a pistol at regular intervals in counterpoint to the irregular, broken screams, and at last Lucy saw the victim: a black man on his knees, tied to the trunk of a tree at one side of the crossroads. His shirt was red, completely soaked in blood.

'Oh, my God,' Lucy said, 'they're whipping him to death.'

But the whipping stopped, as Lucy reached in front of Zag to pull at the reins. Several hooded men turned to look at her with black cavelike eyes.

'Why are you doing this?' She fought to keep her voice hard and unshaking. 'What right have you – '

'Caught us a bad nigger,' one of the men yelled, 'and we aim to teach him a lesson!'

'A lesson he ain't gonna live to forget!' another said with a hard laugh.

'But no other nigger around these parts is gonna forget it!'

'But what has he done?'

There was no answer. A wave of one hooded man's hand was enough to silence the others. He was burly, heavyset, barrel-like, and Lucy thought she recognized him. He mounted a horse as if to put himself on a level with her. Only then did he speak.

'Good evening, Miss Lucy.'

She knew the deep gravelly voice. They could hardly be called friends or even acquaintances, but each had long been aware of the other.

'Mr Jeppson, why are you whipping that Negro?'

If Balbo Jeppson had any objection to being recognized, he didn't show it. The hoods, Lucy realized, were merely a means of terrorizing blacks and a pretext for saying that no one in the group could be positively identified.

'Got caught out after dark without a pass,' Jeppson said, 'and carrying a gun.'

'Who is he? Where does he come from?'

'Don't rightly know – unless he's your nigger, ma'am. Sabrehill is mighty close by, and if he's yours, that's too damn bad. But you better learn your people to stay in at night, and don't let 'em get hold of no pistols.'

'But if you don't know who he is – why, he could be a free person of color.'

'That's what he claims, ma'am, but let him prove it. All we know is we caught an armed nigger without a pass, and he could damn well be one of the blacks that raided the Buckridge place last night.'

'But if you don't know – '

'We know all we need to know. Now, you better get yourself and your people away from here.' Jeppson started to turn away.

'Mr Jeppson, we have laws, we have courts – '

'Oh, yes!' Jeppson whirled back on his horse and leaned toward her. Now she could see his angry eyes behind the

64

hood, and his voice was rich with hatred. 'Yeah, you got your courts, Miss Lucy. Nigger courts that *belong* to the likes of you! Just like you think the whole goddamn state belongs to the likes of you, goddamn chivalry, think your shit don't stink, too goddamn good to sit down with honest farmers! You and your justices and freeholders, whip a nigger and let him off. Well, we all got our own courts, Miss Lucy, and you see one in session right now!' Again, he turned away from her. 'All right, you men know what to do!'

The captive black had been cut free from the tree trunk and his arms tied behind him. Something was being poured over him, and the smell of tar and oil was heavy in the night air.

And for the first time Lucy saw the noose hanging from the limb of a tree.

'Get him up there, men! We'll leave him dangling a few days and teach the niggers around here – yeah, the goddamn Sabrehill niggers!'

Lucy did the only thing she could think to do. 'Mr Jeppson, that man is mine! I claim him! You have no right –'

'Get that rope around his neck. That's right, get him –'

'*Jeppson!*' Lucy brought her whip against Jeppson's shoulders with all her strength. '*Jeppson, you have no right!*'

She had no idea, then, of what she was saying. She saw Jeppson dance his horse around, heard his curses. '*Goddamn bitch, you, whore of Sabrehill, we know you, you nigger-loving goddamn whore!*'

She heard a cheer and laughter and then no more. She was aware only of the black man, no longer screaming, being hoisted rapidly into the air, both legs kicking free, kicking, kicking, until he was over the heads of those who stood below.

He was still kicking when they raised torches and set him on fire.

It was one of those moments that seem as long as all the rest of one's life. She stared at the human torch. She tried to bury her face against Jeb's chest, denying what she had seen, and yet she had to look again. He – it – was still there. It was a nightmare from which she could not turn away. She heard Jeb yell, 'Go, Zag, go, God damn it, *go!*' and the carriage lurched into motion. Jeb tried to pull her face to his chest again, and screaming, she fought him off without knowing why. Then the carriage was hurling along the road beyond the crossroads, while behind them Jeppson shouted 'Whore! Whore!' and Lucy tried to lose herself in the surrounding darkness.

But eyes open or closed, there was no darkness. Wherever she looked, it was lit up by the dangling, kicking, burning man.

To get to his room, there was all that mattered. To get to his room and bury himself in it, to go to it like a return to his mother's body, and not to know. To forget. No longer to see. It seemed to Zag now that along with the scent of resin and oil and tar he could smell human flesh cooking, the scent of burning pork, and he clinched his teeth to keep from wretching. To keep from vomiting, as Miss Lucy was doing in the darkness behind him.

To get to his room.

The gate. The long oak-lined avenue that led up a slight rise to the courtyard and the big house. Then they were there, and Cheney and Jeb were helping Miss Lucy from the carriage, and Jeb was sweeping Miss Lucy up in his arms like a child and carrying her into the house.

To get to his room.

The horses. Running blindly in the paddock to cool the horses, while Cheney put away the carriage. Running. Choking. Vomiting at last. Vomiting, wretching, falling to the ground, crawling.

To get to his room.

Vidette in the coach house with Cheney. Vidette looking puzzled, somehow frightened.

'Not tonight, Vidette.'

'What's the matter? What happened? What they do to
you?'

'Please. Not tonight.'

'But – '

'Vidette,' Cheney was saying, 'you just leave Zag alone
now. You leave old Zag alone. He tell you all about it
tomorrow.'

Vidette left. He had to get to his room.

But suddenly, surprisingly, there was Cheney's big
leathery hand slamming him across the face, a stinging
ear-ringing, vicious blow, and it was as if, for a moment,
he were abruptly wake. He was staring at the angry old
bull of a fighter as Cheney grabbed his shirt front and
slapped him again.

'Cheney, why you – ! Why you do that?'

'Give you something to think about, boy!'

'Cheney – '

The chief driver hit him a third time. 'You think you got
something to think about? I give you something to think
about. Come on, damn you, fight Cheney!'

'Cheney, I got no fight with you!'

'You going to fight! Come on, dumb nigger bastard!'

Zag saw the blow coming that time. He blocked it and
threw a punch that turned Cheney's head on his thick
bull-like neck and staggered him back. Cheney laughed
and gave him another open-handed blow that threatened
to wipe Zag's face off.

That was too much. Zag swiveled left, raised his right
leg, and shot a foot hard, straight into Cheney's guts.
Cheney bounced off a wall and came back roaring.

It didn't last long, not more than five minutes. Then
Zag was down on one knee against the wall, wiping blood
from his face with the back of his hand. Cheney stood over

him, sweat pouring down his face, his big chest heaving. He grinned.

'Want to try one more time?'

Zag shook his head.

Cheney chuckled weakly. He leaned down and helped Zag to his feet. 'Reckon you'll sleep a little better now,' he said. 'Reckon we both will.'

Zag nodded. The burning man was still in his head – he probably always would be – but some of the terror and the madness had faded now.

'Go on,' Cheney said, 'get your ass to bed. I'll put out the lamps.'

He went to his room and lit a single candle. Tonight he didn't want any more light than that.

His nose soon stopped bleeding. He pulled off his shirt and washed, face, arms, shoulders. The water was cool and soothing; Zulie must have again brought it to him, fresh from the well. When he had finished, he took a jug of whiskey from the back of a cabinet and poured a cup nearly full. Then, kicking off his boots, he lay back on his bed against a pillow, sitting up from time to time to sip the whiskey and take long draughts of water.

'Zag?'

It was Zulie on the stairs.

'Come, Zulie.'

She mounted the stairs slowly, almost fearfully. In the dim light, he could barely see her face. She crossed the room silently on bare feet, and when she was at his side, he saw the worry.

'Zag, you all right?'

'Yeah.'

'Vidette, she said you was . . . strange.'

Zag swung his legs over the side of the bed and sat up to drink whiskey.

'What they do to you, Zag?'

'Nothing. Ain't going do nothing. Miss Lucy kept me from a whipping.'

'But what . . . Heard Miss Lucy was sick. And Mr Jeb all upset . . . Zag?'

The fight with Cheney had helped, but her questions were bringing it all back again, and he didn't know if he could talk about it or not. 'It was . . . We was . . .'

She sat down at the head of the bed, facing him. 'What, Zag?'

'That Mr Jeppson you hear about . . . and all those . . . Jeppson people . . .'

'What he done now?'

'At the crossroads, on the way back.' He looked at Zulie and saw her eyes widen as if she knew what was coming. 'They was killing a nigger.'

The eyes closed. 'Oh, sweet Jesus.'

'Hung him. Whipped him first till he was 'most dead, then hung him. And set him on fire.'

'Why?' Zulie asked after a moment. 'Why, why, why?'

'Don't know. Don't care.'

Zag pulled his feet back up on the bed. He lay back again, his head against Zulie's breast.

'I hate them, Zag.'

'I know.'

'Hate them worse than ever now. Hate them all. Going spell them more now, don't care what you say. Put badmouth on them all till they gone and dead.'

'Not Miss Lucy. She saved me from a whipping tonight. Tried to save that nigger.'

'And you know why? Only because you her property, is all. Try to save that nigger for property, I bet. Only reason.'

Zag wondered. Perhaps Zulie was right.

'Sometime I'm going do them like they do us, Zag. They whip, I'm going whip. They hang and burn, I'm going hang and burn. They put the gun and knife to us,

69

I'm going put the gun and knife to them. You know what I can do with a knife, Zag? You ain't got no idea. You don't know all the things our momma taught me, Zag. 'Cause I'm Erzulie, daughter of Erzulie, who was daughter of Erzulie, too. And I know things with a knife – Oh, Zag, you don't know what your Zulie going to do to them when the time comes . . .'

Zag closed his eyes and tried to sleep, tried to forget, while Zulie whispered her vow of hatred.

4

She had been lying on her bed and sipping brandy only a few minutes when Leila came to say that Paul Devereau had arrived. 'I told him I thought you was asleep, Miss Lucy. Said I'd find out. You want me to tell him to go away?'

'No.' She was sleepless, and she found she wanted company. She didn't want to be alone. 'Tell him I'll be right down.'

Her legs were still weak under her as she slipped into a robe and slippers, and Leila had to help her down the stairs. She found Paul waiting in the library. Leila closed the door and left them alone.

'Lucy,' Paul said worriedly, 'I know it's late, but I had to come.'

'That's all right. I appreciate it.'

'It's not just what happened at Kimbrough Hall – '

'I know. You must have encountered Mr Jeppson, too.'

'Then you did see . . .'

'We were there when it happened. I tried to stop it and failed.'

'You mean, they went ahead . . . right in front of you?'

Lucy nodded.

'God, that you had to go through that.' Paul shook his head with disgust. 'When I came along afterwards, they were still there, drinking and singing as if it were some kind of celebration. And that poor black boy hanging there, out of his misery, burnt . . . My God, the smell.'

Brandy boiled up in Lucy's throat, and she choked and sobbed. Paul caught her as she swayed and helped her to a chair. She hardly heard his apology.

71

'Why do we put up with Jeppson and his kind, Paul?' she asked when she had controlled her tears. 'Why do we let him run free?'

Paul Devereau shrugged. He began to pace. 'What is he, Lucy? Basically, he's an ignorant sandhiller who's become a rather successful farmer. He hates the aristocracy, because he knows he can never aspire to its ranks. Oh, many a yeoman has done so, of course, and managed quite well. But not a Jeppson. Never. On the other hand, he can rally the poor white rabble around him.'

'But why do we let him do these things? Why is he allowed to take the law into his own hands? to punish and torture and murder?'

'Why? Because it's useful to allow him to do so, my dear.' Paul's voice took on a satirical tone. 'After all, who does he hurt? His own kind. A piece of poor white trash who steals another man's black, perhaps. Or a free black who gets too far from home. And that frightens all other blacks and keeps them where they belong. Don't you think your people here at Sabrehill are going to be more circumspect after tonight? No, my dear Lucy, don't criticize Mr Jeppson. Why, we all owe him a humble vote of thanks for keeping the niggers in line. I've heard it said that he's rather like a turkey vulture – an ugly bird, but he does help to keep the countryside clean.'

'What a wicked point of view!'

Paul laughed and shook his head, and she saw that he was as appalled by the lynching as she was. She regarded him as a rascal and an opportunist, but she realized now that that didn't mean he was incapable of a decent emotion.

And that reminded her: 'Paul, I do want to thank you for your help at Kimbrough Hall this evening.'

He shrugged. 'You hardly needed it. Why, I never realized, Lucy, what a gift for rhetoric you have. "I reflect on the harsh ironies of this life! Ironies heaped upon ironies, gentlemen, harsh and unjust!" Why John C. Calhoun himself couldn't have been more eloquent.' They laughed together.

'I did put in a word to help you whenever I could, Lucy. It wouldn't have helped you if I had been more direct.'

'I know. And I know that you can be very devious.' She smiled at him and was sorry when he didn't smile back. 'I'm sorry, I forget my manners. Would you pour us each a brandy, Paul? I'm sure you found your encounter with Mr Jeppson as upsetting as I did mine.'

He poured the drinks from a decanter and handed her one, then settled into a chair facing her.

'I didn't come here only because of Jeppson,' he said.

'Then why?'

'Lucy, I'm your lawyer, and I stand by you. I'll plead your case anytime you wish. But speaking privately, I must say that I think Owen and the major and our other friends are right.'

Lucy felt weary. 'You, too, think I should have a white overseer.'

Paul Devereau nodded. 'A white overseer plus another overseer for every fifty blacks. That's the general rule. Now, not everyone lives up to that rule by any means, but not everyone is a white lady living alone on a plantation. And what with free blacks and runaways – '

'It didn't save the Buckridges. It didn't save poor Abbie Buckridge.'

'Isn't that beside the point?'

Yes, Lucy thought, it probably was. There was no doubt that with a few armed white men at Sabrehill she would be safer.

Certainly it wasn't as if Sabrehill could not afford white overseers – it could afford all that might be useful and more. But good ones were difficult to find. No matter how much you admonished them to be just and gentle with your people, they were expected to show a profit, and the

73

only way most of them could do that was through fear and the whip. Thus they tended to be ignorant, brutal men.

And then there was the matter of the black women. To an ignorant, brutal man they were a constant temptation. Even married overseers frequently regarded any black woman, married or single, as their right. And there was always a way to make the women yield – whip them, whip their men or their children, work them naked, or otherwise humiliate and abuse them. Sooner or later, most of them would be broken to the white man's will. It was no wonder that so many plantations had a different overseer each year, as the masters searched for decent management. On the whole, Sabrehill had been fortunate in this respect, but there had been a period of almost five years . . . But that was part of the past that Lucy could not bear to look back on.

And she did have Jebediah Hayes. And Cheney. And other intelligent and responsible foremen and mechanics. And while she was quite willing to admit that there were also troublemakers at Sabrehill, the months since she had taken charge had demonstrated rather convincingly that she and the best of her people were quite capable of operating the plantation successfully.

But if she got the *right* overseer, he could hardly prove to be a handicap. And the pressure from her neighbors would be removed.

'Paul, I suppose that sooner or later I will have to have some white help at Sabrehill.'

'You will, Lucy. There is simply no way you'll be able to avoid that.'

'But I do want to wait until Ash gets here.'

'May I ask why?'

'Let's just say it's a play for time. All right, I must get a white overseer. But I'm in no hurry. My neighbors know that Ash is coming, and that gives me time, and when he gets here . . . well, we'll see what happens.'

74

'And after he leaves?'

Paul had at one time been her suitor. That was all over, but she suspected that he wouldn't mind reviving the situation, and she couldn't help teasing him. She shrugged. 'Who knows?' she said. 'We've had such a nice correspondence, maybe he'll come to stay.'

Paul didn't even try to squeeze out a smile, as she might have expected him to do. He merely looked at her in that measuring way of his and said, 'So you implied at Kimbrough Hall. But do you have any concrete reason to believe that he will?'

Lucy made an indifferent gesture. 'We always got along so well, that's all.'

Paul looked as if he didn't believe her. 'Of course, everything would work out nicely for you if he did stay – if the Sabre and McCloud holdings were combined. I don't know that *I* would benefit by such an arrangement.'

'Paul, I commend your growing frankness.'

'I have always been honest with you, Lucy, whether you'll believe that or not.'

'Oh, I don't think you've ever actually lied to me, Paul. And that's one reason why I want you to believe me when I say that I won't do anything to hurt you. Whatever happens to me in the future, I'll try to see that you lose nothing.'

'I appreciate that.'

That was her hold on Paul: the Devereau plantation, under his father's management, had sold much land and gone deeply into debt to Sabrehill. Paul Devereau wanted the land back and the debts cleared, and for various services Lucy was giving him what he wanted – a little at a time.

'And now,' Paul said, 'I have another suggestion, if I may.'

'Of course you may.'

'I want you to go to Charleston until your cousin Asher arrives here.'

The idea was so unexpected that she automatically resisted it. 'Why in the world should I do that?'

'First of all, for the very reason we've been discussing. For your safety. Here, you're an easy prey for any runaway black with a gun or a knife. If the Buckridge plantation was so easily raided, what about Sabrehill?'

'But I have Jebediah – '

'Are you going to start arming your people? My God, what an uproar that would cause! No, Lucy, since you have no armed whites on the place, you'll be much safer in Charleston. After your cousin arrives, maybe he can talk some sense into you, and we'll find you some good, reliable help.' He smiled slightly. 'We men will gang up on you.'

'Some men already tried it this evening, remember? I don't think they got very far. And you've overlooked one thing, Paul. If I go to Charleston, there won't be *any* white person at Sabrehill, and I'm sure our neighbors won't approve of Jebediah running the plantation by himself.'

'You're wrong,' Paul said. 'I'll be here. I'll live in one of the guest houses, or, if you wish, right here in the big house. And I'll bring one of my overseer's sons to watch the place in my absence.'

Lucy was immediately uneasy. She couldn't have said exactly why, but she didn't like the idea of Paul Devereau actually residing at Sabrehill. Maybe it was just that she suspected him of still wishing to become a permanent member of the household

He saw the uneasiness on her face and held up a hand as if to ward off an objection. 'I shall not interfere with Jebediah's operation of Sabrehill in any way, Lucy. I shall offer advice only when asked, just as I have in the past – or when I see something definitely going wrong.'

'But wouldn't you find staying at Sabrehill for such a period – perhaps two months or more – an inconvenience?'

'Yes, I would – and shall. But I want you safely away from here, Lucy. Would to God that Callie and Abbie Buckridge had been in Charleston for the summer.'

'You said, "first of all." For what other reason should I leave?'

'The obvious one. People are becoming increasingly irate over your being here alone. Now, with the Buckridge raid, you have a perfect excuse to leave. And after all, most people do leave their plantations, summer and winter, when the countryside isn't so disrupted. And if you aren't here, but a couple of armed white men are, clearly there'll be nothing to complain about. Or at least very little, until Mr McCloud departs, and you say he may be here permanently.'

'I was joking.'

'Even so. The principle stands.'

Lucy did not wish to leave Sabrehill. The day might come when she would; in fact, she looked forward to it. She would put the worst of the past behind her. She would abandon her black dresses for beautiful gowns, she would throw balls, she would gallivant in Charleston. She would *dare* the beauties and gallants of the chivalry to stare at her scarred face. But not yet. She was too tied to Sabrehill. She had put such efforts into keeping it going, and she was still far from done. She had much to learn, much to do.

But, still, if going to Charleston would make things easier . . .

'I'll think about it,' she said.

'That's all I ask, only that you consider the idea. I think you'll see its merits.' Paul finished his brandy. 'And now I suppose you'd like me to go.'

He waited for her to stand up, but she didn't. Something Jeppson had said had come to her mind, something that might be connected with her reputation as the sole white person – a woman alone – on a plantation.

'Paul,' she said, 'what do people around here think of me? I mean, really think of me?'

'I don't understand.'

She avoided his eyes. 'Well, there's not only my being here alone, there's also this business out of the past . . . with Mr Turnage.' *No, no, she didn't want to think about that!*

'Why do you ask, Lucy?'

'Well . . . Mr Jeppson said something . . . called me something . . .'

'What did he say?'

'He called me a whore. The Whore of Sabrehill, I think he said.'

The room was quiet. The ticking of two clocks could be heard, one in the library, the other all the way from the central passage.

Paul Devereau was almost to the door before she realized he had stood up from his chair.

'Paul, where are you going?'

He turned and looked around. His face was strained. 'To kill the son of a bitch,' he said quietly.

And she knew he would do it. Opportunist and rascal he might be; he might cheat her or blackmail her. But, oddly enough, he would also kill for her. Obviously he could never fight a duel with a man like Jeppson, so plain killing, face to face, was all that was left.

'No, Paul,' she said, as quietly as he, 'you will not kill him.'

'When a sandhiller like Jeppson dishonors a lady – '

'You will not kill him, because I do not approve, and I tell you not to.'

'Lucy – '

'Do you understand?'

He was silent, looking at her angrily. She stared back until his shoulders slumped and the breath went out of him.

She smiled. 'Besides, Paul, you might actually be indicted. You might even be tried, and hung. Even over a Jeppson. And I can't afford to lose you.'

She rose from her chair and went to him. Smiling, she kissed his cheek.

'We're still friends?' he said huskily.

'I should hope so.'

'Sometimes in the last year I've wondered.'

'So have I. But here we are, aren't we? After all this time. I've never found a friendship an easy account to close out . . . And now, good night, Paul.'

'Good night, Lucy.'

Leila saw Paul Devereau out and locked the door, then rejoined Lucy on the main staircase in the passage.

'Did you hear everything we said?' Lucy asked.

'Why, Lucy-child, you think I'd eavesdrop on you like that?'

Lucy laughed. 'Well, what do you think, Leila. Should we go to Charleston?'

'Yes,' the young black woman said flatly, 'I think we should. Do you good to get away for a while. Take me, do me good too. Open up the house on Lynch Street, have us a fine time.'

Leila entered her bedroom with her. The brandy Lucy had left behind was still on the table, and she sipped it. Yes, she would sleep now, she thought, slipping into bed.

'Turn out the light, Miss Lucy?'

'Yes, please.'

'Want me to stay with you tonight? I can make me a bed on the floor.'

'No. That's kind of you, Leila, but it'll be enough to know that you're in your room across the way.'

Leila turned out the light and crossed the room. 'If you want anything, now, you just call.'

'Thank you, Leila.'

She lay in the dark, her thoughts drifting.

To go to Charleston . . . She didn't really want to. Not yet. But maybe it would be for the best. She wouldn't have to go immediately, of course – in fact, she couldn't; she would have to send someone to open up the house, to dust and clean and make ready. Maybe a couple of girls and Zagreus and another man. She could make gestures, while delaying as long as possible.

She would talk to Jebediah about it. Tomorrow.

Remembering that Paul Devereau never had told her what her neighbors really thought of her, she drifted into sleep.

So she wondered what her neighbors really thought of her, did she?

Paul Devereau urged his horse back toward home, riding much too fast for the darkness. He was angry with himself, angry with Lucy, angry with the world.

Well, what the hell were her neighbors supposed to think of her? There she sat, all alone in that big Sabrehill mansion, without husband, father, or brother, trying to run a plantation with the help of a smart nigger or two. A *woman* trying to run a plantation – and without any protection from her blacks. Wasn't that scandal enough?

But there was more. This was the same Miss Lucy who, only a year before, had become involved with an overseer. With an *overseer*, for God's sake, and one known to be scum, at that! What do you think when one of the finest ladies in the district starts behaving in such a way? If she's reached a certain age, you start wondering if she's mad. You start wondering if she isn't capable of anything.

Yes, anything. Even messing around with her goddamn niggers. So what the hell did she *think* people thought of her? Angrily, he dug at his horse's belly with his heels and whipped its rump with his reins.

Just the same, he was still ready to marry her at any time. That would serve both of their purposes and also stop the goddamn whispers, and he didn't understand what the hell it was she held against him. He had courted her faithfully for years. He had been her friend and ally in every way she would allow. All right, it was true that once she became involved with another man he hadn't wasted any time, but what the hell had she expected? A man had to look after himself.

As he planned to do now.

But why, he asked furiously, why had the bitch had to call on Asher McCloud, of all people, for help? He remembered McCloud very well. Tall – taller than himself. Slender. A crack shot. Good-looking, he supposed, and attractive to women, no doubt. Oh, very much the toast of the ladies, Asher was. Paul remembered that young Lucy had given every sign of being driven witless by him. In his presence she had rolled her eyes, flounced, and lolligagged as she never had – to Paul's knowledge – with any other man in all the years since.

That had been long ago, but Paul had not forgotten, and he doubted that Lucy had either. And now, fifteen years later, if there was the same spark . . . Well, he didn't intend to let McCloud get in his way. There were things to be done, steps to be taken, and first of all, he needed more information.

The Devereau mansion and outbuildings came into sight, a few lights still burning. He rode around to the stable and put his horse into the care of one of the boys, then hurried into the mansion, hoping that his Aunt Junella was still up. His mother's sister, she spent most of her time visiting relatives, and now it was his turn. He had not been thrilled by her arrival, but her encyclopedic knowledge of the Virginia gentry might prove to be a godsend.

He found her at the piano in the music room. She broke off in midpassage as he entered.

'Aunt Junella, I'm sorry I had to desert you this evening. It was a rather urgent matter.'

She turned a wide smile and malicious yellow catlike eyes on him. 'That is quite all right, Paul. Mr Haydn and I have enjoyed each other's company considerably.'

'I'm surely glad to hear that.' Paul doubted that the enjoyment had been shared by Mr Haydn. 'Aunt Junella, I'm curious. Weren't you down here, oh, about fourteen, fifteen years ago when a certain McCloud family came visiting? There were parties for them at Sabrehill, Kimbrough Hall, I don't know where all.'

'I was not here,' Aunt Junella said, 'but you're undoubtedly referring to Gavin McCloud's family. I know Mrs McCloud rather well. I understand that the name was once spelled m-c-c-l-e-o-d, but they changed it to l-o-u-d. I don't know why. They were Dublin people, but before that one or both sides of the family came from the low country of Scotland. Of course, that was long ago.'

'Aunt Junella, you're a wonder.'

'Hated the British, as you can understand. Despised them. Thought they deserved George III. Looked forward to the Scotch and Irish driving the English into the sea.'

'They sound amusing.'

Aunt Junella shrugged and played a rapid arpeggio. Her nose appeared to detect a displeasing odor. 'Gavin had a bad habit of becoming involved in *trade*. Though why he should have, with that big plantation, I shall never understand.'

'Oh? It's quite large? I had forgotten that.'

'Magnificent. The house is one of the finest on the James River. It's called, simply, the Castle. Gavin is gone now, of course, but young Asher still manages the plantation. I understand that he, too, has become involved in *trade*. I suppose that it's something ingrained in the Scotch and the Irish that's just not quite nice.'

'I remember him as being quite a likeable fellow.'

'Oh, I suppose he is, actually. And, from all accounts, quite a devil with the ladies.'

'Is he, now!'

Aunt Junella accompanied herself with a few bars from a Haydn sonata, which hardly seemed fitting. 'There has been some scandal,' she said. 'In fact, it led to three duels. He lost none, and created two rich widows. Not truly ladies, I should say – I'm sure they found the means to thank him.'

That kind of man. Not the kind of man Paul wished to see at Sabrehill. Not at all.

'Why are you interested in the McClouds, Paul?'

'Not interested, just curious.'

'Oh, nonsense. You ride off in the evening on some business having to do with that Sabrehill woman. You come back and immediately inquire about the McCloud family, who visited here years ago. How old was Miss Lucy at that time, about fourteen or so? And you and young Asher were about sixteen or eighteen, I suppose.' She looked at Paul; she blinked and frowned. 'My word, I just remembered. Asher and Miss Lucy are cousins, aren't they?'

'Oh, we're all cousins, Aunt Junella. Lucy and I are cousins, for that matter. Her mother was a Devereau.'

'But you're more distant than Asher, as I recall. Paul, I repeat. *Why* are you suddenly interested in the McClouds?'

Aunt Junella might seem to babble at times, as wellbred ladies often did, but she was shrewd. He decided to tell her the truth.

'Because Miss Lucy has asked him to come visit her, Aunt Junella, at the end of the summer.'

'She, alone with that man in that house? That's hardly a respectable situation.'

'I don't know that she'll be alone. And anyway Miss Lucy has no great regard for public opinion.'

'Typical of Sabrehill people. Aristocrats, but not really very nice. No, not nice at all, though I did like Aaron Sabre in his day – ' She broke off. 'But of course you're worried that Asher might take advantage of Miss Lucy's loneliness.'

'You could put it that way.'

'And you wish to marry her yourself?'

'The thought has passed through my mind, but I don't think the lady intends to so honor me.'

'But you would like to, and you sense that Asher might prove to be an obstacle.'

'Aunt Junella, you are positively prescient.'

'Your marrying that young woman would solve a lot of problems, wouldn't it?'

'Problems, Aunt Junella?'

Fluttering a fan before her face, the lady arose from the piano. Her smile widened, and her yellow eyes glittered. 'Oh, I am quite aware that my sister's husband was not the most astute manager of this plantation. Your mother was not quite the pretty little featherhead your father demanded, and what she didn't tell me, I could easily guess.' She played with her fan and thought for a moment. 'Paul, would you like me to help you?'

'In what way, Aunt Junella?'

'I know a certain amount about Asher and his family, but perhaps not enough. Not all that could be useful to you. Now, I could write some letters.'

Paul shrugged and tried to look indifferent. 'We wouldn't wish to inspire gossip.'

'Oh, my sources would be quite discreet. My lawyers, for example. They are quite reliable, and if I were to write to them . . .'

'That would be very good of you, Aunt Junella. As Miss Lucy's lawyer, I do consider it my duty to look out for her welfare.'

'But of course, Paul. I shall write tomorrow.'

And Mr Asher McCloud, Paul thought, shall not find me unprepared.

* * *

At the second dawn after the raid, they raped and killed the girl.

It was inevitable, of course. Quinn had looked into her eyes in that first moment upstairs in the Buckridge mansion and known she was to be their victim, known she was doomed, but he had come to have a faint hope. Occasionally we outlive our doom. Perhaps Abigail Buckridge would be the one person in this nightmare to awaken and think, *It was all a dream. I live.*

He had watched her so carefully the previous morning. The sky had slowly lightened, revealing Quinn's and Harpe's stained faces, and she had hardly given them a look. She had ridden with her head hanging forward and her eyes closed, and when she had lifted her head and opened her eyes, Quinn had leaned toward her grinning as if to challenge her: *Know me. Know what I am. Dare to do that, and you die. As you must.*

Her head had fallen forward again, and her eyes had closed.

They had rested during the day, taking turns at the watch, and traveled again through the night. Now, near dawn, the time had at last come.

They formed a triangle in a clearing: Xenos, the Negro; Harpe, with his black-stained blond mustache; Quinn, with his thick black beard. The girl, untied from her saddle, had fallen to the ground. She looked like one of the wisps of fog that rolled slowly among the trees. Her gown was torn and twisted around her, her arms, legs, and face were smudged with dirt, and her eyes were dark with exhaustion. Those eyes still held doom and terror as they looked up at the points of the triangle that held her captive.

'Now, Miss Abbie, honey,' Quinn said quietly in his thick field accent, 'Now, don't you be scared. We gon' let you go now. Soon you home wi' your momma and papa.' He believed it could be so; he thought it just might be so.

'But first, honey,' he added, 'they's something we gon' do to you.'

Even in that dim light, he saw that she knew what he meant. She had known from the very beginning.

He expected her to say *No* or *Please*, to beg or to weep, but she didn't. She whimpered. She waited as one might await a surgeon. What had to happen would happen. She might fight it, but it was inevitable.

Quinn reached for his belt buckle.

'No,' Harpe said.

Quinn, surprised, hesitated. He was the leader; to take the girl first was his prerogative, a right that Harpe had never challenged. But now Harpe was looking down at the girl with the same fascination that he himself felt.

'No,' Harpe repeated, as if the matter were settled, 'not this time. This one belongs to me.'

Quinn nearly dropped his accent. 'What the hell? I found her!'

'We found her. This time it's my turn. I'm first.'

Control was slipping from Quinn's hands. He felt as if all the time they had been together, Harpe, the older man by almost twenty years, had been playing with him. Now at last there was a prize Harpe wanted, and he was claiming it. Harpe was taking over.

And Quinn could not let that happen. He looked around, looked for some alternative possibility. And saw Xenos.

The black man was drawing back as if he wanted to disappear into the shadows. He had ridden in on the Buckridge plantation with as much nerve as Quinn ever hoped to see, but now there was something cringing and frightened about him.

'Wait,' Quinn said to Harpe, grinning. 'Our friend here. Ouah new frien'. Ought'n him be first? Gotta baptize'm.'

Harpe didn't answer. He might not have heard. He went right on staring at the girl.

86

'Ain' dat right?' Quinn asked the black. 'You gon' take care duh gal, ain' so?'

'Don't want her,' Xenos said, drawing still further back into the darkness. 'Don't want her.'

'Why, what you talkin' 'bout, boy? Everybody know duh black boy wan' take care duh white gal!' Quinn looked at Harpe, inviting shared laughter at Xenos's expense, but Harpe might not even have heard. His gaze was locked with the girl's.

'Never had no gal didn't want me in my life,' Xenos said. His voice was shaking. 'Don't need no gal don't want me. You say you gon' let her go – '

'Why, we gon' do dat – '

'Then let her go!' The shaking disappeared as Xenos's voice rose in anger. 'You got no call to hurt no gal-child! We got the silver, even some gold, we got everything – '

'You don' like what we gon' do dis gal?'

'No, I don't like – '

Quinn showed him the pistol, and the clearing in the woods was silent. Dawn was pinking the horizon through the trees, and at some distance the birds began their hungry morning chatter.

'All right,' Quinn said, 'you just stay where you are and watch.' To Harpe he said, 'You go 'head. I keep ouah frien' heah covered.'

It was a face-saving gesture, but it might have been wasted. Harpe still appeared deaf and blind to all that went on around him. The only thing that mattered to him now was the girl, and he went down on one knee beside her as if genuflecting. And, after a moment, reached for her.

She whimpered and tried to escape him: tried to roll away, tried to climb to her feet, tried to crawl on her knees. It was no good; he held her effortlessly, not toying with her or tormenting her, simply taking his time, as if this were some ritual which had to be enacted. There seemed to be no great lust in it, only an intention and a determination.

He put her sobbing onto her back again and ripped down the front of her gown. She kicked and clawed, but he held her easily, and she didn't scream until he took her: not so much a scream of pain as a despairing wail. When you rape an innocent, Quinn knew, you took something more than her body, and the knowledge gave him a kind of sad gratification. Harpe's taking the girl first didn't rob him of quite everything he had looked forward to.

Once impaled, the girl no longer resisted. Kneeling and leaning toward her. Quinn saw that her eyes were blank. Even now, with Harpe mounting her, there was not the slightest sign that she recognized him as anything but a black – or recognized anything at all. Quinn sat back on the ground and kept his pistol trained on Xenos, who stood with his back turned and his head lowered.

Harpe, taking his time, finished.

With a groan, a sigh, he sank down on the girl.

Quinn saw clearly what happened then. The girl might have been dead. She and Harpe both lay perfectly still, and her eyes were as blank as before. Harpe's arm lay near her head. She turned her head slightly until her mouth was against the arm. Then, with all her strength, it seemed, she sank her teeth into it.

Harpe screamed. It was a tearing, ripping agonized scream, and he screamed again as he tried to pull his arm lose. But the girl would not let go. Like an animal, like a maddened bitch dog, she hung on, though Harpe pounded at her head and tried to pull away. Finally, with another roar of pain, he gouged one of her eyes, and her teeth came loose.

He rose up on his knees then, and he seemed more caught up in a fit of passion than he had been while raping the girl. He caught her small head in his two big hands and half lifted her from the ground. He gave the head a sharp hard angry twist to one side, and there was the sound of snapping twigs. He threw the girl back down on the road – dead.

Xenos had turned and now stared with horror.

'Jesus Christ,' Harpe howled, clutching at his bleeding arm, 'she *bit* me! The goddamn bitch *bit* me!'

'You killed her,' Quinn said softly. He felt shocked, numbed – and yet somehow thrilled and vindicated. He had been right. The girl had had to die. 'You killed her,' he repeated.

'I don't give a damn, the goddamn bitch bit me! Goddamn fucking bitch!'

His face still taut with pain, Harpe fell away from the girl and rocked from side to side as he nursed his wound. Quinn stood up and walked toward the girl. He bent down to look at her more closely. No, not at her – at it: at a naked body with a bit of rag at the shoulders, a gouged-out eye, and a grotesquely twisted neck. Small. Broken. Not her; it. Abigail Buckridge was no more, and it was as if she had never been. When you kill, you wipe out reality, and only illusions are left. Killing filled Quinn with sadness – and a sense of power. Godlike. He felt it now, even though he was not the one who had actually killed Abigail Buckridge.

Quinn sighed. He straightened up and scratched his head. 'Yeah, she bit you,' he said, 'and she's dead.'

'Bitch had it coming to her.'

Who doesn't, Quinn thought, sooner or later? But a man could kill more often than he could die, which might be a consolation of sorts.

'Don't reckon it does,' Quinn said. 'It would have been good if she had got back home and told how the bunch of goddamn niggers who stole her fucked hell out of her, but I reckon they'll figure that anyway. And we can make sure they know it.'

He had let the muzzle of his pistol drop. Now he raised it again.

Xenos saw what was coming. Eyes widening with fear, he looked desperately about. He reached for his belt but there was no pistol in it at that moment, only a knife that he hardly dared to draw. He clutched the handle, but looked toward a rifle that leaned against a tree. It was far away, about five yards, much too far.

'Nigger,' Quinn said calmly, 'don't you know better than to put your black hide on a white woman?'

Drawing the knife, Xenos sprang. Quinn shot him in the chest. The bullet stopped him, seemed to pick him up, and set him back a yard. Then, for a horrible moment, Quinn thought he hadn't been stopped. Raising the knife high about his head, Xenos took one step forward.

Quinn waited ready to strike again, to kick or to stab if Xenos moved but he was perfectly still.

He fell to the ground.

'Goddamn niggers,' Harpe said after a moment. 'Just can't keep away from the white stuff. Well, this one will never touch another.'

'He never did,' Quinn said, trying to recapture the feeling he had had with Abigail Buckridge. 'He never existed. Never even really existed.' But it was no use – not when you had been trained early in life that niggers were hardly human and therefore hardly existed in the first place.

Harpe gave him a queer look, but Quinn thought to hell with him. He was a damn good man as long as he stayed in his place, but there were things he didn't understand and never would.

Quinn looked up at the rapidly brightening sky. 'Somebody might have heard that shot,' he said. 'We'd better get away from here.'

'Lucky for us if they did hear it. Maybe they'll get here before the damn birds tear her up so you can't tell who she is.'

'Yes. And we'll leave word somewhere. "Saw three niggers with a white woman. Heard a shot." They'll find 'em, and by God there'll be hell to pay.'

And meanwhile he and Harpe would be in Charleston lining their pockets and getting ready for the next raid. Everything was working out fine, Quinn thought, just fine.

Part Two

1

The bugle call awakened Zulie. It was repeated again and again, dispirited and drifting off key, as if the bugler were being urged to work against his will. It lifted Zulie to consciousness, frayed her nerves, and brought a half-hearted curse to her lips.

Where was she? She was in her cabin, the Voodoo oum'phor in which she had always lived, and she sat up on her bed and looked around the room for her brothers. But of course they were not there. Orion and Paris preferred the men's barrack – except when one of them got a girl here alone – and Zag lived over the coach house.

And Zag was in Charleston right now. Lucky Zag.

The goddamn bugle blew again, and what the hell was a goddamn bugle blow for on Sunday afternoon? Wet with sweat, her single garment clinging to her, Zulie arose from the bed and went to the door of the cabin. She hadn't meant to fall asleep. Much better on an afternoon like this to soak in some gentle stream and rest on the bank with her admirers surrounding her.

Fucking bugle blew again!

She left the cabin and walked between the rows of cabins that faced the central square of the field quarters. There in the square, as she had half expected, was Mr Buckridge and his son Royal. Royal had driven a buggy up by the whipping post, and Mr Buckridge had collared the boy with the bugle and was urging him to blow again. Royal, in the buggy, looked hot and dispirited, and Mr Buckridge, standing nearby, was red-faced with a forced enthusiasm that quickly faded as he looked about at the mere thirty or so people who had answered the call.

'Where the hell is everybody?' he asked.

It was common sense to keep her mouth shut and look dumb, but Zulie took it on herself to answer. 'Mr Buckridge, sir, it's Sunday afternoon. People out tending their gardens. People out fishing and catching rabbit for supper. People swimming and pleasuring and saying their prayers. It's the *Lord's* day, Mr Buckridge, sir! Just ain't nobody much here!'

She expected Mr Buckridge to turn angrily on her, and she was ready to defend herself at risk of a whipping, but instead he looked frustrated and near tears. He looked from one face to another as if begging help, and abruptly she felt sorry for him. She hated herself for it; after all, he was one of *them*.

'Well,' he said fumblingly, 'well – well, can't you call them in?'

'Mr Buckridge, sir, I'd dearly love to do that to 'blige you, but they are *all* over the place – some maybe at Devereau or Kimbrough Hall or even clear to your place – couldn't *never* get them all here afore sundown. Now, whyn't you tell us what you want to say, then we tell all the others. I promise you, we tell 'em all.'

Hope brightened Mr Buckridge's face, though not Royal's. 'That's a good idea,' he said. 'I'll tell you, and you tell the others. Because they are going to want to know what I've got to say. I have got something very special I want to tell you, and you all are going to want to hear it.'

Zulie doubted that. This was the third time Mr Buckridge had spoken to the people at Sabrehill in the two weeks since he had buried his daughter. He went from plantation to plantation, she had heard, making the same speech. It wasn't possible that he had anything new to say.

She was wrong.

'How would one of you here like to be free?'

He looked around the small crowd, a bright false smile on his face.

96

But what the hell did he expect them to say to that? *Yes, master, I'd sho' like to be free*, like some troublesome nigger? And what good was freedom, some of them might have thought, without knowing numbers and letters and a trade? Here at Sabrehill, at least they had good food and adequate clothing.

Buckridge seemed to see the doubts behind their blank faces. 'I mean *really* free,' he said, a note of protest in his voice. 'I've already made an agreement with Miss Lucy. Any of you can tell me for sure who the men were who killed my daughter, I'll pay for your freedom. More than that – you have a husband or wife and pickaninnies, I'll buy them free too! How'd you like that? Why, you can go to Charleston and live off the fat of the land! Because I'm going to give you one thous – no, sir, I am going to raise that right now! I'm going to give you *two* thousand dollars for your very own. And if you don't know a trade, I'll see you learn one. Put you in business in Charleston, how you like that? Man could become a carpenter, make a lot of money. Woman could become a seamstress, open a dress shop. I am telling you, there is a lot of money to be made in Charleston! And one of you could do it! Any one of you!' Again, Mr Buckridge looked around the crowd, looked desperately. 'Now, how about it? Is one of you going to earn that money? One of you going to go free and go live in Charleston? Because I'm convinced, the way those men disappeared, they're being sheltered somewhere right in this countryside. And you people, you all know a lot more than you ever let on. Don't ever tell me niggers don't know a lot that white folks don't know!' He tried futilely to generate an infectious laugh. 'Oh, you know plenty, let me tell you! Why, I could tell you stories . . . Now, how about it, somebody here got something to tell me?'

No one spoke.

'Please . . . somebody . . .?'

Charleston, Zulie thought, to go to Charleston and be free . . .

'We going tell everybody what you say, Mr Buckridge, sir,' she said, to be rid of him. 'Don't you worry – me, I tell 'em all.' She thought the old fart had gone plumb crazy.

'Thank you.' Mr Buckridge looked genuinely grateful. 'Thank you. What's your name, girl?'

'Erzulie, sir.'

'Erzulie, I'm beholden to you. If you learn anything . . .'

'Yes, sir.'

'You get the men that killed my daughter – and I'll do *anything* for you!'

'Yes, sir.'

Mr Buckridge climbed into the buggy with Mr Royal, and they drove out of the quarters square, headed, no doubt, for another plantation – telling one and all of this grand chance to be free and to go to Charleston.

They ain't never going catch them maroons, Zulie thought as she headed for a swimming hole.

But, oh, to be free and in Charleston . . .

Buckridge could have no idea of what a dream he had brought back to Zulie's mind, what a lust for a different kind of life. She had had it for years, ever since she had been taken to Charleston years ago with her mother. She would never forget the shops along King Street, the tall white steeple of St Michael's church, the marvelous Sabre house on Lynch Street. And the free blacks. They had walked along Meeting and Broad and Trapp Streets as if they had owned them, hardly even stepping aside for the resentful-eyed whites.

And some of those blacks were rich, it was said – not many, perhaps, but some. They no longer had to work like the carpenters and the seamstresses Mr Buckridge had mentioned – they wore white gloves and had money in the banks, the same as the white folks. They, like the rich whites, had large, fancy houses, and some even owned slaves and planted cotton and rice. So Zulie had heard.

To be free and in Charleston . . .

Now that she was older, she knew that the dream could never be fulfilled. All of her magic had failed to make it come true, and yet it refused to die, and it flooded her mind now, as she crossed the fields. She would live in her own house, three stories high, with an enclosed yard and shady piazzas. Her husband would be handsome and rich, and she would have only the finest silken clothes, the finest carriages, the finest horses. She would be fawned over in the best shops, and she would dine with the other rich people of color. She would give balls such as she had seen both in Charleston and in the plantation mansions – and, yes, Charleston would *belong* to the people of color!

The vision grew, and Zulie smiled. She knew that white folks frowned on voodoo and had even killed mam'bos for being witches. But with Charleston in the hands of the people of color, there would be nothing to fear. She would be mam'bo for the whole city and have the greatest oum'phor that ever was, oum'phor and peristyle, and there she would perform all of the half-forgotten rituals her mother had taught her. She would be paid tribute by all the people of the city.

And what else? Oh, yes – Zag and Orion and Paris would be with her, of course. They would be her guard, sharing her luxuries. They would all have many servants, and in the heat of the day the servants would fan her and pour cool baths for her. White servants? The idea made her smile. Yes, she would have little white maids and little white houseboys to do her bidding. Her slaves. She was rich and in Charleston with her slaves –

Thunder rumbled in the distance.

And suddenly the dream was gone. She was standing on the edge of a dusty field, and looking up, she saw storm clouds rushing across the sky as if to overtake her. She was not in Charleston, and quite likely she never would be again. Never again in Charleston, and never free.

'God damn them,' she said dully, aloud. 'God damn them all.' She didn't care what Zag said, she would continue to put badmouth on the whites until they were all dead. She would curse them and spell them and call upon the *loa* for vengeance until the whites had paid for every last injury and pain and indignity that she and hers had ever suffered. 'God damn them all.'

Suddenly the sky was blackening. Lightning ripped through the darkness, and thunder exploded in a ragged salvo. Zulie turned and hurried back toward the field quarters. The storm made her worry about Zag – she hoped he would be back from Charleston soon, so that she could look after him.

'God damn them all.'

The rain came down in a torrent, in a deluge, and the hood of the buggy gave him no protection at all: almost from the moment the storm burst, he was soaked, cold, and miserable. Everything seemed to be conspiring to keep him from reaching Sabrehill. The mud of the rutted road sucked at the wheels, slowing his tired horse down to a walk. In the darkness he heard a stream rushing against a small bridge he had to cross, and he was hardly over it when he heard the breaking of timbers and it washed away. Then, not five minutes later, lightning threw a tree across the road ahead, and he had all he could do to control his panicky horse.

He managed to get around the tree, twice nearly tipping the buggy over, but he knew he had to find shelter. He should have done it before, but the storm had come up fast, and he had been eager to get back to Sabrehill. Now, however, it had become downright dangerous to remain on the road.

100

He soon spotted a farm house, but he had no luck there. He tied his horse out front, but he must have been seen coming, for the moment he stepped onto the veranda, a door was flung open and he found himself staring down the barrel of a musket.

'Nigger, you ride on,' a man's voice said.

In spite of the light behind the figure in the doorway, Zag saw that he was talking to another black man. 'Brother,' he said, 'a little mercy. My horse is cold and wet, and I'm cold and wet, and – '

'Ride on, I say!'

' – it's a long, long way to Sabrehill plantation. A night in your barn, that's all I ask – until the storm lets up.'

The musket wavered, and Zag sensed the man's hesitation. Maybe he had heard of Sabrehill.

'Please, master, sir.' Maybe the man was free; a little flattery could not hurt.

'Got any money?'

'Yes, sir. I pay – '

'Don't want your money. There's an old inn on an old road people don't use much anymore. It's called The Roost – Keegan's Roost. You go west maybe two, three furlongs and turn north for maybe a mile. Then west again. You try there. Nobody 'round here gonna let you in.'

'Yes, sir.' Zag started to turn away.

'And, boy . . .'

'Yes, sir?'

The man's voice softened, became almost friendly. 'You be careful there. Nobody I know goes to Keegan's Roost that don't have to.'

'Yes, sir.'

The door closed, cutting off the light, and Zag staggered back through the drenching rain and the darkness to the buggy. He felt angry and bitter toward the man, yet he didn't altogether blame him. In the other's place, Zag,

101

too, would have been reluctant to welcome a strange black on a night like this – though he probably would have done it.

It was a full hour before he found The Roost, an old building, large and ramshackled, with a washed-out sign of a rooster hanging out front. Late though it was, a light or two burned dimly within. This time Zag did not approach from the front but drove around the back, as he thought would be expected. There he found a kitchen house, with a light burning, a stable, and various other buildings that indicated the Roost functioned as a farm as well as an inn. In this out-of-the-way place, it probably could not otherwise have continued to exist.

From somewhere in the house, distantly, Zag heard a wail of pain. It was the kind of cry, short and sharp, with which he was all too familiar, and he remembered the black farmer's words: 'Nobody I know goes to The Roost that don't have to.'

But he had to have shelter. He heard the cry again as he climbed down from the buggy.

He dashed through the rain. The third cry came as he reached the door. They were well spaced, and Zag knew instinctively that they would be interspersed by a master's threats and curses. He raised a hand to bang on the door, but, suddenly, hesitant, he held back. He stepped to one side and looked through a window.

He could see only through one small pane, where a drape had been pulled aside, but what he could see was enough. A girl lay on the floor. The light was dim, but she seemed to be light-skinned. Over her stood a white master, tall, bald, and fat, and as Zag watched, he brought a whip down on the girl's buttocks one more time. A bit of broken crockery on the floor beside her explained the whipping.

For some reason, he had no idea why, Cissie came to Zag's mind. He remembered how she had come in from

102

the fields with welts on her butt and how he had wanted to kill the driver who had put them there. And now, as he waited for the whip to rise again, he felt a return of that same anger, that same hatred, and he thought of how he might burst through the window – or how he might seize the white master's throat, how he might choke, strangle, kill the man –

But then it was over. The man tossed the whip aside, said something, and half-heartedly kicked the girl. He walked away, and the girl slowly began to get up from the floor. Trembling with fury more than with cold, Zag hurried back to the buggy.

He sat there, not knowing why. He should either leave and seek another place – but where? it would take hours – or go back to the door of the inn and knock. But he knew in his bones, somehow, that The Roost was no place for him tonight.

But the girl. He wanted to see her again. He could think of no reason why – he had not even seen her face – except that she had made him think of Cissie.

As if in answer to his wish, the door of the inn opened. A girl emerged and closed the door – it had to be the same girl – and hurried, head lowered, through the downpour toward the kitchen house. She never looked up, never appeared to see Zag.

That settled the matter without his giving it another thought. The stable door was already half-open, and, opening it the rest of the way, he drove in. The relief from the rain was so profound that for a moment he forgot both the girl and his anger.

But then his stomach gurgled, and Zag had to laugh. A man's stomach didn't give a damn about anything but itself.

He climbed down from the buggy again. After setting the stable door exactly as it had been, he slogged hurriedly through the mud and the rain toward the kitchen house, where a light still showed through a window. When he pounded on the door, it swung open under its own weight.

He saw a typical kitchen house: a large fireplace with the usual spits and hoists and trivets; in the wall beside it, an oven; heavy pans hanging on the walls; a table with cutlery scattered over it.

And in the middle of the brick floor stood the girl looking over her shoulder at him. With a startled cry, she grabbed a wicked carving knife from the table and whirled around to defend herself.

Cissie, Zag thought, though not in a thousand years would he have mistaken this girl for Cissie. Cissie had been dark; this girl, if she were a mulatto, was as light as any he had ever seen; she might have been one of the Spanish or French girls he had seen in Charleston. Their features were quite different; Cissie had been taller, her face and figure rounder and fuller, while this girl looked like a skinny, half-starved little swamp rat. She was much younger than Cissie had been at the time of her death, and a good ten years younger than Zag himself. There was simply no resemblance between the two women, and yet Zag felt a sharp pang of sympathy, and again he thought: *Cissie*.

Scraping the mud from his boots, he stepped through the doorway, and the girl brandished the knife.

'What you want, boy? Why you come sneaking in here?'

'Not sneaking – '

'You speak up! What you want? You got no business here!'

'Saw your light,' Zag said patiently. 'Looking for shelter, my horse and buggy and me. If we can stay in your stable – '

'You got a pass? What business you got around here?'

'Course I got a pass.'

Zag watched the girl calm herself, watched the tear-reddened eyes become more cunning.

'Got money?' the girl asked.

'A little.'

The girl took a step toward him, her knife still raised but fear evaporating. 'You got to pay.'

'Yes, ma'am. For something to eat and a place out of the rain, I pay one dollar for me, my horse, and my buggy. I see you got a nice big empty stable – '

'Three dollars!'

Zag looked with astonishment at the girl – with more astonishment, in fact, than he actually felt, for a little dickering was not out of order. 'Three dollars!' he said. 'My mistress don't give me no three dollars for a itty bit of oats and johnnycake and a night in a stable! She going think I'm cheating her! You trying to get me whipped, gal?'

'Ain't no *gal* to you,' the girl said indignantly. 'I'm *Miss* Bonnibelle to you, you hear me, nigger?'

'Yes, ma'am,' Zag said sceptically. '*Miss* Bonnibelle *what*, ma'am?'

The girl's eyes wavered. 'Ca . . . Calhoun.'

The girl had hesitated and then picked a famous name, a name often heard in Charleston and in the mansions of the great plantations. Zag doubted that it was hers or that she even had a last name. He suppressed a smile and said, 'Yes, ma'am, Miss Bonnibelle Calhoun, ma'am. But anyway, I can't pay you no three dollars. Pay you dollar and a half.'

The girl brandished the knife. 'Start running, nigger.'

'Tell you what,' Zag went on, as if he hadn't heard her. 'Don't think nobody saw me come here, did they? Buggy's already in the stable. Now, if you was to let me feed my horse, and if you was to give me a little something to eat, I could give you two whole dollars, and you could keep it all for yourself. Long as nobody didn't find out. I wake me up real early in the morning and be gone before anybody know.'

The girl looked at him warily for a long moment, as if suspecting some kind of trick. She lowered the knife a few inches.

'Two dollars,' Zag urged quietly. 'Two dollars all you own. I pay you, not them. I want you to keep it.'

The girl's face was visibly pulled between hope and distrust. Under the bitterness and the tears, Zag saw, there was a kind of remnant sweetness, and he almost wished he had agreed to three dollars.

The girl grinned crookedly. 'You don't look like no mean nigger,' she said.

'Not mean. Just cold and wet and hungry and tired.'

'And if my master catches you, you won't tell on me?'

'No. I'll just say I was scared to wake him in the middle of the night. I'll pay him what he wants, and you can still keep the two dollars.'

'Show me your money.'

Zag took two dollars from his money poke and gave them to her. She looked at them carefully as if to make certain that the money was genuine.

'Keep it,' he said again, and when she looked up at him, he figured she was remembering the beating she had taken only a short time before. This was payment.

'You go on back to the stable,' she said. 'It's big and mostly unused. Put your buggy way to the other end and your horse in a way-back stall, and feed him. Then you be quiet and wait for me. I'll bring you something to eat in a little while.'

She might or she might not. He thought she would. He smiled and said, 'I thank you, ma'am.'

For a man who claimed to be cold and wet and tired and hungry, Zag returned to the stable feeling curiously good. The image of Bonnibelle's crooked smile stayed with him as he made his way back through the mud, and in the darkness of the night he returned it. Damned little blanched-out swamp-rat girl, cheating her fat-ass white master out of two dollars. He liked her.

The rain was letting up, and the thunder had grown more distant. After five minutes alone back in the stable,

106

Zag decided that no one but Bonnibelle had seen him crossing back from the kitchen. He was safe.

He did as Bonnibelle had instructed him: put the buggy far back in the stable, then put the horse in the back stall and fed it. He was beginning to think that she was not going to bring him food after all, when, after half an hour, she appeared. She handed him a plate heaped with beans, corn, and ham and gravy, and with delight he discovered why she had taken so long: the food was not only good, it was hot.

'I do thank you again, Bonnibelle Calhoun.'

'A man shouldn't have to come out of a night like this without getting a hot meal.'

Explaining that it could not be seen from the inn, she lit a lamp, and they sat down together on the floor while Zag ate.

'You ain't even told me your name,' she said.

'Name is Zagreus.'

Zagreus? Never heard of such a name. Is that all there is to it?'

'Zagreus is all. Unless it's Zag Sabre or Zag Sabrehill. 'Cause they're my people, and that's where I'm heading.'

It seemed to Zag that in the lamplight Bonnibelle's smile was almost as pretty as Cissie's.

'Zagreus Sabrehill – that's a mighty fancy name.'

'Not nearly as nice as Bonnibelle.'

The smile widened. 'And where you coming from, Zagreus Sabrehill?'

'Charleston. Sent there by my mistress to help open up her house.'

'Oh, my, you musta had a fine time there.'

'Some,' Zag said hesitantly. 'Some.'

The smile faded. 'Why, I always thought Charleston must be the grandest place in the world to visit. I never been there, but I heard all kinds of things about it. You have troubles there?'

'No, not troubles, 'zactly.' How could he tell her about the hollowness in the life he was trying to rebuild, the hollowness that Cissie had left? He thought he would like to tell her, because something about her had touched him, but not yet; she was still a stranger. He settled for a partial truth: 'Sometimes, Bonnibelle, when things been nice, you think they going to be nice again. But mostly they ain't. Not like the first time.'

Bonnibelle laughed and shrugged. 'I sure wouldn't know about that. Never been in Charleston, never had my first time yet.'

No, Zag thought, you ain't had your first time for lots of things.

He savored the food; perhaps the miserable night made it seem better than it was – warm and peppered and salty. He needed water, and Bonnibelle disappeared for a few minutes to bring back a pitcher, fresh from the well. She watched with pleasure as he ate, knowing that the food was appreciated, and as he returned her smiles, desire came, as it often did after a long hard day: the need for the final comfort. But he thought of Cissie and listened to Bonnibelle's voice and put the need aside.

They talked. He told her first of Charleston – of the grand houses with their sheltered piazzas, the shops on King Street where you could buy anything in the world, the ships' masts as seen from the cobblestones of East Bay Street and the Battery. He told her about the music and the night laughter and about the grand balls in the mansions and the even better parties among the house servants and the free people of color. He tried to give her some idea of the smell of salt air that wafted in from the harbor and the sense of near-freedom he had when he was in Charleston.

Then he told her about Sabrehill – about the white Miss Lucy and the black Mr Jeb who ran the plantation, about the fine big house overlooking Sabre's Landing and the

108

wide slow river, about the dozens of glistening white outbuildings and the vast cotton fields and the rice tracts. He told about his sister and his brothers, about Momma Lucinda and her son Irish and Leila the housekeeper. He spoke of hard days in the fields and fine Saturday nights. Tired as he was, he talked for an hour and then another hour and hardly knew the time was passing.

'You sound 'most like you plumb like being a slave at Sabrehill.'

Zag looked at the girl with surprise. 'No,' he said after considering the thought, 'I sure don't. Don't enjoy it at all. I remember Mr Turnage, worst overseer ever at Sabrehill, and I hate it. I think about when damn buckra Mr Jeppson whip a nigger then hang him and burn him to death, and then . . .'

For a moment, all the terror and rage of that evil evening returned to Zag, and he found he could not speak.

'People around here do that, too,' Bonnibelle said. 'My master, he as soon kill a nigger as look at him.'

Zag nodded. 'So don't say I like being a slave. But, Bonnibelle, I hear tell a story once about a man whose ship is lost at sea. Everybody die but him, and he swims to a little island, way out there 'most to Africa. And he's all alone, and he figures he might as well die. And then he thinks, "No, by God. Ain't going die." Thinks, "This all I got, it ain't going beat me. Going make me a life out of it somehow." '

'How does the story end?'

'Don't know. Forgot. All I know is, I got what I got, and going make me a life out of it, and to hell with every Turnage and every Jeppson. Most of the time I don't even think about being a slave. Don't want to hurt nobody, don't want to be hurt, just want to do what I can to be happy.'

Bonnibelle's eyes were wistful and distant. 'Guess that's all a body can ask for. Someday I'm going away some place where I can be happy.'

So this girl, too, had a dream. And, whatever the miseries of her life, the dream had not yet been killed.

'He whip you much?' he asked gently.

The girl nodded. 'Most every day.' Her answer was automatic, as if her mind were far away and she had not really heard the question.

'You got no family?'

'Got some somewhere, I guess.'

'Gone off and left you here?'

'There was lots of us kids, and I was littlest. My pa, he said for two hundred dollars he'd let me stay here and work at the inn. Been here ever since. About five years.'

Zag was shocked. 'You own pa – *he* sold you?'

Bonnibelle seemed to awaken. Her gaze moved to Zag's eyes, and she frowned. 'No, he didn't *sell* me. He just took some wages for me and left me here to work them out.'

'Forever?'

She saw the implication and was offended. 'No, just till – till I'm ready to leave.'

'And when you going be ready?'

Bonnibelle bit a lip. 'When I'm ready.'

'When your master lets you go, you mean, and when that going be?'

She got onto her knees. Her eyes hardened and her voice rose. 'What you talking about? You talk like I'm just a – a nigger slave! Just like you!'

Well, there was that question. The notion had crossed his mind that she was probably white and free. But she could have been a person of color, and in those first seconds that he had seen her, she had been under the whip. And he had thought of Cissie.

And she had been sold, sold by her own father, sold like any common nigger slave – and she knew it. And now she was trying to save a small shred of pride by putting herself above him. He should have felt a sharp resentment, but

110

somehow the resentment would not come. Just a poor damn white-trash girl-child, he thought, sold like any black pickaninny. One of us, and she don't even know it. Can't make herself believe it.

'I'm sorry, Bonnibelle,' he said.

Angrily, she got to her feet, gathering up his plate and the pitcher and banging them together. 'I *told* you! I'm *Miss* Bonnibelle to you, boy, and I ain't no nigger slave! Maybe I'm just common, but I'm *white*, and don't you forget it! You understand me, boy? I'm *white*, you hear?'

'Yes ma'am. I hear.'

She tramped to the other end of the stable. At the door, she turned to him again.

'You are just a goddamn nigger slave, you hear me, and you better remember your place. You understand?'

'Yes, ma'am.' Zag thought the girl was crying or close to it.

'I'm white!'

And that's all you got, Zag thought sadly, as he watched the girl leave. You got a white skin and that's all – not even a trip to Charleston or a home like Sabrehill. A white skin and a pa who would sell you away for two hundred dollars.

He wondered what revenge she might take for the hurt to her pride. She could have his hide or even his life if she wanted to, yet Zag had a feeling that nothing at all was going to happen. The girl had the money he had given her, and she would take no chance on losing it. Besides, they had had a good time together for a couple of hours, and that had to count for something. In spite of her parting insults, Zag continued to have a good feeling for the girl.

He felt safe.

If he had not, he would have left at once; instead, he checked his horse one last time, then found an empty stall and made himself a bed of hay covered with an old blanket. He put the lamp out and settled down to rest under the quiet, comforting sound of the slackening rain on the roof. He meant to think about Bonnibelle, but he fell asleep almost instantly.

He had no idea of how long he had slept when he awakened. It could have been a few minutes or an hour or more. The thinnest ray of light from the front of the stable passed his stall and awakened him like a fire alarm.

He didn't move, didn't make a sound.

Door hinges creaked.

Zag heard the shuffling of men's boots and the thump of hooves from the front of the stable.

And voices.

'Damn . . . never thought we'd get out of the rain . . . shoulda stopped hours ago . . .'

'Safer here.'

'. . . get a nigger take care the horses?'

'Don't trust 'em here. Do it ourselves.'

'You're the boss, like they say . . .'

Horses were rubbed down; hooves were cleaned. The lights went out. Hinges creaked again as the strangers left the stable. Zag drifted back to sleep.

2

There is no law.

That was the lesson of Quinn's life, the belief that he lived by. Oh, there were courts and judges and juries of one's peers, there were constitutions and regulations and decrees of every kind; but that was merely a game that men played. There was no law. There was no ultimate principle, no rule, no God to be answered to, unless it was Quinn himself. The world was dark; he himself was his only light.

It was a lesson he had learned as a youth in the darkness of the forests, not one he had been taught by others. He had been brought up, conventionally religious, as a young gentleman of the town and the cultivated countryside. Like most of his fellows, he supported the Church, went to communion three times a year, and took God for granted. He fought an occasional duel and always won, which proved that if there were a God at all, He was on Quinn's side. God's world, taken all in all, was good, and it was a gift to Quinn. It contained good food, good wine, good times. It gave him women – an occasional lady and many a wench. There were horses to be bred and raced, races to be won. God was an indulgent Father.

And then one day, in the darkness of the forest, Quinn lost a race.

He liked the forests. Just what their fascination was for him, he could not have said, but their darkness, their loneliness, their *unknown apartness* drew him. He had an inkling, when he thought of it, of why a man like Boone might wander deep into the wilderness. D.BOON CillED A BAR ON THE TREE IN YEAR 1760. It was not bear Quinn was

113

after, but on the pretext of hunting he frequently disappeared alone into the woods for days at a time.

'Self-reliance,' his father had said, 'that's what he's learning. We may be gentlemen, but, by God, we are pioneer stock. No English king could tame us, though we tamed Northern Ireland for him, and we tamed a wilderness in America. The boy shows he's a true pioneer.'

But he had no idea of what the boy would find in the forests, of the race he would run and how it would end.

Quinn had been out almost three days when his path crossed that of Henry Brandon, a Williamsburg acquaintance. It was a sunny afternoon, and the two of them walked their horses along a smooth trail by a riverbank. Henry was a freckle-faced, pleasantly ugly man, always a good companion, and since Quinn had spoken to no one for most of the three days, he didn't mind the company.

Henry admired Quinn's horse, Cincinnatus. He had reason to. Though Quinn rode Cincinnatus everywhere, even into the deep woods, he was famous as a race horse and had beaten Henry's own horse, Cara, several times.

Now Henry suggested a wager.

'Do you know that old abandoned shanty up the trail about a quarter of a mile from here?'

'I never been along here before.'

'Well, the shanty's there, or it was the last time I came by, and I'll bet you my old nag here plus the pick of my stable against Cincinnatus that we can beat you to it.'

Quinn was puzzled. 'How could you hope to win such a wager?'

Henry grinned. 'Well, Cincinnatus is the faster horse, I guess, but Cara and me, we know the trail. Been over it often, though we never raced it. Nothing tricky about it except that it turns a lot, but since you don't know it at all . . .' The grin faded; Henry shook his head. 'No, I guess the wager wouldn't be fair. Since you don't know the trail at all, you wouldn't have a chance. You'd be sure to lose, and that wouldn't be right.'

'Well, now, I don't know . . .'

Cincinnatus was Quinn's pride and joy, and the thought of losing her was intolerable. But the pick of Henry Brandon's horses was a temptation; the man had more than one that Quinn would dearly have loved to own. And Cara was hardly an 'old nag,' as Henry had called her. Though she was no match for Cincinnatus, Quinn had seen her win more than one race.

Furthermore, Henry had the look and the sound of a man who had spoken too quickly, a man who had suggested a wager he regretted.

'Don't back down, Henry. If I'm willing to gamble . . .'

A race was arranged; reluctantly, on Henry's part. He even insisted on adding five thousand dollars to his side of the wager, and Quinn had to start at least a full length ahead of Henry. Since Henry knew the trail so well, he would have felt badly about winning if Quinn had no comparable advantage.

They raced.

They had not gone a hundred yards before Quinn realized that he had made a fool's bet. The trail, though level and wide, twisted and turned far more than he could ever have expected, and Cara anticipated every curve and corner. She soon passed Cincinnatus, and Quinn was left to dodge low-hanging branches that threatened to sweep him from the saddle. When he at last reached the shanty, Henry was already dismounted and was waiting for him.

'We shouldn't have made that wager,' he said, looking troubled. 'I didn't realize that Cara knew the trail all that well. I'd be obliged if we could call the bet off.'

It was a safe enough statement, in that a gentleman, having lost such a gamble, would insist on paying the debt. In fact, it was almost insulting in its suggestion that he might do otherwise.

Quinn forced a smile. His heart beat sickeningly as he dismounted. He had never seriously thought that Cara could beat Cincinnatus, and he felt that he had been made a fool. Henry's protestations were hypocritical. He was no better than a thief. Or if his protestations were quite honest . . . What difference did it make out here in the dense woods where no one watched?

Quinn continued smiling; he insisted on paying the wager. Henry must have Cincinnatus and must take him now. 'But that leaves you here without a horse,' Henry said. 'Let me lend you Cara. She'll see you safely home, and you can use her until I see you again.'

Quinn agreed. The two men exchanged horses, as they stood there on the sunny river bank, and the debt was satisfied. Honor, such as it was, was satisfied.

Both men were still smiling when Quinn drew his pistol.

That was when Quinn discovered that the forests were dark even on the sunniest of afternoons. The forests were dark, and there was no God in them to say *no*, and not even a devil to say *yes*. There was only *you* with a smile on your face and the butt of a pistol in your hand and the business end pointing at your friend's heart. There was only *you* to make the decision, and no God and no law, and you hesitated to act only because of the fascination of watching the smile disappear from your friend's face and the fear come into his eyes.

Henry began to talk, asking him what the hell he thought he was doing, what in God's name –

Quinn pulled the trigger.

There was nothing to it. The bullet picked Henry up, and he winced with hideous pain, and he went down. He rolled in the weeds and tried to get a knife out of his belt and couldn't do it. He rolled onto his back, and, still alive, looked up at Quinn as if Quinn might grant him some remission, might undo the deed. Quinn looked back into his eyes and felt a kind of pity for him, and smiled.

116

What to do with Henry now?

He remembered that the land pirates often gutted their victims and filled the cavity with rocks to weigh the body to the river bottom. Should he do that to Henry Brandon? Should he do it now – or wait until Henry was dead?

But he was already dead, the eyes going flat and empty as Quinn watched them, and an ant crawling across the freckled sunlit face. He pushed the body into the water without bothering to gut and weigh it down.

Then, looking about at the peaceful sky, Quinn saw that there was still no God watching. No God and no law. There was only the hot sunlight of the slow river and the high tree tops, only the cool darkness of the forests.

Somehow, he was not surprised. It was as if at some level he had known it all along, and only this incident was needed to bring the knowledge to the surface of his mind. When you entered the deep woods, you left God behind.

He was surprised, however, when he reached home. He had expected to return to God and the law. Even if there were no God in the forests, surely He lived in the libraries and salons of the great plantation mansions and in the houses and byways of Williamsburg. God walked the cobblestones; He was the Lord of Civilization. But when Quinn returned, he found that God had vanished. He looked about with a kind of astonishment; did no one but he understand? God and the law, if they had ever existed, had been murdered by Quinn on a lonely river bank in the deep forest.

And that left Quinn as the only god.

Which, he thought now, was an important difference between him and Lacy Keegan, keeper of The Roost. Old Lacy, fat and bald, might do anything that Quinn would do, any crime, any villainy, but he would always glance back over his shoulder to see if God were watching. Quinn never did that. He was his own god, and there was no law.

'Well, what are you staring at, man?' He dropped his saddlebags and stood dripping in the middle of the public room. 'Did you think we weren't coming back? Hot food and get it fast. And build a fire – we're cold and wet, and we'll burn this place down if we have to dry out again.'

Keegan, lard-faced, tried to grin, but the fear stayed in his eyes. He yelled out the door to the girl, Bonnibelle, telling her to hurry food. He bawled at his wife, Dora, to fetch brandy. Harpe seized Dora and kissed her. He danced her around the room before he released her, frightened but excited and laughing, to run to the cellar.

Quinn slumped into a chair at a table near the big fireplace. How often did you want a fire on a summer night, he thought with a silent laugh, but God, the rain was *cold!* and he had been out in it so long he was shriveled and shaking. While he watched Keegan pile wood on the grate, he kicked off his boots and slipped out of his soaked coat and shirt. He wrapped a blanket Dora had brought around his shoulders and waited shivering.

The wood was dry, and Keegan was good with a fire. It snapped and crackled, and Harpe leaned over the flames, rubbing his hands together. Quinn thought of the last time they had visited The Roost, some weeks before. There had been a storm then too, by coincidence, and it had driven a Charleston merchant to seek shelter here. It had been a night that none of them would ever forget.

'And now, Keegan,' Quinn said when the man had finished.

Keegan looked around, still frightened. He was a tall man and strong, but he carried fear like the white blubber that encompassed his body.

'Keegan, sit down.'

Keegan slowly eased himself down into a chair on the opposite side of the table. He was careful to face Quinn; he would never in his life have turned his back on Quinn. He leaned forward, giving his full attention.

118

'You say you have no other guests?'

'No, like I told you.'

'No rich merchant, driven in by the storm?' Harpe asked, standing by the fire.

Keegan's lard face became whiter, if that was possible. 'No. There's no one else.'

'What a pity,' Quinn sighed. 'Don't look so frightened, Keegan. Wouldn't you like to fatten your purse again?'

'I never done nothing like that before, Mr Quinn. Honest to God, I never did – '

'Never, Keegan?'

'Not since I was hardly a lad, sir. Not to a white man. I'm an honest innkeeper. If I hadn't been drunk . . .'

Yes, if they hadn't all been drunk . . . here in this same room . . . Harpe with Dora on his lap as he played with her bare breasts and told of his plans for her . . . Quinn fondling Bonnibelle and trying to shock the merchant with his blasphemies . . . Keegan running in and out of the room, laughing, laughing, afraid not to laugh . . . All drunk but the merchant, who could not finish his meal and retired to his room, sick with disgust.

Rich merchant, Harpe said, too good for the likes of us. Hypocritical bastard.

Ought to whip him like a nigger, whip his goddamn pride away.

Ought to be hung.

Ought to cut his balls off.

What about it, Keegan? Want to cut his balls off?

It started as a drunken joke, their urging the swaying, staggering, giggling Keegan on. Come on, Keegan, cut the bastard's balls off – we'll help you do it. Up the stairs, Keegan, let's go. We'll hold him for you while you clip the bastard's balls.

It was a childish, a schoolboy's jest, a way of toying with Keegan and perhaps hazing the merchant, but all the time Quinn felt a growing certainty that something final and deadly was really going to happen. There was no God and no law to say that it should not. The gray-bladed knife in Keegan's hand was going to be used.

The merchant did not answer when, snickering to themselves, they knocked at his door. They knocked three times before Harpe, with one swift kick, sent the door flying open and they burst into the room. The merchant, fully clothed, brought up a pistol and fired before Harpe could knock it from his hand, but the bullet went wild.

Why, he tried to kill you, Keegan! Son of a bitch tried to kill you!

Quinn and Harpe grabbed the man's arms. He kicked and screamed, seeing what was coming.

Kill him, Keegan, kill him! Son of a bitch will see you hanged if you don't kill him!

Keegan was almost too weak with drunken laughter to move, but one of the merchant's feet caught him squarely between the legs. He screamed.

Kill him, the son of a bitch! Or he'll kill you!

Still crying with pain and rage, Keegan gut-stabbed the merchant. He stabbed him more than a dozen times before the man slid to the floor and died.

'. . . no, sir, I swear to God. If he hadn't kicked me the way he did – liked to kill me, he did – I swear to God – '

'Stop sniveling to God, man.' But Quinn knew that Keegan was not sniveling to God. He was sniveling to Quinn. And quite likely he was thinking of John Fisher and his wife, keepers of the infamous Six Mile House, who had been hanged only a few years before. From the pirate Stede Bonnet to the Vesey Conspirators, Carolina had never been slow to take vengeance with the noose.

'We helped you bury him, didn't we, Keegan?'

'Yes, sir. That you did.'

'Out behind the pig pen. And has he ever been found?'

'No, sir. The state sheriff and the militia came by – '

Quinn stiffened. 'And what did you tell them?'

'Nothing! I swear to God, sir! I said I had no visitors that night. They cursed me out, like they always do, and they looked around, but they found nothing. And I told them nothing – if I had, would I be here now?'

Quinn relaxed. What the man said was quite true. The murder had taken place weeks before, and what danger there had been was now past.

'He lies where we planted him? I warned you not to move him.'

Keegan nodded vigorously. 'Right behind the pig pen, and still under them rocks so he can't be dug up, and under the dirt. Oh, I wouldn't open that grave for anything in the world, Mr Quinn!'

It was probably true. The man would be too cowardly to open the grave. Nevertheless, Quinn said, 'I may just look in the morning, Keegan.'

'Oh, Mr Quinn, I swear – '

'All right, Keegan, I believe you. But remember, at any time I may just come back and look. If you get any fancy ideas about moving the body away from here, you could cause trouble for all of us. You let our departed friend sleep in peace.'

'Oh, I shall, Mr Quinn!'

Quinn watched Keegan carefully. There was something odd about his eyes, something in the way they shifted from Quinn's and took on an empty look. He muttered something under his breath; Quinn thought he said, 'I only wish he would.'

Quinn stared at him. 'You wish what, Keegan?'

Keegan's gaze jerked back to Quinn's. He looked guilty. 'What, sir?'

'You said you only wish our departed friend would sleep in peace.'

'Did I say that, sir?'

'You did.'

Keegan's hands fluttered impotently over the table.

121

'Well, I only meant . . . I meant I have these dreams, Mr Quinn.'

'Dreams, Keegan?'

'Dreams, sir, about that man – '

'What kind of dreams, Keegan?'

Keegan obviously did not want to answer, but he knew he had no choice. 'Dreams . . . that he's clawing the rocks and the dirt away . . . clawing his way up out of the grave . . .'

Harpe, moving closer to the table, stopped. Keegan looked back and forth between the two men, new fear in his eyes.

My God, Quinn thought, the old bastard is getting a conscience. After all he's done in this bloody world, his guts are turning to water, and he's getting a conscience.

'You're a fool, Keegan,' he said, when Keegan's eyes had dropped. 'Have a drink or two before bedtime, and you won't have such dreams. Pretend it never happened. There's no grave and no body, do you hear me?'

'Yes, sir.' Keegan did not look any happier.

'And now get out of here and get us our food. And tell that girl Bonnibelle to stay close enough to hear my call.'

'Yes, sir.'

Keegan arose from the table and left the room. Harpe, hard-eyed, slid into the chair he had occupied.

'We gonna have to do something about him.'

'I know.'

'This place was supposed to be safe. We pay him plenty to keep his mouth shut about us, but if he's gonna turn into a crazy, talking about the man he killed clawing his way out of the grave – if he's gonna start talking about *us* and how we helped kill that man – '

'I know.'

Harpe sat back in his chair. 'When?'

Quinn felt utterly calm, able to deal with any situation. 'We've been traveling in the open,' he said, 'and we may

122

have been seen. We'd best continue on, then circle back in a week or two. We'll do what has to be done, then head south to Georgia. Fill our pockets some more, and not come back this way till fall. It won't change our plans much. Hardly at all.'

Harpe looked uncomfortable. 'I don't like it. The longer we wait, the more likely he'll spill his guts.'

Quinn shrugged. 'You want to do it and get out of here tonight? It means killing them all, but that might be best anyway.'

'No. No, I reckon not. Your way's best.'

'Then we'll do it my way.'

'You're the boss.'

Quinn smiled. Life or death decisions, for himself or others – he handled them easily. And there was never any looking back over his shoulder for God.

Bonnibelle brought their food, and Dora put a bottle on the table, and they ate and drank in great comfort. The chill left their bodies, and the rain-wet was replaced by sweat, and Quinn's thick beard began to itch. He tossed the blanket from his bare shoulders, and unfastened his pants, the better to fill his belly. All but Bonnibelle laughed and joked and cursed Keegan for building such a large fire, and Harpe, his meal finished, reached for the giggling Dora.

Bonnibelle was ordered to clear the table and to return from the kitchen at once. Keegan was ordered to bed. Harpe, belching his comfort and pleasure, pulled Dora down onto his lap and began unfastening her clothes and his own. Quinn told him to get his woman the hell out of there, and the two went drunkenly up the stairs. Quinn waited until he could no longer hear their voices.

He was alone, sprawled out in his chair before the dying fire. He was half asleep now, almost satisfied. But not quite.

'Bonnibelle . . .'

He didn't say the name loudly; he didn't have to. In three previous visits to The Roost, the girl had been trained – trained as well as any dog Quinn had ever known. And what was a woman anyway, Quinn thought, but a kind of dog, a kind of bitch that somebody owned? Wench or lady, they were all the same – talk all you wished about a Southern lady's purity and fineness, underneath it all she was still a possession, a bitch, a chattel. And that meant, when all was said and done, that she was not much more human than a nigger.

So why not be done with hypocrisy and treat her like the kind of thing she was?

Bonnibelle: he didn't have to say the name loudly, and he didn't have to say it twice. Like a frightened child who dared not disobey, she came from the darkness of the room beyond, where she had been hiding. She crossed the public room and stood at his feet. Without a word, she knelt. She lifted a mud-incrusted boot and, with some care, pulled it from his foot. She placed it to one side, and then, just as carefully, removed the other boot. When he reached out and ripped open the front of her dress, she winced, but she did not move away, and she still said nothing.

Quinn touched her half-naked body. There was no response, not even a quiver of fear. He frowned. Leaning toward the girl, he seized her face and turned it so that he could see her eyes in the dying firelight. He looked for the knowledge that she was absolutely in his power, that there was no escape, that her life was his to take or to give.

He found what he wanted: her eyes were dry, but the terror was there.

Laughing softly, he slid an arm around the girl's shoulders. 'Poor Bonnibelle,' he whispered as he drew her to him, 'poor, poor Bonnibelle . . .'

* * *

First Harpe, Keegan thought as he lay in the darkness of his room. *First kill Harpe and then Quinn. Kill them both*. It was the only way he would ever escape them, he had decided, the only way he would ever be free of those two murderous bastards who kept coming back to take over his inn, his women, his life.

'You'll leave the old boy buried right where we put him,' Quinn had said on the night of the murder. 'I don't want to come back and find that he's been moved.'

'But if he's ever found here – '

'He won't be. Unless you cross us, Keegan. Or say anything at anytime that might betray us. We're your special guests, your special friends, Keegan, and we like to think we're safe with you. But if I ever get a whiff of the Judas about you, I'll see that the old boy is dug up and that you hang for him. If I can't kill you, I'll see that the law does.'

So Keegan had to get rid of the body, but he didn't dare. Not when he thought of Quinn's threats, not when he thought of those blue eyes with death in them.

Those damned eyes, he thought. *Well, I'll put out their lights tonight!*

Sweating, his nightshirt clinging to him, Keegan got up from his bed. He fumbled in the dark for bottle and tumbler and poured himself a drink. It was nearing dawn, but anger and fear still pulsed through his body, driving away sleep and keying him up for the bloody job to come.

He had thought it through quite carefully. Harpe and Dora had bedded down first, and Quinn and the wench had followed within half an hour. The sounds of passion, the bawdy laughter, had long ago ceased, and the chances were they were all in deep sleep now. Their doors might be barred, but there wasn't a room in the inn that Keegan could not enter silently and easily with the aid of a bit of wire. The merchant, after all, had not been the first to disappear from The Roost, though the others had been long ago.

First Harpe. One blow of an iron bar would do for the big blond man, and there would be a little blood. The big danger was that Dora might awaken and scream, but Keegan thought he could deal with that: one hard hand over Dora's mouth and if necessary a blow to her head too.

Then Quinn, the same way. With Harpe out of it, Keegan would have less fear of Quinn. He could deal with the man as he slept, but by God he might just welcome Quinn's awakening. Keegan would have pistol and knife with him – let Quinn know what it was like to peer into the barrel of a flintlock. Let the bastard see the ball coming.

The rest would be easy. He could have the two bodies in the swamp by the time dawn broke. The niggers, if they saw, would never dare talk – he could even force them to help him. And tonight he would overcome his fear of the merchant's decaying body and dig it up and take it to the swamp too. He was convinced that once the merchant was away from The Roost, the bad dreams would stop.

And Keegan would have the riches in his guests' saddlebags.

Now, he thought, pouring himself another drink. *Do it now.*

He drained the glass. He pulled on a robe and tightened the cord around his waist. From under his pillow he took a loaded pistol, and from a cabinet another, placing them carefully in the pockets of his robe. His knife, the same one that had done in the merchant, he stuck under his waist cord. But the pistols and the knife were only insurance. From under the bed he took his favorite weapon, the two-foot iron bludgeon that more than once in the past had served him so well. He stroked it, caressed it, thinking that he felt its cold weight warming and hardening in his hand. It was like a thing alive, a thing

126

with a will of its own, and he trusted it as he did nothing and no one else on this earth.

Now, he thought again. *Do it now*.

He needed only one more thing: the bit of wire, which he took from a drawer. Then he crossed the room and opened the door into the hall. He took his time, lifting the weight of the door and swinging it slowly so that the hinges made no sound. The hall was dark, but that was just as well. He had the eyes of a cat, and some things were best done in the dark.

Heart churning, he went along the hall toward Harpe's room. Each step was carefully calculated to avoid any noise; Keegan's bare feet knew every creaking board in the inn.

He came to Harpe's door, and he could hardly believe his luck. The wire would not be needed, for the door was ajar. Harpe had drunkenly, stupidly, failed to close it, and now all Keegan had to do was to ease it open just a little farther, ease it quietly, slowly . . .

Keegan reached for the door.

He hesitated. What if Harpe heard him? People like Harpe and Quinn slept like watchdogs; they hardly slept at all. The merest sound, the slightest breath, was enough to awaken them instantly, and then they might strike out, strike to kill. Harpe might be an old dog, like Keegan himself, but Keegan knew he could move like lightning and had the strength of an ox. And if he made even a sound before Keegan killed him, Quinn would be instantly awake. And what chance did Keegan have against Quinn awake if he didn't have the man under the gun?

Fresh sweat came to Keegan's forehead and to the hand that held the bludgeon. He had thought the killing through, but perhaps he had thought it wrong, perhaps he had overlooked something. Of the two men, Quinn was the more dangerous. Surely it made sense, then, to deal with Quinn first. Get him out of the way. Then he could take care of Harpe. He had two pistols and a knife as well as the iron bar, and he would dispose of Harpe quickly.

Or would he?

Harpe was no fool, and he had his own pistols, his own knife. And he knew how to use them.

Keegan was suddenly wracked by indecision. He felt wet with sweat, and his bladder was full. The iron bludgeon hung from his hand like something cold and limp and dead.

He dared not try to kill Quinn and Harpe, he realized. All the raw whiskey and brandy he could drink would never give him the nerve. He was terrified of them, especially of Quinn, and he would always be in their power. If they found him in the hallway now, armed as he was, God only knew what terrible thing they would do to him. All the weapons in the world could not protect him.

Frightened of making a sound, he slowly turned and crept back towards his room. He wanted to bolt toward it, but he dared not. Tears of rage and frustration came to his eyes. Once his door was closed, he sat on the edge of his bed and thumped his knees with his fists. Sobs struggled to escape his throat, and he fought them back.

He put away the pistols, the knife, the bludgeon.

He poured another drink.

He was standing by the window when a movement in the darkness below caught his eye. It was the wench, on her way back to the kitchen. The useless goddamn wench for whom he had paid two hundred dollars. The useless goddamn wench who had been in Quinn's room, and Keegan had not even heard her leave. That meant that Quinn might have been awake all the time, just waiting for Keegan to make his move. Waiting, so that he could kill Keegan. And the useless goddamn wench in on it, as likely as not, both of them laughing at him. *All* of them laughing at him.

Well, he would show her who had the last laugh.

It had been weeks since he had last had his way with her. It was time she was reminded who was the master of The Roost. There were other ways to teach a wench than with a whip, and he knew them all. He would have his way with her, he would, and then take the money Quinn had given her, and Quinn had damned well better have given her enough. If he had not, there was always the whip again to teach her to get her price.

Raging, no longer striving for silence, Keegan left his room and headed for the kitchen.

As always, she clung to the one thing that saved her sanity: the thought that she would not always be at The Roost; the thought that one day she would leave, never to return again. Perhaps it was only a dream, but she could never admit that. She had to believe that somewhere there was a better life awaiting her and that someday she would leave The Roost and find it.

Her stomach cramped. Clutching the few coins Quinn had thrown contemptuously on the floor, pulling her torn dress over her small breasts, Bonnibelle stopped by the corner of the inn to vomit – to gag and wretch torturously, as if to rid herself through one violent outpouring of all that had happened to her during the night.

Well, at least she was still alive, she thought as she choked on her tears. At least it had been only Mr Quinn this time and not both of them. But Mr Quinn frightened her more than any other man she had ever known, even more than Mr Keegan. She remembered what had happened the last time they had come to The Rost – the screams in the night and the burial out behind the pig pen. But she was not supposed to know about that; she was supposed to have wiped it from her mind. She must never, for fear of her life, speak of it, and she hardly dared think of it.

In the tattered, rotting boots she used to get between

the inn and the kitchen house, Bonnibelle continued to wade through the mud. At least, she thought, she had had one piece of luck: they had not discovered the nigger boy out in the stable. And she still had his two dollars. That in itself was a kind of miracle.

She climbed the kitchen steps and pushed open the door. She slipped her feet out of the dirty boots. Groping in the dark, she found a candle and lit it. Then she looked at the payment which Quinn had thrown to her.

It was better than she had expected. There was a kind of pin – a brooch pin, she thought it was called – consisting of an ivory flower against a silver backing. It should be worth something. And there were eight coins. None of them were American, as far as she could tell, unless they were from the old days, but you didn't see many American coins unless you were rich. A person like Mr Quinn would keep such coins for himself. Several of those he had given her were big and shiny, however, and surely worth a considerable amount. She thought about keeping about three, or even four, of the best looking coins before turning the remainder over to Mr Keegan. Of course, if he ever found out . . .

But he never would. And one day her money would help her to go far away from here. She would disappear during some future night, never to be heard of again. Not by Mr Keegan, not by Miss Dora. Not by Mr Quinn or Mr Harpe or any of the other men who came to The Roost. Her plans were vague, but she thought she would spend part of her money on coach fare to some distant place, and there perhaps she would find work with some good family. There were good people in this world, she knew. Maybe she would even find a man she mattered to, someone who would protect her and care for her. As long as she kept hope, anything was possible, and she would live a completely different life and forget that The Roost even existed.

She went to her hiding place, the place where she kept her secret treasure. It was a good hiding place, in plain sight and yet invisible.

The kitchen's floor was made of bricks, most of them now loose and lying irregularly. Kneeling, Bonnibelle pulled up one brick and then another, setting them aside. This allowed her to pull up a third, which was otherwise more tightly wedged into place and impossible to remove. And from under this brick she took the rusted tin box, tied up with a string, that held her treasure.

The box was pleasingly heavy as she lifted it from its hiding place. She untied the string and lifted the lid. The box sat on the floor where she could just see its contents by the light of the single candle, and the coins glittered dimly. She had no real idea of their total value, but she thought they must amount to quite a lot by now – she had collected over a hundred since she had thought to start her horde – colonial money, foreign money, a few American coins. She even had – the prize of her collection – a heavy gold doubloon that some careless stranger had dropped during a stay at The Roost.

She raked her fingers through the coins. She picked up the doubloon, looked at it, stroked it. She put it back again. She dropped the brooch pin into the box, then turned Quinn's eight coins over in her hand, deciding which of them she should keep for herself, keep for the day when she would take her freedom.

That day would never come.

The scrape of a boot. She heard Keegan before he reached the door of the kitchen, and she knew, sickeningly, that it was too late – there was no time to conceal the box and her secret treasure. She looked up at the doorway, at his tall hulking figure in nightshirt and robe, and wailed – not from fear this time but from anguish and despair.

Keegan's eyes widened. 'You . . . you goddamn little thief.'

131

She wailed again and picked up the box. Coins fell ringing to the brick floor and rolled away as she clasped the box to her naked breasts.

'Bitch . . . thief . . .'

She leapt to her feet and away from Keegan as he reached for her. More coins fell, scattering, and she knew she was going to lose them all, going to lose every last hope she had ever had, every dream. He lunged at her, but fast as a rat she sidestepped, and she found she had a knife in her hand, hardly knowing how it had got there. It was the same one she had used to threaten the nigger boy. Now she was going to use it to defend her dreams. With another cry, she sent the blade slashing through the air.

'Oh, you would, would you, bitch . . . steal from me . . . take my money – '

'It's mine, it's mine!'

'You've got no money, you thieving little bitch. You've got nothing but what I give you. You whore for your meals, you do, and every penny you've held out is mine. Every ha'penny, every cent! Now, you give me that!'

There was no reason in her head, not even fear, only anguish, and she slashed out with the knife again. Keegan jumped back. 'Bitch, I'll knife you, I will! I'll knife you!'

The next time he came at her and she shot the blade out, he did not retreat. She felt his iron grip on her wrist. Her arm twisted painfully, and she cried out again as fear came at last.

'I'll kill you, bitch, I'll kill you!'

Arm bent, back bent. Her head seemed to explode as his fist struck her like a lump of iron. The blow came again, and the knife fell from her hand. The box with its few remaining coins slipped away from her. One more time the fist hit her, and the next blow, she knew, was the brick floor, as she crashed into darkness.

'. . . bitch . . . thieving bitch . . . thieving bitch whore . . .'

She heard his mutterings before her eyes opened. For a

moment she could not move. She could only watch as Keegan, humped over on his knees in the pale candlelight, gathered up the scattered coins – her lost hopes, her stolen dreams.

She wept. Keegan threw a curse at her and looked for more coins.

She struggled to sit up. She looked about her for the knife, but it was nowhere to be seen.

Keegan had it. He was using it to pry a coin out from between two of the bricks.

She managed to her to her feet. Her head spun, and she thought she was going to fall again. She staggered toward the fireplace.

There she found what she wanted – a long iron rod used to skewer and roast game. It was the longest and heaviest of the rods in the fireplace. It was pointed at one end and blunt and heavier at the other. She did not think about what she was going to do with it.

She took it by the thinner end and, turning toward Keegan, raised it over her head.

She brought it down with all the strength she had left. But Keegan saw the blow coming and tried to dodge it. The rod hit a glancing blow on one side of his bald skull, peeling it down, and blood suddenly fountained red over the whiteness.

He howled and drew back, but only for an instant. He threw himself at her.

Sidestepping again, she brought the rod up backhand, and this time it caught Keegan solidly over the right temple. The knife flew from his hand. Bending forward, screaming, he wrapped his arms around his head as if he were trying to hold it together.

She lifted the rod again. She brought it down on the back of Keegan's head, and this time he fell to the floor. He collapsed like a pile of rubble until he was on his knees and elbows, still holding his head.

He slowly lifted that head, now capped with torn flesh and blood. Sounds came from his throat but not words. His eyes, smoky in the candlelight, were a curse. He got one foot under him. He reached for her with red-stained, dripping hands.

She brought the rod down again. This time he flattened out on the floor and rolled over onto his back.

'Don't!' she cried, not knowing what she meant. 'Oh, don't, please, don't!'

He rolled over onto his belly and began to crawl toward her, snarling at her, clawing at the brick floor. He was like an animal, cornered and dying but determined to take her with him.

'*Oh, don't, don't, don't!*'

She brought the rod down again and again. It was like trying to scotch a snake, a great fat monstrous cottonmouth that refused to die.

'*Don't, don't!*'

She struck again.

Keegan's head sank to the floor. He seemed to stretch out. His arms went limp. He sighed.

She waited, but he didn't move. His eyes were open but sightless. He was dead. He had to be dead.

But it couldn't be, she thought. It never happened. Because if it had happened, she would be dead too. She would hang for it. They would take her away and put a rope around her neck and kill her. No, it couldn't have happened, it never happened, it was all an evil dream.

But then she knew it was no dream. Dreams had no witnesses. And there, outside the kitchen doorway, stood Zagreus Sabrehill – watching her.

3

It was his instinct for danger, his fear of being discovered, that awakened him. He was deep in sleep, and the cries, the voices, were distant, and yet he heard them. They penetrated his curtained mind, and an alarm went off: *Beware!*

He had to fight to come awake. He heard the voices and knew they were no dream, and he struggled in the darkness of his mind until, with one final wrench, he at last found himself sitting up in the stall. It was night still, he saw, but surely by now dawn was not far away.

Distantly, more cries:*Beware!*

One voice, he knew, belonged to Bonnibelle. He recognized it as easily as if it had been Cissie's. Hurrying from the stall, he went to the door of the stable and looked out toward the inn and the kitchen house. There was an angry male voice and a long moan. Zag's fists clenched. Bonnibelle was in trouble, and if the man with her was her master, there was nothing he could do about it. Nothing in the world.

But perhaps the man with her wasn't her master. Perhaps he wasn't even a white man. And perhaps Zag could help.

He knew that he should remain hidden – either that or harness up and hope to escape unobserved. He was a stranger here, and it was dangerous for him to become involved in the troubles of anyone else, black or white. And yet, against all reason, he found himself running across the yard toward Bonnibelle's cries.

He saw no light anywhere, but the cries seemed to be coming from the kitchen house, and he rushed toward it, the mud sucking at his boots. As he got nearer, he saw the faintest glimmering, the flickering of a candle from within. He slowed as he approached the door.

He could see inside: Bonnibelle like a shadow within shadows and, on the floor, something monstrous, crawling.

'Oh, don't, don't, don't!'

Bonnibelle had a weapon in hand, and she brought it down on her crawling enemy in sickening thumps. The crawler tried to rise, but she struck him down again.

Don't, don't!'

A final blow. A sinking to the floor. A sigh, and then only Bonnibelle's painful sobs against vast silence.

Zag knew the man was dead.

And he knew that, simply because he was there, he might die as well.

He stared at the bloody figure on the floor as if entranced by it, until Bonnibelle turned and saw him. She whimpered, and her weapon dropped to the brick floor with a metallic ring.

Run! he thought. *Run!*

But he knew that if he ran now, they would be after him – *they,* all the whites in the world – after him for the murder of this bloody bundle of rags lying on this floor, and he would die within hours. He knew, because that was a black man's life.

No, he dared not run, not yet. Not if he wished to survive.

He went up the steps, and one pace into the kitchen. He looked closer at the mess on the floor. The candle's flame was small and unsteady, but he was reasonably certain that this was the man he had seen earlier through the inn window, the man who had stood, whip in hand, over the fallen Bonnibelle.

'You killed him,' he said.

The girl whimpered again and shook her head.

'Why? Why you kill him? Because he whipped you, is that why?'

'No, no, I didn't!'

'Miss Bonnibelle, I stood there and watched you – '

'No! I didn't kill him!' She rang her hands, twisted her arms, writhed as if in pain. Her words came out as an agonized squeal, a denial of reality: *'No, no, it didn't happen, nothing has happened at all!'*

But Mr Keegan still lay there, bloody and dead.

Zag stepped back to the doorway and looked around outside for signs that anyone else might be awake. He had heard the voices in the night; surely someone else might also have heard them. But he saw no one.

'I didn't kill him!' the girl repeated. 'I didn't, I didn't!'

Zag turned back to her. 'Miss Bonnibelle – '

'Don't you say I did! You were the one, I'll tell them that! I didn't kill him, I'll say you did! You, you, nigger – you killed him for the money! I'll tell them!'

There it was, the accusation. Absolute terror was in the girl's eyes, she was almost beyond reason, and she would say anything to save her own life. If he ran now, she would have others after him in a matter of minutes.

He remembered a night not long before on a dark road. He remembered the hooded figures and the torches . . . the black man, tied to the trunk of a tree and whipped bloody . . . the noose being fitted around his neck, the rise of the kicking body into the air . . . and then the flames and the human torch . . .

Christ, she could bring him to that . . . anything might happen to him . . .

She had seen the fear on his face. She had seen the weakness, the reminder that he was only a nigger and she was white, and it had given her a desperate hope.

'You done it to him, nigger!'

He had never felt so trapped. The whipping he had

137

come close to after the Buckridge fire was nothing compared to this.

'What I ever do to you? Why? Why you do this to me?

'You killed him! You killed him!'

With one great effort he pulled himself together. He felt anger flooding through his mind and body, and anger was strength. He had nothing to lose now, no reason to bow to this girl's whiteness.

'All right, you say I killed him – and what about you?' He moved toward her so that he could look down on her – force her to look up at his fury. 'What about you, *Miss* Bonnibelle? You think I'm going hang alone? You think they won't hang a wench like you?'

The hope in her eyes faded, and the fear flooded back. 'You better start running – '

'Ain't running nowhere.' The coins, dull and shiny, scattered about the corpse, had caught his eye. 'What's all this money on the floor?'

'It's mine, all mine!'

'That what you killed him over, *Miss* Bonnibelle?' Zag looked desperately for a way out. 'That why you killed him? He found you here whoring for money and tried to take it away from you. And you killed him, whore! You killed him!'

The way she crumpled, he thought he must have struck somewhere close to the truth. Her eyes widened, and her hands went to her face. A long, stricken moan came from behind the hands.

He pressed on: 'And they going hang you for it!'

Her eyes seemed to dim as they closed. She turned from him, and her cry was like the wail of a ghost. He caught her in his arms as her knees buckled.

It was no time for compassion. Both of their lives were in jeopardy, and he knew well that Bonnibelle would sacrifice him without hesitation to save herself. But he felt a stroke of pity in spite of himself. She was such a skinny, pitiful little swamp rat, and all of her struggles to make a life had come to this.

He gritted his teeth. *It's me I got to save,* he thought, *Me!* And he said, 'Yes, Bonnibelle, they go hang you!'

'Don't let them,' she whimpered, 'don't let them!'

It was like a capitulation of sorts. Not final, perhaps, but useful.

There was a chance, then. Just a chance.

He dragged her to the one chair in the kitchen and sat her down. She was like something made of rags, limp and hardly conscious. He went to the door, and still he saw no one. But was there a hint of dawn in the sky?

He returned to Bonnibelle. He shook her. 'Listen. Listen to me! You say you got niggers here?'

She nodded. 'Where? All in the quarters?'

'Yes.'

'How far? Can't they hear you yelling?'

'They scared to come.'

That made sense. Most field hands minded their own business and to hell with their masters'. The more trouble at the big house, the more reason to stay away and hear nothing, see nothing.

'And those travelers I hear come last night. And you mistress. Don't they hear nothing? Why ain't they here?'

'Tired and drunk. Been pleasuring. They going sleep a long, long time.'

Yes, there was a chance. Maybe not much of a chance – but hadn't Zulie put a good luck spell on him to bring him safely back to Sabrehill?

'Maybe we can get away,' he said.

The girl looked up at him slowly. Her eyes said that she hardly dared to believe him but that she wanted to, wanted to desperately.

'Maybe we can get away, Miss Bonnibelle. You want to? You want to come with me? I ain't going without you.'

She understood. She nodded. 'I want to.'

139

Like it or not, they were tied to each other. If he hung, she would hang with him – or so he wanted her to believe. But if she let him run, he would take her with him and try to save her.

'All right. We leave now.'

New life seemed to flow into the girl. She stood up and looked about the room. Zag tried to pull her toward the door, but she resisted.

'My money . . .'

'We gotta get out of here!'

'My money! I can't leave without my money!'

Tearing away from him, she stooped and picked up an old tin box that lay on the floor. She began searching for the coins and snatching them up. It was something sacred to her, that money, he realized – something she had killed for. He knew that he would never be able to make her leave without it.

He helped her. They hardly paid any attention to the corpse that lay sprawled on the floor. The urgency of the moment drove it from their minds. Without hesitation, hardly thinking of what it was, Zag rolled it to one side to see if any coins lay under it.

'You got 'em?' he asked. 'You got 'em all?'

'I think so.'

Standing with her near the burned-down candle, he noticed for the first time the crimson stains on her bare body. He didn't think of her nakedness, only of the incriminating blood.

'Water! You got water? You got to get the blood off!'

She had a bucket of water, but it seemed to take forever for her to wash herself and sponge her torn dress.

'Let's *go!*'

'My things. . .'

Her things were a pathetic bundle of a few small items – an old comb, a piece of broken mirror, another old torn dress. She tied the bundle up, together with some odds

140

and ends of food, and stepped into her delapidated boots. Zag was frantic. It seemed impossible that no one had yet discovered them – and the body of Mr Keegan.

He dragged Bonnibelle out the doorway and down the kitchen steps. There wasn't a sound anywhere, not a light in the inn, yet all the time they were crossing toward the stable he felt that they were being watched. At any instant, the figure of a white man would step out of the inn, they would be seen and hailed and challenged.

Then they were in the stable, and he was pulling the reluctant horse from its stall. Bonnibelle helped him to hitch up. They worked wordlessly. She opened the stable door wide enough for him to drive out, then closed it most of the way behind him, just as it had been before. She climbed up onto the seat beside him.

All the time that they were leaving the innyard, Zag felt as if gun sights were on his back, aiming squarely between his shoulder blades. There would be an outcry, a command, and then a shot. He would be blown from the carriage seat. The carriage, the horse, seemed incredibly loud, and they would be heard.

But nothing happened. He drove around to the front of the inn. They rode out of the innyard and onto the road. They left the inn behind them.

After a few minutes, he dared to turn and look back. The inn was nowhere in sight, not even as a shadow.

Neither of them said a word. Zag could hardly believe that they had gotten away from The Roost. Their escape was not complete, of course, but at least they were on the road. They were on their way to Sabrehill.

Dora awakened slowly, hating the morning. The light hurt her eyes, and her mouth was foul. She was vaguely aware that she was not in her own bed and the man beside her was not Keegan, but she did not know who he was. She

141

groaned and buried her face in the bed, trying to shut out the light and escape back into sleep.

Then the night came back to her. Mr Quinn and Mr Harpe had returned to The Roost – exciting men, but fierce and frightening and deadly. They would do anything, those men, anything at all, and her one thought had been to please them and stay alive . . . and not end up in a grave of mud.

Well, she had survived. She had bedded with Mr Harpe, and it was daylight again, and nothing bad had happened. And she was safe now. The really bad things did not happen in the daylight, only at night. All she had to worry about was Keegan. He would be in a nasty mood, as he always was after she had pleasured another man – even though he insisted that she do it and, himself, rarely touched her. He would curse her for bedding with Harpe, then curse her again for not getting enough money from him.

She often asked herself why she had married Keegan, but she knew well. She had been a mere barmaid, a girl without a family, an ignorant wench from out of the hills. Keegan had seen her and wanted her, and Keegan had been a man of property. He owned The Roost and the farm that went with it and more than a dozen slaves. She could never have aspired to anything better than being his wife. His wife and whore, she thought bitterly.

She groaned. Sleep evaded her. Raising her head, she saw by the light that it was even later than she had thought. Keegan would be angry that she wasn't up. He would be banging on the door by now if he dared – but he didn't not with Mr Harpe sleeping here beside her.

She sat up. She had pulled her dress back on during the night, but Mr Harpe still slept naked, and she looked at him and grinned sourly. A handsome man he was for his age, and mighty powerful, but it was funny how wizened and small even a powerful man could become by the end of the night.

142

Creakily, she got up from the bed. She had best find Keegan, she decided, before he became any angrier over her having slept so late. Well, she'd soothe him with the thought of the money that was yet to come. Mr Quinn and Mr Harpe were frightening men and often mean, but they paid far better than any other guests that The Roost ever had.

With reason.

Silent on bare feet, she went to the door. It was ajar, she saw, and Mr Harpe wouldn't like that. Neither would he like her leaving it unbolted, but that was too bad. Maybe he wouldn't think about it. If he only knew it, there wasn't a bolt or a lock in the inn that could stop Lacy Keegan.

She left the room, closing the door behind her. She stood for a moment listening, but she heard no sound anywhere in the inn.

She walked to the innkeeper's chamber, the room she shared with Keegan. There was just a chance that he was still asleep, though he usually awakened before her.

No luck. He wasn't there. Looking out the window, she saw some of the slaves in the fields but no sign of Keegan.

She went down the stairs, still being quiet so as not to disturb the guests. She wondered if Bonnibelle was still with Mr Quinn. The thought of the two being together brought a momentary sick feeling to the pit of her stomach. Of the two guests, Dora preferred pleasuring with Quinn, even though he was the more dangerous. But he had a definite preference for Bonnibelle, and what he saw in the skinny little bitch, Dora could not understand. Well, whatever it was, she would make Bonnibelle suffer for it. She hoped that Mr Quinn had kicked her out after being done with her and that she was at work in the kitchen house.

'Mr Keegan? Mr Keegan?'

She was afraid to call too loud. There was no answer.

Keegan didn't seem to be in the inn. He might be out in

143

the fields with the niggers, or perhaps in the kitchen house with Bonnibelle. It would be like him, on the morning after a night like last night, to please himself with the wench. Dora laughed to herself. Let her catch them at it together – it wouldn't be the first time! Her stomach growled loudly, and she decided to go out to the kitchen house and find some breakfast.

She looked about for something to put on her bare feet. There had once been a board walk to the kitchen house, but it had long ago disintegrated, and Keegan had never replaced it. To reach the kitchen house, she had to cross a field of mud. To hell with it, she thought, and started toward the kitchen barefooted. She rather liked the feel of the mud between her toes.

She reached the kitchen steps. She laughed silently again as she thought of catching fat old Mr Keegan forcing his pleasure on Bonnibelle. Yes, she just might catch them at it. Her eyes on her muddy feet, she went up the steps and into the kitchen.

She screamed.

Quinn was angry – sick with anger, head throbbing with anger, and gut ill. It was one of those times that seemed to mock his control of events: control was only an illusion. Looking at Keegan, bloody mess that he was, there on the kitchen floor, he wanted to kick the body, to curse it, to defile it.

'Stop your sniveling!' he called angrily to the red-eyed Dora. 'You're a rich widow now. Enjoy it!'

He toed the body. Keegan. The fool who had let himself be murdered by a wretched little slut.

He left the kitchen, walked down the steps to where Dora stood with Harpe.

'You're certain she's gone?'

Dora, white-faced, ugly by the morning light and uglier in her fear, nodded.

'Any of your niggers gone?'

A pale whisper: 'I don't know.'

'Maybe it wasn't the girl at all. Nigger could have done it. And carried her off. Or she ran off to hide. You got any bad niggers?'

'They're all lazy . . . worthless.'

Of course they were. What other kind of nigger would a man like Keegan have? Niggers were like dogs: they reflected their masters. It followed that Keegan's were vicious and cowardly as well.

'Get some law, Dora,' Quinn said, and Harpe gave him a quick look. 'Get some law, God damn it,' Quinn repeated, feeling a wave of anger building. 'Go yell for a nigger and send him. There's been a murder committed, you stupid bitch, and we've got to have some law, what kind of a stupid bitch are you, you bitch?'

Frightened, Dora backed away from Quinn.

'Wait a minute.'

She stopped. Quinn stamped through the mud toward her. He stopped less than a foot from her and stared down at her, his hands on his hips. His look told her that, no matter what he said, he acknowledged no law and knew no God and if he wanted something, nothing in the world, would stop him from getting it.

'Who are we?' he asked.

'Mr Quinn and Mr Harpe.' Dora's voice shook.

'And what are we?'

'I don't know. You – you're planters, I think. You're looking for land – to invest.'

'That's close enough. And have we been here before?'

'No.'

'That's right. We've never been here before, and don't you forget it. And the only reason we were here last night, we were forced here by the storm. Lost our way and found this miserable place. That's all you know.'

'Yes, sir.'

'And if you should remember anything else, Dora, we're likely to remember a grave out behind the pig pen. Think about that grave, Dora. Keegan killed that miserable bastard, and you helped bury the body. You're as guilty as he was, and you'll hang for it.'

Dora shook her head vigorously, 'I don't know a thing, not a thing, just what you said.'

'That's right. Now, go yell for a nigger and send him for a magistrate, a sheriff, whatever you've got around here.'

Dora hurried through the mud, headed for the fields.

'How can we trust her?' Harpe asked. 'Ought to kill her and clear out of here.'

Sometimes Harpe was a fool. And his foolishness stoked Quinn's anger, made his head throb harder and his stomach feel sicker.

'All right, we kill her and clear out, and then what?' he asked harshly. 'Sooner or later the law will come here anyway. The niggers will talk. A blond man with a mustache and a man with a black beard were here. They've been before and scared hell out of ol' marse and missus. Must have killed the both of them and carried the wench off. And then they'll be after us –'

'All right, all right, you're the boss.'

'This way we're just what we seem to be. A planter with plenty of identification and letters of introduction and credit. And his right hand man. Looking for a good property.'

'All right.'

'The law comes, and we answer their questions, and we clear out. Head for Georgia as fast as we can go.'

Harpe nodded. 'And fill our pockets even deeper down there, before we head back this way. I'm for that.'

'Then just do what I tell you.'

Quinn dared say no more.

Was his control only an illusion?

The anger burned, sick and deep and murderous.

After a couple of hours of hard travel, Zag insisted, against Bonnibelle's protests, on going slowly and resting the horse for a few minutes every hour or so. 'There's hands out in the fields and foremen and overseers, and they see us running along the road, they going say, 'Something wrong – go get them niggers!'

'But we got to keep moving – '

'We going keep moving. But not if'n we break down this here old horse. He had a hard day yesterday and not much rest in the night, and if'n we don't rest him, he ain't going get us to Sabrehill. You wan' get there, don't you?'

The day dawned hot. By the time the sun was full-up, the day was sweltering. Sweat ran into Zag's eyes, blurring his vision; he licked his lips, and it ran salty onto his tongue. His clothes stuck to him, and the hot air left him gasping. Fatigue weighed him down. He tried to alleviate his discomfort by dozing, but without success. The carriage, jolting along the rutted road, constantly shook him awake. He saw the hands moving into the fields, saw them bending over their hoes and wiping the sweat from their faces. Back-breaking work. Zag smiled wryly. At least he was out of that – working in the fields. All he was doing now was fleeing from a noose. He counted his blessings.

'Zag! Zagreus! Those men, they're watching us!'

Bonnibelle shook his arm. He had not been asleep, but his attention had been dulled. Now he saw two white men on horseback in the fields ahead of them. They were moving slowly toward the road, with plenty of time to intercept the carriage. And, as Bonnibelle had said, the two men were indeed watching them.

Zag patted her hand. 'It's all right. Just let me talk to them. If they ask you anything, just say to them like I told you.'

'But if they know what happened at The Roost – '

'They can't know yet, Bonnibelle. Just ain't no way.'

Nevertheless, he was nervous, though he tried to conceal the fact, as they approached the riders. He lacked the confidence with white men that was bred of city living, and in the country you could never be sure how a strange white would treat you. He tried to assess these two. The older had the appearance of being an overseer. He was rugged-looking, mustached, and hard-faced, but not mean-eyed. The other, riding somewhat behind, could have been his assistant or his son – or likely both. He was perhaps eighteen, with a sloppy grin and eyes too big for his face. Zag thought he looked somewhat stupid. His big eyes were on Bonnibelle as they halted the carriage, and Zag felt her fingers dig into his arm.

The overseer rode to Zag's side of the carriage. Smiling slightly, he held out his hand as if to take something. 'All right,' he said, 'who are you, where do you come from, where are you going?'

'I'm Zagreus Sabrehill, sir – '

'Oh, a Sabrehill nigger, eh?' He moved his fingers impatiently. 'Come on, boy, you know what I want. Give me your pass.'

Zag dug out his money poke. 'Yes, sir. On our way back home from Charleston.' He got the slip of paper out of his poke and handed it to the man. The man looked at it.

'Four names here,' he said without looking up.

'Yes, sir. Me and Big Lida and Little Lida and Genevra. This here is Genevra. Left the others back in Charleston at the house.'

'The pass don't say nothing about that. Just says to let you all go back and forth between Sabrehill and Charleston.'

'Yes, sir.'

Zag barely heard the overseer's words. He was distracted by the younger man. He had ridden to the other side of the carriage and, with a silly grin on his face, was staring openly at Bonnibelle.

Zag had suggested that she change her dress, but she had said that the one in her bundle was no better than what she had on. Instead, therefore, she had fastened her dress closed with a couple of pieces of string and a pin that she had taken from her tin box. Her dressed gaped badly, but actually she looked no worse than many a field wench. Now, as the overseer talked, the younger man's eyes explored the openings of the dress. The sloppy grin widened, and Zag saw him lean back in the saddle and reach down to massage his crotch. Then, still grinning, almost panting, he lifted himself in the saddle and thrust his crotch toward Bonnibelle, showing her the outline of his bone.

Zag could have killed the man.

Hatred welled up sickeningly. He found himself clutching at the carriage seat, trying to control himself. If the overseer had asked a question at that moment, he would not have trusted himself to answer. Only once before had any man ever dared to do such a thing to his woman before his very eyes – a slave called Luther had exposed himself to Cissie, and Zag had spent the better part of half an hour beating him into a bloody mess.

'You all right, boy?' The overseer had noticed that something was wrong, and he sounded genuinely concerned.

'Just the heat, master, sir. Me, all tuckered out from the storm last night, and now this heat.'

'Didn't you find a place to stay?'

'Wouldn't nobody let us in. Found an old shed, kept some of the storm off us.'

It was a safe enough lie, and the overseer nodded sympathetically. He handed the pass back to Zag. 'Well, you go on, now. But better be easy with that horse, he looks plumb worn out. You don't take care, you're gonna ruin it.'

'Yes, sir.'

'Heat of the day comes, you all rest, you hear?'

'Yes, sir. Thank you, master, sir.'

Giving a friendly wave, the overseer rode off. The younger man snickered at Bonnibelle, then followed the overseer. Zag shook the reins, and the carriage rolled on.

He looked at Bonnibelle. She had put her forehead against his shoulder and closed her eyes as if in doing so she could hide. Though his anger remained, it was well under control now, and he smiled. He still hardly knew this girl, but there for a moment he had thought of her as his woman. Even if she was white and a threat to his life. He had wanted to defend her, to protect her. It was a good feeling. It made him feel like a man.

Again, he patted the hand that gripped his arm. 'It's all right, Bonni-child,' he said. 'Told you it was going to be all right.'

'Don't like pretending to be no nigger,' Bonnibelle muttered against his arm.

Zag laughed. 'Well, Miss Bonnibelle, what you want to be? A live nigger or a dead white gal?'

Bonnibelle didn't answer, but after a moment she managed to smile back at him.

The day grew hotter – it was the hottest, Zag was certain, since the summer had begun. The landscape seemed to waver before his eyes. Hunger struck, but it took only a few bites of dried meat from Bonnibelle's bundle to satisfy it, leaving a desperate thirst to clog Zag's throat. He had filled a jug at a stream, but the water that came from it now was hot and tasted slimy.

He kept his eyes open for another stream. When the sun was past its zenith and the worst heat of the day was on them, he found one that satisfied him. It passed sparkling under a bridge and through a small empty field into some woods. After crossing the bridge, Zag pulled off of the road and followed the stream.

150

Bonnibelle, startled, looked around. 'Hey, where you taking us?'

'Into them woods over there. Where we won't likely be seen from the road or by any field hands.'

'But we got to keep going!'

'Bonnibelle, if we don't rest some, we ain't never going get to Sabrehill. We going kill this here horse. Like that white man said, we got to rest in the heat of the day.'

Bonnibelle didn't protest further, and he saw the weariness on her sweat-streaked face.

He found a nice place for them, shaded and grassy. The water was shallow, but it ran fresh and clear over pebbles, and Zag saw no snakes in it. After beating the grass for snakes with a switch, he unhitched the horse and took it downstream to water, then tied it so it could graze.

He had an old blanket in the carriage, and he spread it out on the ground. Bonnibelle already had her boots off and her skirt fastened up and was wading in the water. Zag took off his boots and his shirt and went to join her. The stream was a blessed relief. Zag drank deeply from it, splashed it over his face and shoulders, and finally just lay down and rolled over in it. Bonnibelle laughed at him and he spouted water into the air.

When they had had enough of the stream, they slopped wearily down onto the blanket. Zag put his shirt over his shoulders and sat back against a tree. Bonnibelle lay on her back, her eyes closed and a faint smile on her lips, and he wondered why it was that she made him feel so sad for her. He didn't want that feeling. He owed the girl nothing. He had to remember that she had threatened to accuse him of a murder that she had committed, and his own first concern was to save his own hide. He must never forget that.

And yet he could not get over his protective feeling for her. He had been dangerously angered by a stranger's making an obscene gesture toward her. If she had been the real Genevra or Vidette or one of the Coffey sisters, he might only have been contemptuously amused and a bit disgusted. He told himself that this Bonnibelle was really nothing very special, but something else told him that maybe she was. Maybe, after all, she really was.

Special to him.

He shook his head. Impossible.

He shifted his mind to more important things. 'Bonni-belle, honey,' he said, 'before you go off to sleep, there's things you maybe best tell me.'

She lay perfectly still, but he knew she wasn't asleep. Her smile vanished.

'Bonni-child, tell me,' he said as gently as possible, 'tell me why you kill him.'

She sat up abruptly. Avoiding his eyes, she looked down at a bare foot and picked at a nail. Like a child, Zag thought. She ain't nothing but a child.

'Bonnibelle?'

'Why you wanna talk about it?'

'I got to know. I got to understand. So I can take care of you.'

She twisted, turned away from him.

'Was it like I said, Bonnibelle? For the money?'

Her head still averted, she nodded. 'He said it was his. Said I stole it from him.'

'And did you? I wouldn't care if you did, but did you?'

For a long moment, he thought she was not going to answer. She sat perfectly still, keeping her face hidden from him. Then she shook her head. 'You shouldn'ta called me what you did. You called me a whore. But I ain't no whore.'

Zag was silent, waiting.

'Men who come to The Roost, they give me money sometimes for doing things with them. But that ain't because I want to do them. Old Mr Keegan, he made me

152

do them. And then, when they gave me money, he took it away.'

Yes, she was a child. He had called her a whore, and she had thought that he had seen right through her, that he had seen *whore* written on her face. But she didn't want to feel like a whore, didn't want to be one.

'Mr Keegan took the money,' Zag said, 'but you hung onto some of it, didn't you?'

'Only because I figured I had a right. And only because I wanted to go away from The Roost some day and live some place where nobody could make me do them things. Not because I'm a whore. You had no right to call me that.'

'No, I didn't. And I am sorry I said it, Bonnibelle. I am truly sorry.'

'But when Mr Keegan caught me with the money and tried to take it away from me, I knew I wasn't never going leave The Roost. No use dreaming about it. Going be there all my days, acting like a whore. *Being* a whore.

'So I killed him. Had to. Wasn't no other way.'

She was silent for a time, her eyes blindly on her toes. She didn't seem to notice when he reached out to stroke her foot.

'Is there something wrong with me, Zag?'

'Ain't nothing wrong with you, Bonnibelle.'

'Yes, there is. I seen other gals, they don't get treated like me. Me, I wasn't at The Roost no more'n a week before old Mr Keegan was trying to spread me. There was a old nigger cook there that kept him away from me for a time, but when she died, wasn't nobody. So he finally done it and done it plenty and made me do other things too. Then when men came to the inn and took a shine to me, he made me do it with them. Other gals don't get treated like that.'

'Nobody going treat you like that no more, Bonnibelle. No more, now. You'll see.'

'Yes, they will. Like this morning. Like that young feller we saw on the road. Did you see how he acted with me?'

'I saw.'

'How come he acted like that with me? What give him the right?'

Zag found his hands gripping the blanket as they had gripped the carriage seat that morning. 'Nothing give him the right, Bonni-child. Nothing give him the right, and if I could, I'd damn well killed him for you.'

She threw him a surprised look. 'You would? For me?'

'I'd killed him for you,' Zag repeated flatly.

Bonnibelle stared at him as if she could not quite understand what she was hearing. Why in the world would anyone ever kill for her? Why would they even say it? She shook her head. She smiled.

'You kinda like me, don't you, boy?'

'I kinda like you.'

'I like you, too.'

Hot or not, it was a nice afternoon, there under the trees by the clean, clear-running stream. A nice afternoon, and far from The Roost. And Zag at last understood that he was not helping this girl because he had to. He was doing it because he wanted to.

'Miss Bonnibelle, honey,' he said as he scooted down onto the blanket, 'will you kindly shut up your mouth for a while now and let a man get some rest?'

Bonnibelle laughed and stretched out beside him. When he looked at her again, she was asleep.

4

They came at dusk, three riders walking their horses abreast up the long avenue of oaks that led to the courtyard and the mansion, and Lucy, watching from the north parlor, was reminded of the three raiders on the Buckridge plantation. These were not raiders, but she knew that they signified trouble.

Paul Devereau, Owen Buckridge, Major Kimbrough. She was certain that they would be together, and approaching Sabrehill together, for only one reason: something to do with her rule of the plantation.

She watched as they circled the courtyard and dismounted. How old Mr Buckridge looked, she thought; shattered and old, yet filled with a kind of mad, murderous energy. The major was his usual self: well-tailored, soldierly, confident, his short bar of a mustache neatly trimmed. Paul looked grim; more handsomely leonine than ever, with his thick white mane and shaggy brows.

Leila had also observed the visitors; Lucy heard her greet the three at the door. She left the parlor and went into the central passage.

'Mr Buckridge . . . And how is Callie?'

'Bearing up . . . bearing up.'

'I hear you're building again.'

'As soon as possible. It gives Callie an interest. Best to put away some old memories.'

'Of course.'

Small talk. Sometimes it was the kindest talk, and in any case it had to be made. Lucy settled her guests in the unlit passage; the open doors on the courtyard and the piazza made it the coolest room in the house.

Lucy brought them to the point. 'It was kind of you to stop by, though I'm a little surprised . . . the three of you together. Hardly a coincidence, I dare say.'

'No, Miss Lucy, not . . . a . . . coincidence.' Paul spoke in the measured, pedantic manner he sometimes assumed. It usually portended no good.

'As old neighbors,' the major said, 'we felt an obligation to inform you of certain developments.'

Trouble it was, then. Lucy felt her nerves tightening. 'Well . . . I have braced myself, gentlemen.'

'There was a meeting in Riverboro this afternoon, Miss Lucy,' the major went on. 'Most of the nearby planters who haven't left for the summer were there.'

'I was informed of no such meeting.'

'No. The fact of the matter is, you were the meeting's principle subject.'

Lucy's cheeks warmed. 'All the more reason, I would say, that I should have been informed. Am I to be talked about in public behind my back? Am I to be tried for my high crimes and misdemeanors *in absentia?*'

'Now, Miss Lucy,' Buckridge said, 'it wasn't anything like that.'

'Well, in a sense, Owen,' Paul said, 'it was.'

'And what was the verdict?'

Buckridge waved his hands placatingly. 'First of all, Miss Lucy, I want you to know that this was not my idea. You're bound to think it was, after that meeting we all had at Kimbrough Hall. Now, I admit I've been unhappy about the way things have been here at Sabrehill. However, I have never at any time – '

'Mr Buckridge, whatever our differences, I have never at any time doubted your personal goodwill.'

'Thank you, Miss Lucy.'

'But I nonetheless gather that I have been condemned. I would like to know the punishment that is supposed to fit my heinous crimes.'

'It's Pettigrew and McClintock behind all this,' Paul said. 'Briefly, they've mustered a majority opinion in these parts that legal action should be taken to put Sabrehill under professional management.'

Lucy looked from one face to another. They told her nothing. 'I don't understand,' she said, though she feared that she did.

'What it means, quite simply,' the major said, 'is that they intend to get a court order putting Sabrehill into some kind of trusteeship for you until such time as you marry. Until then, it will be rather as if you had a legal guardian. He will be responsible for seeing to Sabrehill's business affairs, including the hiring of white overseers, overseer's assistants, and so forth. He will be paid, of course, and perhaps take a share of the profits.'

'In short, they are trying to take Sabrehill away from me.'

'Well, not actually.'

'But in effect. I may or may not derive an income after this – this manager deducts his own tidy sums. Meanwhile, my people may be sold without my consent, and I will be unable to discharge an overseer if I consider him inadequate or cruel.'

'Oh, I'm sure this manager, whoever he may be, will consult with you.'

'Major, you know better. No manager is going to consult in good faith with a "mere woman." Who is supposed to occupy this exalted position?'

'Court appointed. But I'm sure you'll have a say in that, too.'

Lucy looked at the three men with a certain amazement. Were they naïve, or did they merely think that she was naïve? She knew perfectly well that any court-appointed 'manager,' even a relatively honest and well-intentioned one, would be likely to seize on Sabrehill as on the goose that laid the golden egg. Never knowing

157

when she might marry, he would soon be squeezing that goose for all it was worth. And she would be expected merely to sit by and watch.

She turned to Paul Devereau. 'Paul, can they do this to me?'

'I'm afraid they can. They have the law, precedent, everything on their side – as long as you don't have even one responsible white male in charge here at Sabrehill.'

'That's what they want,' Buckridge said, 'a man in charge here. And the fact is, they're right. I haven't changed my mind about that. But I don't approve of this business of setting the law against your neighbors. You all know how I feel about the law – it's a necessary evil for keeping order among the ragtag and bobtail. But all of us folks close by here, we always got along just fine, and we can always settle our differences over a drink or a brace of pistols. With all respect to our lawyer friend,' Buckridge nodded to Paul, 'we don't need the help of any goddamn courts.'

'I must say, Lucy,' the major said, 'Paul here did defend your interests this afternoon.'

'I told them,' Paul said, 'that if they would forget this court business, I would immediately send my assistant overseer – my overseer's son – to Sabrehill to furnish the required authority. But they wouldn't accept that. No callow youth, they said, no mere assistant. And beside, they said, he was needed at *my* place, which has none too many whites.' Paul bristled. 'As if to tell me how to run my own plantation!'

Silence filled the darkening room.

'Well . . . what am I to do?'

Paul leaned toward her. He looked very intent, as if to persuade her. 'There's only one thing you can do. Implement the plan we discussed a couple of weeks ago, and do it as soon as possible.'

'But I'm not ready to go to Charleston yet. There was so

much to be done to the house there, and Zagreus hasn't returned with word that it's ready.'

'When will he be back?'

'Why, anytime.'

'Within a week?'

'I should think so.'

'Be ready to leave as soon as possible after his return. Meanwhile, I'll tell Pettigrew and McClintock that you're leaving almost immediately and that within the next day or two, *I* am assuming charge of Sabrehill until your McCloud cousin arrives. Then they will have nothing that they can complain about.'

'Except,' the major said, 'that they'll still say there aren't enough white men here to handle several hundred people.'

Paul shrugged. 'That doesn't worry me. If it comes to it, I'll actually hire a man or two, with Miss Lucy's permission. Better that than that she should lose control of Sabrehill to the courts. The key element is that *I* am physically here. A white man of authority, at Sabrehill.'

Lucy was still not happy with the idea of having Paul lodged at Sabrehill, and she had the feeling that she was being manipulated by her friends no less than by her enemies.

'It occurs to me, Paul . . . as long as you're going to be here . . . is it really necessary for me to go to Charleston?'

If she could not always read Paul's eyes, she could almost always see the veils he put before them. 'No,' he said slowly, considering the matter, 'if you want to stay here –'

'Respectfully, Paul,' the major cut in, 'I must disagree. This whole business is going to calm down much faster if Miss Lucy leaves Sabrehill so that there is absolutely no doubt as to who is in charge. Everybody has been upset for too long over her living here all by herself. If she stays, there's going to be an element of doubt. Some people are going to say that your being here is just a gesture and that you're not really devoting your attention to Sabrehill at all. Miss Lucy should go to Charleston.'

'Well, you may be right. Owen?'

'She should go to Charleston,' Buckridge agreed. 'She'll be safer there, anyway. I'm sending Callie.'

Paul shrugged. 'You now have our opinions, Miss Lucy. You'll have to make up your own mind.'

It seemed that she would make a number of people happier if she were out of the way, and at this time it was in her interest to make them happy. 'Very well,' she said. 'You may inform the world at large that I intend to leave for Charleston within a week.'

Paul nodded. 'And I'll tell people, too, that I plan to move over here in a day or two. It will all work out, Miss Lucy.'

And so it was settled. Chairs scraped back. Lucy's hand was kissed. Paul lingered an extra moment, then departed with the others.

Strange, Lucy thought as she watched the three men ride away, disappearing under the night darkness of the avenue of oaks. Strange how they had no faith in her ability to run Sabrehill. *How could a* LADY *possibly do such a thing?* How often she had heard that. Oh, an up-country yeoman's wife might do very well at running a farm, with or without slaves, but such a person hardly qualified as a gentlewoman. And yet when Owen Buckridge had gone north on business and his overseer had died, Lucy had seen Callie Buckridge in the saddle twelve hours a day, day after day, riding in the fields, directing the hands, keeping the plantation going and in fine shape. Only after Owen had returned was she once again the delicate lady who could not possibly function as a planta-tion mistress without benefit of male direction. And Callie Buckridge was hardly an exceptional case; Lucy had observed similar instances a number of times. Strange . . .

160

But God damn it, she thought fiercely, *I do not* want *to go to Charleston!*

Going be my ass, I get caught with her, Zag thought. *God* DAMN, *going be my ass!* And yet somehow he had not felt so happy in years. Not so happy, so excited, so adventurous.

His next task was to get Bonnibelle unseen to his room over the coach house and to keep her hidden there. He had considered hiding her in the gin house, but that would present certain difficulties in the morning, and besides he wanted to keep her close to him for as long as possible.

As he had planned, they did not reach Sabrehill until well after dark. In the last miles, he left the main road and followed the less used river path. When they were at last on Sabre land, he turned north from the river until he came to a wagon path that would lead to the east service lane and, finally, home.

'Nearly there,' he said. 'Time for you to scrunch down behind me under that old blanket. You remember what I told you to do?'

'Yes.' He had instructed her carefully.

'Just don't you move or make a sound till it's time.'

Once on the service lane, Zag's heart seemed to pound a little harder with each few feet they traveled. There was a faint glimmering to the north in the field quarters, and a light in the plantation office, but most of the buildings were dark, and the lane appeared deserted. Fortunately, hands and servants who had to rise at dawn tended to bed down early.

They passed the barn. The stable was ahead on the right, the coach house on the left. Only a few more yards to go.

'We nearly there?'

'*Shut up!*'

The instant he reined up, Zag was out of the carriage

161

and opening the door just far enough to enter. Bonnibelle followed him like a shadow, her few possessions in her arms. He grabbed her hand and, with pausing to light a lamp, led her up the stairs. He pushed open the trapdoor and pulled her into his room. He closed and locked the door, and only then groped around in the dark for a candle.

'Welcome to Sabrehill,' he whispered. Somehow he could not help but whisper. 'Welcome to the abode of the famous Zagreus Sabrehill hisself.'

'Thank you, Zagreus Sabrehill.'

'Just you stay away from the windows, you hear?'

The candle flame blossomed. Zag laughed. 'We got here,' he said, speaking louder. 'We done did it, we're home!' And Bonnibelle grinned her crooked grin back at him. She looked around the room, a sparkle in each eye from the glow of the single candle. 'Oh, my,' she said, 'this is real nice!'

Zag warmed to her approval. 'You hungry?'

'Me? I'm just starving to death, is all.'

'Me, too. Now, I'll tell you what. I got to put the old nag to bed, and then I can get us some food. You just stay right here and be quiet as a mouse, and I come back real soon. That all right?'

'Yes, sir, boy!'

'And don't open the door for no one but me.'

He went back down the stairs, closing the door above him. Rather than risk drawing attention, he decided to forego a lamp and work in the dark. He opened the coach house door the rest of the way and began unhitching the horse.

'Here, whyn't you let me do that for you.'

The voice so startled him that he damned near jumped out of his boots. The voice laughed softly.

It was Hayden, stepping out of the shadows, and Zag had to restrain an angry impulse to lash out at him. How long had he been standing there, and how much had he seen?

Zag had little liking for Hayden. He wasn't quite sure why – maybe it was just because the big, brawny man had occasionally been his driver when he was in the fields and had used the whip more often than Zag liked to remember. Of course, Zag had had other drivers, and most of them had been more or less forced to do what they did, but still . . . Hayden had seemed to enjoy it too much.

Or maybe it was because there was something sly about the man's handsome, impassive face – the little smile, the veiled looks. Since Mr Jeb had taken Hayden's whip away from him, he had taken to hanging around the stable and making himself useful, but Zag always had a feeling that he was just waiting for his chance. His chance for what, Zag had no idea, but just the same, he didn't like it.

'Didn't mean to scare you, Zag. Have you a nice time in Charleston?'

Zag calmed himself. 'Nice enough.'

'Me, I ain't been to Charleston since my pa was a houseboy and I wasn't no more'n a pickaninny. I ever get to Charleston again, I going have me a high old time.'

'Reckon you would.' Zag busied himself with the harness. He wanted to be rid of Hayden.

'Here, like I said, let me do that. You must be plumb wore out after a long trip like that.'

'I can – '

'Never you mind, boy. You go get yourself some supper. Bet you ain't even ate yet. You go on, now.'

'Well . . . I thank you, Hayden.'

'Ain't nothing.'

The man was being pleasant, thoughtful. There was no reason to distrust him. Yet somehow Zag did. As he walked along the service lane, he could not resist looking back over his shoulder, and when he passed the carpenter shop, he quickly stepped around its corner and looked

163

back. He watched as Hayden, a dimly seen shadow, led the horse to the stable. He waited until Hayden had pushed the carriage into the coach house and closed the door. Only then, when Hayden disappeared into the darkness, apparently on his way to the field quarters, could Zag force himself to continue on his way. If Hayden had seen Bonnibelle and intended to take a closer look in Zag's absence, he probably would have done so by now. Just the same, Zag felt a panic to get the food and return to the coach house as quickly as possible.

It was not to be. As he passed the plantation office, he heard his name called: 'Zagreus.'

He stopped and looked around. It was Miss Lucy, stepping out of the office doorway, and he went to her. He had no choice. He could only hope that she would not detain him for long.

'Zagreus, welcome home.'

'Thank you, Miss Lucy, ma'am.' In the light from the office he saw her smile, but her eyes were not happy.

'I take it that everything is ready for me in Charleston?'

'Yes, ma'am. We cleaned the house good, top to bottom, and Big Lida laid in staples, and I got in a good carpenter for repairs . . .' Zagreus hurriedly gave his report, wishing that it could have waited until the next day. It seemed to him that every moment he was away from Bonnibelle, with Hayden perhaps nearby, was dangerous.

'I hope it wasn't all work, Zagreus. I hope you found Charleston enjoyable.'

'Oh, yes, ma'am. I had me a good time there.'

'And you're looking forward to getting back?'

'Why, yes, ma'am.' He was surprised by the suggestion.'

'Well, that's good. Because we'll be leaving very soon, in just a few days.'

He hardly heard her next words. For the first time since

164

he had encountered Bonnibelle, he remembered that as Miss Lucy's coachman he might be required to go to Charleston. One of the hands who helped him could take care of the coach house and the stable while he was away.

Maybe Hayden.

And if he had to leave Sabrehill, how could he take care of Bonnibelle?'

'. . . but you don't look very happy at the idea of returning to Charleston, Zagreus.'

'Oh, I am, Miss Lucy, ma'am. I truly am. I'm just surprised, kinda, 'cause you want me and not one of the other boys – '

'Zagreus, how can you say that? You've been such help these last months, I'd hardly know what to do without you.'

'Why, thank you.'

'And you take tomorrow off and rest from your trip, you hear me? I'll tell Mr Jebediah.'

'Thank *you!*' God, he thought, a nigger had to say a lot of *thank-you's*. But at least he could stay close to Bonnibelle tomorrow.

'Now, I suppose you were about to get yourself some supper. Get one of the kitchen girls up and tell her I said to feed you well.'

'Yes, ma'am. *Thank* you, ma'am.'

Free at last, Zag hurried across the courtyard. He had visions of Hayden returning to the coach house, going up the steps, pushing open the trapdoor. Had he told Bonnibelle to bar it or not? He couldn't remember.

He ran down the west service lane between the white outbuildings – ice house, spinning house, wash house, and others – until he came to a long brick building called the big-house quarters. To his surprise, Momma Lucinda was still up and sitting on the porch. She got up and started toward him. 'I know what you want,' she said without a word of greeting. 'Food!'

She led the way back toward the courtyard and the kitchen. She opened the kitchen door and lit a lamp with aggravating slowness. 'Now,' she said, 'what you need after a trip like that is a good hot meal. You just sit yourself down for a little while – '

Zag didn't think he would ever get back to his room. 'I don't need no hot meal, Momma Lucinda. It's a hot night, I don't want no hot meal.'

'You got to eat right. You just rest yourself – '

'Aw, no, just give me something cold, Momma! Something cold and lots of it!'

'Got nothing cold but pot of hop-in-John and some cracklin' bread. Now, you wait'll I make a fire, I'll heat it up – '

'Cold hop-in-John, that's wonderful! I *love* cold hop-in-John!'

Against Momma Lucinda's protests, Zag at last departed with the cold food and a pitcher of milk. He crossed back over the courtyard and ran along the east service lane, expecting at any instant to see Hayden dragging Bonnibelle away from the coach house.

It's all right, he told himself, *it's all right!*

But when he entered the coach house, he nearly cried out. The trapdoor he had so carefully closed behind himself was now open, bright light streaming out from it.

'You have got to be plumb out of your mind!' Zulie said. 'You have got to be departed from every last bitty sense you got!'

To find a girl in Zag's room – that was to be expected. It happened frequently. But a *white* girl! And a fugitive white girl, at that. It was as if Zag were deliberately putting his head in a noose.

'I couldn't just run away and leave her,' Zag said. 'Don't you see that?'

Zulie walked the room like a caged animal, and the white girl cowered as if the animal might turn on her at

166

any instant. That was what Zulie wanted to do – turn on her and tear her apart for the danger she was causing Zag.'You mean if you run off she woulda put the blame for the killing on you. She woulda got you killed too, and yet you act like you want to help her.'

'Well, what else could I done, Zulie?'

Zulie stopped pacing and turned hard, mean eyes on the frightened Bonnibelle. It had occurred to her that this was probably the one white person in all the world that she could safely treat with the same cruelty that she had received from certain whites.This was the one white person on whom, without benefit of voodoo spells, she could take revenge.

'I know what I'd done,' she said, thrusting her hand into the top of her dress and down toward her waist, and from a hidden sheath she drew out a knife with an eight-inch blade. It had belonged to her mother and to her mother's mother before her, and over the years it had been honed down until it was needle-thin and razor-sharp.

'Zulie, put that thing away.'

Zulie's eyes stayed on Bonnibelle. 'I ain't scared of no poor white gal trash. If I been there, I'd stuck my knife in her. Make it look like that old man she killed done it 'fore he died.'

'Aw, I couldn't – '

'Or if she was like to scream, I'd run off with her just like you done, then stuck her when I got her away – '

'Zulie, will you put that goddamn knife away and settle down! Bonnibelle, honey, don't pay her no never-mind. She don't do like I tell her, I bust her ass.'

'We can still rid us of her,' Zulie persisted. 'Do it tonight. Wait till later, then bury her out in the fields. By Jesus, I like to do it – '

'Zulie, we going help this gal! You understand me?'

Zulie turned her glare on Zag and felt the tears of frustration come to her eyes.

'We going help this gal! Now, you put away that knife!'

She did as she was told. She had always found it difficult to disobey her older brother or to refuse him anything he wanted.

'You going get yourself killed,' she said.

'Ain't nobody going get killed,' Zag said patiently. 'Thing is, if anybody see her running now, they think, "That's maybe the gal killed Mr Keegan at The Roost." So we just hide her a time till the patrol looks all around here, and everybody knows she ain't here. Then when nobody ain't thinking about Mr Keegan and Bonnibelle no more, she can go off to Riverboro or somewhere, like she just wandered down out of the hills. Find work. Take a coach, go anywhere she wants.'

Zulie shook her head. 'You are plumb crazy. Buckra wench like that, anybody see her alone, they know she ain't up to no good. No man of her own, no nothing. She ain't no better off than some poor nigger.'

'That's right,' Zag agreed emphatically, 'right now she ain't no better off than you or me, we get caught away from Sabrehill without a pass.'

'Not now, not ever. And if'n you get caught with her –'

'We just got to hide her good. Make you mind up to it, Zulie. You got a better idea?'

Zulie shook her head. She was having difficulty in holding back tears.

'You don't want to help, you don't have to. Only you promise to forget you know about Bonnibelle.'

'I'll help.'

'Good. Now, the way I figure, right here in my room is safe for a day or so, but the patrol going come looking, you know that. And we got to have her hid some place good. So you think on that, Zulie. Think on where we going hide her.'

Zulie nodded. Then for a minute she put her arms around her brother and held him, her face pressed against

168

his chest. He seemed to have no idea of how frightened for him she was.

'Be all right, Zulie.'

'I hope so. I hope to Jesus so.'

She knew there was nothing further she could say to dissuade him, nothing she could do. She had released him and started for the trapdoor when his voice stopped her.

'Zulie, try to understand . . . You remember Mr Turnage?'

She didn't answer. She didn't have to. Zag knew perfectly well that neither she nor anyone else at Sabrehill would ever forget the departed overseer.

'Well, this man that Bonnibelle killed, this Mr Keegan, he was like Mr Turnage. Maybe even worse. He treated Bonnibelle maybe even worse than Mr Turnage treated you.'

'No – '

'Yes, I think maybe he did. You got to understand that, Zulie. This little gal ain't with them, she is with *us!*'

'She's white – '

'She's with us! And I aim to take care of her. It's something I got to do, Zulie. Something I just got to do!'

Zulie shook her head. 'Crazy. Plumb crazy.'

'I reckon.' Zag grinned. 'Bonnibelle, honey, looks like Zulie is leaving. Say good night to her.'

The white girl, still frightened, still cowering, murmured something. Zulie didn't trust herself to reply or even to look at Bonnibelle. She opened the trap and went down the stairs. Over her head, the door closed, cutting off the light.

She looked up and down the dark service lane, half-expecting to see Hayden somewhere about. It was Hayden who had informed her of Zag's return, and she wondered if he had caught a glimpse of the girl. If he had, surely he would have mentioned her? No, not necessarily. There was something sneaky about Hayden, something

169

secretive and treacherous. It was hard to say why, but there was probably no one else, black or white, in whom she would put less trust. Not even Bonnibelle.

Goddamn buckra wench, she thought as she walked toward the field quarters. *Damn wench going get Zag killed! Going get us all killed!*

No. She could not allow that to happen. Oh, she would help Zag to hide the girl all right, but if the least harm came to him . . .

She touched the knife beneath her dress.

5

She awakened feeling happier than she had ever before been in her life. At first she had no idea why; she simply came to consciousness in a warm glow. Then she remembered that she was in a new place and a new life and that she would never again see The Roost or the Keegans.

Mr Keegan was dead.

She quickly put that thought out of her mind – the thought of Mr Keegan lying on the floor of the kitchen house, his eyes flat and glassy, his head crimson and torn. If she let the thought linger, the happiness would disappear, and the fear would return.

The room was hot, but the faint cross-draft from window to window was pleasant, and Bonnibelle lay still for a moment enjoying it. Then she opened her eyes and sat up to find that Zag, like herself fully clothed, was lying on the bed beside her. The pallet he had made for himself on the floor must have gotten hard during the night. He blinked and stretched, and they smiled at each other.

Zag sat up, got up from the bed. He poured some water into a bowl and splashed it on his face, sputtering and humming a song at the same time. He grinned at her.

'Sleep good?'

'Real good.'

'Late, too. Sun way up. Well, don't matter, long as we got a good sleep.'

'Zag . . .' Bonnibelle discovered she had a problem, and to her surprise, it embarrassed her. She had for so long been pushed beyond embarrassment.

'Yes, Bonnibelle?'

'Hiding like this . . . how am I going to get to a . . . well, to a "necessary house"?'

Zag blinked. 'Can't you hold it?'

'All *day-y-y?*'

Zag considered the problem. Then he reached under a table and produced a battered old chamber pot. Bonnibelle took it and peered into it as if to judge its trustworthiness. To her consternation, a very worried fat white face peered back at her from the bottom of the pot. On the painted face there was a crown.

'There's somebody in there,' she said.

'Course there is, honey. Don't you know King George III when you see him?'

Bonnibelle's knowledge of history was scanty at best, but she had heard many an Independence Day oration. She took another look into the pot and burst out laughing.

Zag said he would find them some breakfast. He warned Bonnibelle for perhaps the dozenth time to stay away from the windows and to make no noise. Usually, he said, he left the trapdoor unbarred or even open, because nobody but Zulie ever entered his room without his permission, but he wanted her to bar it and to open up only when she recognized his or Zulie's voice. If she heard him talking to anyone else down below, she was quietly to unbar the door and immediately hide as best she could in the dusty old harness and other gear in the next room. Did she understand? She understood.

When Zag had left, Bonnibelle splashed water on her own face and made use of George III. Her stomach began to growl, and she wondered what Zag expected her to do about *that* noise. Well, she had no doubt that he would return with food before long. She was beginning to think that Zag could manage anything. She was hiding, she knew there was danger, and yet somehow she had never felt safer.

172

Mindful of Zag's admonitions, she settled herself in a chair at one side of a winow, where she was quite certain she could not be seen, but could see just a little of the service lane. The stable was right across from the coach house, and beyond it, the paddock. The blacksmith shop was beside the stable, and she could hear the ringing of a hammer on an anvil. Another hammering, metal on wood, told her that a carpenter was at work nearby. A wagon clattered along a lane. A boy shouted a greeting to someone, and the greeting was returned. The day was in full swing.

Exactly how it happened, she had no idea. She thought she was being as cautious as Zag had warned her to be. She didn't understand how anyone could see her. Yet she knew that Zulie did.

The black woman was coming along the lane and had reached the blacksmith shop when Bonnibelle noticed her. A tall woman in a somewhat ragged cotton dress and a yellow kerchief, she was barefoot and walked with long strides. Perhaps Bonnibelle leaned forward slightly to be sure it was really she. And at that moment Zulie looked up, straight into Bonnibelle's eyes.

She came to an instant halt. Then, her eyes still on Bonnibelle's for a few seconds, she quickly crossed the lane toward the coach house.

Bonnibelle was in a panic. She feared the black woman, who seemed so much older and wiser and fiercer than she, and she remembered the threats of the previous evening: 'We can still rid us of her. Do it tonight. Wait till later, then bury her out in the fields. By Jesus, I like to do it . . .'

She stared at the barred trapdoor. She heard nothing from down below, but she saw the door raise the merest fraction of an inch until the bar stopped it.

The voice was muffled: 'You open this door, you hear me?'

Bonnibelle didn't move. The room was becoming in-

173

creasingly hot, and she felt fresh sweat break out. She remembered Zag telling her that Zulie was a voodoo witch.

'Ain't going ask you again, Bonnibelle. This is Zulie, and you know it. Now, you open this here door. Got something to tell you.'

She wanted to wait for Zag, but she didn't dare refuse Zulie. She removed the bar. She backed away as Zulie came up the steps and closed the door again.

'Zag told you,' Zulie said quietly. 'Tell you, stay away from window.'

'I did – I was – '

'I see you. Right at the window.'

The bigger taller woman kept coming closer; Bonnibelle felt as if she were cornered by an enraged animal. 'I didn't mean – '

'I don't care. But they hurt Zag 'cause of you, you know what I do?'

Bonnibelle never saw the blow that hit her. Zulie shrugged her right shoulder, and it was as if Bonnibelle's head blew apart, then blew apart again as it hit the floor. She found Zulie straddling her, and she tried to scream as she saw the knife appear, but long brown fingers clamped down firmly over her mouth.

'You don't lie still, I cut you!'

Bonnibelle dared not move. The point of the needlelike knife moved over her forehead, her eye, her cheek, never quite touching.

She felt it touch the opening of her ear.

'Now all I got to do, I push it in a bitty bit more. Don't hardly even cut you. But it hurt more than anything you feel in your whole life. It hurt so much – and if'n you scream once, I shove it through your head. It hurt, and you never scream no more.'

Bonnibelle felt the knife-tip entering her ear. She twisted, tried to move her head, tried to escape the

174

probing needle point, but she could not. The tip went in still further – it seemed to go in so far, so very far - and then she dared not move.

'Little more, white bitch, just a little more, and you going want to scream like never before in your life.'

Paralyzed by fear and the anticipation of pain, Bonnibelle waited.

Zulie made a sound that could have been a laugh. She withdrew the knife-point from Bonnibelle's ear. She took her hand from Bonnibelle's mouth and slapped her hard across the face.

'Next time,' she said, 'I do it. Next time I cut you up, and I do it so it hurt.'

She stood up. She looked at the white girl contemptuously. Bonnibelle continued to lie where she was on the floor, trying to muffle her sobs.

Danger and pain pursued her. Even here, where Zagreus had brought her, even here at Sabrehill, there was Zulie with her knife. Zulie had promised to help them, but Bonnibelle had felt the knife-point in her ear and heard the promise of pain.

But she was a survivor. She had survived all this way – her sale to Mr Keegan, the years spent at The Roost, the killing of Keegan. Now she had to find a way to deal with Zulie. Having gotten up from the floor, she sprawled on the bed and listened intently while Zulie paced the room and muttered.

'Don't know why Zag brought you here. Swear to God I don't know why. Could have left you there. Could have killed you and run off just like I said, and nobody ever know. Now, ain't that so?'

'Yes. That's so.'

'If'n I been there 'stead of Zag, you sure as hell ain't here today. You know where you be? You be dead.'

'I know.'

175

'Me, I stick you so quick . . . Him, he don't even think of killing you. Ain't 'cause he's like some black folks, scared even touch white folks. And ain't 'cause he's slow in the head. Zag is right smart. But he just don't look out for hisself right.' Zulie's voice took on a special vehemence. 'Even with goddamn white folks.'

'Zulie, how come you hate white folks like you do?'

Zulie's laugh was a single syllable, a harsh bark. It was her only answer.

'Please,' Bonnibelle said, 'tell me. I ain't saying you shouldn't. I just want to know why. If your master was somebody like Mr Keegan, I guess I'd know why, but Zag says that ain't so. Then how come?'

She raised her head from the bed and looked at Zulie, who was now gazing out the window into the service lane. Bonnibelle's instinct told her that it was her turn now: her questions could be a knife-point in Zulie's ear.

When Zulie didn't answer, she looked for something else, another question, something in what had been said the evening before.

'Zulie. Who is Mr Turnage?'

'He was overseer here a while back. For maybe four, five years.'

'Zag made him sound almost bad as Mr Keegan.'

Zulie flashed her a hard look. 'No. No, Mr Keegan never bad as Mr Turnage.'

'Why? What he do?'

Zulie shrugged, as if it were a matter she didn't care to go into. 'Like lots of overseers, I guess. Mostly they all the same.'

'Tell me. Mr Keegan didn't have no overseer. I don't hardly know about them.'

'Oh, I guess you know how they do. Tell the driver whip you, you don't dig enough potatoes, don't shuck enough corn. Overseer gets down on you, you don't never get out

176

from under the whip. Take your rations away from you, make you work through the heat of the day. Complain to the master, and he say you're a bad nigger, and you get some more whip.'

'That don't sound no worse than Mr Keegan.'

'He ever make you work naked to shame you?'

'No. Mr Turnage did that to you?'

For a moment Zulie was silent, still looking out the window, and Bonnibelle thought she was refusing to answer. Then she began.

'Mr Turnage . . . always after the wenches, that man. After any wench catch his fancy, don't matter they got a man their own or not. He want you, you don't want him – too bad. If'n he don't whip you, he whip your man. And you tell at the big house – too bad. Someday he get you. Overseer always win, don't you worry.

'Like there was this one gal he want. Worked around the big house, this gal, but lived in the field quarters, so after a time Mr Turnage, he see her. But she don't want no damn thing to do with him. Him, he keep sniffing around her, sniffing around, but she kick dust in his face. Ain't going have nothing to do with that man.

'Only trouble is, she got brothers, and they work in the fields. So Mr Turnage, what he do? Little brother can't never do *nothing* right. Driver, use your whip on this here boy. And use it again and again. Kick him, kick him where it *hurt!* Then make this here boy shag down and work naked in the field, off where master won't see, and whip him again.

'Whip him till he run off or die!'

Zulie took a deep breath. She had sounded almost as if she had forgotten about Bonnibelle, but now she turned to face her, and she sounded more like the house servant that she was.

'So what is this here gal going do 'bout her little brother? I tell you what. After a while, she is going go to goddamn Mr Turnage and lift her skirt and say, "All right, then, hurry up and get it done with!" '

'Only it don't end there,' Bonnibelle said softly.

'It sure don't. It go on and on, and Mr Turnage, he don't like it like he thought he going to, so he puts the whip to you. And it still go on till he's tired of the gal. Then when his white friends come over, drink and have cock fights, he lets *them* have their pleasure with the gal. *That* is goddamn Mr Turnage!'

Zulie fell silent.

Bonnibelle thought of what she had done to Mr Keegan. 'What did you do about him?' she asked.

Zulie gave her a quick look. 'Did I say me? I said a gal, was all.'

'Don't matter. What happened?'

'I put spells on him. Plenty spells.'

'Don't sound like they work so good, that gal had to go through all that.'

'They work. Mr Turnage, he was 'gainst Danbhalah, and I call the bad *loas* of Erzulie against him to settle things. My own Danbhalah curse. It work.'

'What happened to Mr Turnage?'

Zulie looked steadily at Bonnibelle. Something like a twisted smile spread over her face. 'Well,' she said, 'he ain't here no more, that's for sure.'

Bonnibelle shook her head regretfully. 'Sure wish you was around The Roost to make a spell on Mr Keegan. 'Cause he done just about the same as you said to a white gal I know. Only it wasn't no brother that got whipped, it was her.'

'You?'

Bonnibelle nodded reluctantly. 'Only don't you say I'm no whore on account of that. 'Cause if you do, I'll say you're another.'

'He hurt you bad?'

'Bad enough.' She hesitated, then blurted it out. 'Guess

he musta put five or six pickaninnies in me the first two or three years, maybe more. But none of 'em got born right. Now I don't get 'em no more, so I guess I ain't no good for that. He always said I wasn't good for much.'

Zulie sank into a chair. 'Oh, shit,' she said.

'What's the matter?'

'Nothing, honey.'

But Bonnibelle, the survivor, shrewdly observing, knew what the trouble was. Zulie had been intent on hating her, not only for endangering Zag but because of her white skin, and Bonnibelle was making that difficult. Bonnibelle was beginning to seem human to Zulie.

And Zulie to Bonnibelle.

'You had any babies?' Bonnibelle asked.

Zulie shook her head. 'Ain't gonna neither, if'n I can help it. Not till I find me a good enough man, and I reckon that ain't never. Around here they ain't none of them half as good as Zagreus.'

'Trouble is, maybe they ain't no good. But, white or nigger, they *is* the men. And us, all we is is just women.'

Zulie nodded. 'Just women.'

The moment Zag lifted the trapdoor he knew that something had happened. He felt it in the way that neither woman looked at him, in the lack of any greeting.

He lowered the trapdoor. He carried the pot of food to the table and set it down. He went to Bonnibelle, who lay on her stomach across the bed, and, reaching under her chin, he tilted her face up toward him. Her eyes were streaked, and one cheek was swollen. God, he thought, someone was always slapping someone else around. Always.

'All right,' he said, 'what you do to her?'

'Hit her. Stuck my knife in her ear and said I'd cut the hell out of her if she let herself be seen at the window again.'

179

'Bonnibelle? Is that what happened?'

Bonnibelle nodded. 'Thought I was being careful, but I guess I wasn't.'

Zag withdrew his hand from the girl's chin. 'Zulie, I didn't bring this gal here for you to slap her face off and stick her with your knife.'

'It's all right, Zagreus,' Bonnibelle said softly.

'It ain't all right!'

'Zagreus, it was my fault, really it was. Zulie got cause to be mad. Don't you blame her, 'cause I sure don't.'

Zulie looked at him as if he were stupid. 'Well, Mr Zagreus?'

Zagreus shrugged and decided to let it go. Women – even rivals, even enemies – often fell into these unexpected alliances. What could you do? Nothing. At least it was helpful in this instance, and they were not fighting.

He found a couple of wooden spoons, picked up the pot of food, and carried it to the bed. Bonnibelle sat up beside him and looked into the pot. 'My, don't that look good!'

'Yams and 'lasses and ham. Momma Lucinda asked me why I wanted so much. Wouldn't give me no more milk, 'cause she said it would make me bilious.' Zag sniffed the air. 'Zulie, go empty the chamber pot.'

'Go empty your own pot.'

'Not mine, hers.'

Zulie was shocked. 'I got to empty her slops?!'

'Please, Zulie.'

'I ain't!'

'Zulie, empty the goddamn pot!'

Zulie found the pot and snatched it up. 'On you, I empty it – '

'*Zulie!*' Zag snarled, and Zulie snarled right back at him. For a moment he thought she was really going to do it. When Bonnibelle stuck her tongue out at Zulie, he was certain of it. But then, to his surprise, she merely laughed, shrugged, and headed for the trapdoor. No, he would never understand women.

If Bonnibelle had any reservations about eating with a Negro, she had evidently forgotten them. Zagreus knew there were white people who would never eat off the same plate, but that had always struck him as silly. White man says, 'Boy, you go out to the kitchen and fetch me a plate of food, you no-count rascal, you.' No-count rascal runs out to the kitchen, mixes up a plate of food with a lot of nigger spit and voodoo curses and comes running back. 'Eat up good, master, sir! Eat up good!' Master eats. 'By God, that's good food!' Plumb silly.

By the time Zulie returned, they had finished their meal.

'Now we've got to decide where to hide this here gal,' Zag said. 'We don't dare keep her here more'n today. I been thinking about a lot of places – like the gin house and the old schoolhouse – '

'No good,' Zulie said. 'You can't take her food places like that 'thout people seeing you, wonder what you doing out there. And the kitchen garden people, they work real close to the schoolhouse. They going see Bonnibelle.'

'I know that. But I think I know a good place no patrol going look, a place nobody ain't never going think of.'

'Where?'

'Big house.'

Both women looked at him as if he were crazy. 'How'm I going stay in any big house?' Bonnibelle asked.

'Under it, down in the cellars. There's cellars down there don't nobody hardly ever go in. Miss Lucy, she ain't even using the summer dining room that's down there. When I was a tadpole, I learned how to work the lock on the east cellar door, and all we do is put her down there in one of those storerooms.'

'No good,' Zulie said.

'Why not?'

'Same as before, someone see us bringing her food – '

'Not if we're careful.'

'And we got to empty the chamber pot for her, same as in this room. And you never know when Miss Lucy or Leila is going down there. Sure, maybe days and days go by, they don't. Then all of a sudden, six times in a day.'

Zag felt frustrated. He had thought his plan so brilliant. 'Then how about up under the roof? We wait till Miss Lucy and Leila is out – '

The instant he said the words he knew they were nonsense. 'You got a goober head? How we going feed her up there? How we going get her out? You just going leave her and George III all alone together up there to keep each other company?'

'All right,' Zag sighed, 'where we going hide her?'

'I been thinking, and there just ain't no place right close near the big house.'

'How 'bout them guest houses out the other side of the big house gardens?'

Zulie considered. The Sabrehill mansion was flanked by extensive formal gardens, each with its gazebo, and beyond the western garden were several small buildings known as the guests houses. In an earlier day, one had lodged a doctor and another a schoolteacher, and they had all been used for guests at a time when the Sabres had entertained extensively.

Zulie shook her head. 'No good. Them patrollers, ain't no good telling 'em those ain't nigger houses. They going go through everything but the big house, and that's for sure. What we got to do, we got to take Bonnibelle out into the fields. Find her a little old shanty in fields that ain't planted, some place where she can watch and see if the patrol is coming. Where there's woods she can get to if she sees the patrol. That's best where to hide when the patrol comes – in the woods.' She turned toward Bonnibelle. 'Go up a tree. Runaway nigger, he knows to hide

182

in lots of leaves. High up is best, 'cause patrol hardly ever looks up.'

Zag realized that Zulie was thinking of a specific cabin. It was a ramshackle affair, its earliest inhabitants long forgotten, but it served as midday shelter when the nearby fields were under cultivation. The fields were lying fallow now, however, and no one went near them. He didn't like the idea of Bonnibelle being so far away, but he knew that Zulie was right: it was probably the best place.

'I know where you mean. We get her there, she should be all right. There's a stream close by where she can get water, and it ain't too far to take food to her.'

'And all you got to do,' Zulie said to Bonnibelle, 'is keep your eyes open for the patrol. Think you can do that?'

Bonnibelle nodded. 'I can do that.'

'It won't be for long,' Zag assured her. 'Maybe three four days at most, then the patrol gone by, and I bring you back here again to hide.'

'We talk about that after,' Zulie said. 'First we got to get her out there – tonight. You got a blanket she can use.'

'She can have all mine. I don't need 'em.'

'You give her one, and I give her another. And now I been here too long. I got to get back to the wash house and hang out laundry.'

The day was pleasant. Zag left his room only to fetch afternoon and evening meals and to visit the necessary house. In the kitchen Momma Lucinda complained about his vastly increased appetite. Hadn't Big Lida fed him while he was in Charleston? Hadn't she fed him *any*thing? Irish, the houseboy, opined that servicing the beautiful Charleston wenches had caused Zag to lose much sleep and a great deal of weight, and Momma told him to hush his mouth and not talk like that.

On his way back to the coach house, Zag encountered

Jeb Hayes, who regarded his heaped plate with amusement and awe and wondered where Zag would put away such a meal. He also wondered why Zag would spend the heat of the day in his room when he could be taking a swim. 'Why, all those pretty girls – Vidette, the Coffey sisters, I don't know who all, they've just been waiting for their Zagreus to get back from Charleston and take them to a nice, secluded little pool – '

'Can't help it, Jebediah, just don't care to swim. Just going go back to my room and eat all this here food and have me a nice long snooze for the rest of the day.'

Hayden, Zag saw, was taking his place in the stable. Somehow he wished it was almost anyone else.

He and Bonnibelle spent most of the day talking and trading anecdotes. She had far less to say than he, because there was little that she wished to remember of her childhood, and she was obviously trying to put The Roost out of mind completely. Yet she retained a zest for living that the world had not yet been able to kill.

'What you say your daddy's name was, Bonnibelle? James Monroe, did you say?'

The crooked grin. 'I said Calhoun. As in John C. Calhoun.'

'Could have sworn you said Monroe. As in James Monroe.'

'No, you thinking about the time he was Pinkney. As in Charles C. Pinkney. Can't say much for Daddy, but he sure could pick pretty names!'

Zag continued his description of Sabrehill and its people, and talked of his own early life – of childhood with Zulie, Orion, and Paris, of his marriage to Cissie, and of the great hatred between Jebediah Hayes and Mr Turnage, the overseer.

Twice in the evening, after supper, Zag had unwanted visitors. First there were the Coffey sisters, pounding on the underside of the door and calling to him, while he and

Bonnibelle held their breath. 'They're twins,' Zag said afterwards, 'and they look 'xactly alike and ain't never apart and even *do* everything together. And I mean e-e-*ev*erything, which means if they get in a man's bed, he don't get *no* sleep!' Then, a little later, it was Vidette knocking at the door. 'Zagreus, you up there? Hey, there, candy man! You want Vidette put out your fire, honey?' Zag snored softly, pretending to be asleep, while Bonnibelle gasped and turned red and chewed on the corner of a blanket to control her laughter. 'Hey, there candy man,' she mocked in a falsetto voice when Vidette had gone, 'you want Vidette to put out your fire, honey?' and they tortured themselves with silent howls of mirth until the tears ran.

Zulie led the way, waving to them from the corner of the barn to follow: the way was safe. But in the moonlight, Zag felt like the most visible of creatures, nerves tight and breath short. He kept Bonnibelle close to him, as if he could hide her with his own big body. Zulie went on ahead. If she were to encounter any wanderer from the field quarters, they would hear her voice.

They met no one. Following a northerly course and staying close to timber, they walked almost half a mile before they came to the cabin. Once, perhaps fifty years before, it had been a stolid structure; now it was a moldering ruin, windows unglazed and roof sagging. But at least it had a roof, and the floor was built up off of the ground, and the windows and doorway provided a view of the surrounding fields and the nearby woods. 'Patrol ain't coming at night,' Zag had told Bonnibelle, 'only in light when they can see. You see 'em coming, you head quick for the woods, keeping the cabin 'tween you and them. Then do like Zulie says, and find yourself a good tree. Take everything with you – the blankets, your clothes, the tin box, everything. Don't leave nothing behind.' Zag had offered to take care of Bonnibelle's possessions for her, but she had insisted on bringing them along with her. They were all she had in the world: her treasure.

They approached the cabin carefully. The surrounding ground was hard and took little in the way of footprints, but the thick growth of weeds immediately around the cabin would easily have given away Bonnibelle's presence. Zag had warned her: disturb nothing, trample nothing, leave no paths, no signs.

Inside the cabin, starlight came through one corner of the roof.

'I sneaked out here earlier with an old broom and scared off the spiders,' Zulie said. 'Wasn't many, 'cause it's fair dry here, but you got to be careful.'

'Zulie, stop scaring Bonnibelle with talk of spiders.'

'I'm just telling her. Some skeeters here, but not too bad. And this weather you don't have to worry about no snakes crawling into your blanket with – '

'Zulie, will you shut your mouth!'

'It's all right, Zagreus,' Bonnibelle said. 'Reckon I'll be right cozy here.'

'Course you will.'

'It ain't much,' Zulie said, 'but I guess it'll keep the rain off you . . . or most of it.'

'I'll be fine.'

There was nothing more to be said. They had delivered Bonnibelle to the cabin. She had in her bundle enough in the way of smoked meat and johnnycake, stolen by Zulie, to last her until they could bring more food. But the thought of leaving Bonnibelle alone out here worried Zag. Something bad was going to happen to her, he could feel it in his bones.

The words came out before he had even thought them: 'Bonni-child, you want me to spend the night with you?'

'You crazy?' Zulie exploded. 'Tomorrow you got to be up and doing and not seen coming in out of the fields at sun up. You let 'em see you working hard, then if it don't look like you're needed, you can come out here. But you want to help this gal, you won't let 'em find her.'

'She's right,' Zag said. 'I better go back to the coach house, Bonnibelle.'

'I know.'

'But I'll come out again soon's I can.'

'I know.'

Standing beside her in the dark, he slid an arm around her shoulder, and she moved against him in a fumbling embrace. It was a gesture of trust, and he wanted to give her some further reassurance, but he felt completely inadequate. How could he take care of her if Miss Lucy was going to take him to Charleston in a few days? Could Zulie do it alone and get Bonnibelle safely away from Sabrehill? What if he had to leave even before the patrol came? No, he could never justify the trust Bonnibelle put in him. More likely he was destroying his own future and the life he was trying so hard to rebuild.

Zulie's right, he thought, *I must be crazy . . . just plumb crazy . . .*

But I do not WANT to go to Charleston.

It was her first thought on awakening. She had slept late, and she felt hot and sticky. Her window was open. That meant Leila was already up and had opened up the house in hope of getting a breath of air off of the river. Her eyes feeling puffed and her mouth gummy, Lucy rolled over on her bed.

I do not WANT to go to Charleston.

Shit.

Lucy smiled sourly at her own childishness. She had a secret vice. Both in public and in private she probably had the most ladylike tongue in all of low country society. Except upon a rare and extreme occasion, none but the fairest words ever passed her unsullied lips. In fact, virtually from childhood she had been known as such a model lady that at times she had grown somewhat sick of herself. Therefore she had secretly collected as many forbidden words as she could. The words that other ladies made a point not to hear, Lucy noted carefully and filed away for future use. She didn't use them often, but they were there when she wanted them.

So – *Shit, shit, shit, shit, shit!*

She forced herself up and out of her bed. She washed the gummy taste out of her mouth.

Oh, hell, she thought, she was really being *too* goddamn childish. It was hardly as if she were indispensable to Sabrehill; Jebediah could keep things running quite well on his own, and Paul would be here to lend a hand if needed. And the fact of the matter was that she would probably enjoy Charleston once she got there – she had been away for too long. She would visit the shops and squander money. She would break her seclusion of recent months and give a grand dinner party. And when she tired of Charleston, she would go to Sullivan's Island, since half of her Charleston friends would be there for the summer. She had a dozen standing invitations which she could accept.

For that matter, why should she stay in South Carolina? If she intended to travel, maybe she should do it right and go up north. She hadn't been north in years. Why not go to Saratoga Springs? Or Newport? She remembered Newport as being lovely at this time of year, and of course she would find old Carolina friends at either place.

Why not go to Europe?

The thought was inspired. She had wanted to go to Italy for years, and there wasn't a reason in the world why she should not do it. People did, every year. She would go to England first, of course and then to France, and then on to Italy and Greece. Maybe she would stay in Europe for a year or more, and as for her neighbors, to hell with them all. If Cousin Asher couldn't look after Sabrehill all that time, then Paul would love to install himself here. She was tired of worrying about it, and to hell with them all.

Europe. France, Italy, Greece.

She dressed and hurried downstairs. Leila was in the dining room. 'You didn't want to wake up,' she said, 'so I let you sleep in.'

'Thank you, Leila.'

'Get you some breakfast?'

'No, wait. Leila, how would you like to go to Europe with me?'

Leila looked startled. 'You serious?'

'Perfectly serious. Why not? We can go anywhere in the world we wish and stay as long as we like. So why don't we go?'

'Well, now, I don't know – '

'You'll probably meet some handsome Frenchman, get married, and refuse to come home. Wouldn't that be exciting?'

'Don't know as I cotton to marry no Frenchie. You trying to get rid of me, Lucy-child?'

Lucy laughed. 'No! I'm just thinking of the exciting time we can have. Oh, Leila, I want to have *fun* again. I'm not a girl anymore, not for a long time, and there's been too much grief in my life. In yours too, Leila, and its time we began enjoying ourselves. I'm not going to worry about Sabrehill and our people any longer. Mr Jeb and Mr Paul can do that until we get back, and I say to hell with Sabrehill – '

'Why, Miss Lucy!'

'You and I are going to have the time of our lives, we are going to visit castles in Spain and green Greek isles, we are going to concerts and balls and dance through the night – '

'You sure you ain't got a fever?'

'And you're going to find that Europe is so different

from South Carolina – there are no bound servants in France anymore, and a beautiful girl like you is just another beautiful girl – really. We are so provincial here, no matter what we may think. Leila, you are going to enjoy it so much – '

'Miss Lucy, something is wrong out there.'

Leila was looking out a dining room window toward the courtyard. Lucy went to her side. A horseman was coming around the courtyard toward the door. His head hung down, and he swayed in the saddle as if he might fall from it at any instant.

'He must be sick, Leila,' Lucy said, 'sick or wounded. Come, he's going to need help.'

They hurried through the passage and out to the courtyard. The horseman reigned up before them. He was a tall, slender man, thin-faced and dark-browed, handsome in spite of a day's growth of beard. Lucy recognized his features instantly, yet somehow she could hardly believe that this was really he, not after all these years.

He doffed his hat in a kind of salute to Lucy, and with effort swung a leg over the back of his horse. He all but fell from his saddle, barely managing to stay on his feet.

He managed a kind of smile. 'I trust my early arrival is not too great an inconvenience,' he said, his voice little more than a whisper. 'And I must say, Cousin Lucy, you look as lovely as ever.'

'Cousin Asher!'

'Yours, my dear lady, until death . . . which would seem to be imminent.'

Lucy and Leila caught him as he fell to the ground, and Leila ran to get help. Lucy knelt and touched her cousin's forehead. It was frighteningly hot.

'Cousin Asher,' she said, 'don,t you worry! You're here now, and you're going to be all right!'

'If that is your wish, dear cousin,' Asher mumbled, 'I have no choice but to survive.'

'You will! Of course you will!'

Asher smiled.

And now I don't have to go to Charleston, Lucy thought, with an abrupt surge of happiness. *And I may never get to Europe!*

She searched her memory for an appropriate expression and quickly found one. As with many of her forbidden words and phrases, she was not completely clear as to its meaning, but somehow it had the right feel to it.

BUGGER *Europe! she thought joyfully.*

6

'Zagreus.'

Zagreus looked up at Zulie. He was sitting outside the coach house, mending a broken halter. Zulie stood before him, tall, broad-shouldered, statuesque in the morning sunlight.

'Zagreus, you was out at that cabin way before sun up this morning.' Her tone was not accusatory, just sad.

'How you know that?'

'Saw you. Couldn't sleep.'

'I couldn't neither.'

He had been too worried about Bonnibelle. Bonnibelle frightened, Bonnibelle alone. Something might happen to her while he was gone – a snake, a spider, a wandering poor white or a maroon. And what would happen to her after he left for Charleston? An hour before dawn he had left his bed and hurried back to the cabin. He had found her wide awake, sitting in the middle of the floor, a blanket pulled tightly around her. 'It's the spiders, Zagreus,' she had said, tears in her eyes. 'They been biting me – and I'm scared!' He had sat with her, an arm around her shoulders, for as long as he had dared. Then he had left, assuring her that he would return again as soon as possible.

'Zulie, she can't stay out there long. She just can't.'

'She got to. She got to stay till the patrol gone by.'

'It ain't the days, it's the nights. Zulie, you s'pose we could bring her in nights?'

'No! Now, don't talk foolish. You know you do a thing like that, take her back and forth, back and forth, you going get caught. You just leave her out there, you hear?'

192

Zag sighed. 'I hear.'

'Zag, you was doing just fine before you happen on her. You was getting over your grief for Cissie. You got work you like and a nice place to live and lots of pretty girls knocking at your door. Now, don't let her spoil it! You got to be rid of her 'fore she gets you killed off – now, you know that!'

'I know that.' He knew, but somehow he didn't feel that way at all. 'Zulie, what day is this?'

'Friday. Why?'

He didn't answer. He was counting days, which was something he rarely did. Ordinarily, he took them one by one, enjoying them as best he could without bothering to count. But now they had become important. If this was Friday morning, that meant they had spent Thursday in his room. And that they had reached Sabrehill on Wednesday night. So he had reached The Roost on Tuesday evening, and it was during that night that Mr Keegan had died. So the patrol wouldn't have started until sometime Wednesday.

Tuesday. Wednesday, Thursday, Friday morning.

But God almighty, it felt like a whole month had gone by!

Maybe the patrol would come today. He hoped so. As long as it didn't discover Bonnibelle, the sooner it came and looked around and left, the better. Once here, it wasn't likely to return, and he could bring Bonnibelle back in from the cabin and hide her over the coach house again.

But if the patrol didn't come soon . . .

Zulie's hand touched his shoulder, and he looked up. He followed her gaze down the service lane toward the courtyard, and his first thought was Patrol! Then he realized that the horseman was alone. The man swayed in his saddle as if he were in danger of falling from it.

When Zag looked at Zulie again, he didn't like the

193

expression on her face: the narrowed eyes, the faint smile. He knew that expression: the conjure look.

'What is it?' he asked.

'Trouble,' she said. 'Going be trouble at Sabrehill.'

Poor Asher, he was so sick, he might well have been dying, and yet – guiltily – she almost laughed aloud for joy. Everything was solved. So they would take Sabrehill from her, would they? Sick or not, Asher was here, and she could say the devil take Pettigrew and McClintock and the rest of them. She was triumphant.

But she would not be triumphant for long if anything happened to Asher.

'Leila, get Momma Lucinda. Hurry!'

They had helped Asher into the downstairs bed chamber and laid him down on the four poster. Leila rushed out of the room, and Lucy pulled off Asher's dusty boots. Pale as Asher was, and unshaven, Lucy didn't think she had ever in her life seen a face so handsome – and so welcome.

'I'm sorry,' he murmured. 'Sorry . . . truly sorry . . . arrive here like this.'

'Now, Cousin Ash, you've nothing to be sorry for. If you only knew how glad I am to see you!'

'Finished my business earlier than I expected. Thought I'd surprise you . . . since you said come soon as possible. . . . Then on way from Charleston, this fever . . .'

'Don't you worry about a thing. We'll have you well in no time at all.'

'. . . trunk being shipped . . . Charleston. Always liked travel horseback.'

'I remember, Cousin Ash. I remember so well.'

And remember she did . . . Asher and Paul Devereau racing their horses along dusty country roads . . . dancing with Asher in the ballroom of this very house . . . parties for the McClouds at Kimbrough Hall and in Charleston . . . a spring and a summer of adoring Asher McCloud, the prince from far away. He was older now, it seemed to her that they were both a lifetime older, and yet somehow so little had changed. To her eyes, he looked the same, he was the same, the same Asher McCloud.

Leila returned to the room, followed by Momma Lucinda and her son, Irish. Momma Lucinda didn't waste words or motion. She went directly to the bed and laid a hand on Asher's forehead. She pulled back his eyelid and looked under it. She felt his pulse.

'Your bones hurt?' she asked.

'Just my joints,' Asher said weakly. 'It's not dengue fever, if that's what you're thinking. And so far, it's not flux.'

'Throw up?'

'Some.'

'Throat hurt?'

'No.'

'Let me look.'

He opened his mouth and Momma Lucinda bent down to look as best she could. When she straightened up, Lucy could tell nothing from her face.

'Miss Lucy, you got an old nightshirt left around here from Mr Aaron or Mr Joel or somebody?'

'Why, yes. Leila – ' Leila immediately left the room to fetch the nightshirt.

'Irish,' Momma Lucinda said, 'you go tell Zagreus to take care of this here gentleman's horse, then you hurry right back here and help him get ready for bed. And don't you disappear – you gonna be needed. Lucy-child, you come with me, I want to talk to you a minute.'

With some misgivings at leaving Asher alone, Lucy followed Momma Lucinda out into the passage.

'What is it, Momma? What's wrong with him?'

'Don't rightly know. You can see for yourself it ain't yeller or scarlet fever, and I don't think it's malaria. It seems too bad for bilious fever, and he says it ain't dengue fever or the flux. So I guess he just breathed some kind of miasma on his way here.'

'Do you think he's in danger?'

'Course he's in danger, long as we don't know for sure he's getting better. All we really know now is, before he gets better, he could get worse.'

'I suppose I'd better send of Dr Paulson.'

'Now, why you want to do that?' Momma Lucinda asked in disgust. 'All that man know to do is purge and bleed, purge and bleed. You get a bitty headache, he's gonna purge and bleed.'

'I suppose you're right.'

'You know good as me what we got to do. We got to work the fever out of him. Fill him with hot bark tea, and make him sweat it. Sop him with cold water or witchhazel so he don't burn up. Sop him till he gets the shakes, then cover him till he's all shook out, then sop him some more. He gets a good natural sweat of his own a time or two, maybe he'll start getting better again.'

'All right, that's what we'll do.'

'And he ought to have somebody with him all the time.'

She thought about it. Irish would be helpful, but he could hardly do the whole job himself, and besides he was inexperienced with the sick. Fortunately, there were at least two or three servants who were quite good, and it would be wise to put one of them in charge of Asher. Yes, put one in charge, with Irish as an assistant, so that neither of them would have to work twenty-four hours a day. But who should it be?

Why, of course – Lucy knew at once who should be in charge of Asher. In spite of her silly pagan spells and the superstitious fear some of the people had of her, she was perhaps the best healer at Sabrehill.

Zulie.

* * *

196

'Coffle coming.'

Orion brought the word, and Zulie, Paris, and others hurried to the road to watch. The snap of the whips could be heard long before they got there.

The coffle was guarded by three armed white men on horseback. It was made up of about fifty slaves, male and female, chained together in four groups. Most of them barefoot, they trudged wearily along the road, chains clanking, raising dust. They were on their way from Charleston to the up country, most likely. A long walk.

The coffle stopped at the Sabrehill gate. Zulie and the others watched as a guard, no doubt the leader, rode alone up the long sloping avenue to the big house. Moments later he rode back again. Yes, Miss Lucy would allow the coffle to stay there for the night. She would feed the chained slaves well – for a price. The fifty slaves, heads bowed, defeated, turned through the gate and headed toward the big house. At the courtyard they would head up the east service lane toward the barn at the end of the paddock.

'Jesus,' Paris murmured, 'glad I ain't one of them.'

Later, on her way from her cabin to the big house, Zulie stopped by the barn. She kept her distance and stood in the shadows, but the moaning of the chained slaves came to her clearly. The pain was like her own knife in her guts, and her eyes flooded.

God damn you, why don't you strike your chains . . . slay your masters . . . slay, slay . . .

She had put the coffle out of mind. It was just one more painful memory, buried to fester deep. For now, she had other things to worry about.

Going be trouble . . .

She had called on the *loas* of vengeance, on Marinette-Bois Chè-che and the Erzulies Toho and Zandor and many others, just as her mother had instructed her, and the instant she had laid eyes on this man she had known instinctively that he was the *loas'* answer. But he lay here now on the bed, ill and possibly dying, and she didn't understand, she didn't understand . . .

She had her orders from Miss Lucy. She was to use her skills to make this white master, this Mr Asher, well. She had been allowed to rest during the day, while Irish looked after Mr Asher, but she was to take care of him through the night. A bed had been set up for her in the little hallway between this room and the library, but until the fever died, she could sleep in it only in the daytime. When she rested, someone else would be with Mr Asher, but she must be nearby, night and day, whenever she was needed.

Very well. The gods had sent this man to her. But what good to her could he possibly be? She didn't understand . . .

The lamp was turned low. Miss Lucy and Leila had long ago retired to their rooms, and the house was silent. Mr Asher lay on a thick pad of old blankets, meant to absorb the water that ran off as Zulie bathed him. His nightshirt was pulled up to his armpits, and a thin cotton blanket covered him to the hips. Zulie lifted the blanket off and looked at him – looked long and coldly.

Long-bodied and lean. Hard. The hair shiny black against the white body. He might have been as handsome as Zag if he hadn't been so fish-belly white. She knew of some niggers who envied such white, but not she, not white like this.

Still, yes, he did look good, and she could understand why Miss Lucy was excited by him. She could understand, even if Miss Lucy didn't yet know the reason herself. Zulie had watched her flying about the room, gasping, flushed, happy. Maybe Miss Lucy thought it was just something about that business of having a white master at Sabrehill so that the neighbors would simmer down, but

Zulie knew better. Miss Lucy wasn't the icy-cold proper white lady some people took her for. And Zulie had been about eleven years old the last time Mr Asher had visited these parts – plenty old enough to remember how Miss Lucy had acted. Like any other wench, white or black, come into season.

Zulie put the blanket back. She rested a hand on Mr Asher's forehead. Yes, he was as hot as ever, and he groaned and shook his head as she touched him. Something was riding him, something evil, and she would have to conjure it out. Momma Lucinda had told her to use water and herbs and medicines and 'not no fool voodoo spells.' But Zulie didn't care. As soon as Momma had left, she had spelled the bowl of water to drive out the evil.

Now, sitting on the edge of the bed, she selected a rag from a pile on a table and dipped it into the bowl of water. She partially wrung it out, then moved it gently over Mr Asher's face. He groaned again and moved his head. She swept the rag over his chest, moistened it again, and moved it over chest and belly. Mr Asher's eyelids fluttered. He would awaken now, she knew, as men often did at night when they had a fever.

'Where . . . where . . .?' The eyes were like blue fire.

'You all right, Mr Asher. Miss Lucy say look after you.'

'Lucy . . .'

'You got fever, is all. We make it go away.'

Mr Asher's eyes closed again. He put a hand to his head and moaned. 'Everything . . . fuzzy . . . don't seem real.'

'That's the fever.'

Zulie dipped the rag in the bowl of water and continued bathing Mr Asher – face, chest, arms. He shuddered as if he were cold, but he was still like a bed of warm coals under her hand. His eyes opened again, wider this time.

He smiled slightly. 'You being mighty nice to me.'

'Just making you well, Mr Asher, sir.'

'You know my name. I don't know yours.'

So he didn't remember her, it seemed. Well, she hadn't expected him to.'

'Erzulie,' she said.

'Erzulie. I've heard that name somewhere before.'

'My momma's and my momma's momma.'

'It's mighty pretty. Bet they just call you Zulie, though.'

'Yes, sir.'

'Mighty pretty.' Mr Asher smiled slightly. His fireblue eyes moved. 'Pretty as you are, Zulie.'

The eyes made Zulie suddenly conscious of her body, a tall, strong, desirable body under a thin cotton dress, and she flushed with resentment. Yes, she knew she had a kind of beauty, she knew what she had, but what she had was not for any white man. She said, 'Thank you, Mr Asher, sir,' but her eyes were cold.

'Never seen another like you. Not in Richmond, not even in Charleston.'

Charleston . . .

Something stirred in Zulie, something like recognition, the beginning of understanding.

'Never seen another . . .'

'Charleston? You come from Charleston?'

'Been there. Just came from there.'

'Don't live there?'

He looked at her curiously. 'No. Might sometime, though. Just might.'

'I been there. Mighty grand place.'

'You liked it, did you?'

'Mighty grand.'

Mr Asher smiled. He lifted his hand. When he dropped it, it fell on her thigh. She didn't slip away from under it, as she might have done at another time. Her heart was beating a little harder than it had been, and she wasn't quite sure why.

'You tell me about Charleston sometime?' she asked.

'Why, sure I'll tell you.' He patted her thigh.

200

Zulie smiled as if she didn't mind. They got that way sometimes, men did, when they were sick – long as they weren't in bad pain or half bled to death. And they were worse when the sickness started going away. Got that way, then used you if you let them, then forgot all about you.

Mr Asher's eyelids were falling again, veiling the blue fire. Zulie patted the hand that patted the thigh.

'You better go back to sleep, Mr Asher, sir. Get your rest so you get well.'

'You going to ge me well, Zulie?'

'Yes, sir, I am, sir.'

'Good . . . that's just fine . . .'

'Sleep . . .'

The eyes closed. His head turned away from her. She listened to the rhythm of his breathing until its shift told her that he was asleep.

Charleston . . .

She understood now. She understood why Marinette-Bois Chè-che and the others had sent Mr Asher McCloud to Sabrehill. She smiled.

She waited until his sleep had deepened and he didn't even stir as she brushed him with the damp cloth. Even then she waited a full half-hour before she reached into her dress and pulled out the needlelike blade. Perhaps Miss Lucy and Mr Jeb and some others laughed at her spells, but conjuring, obeah, voodoo – they could get a witch hung or burned. She had to be careful.

Very carefully, she cut some hairs from Mr Asher's head – not a lock, which might be noticed, but just a few hairs from here and there. She put them on the center of a scrap of cloth. Next, she just as carefully took a few hairs from Mr Asher's chest. A few more came from his belly, and still more from down his body until she reached his ankles. All were gathered together on the scrap of cloth, which was then folded and hidden under her dress.

He thought she was a plaything as all white men thought of women. But he was wrong. He would be the plaything. And hers, not Miss Lucy's.

7

The patrol came on Saturday afternoon.

Lucy was in the office with Paul Devereau at the time. He had stopped by to tell her that he had informed various neighbors of her decision to visit Charleston, leaving him in charge of Sabrehill. She in turn told him of Asher's arrival and of the reversal of her decision.

'I'm sorry I didn't let you know immediately, but we've been so busy – first, Asher ill; then, the coffle yesterday evening and this morning – '

'I quite understand.'

'And you do see, don't you, Paul, that there is no longer any need for me to go to Charleston. On the contrary, I'm obliged to stay here and care for Cousin Ash, and once he's well . . .'

Whatever he might be thinking, Paul's face told her nothing. Its expression – attentive, unsmiling – never altered as she gave him her news, yet she was sure it must be a disappointment to him.

'It's simply a matter, then, of getting Mr McCloud well again,' he said almost carelessly. 'For my part, I won't tell anyone how sick he is. Let people think it's just a passing indisposition. Otherwise, they may think he's more a burden than a help to you.'

'I quite agree.'

'I must confess, though, Lucy, that I still wish you were going to Charleston. You'd be safer there, and I still think you could use a rest from Sabrehill.'

Lucy shrugged. 'The time for that will come.' She wondered how long Paul would stay. She had no wish to invite him to supper, and she wanted to get back to the house to look in on Asher. In spite of all she had to do, Asher was rarely out of her mind.

'Now, there's one more thing, Lucy, and I hope you won't take this amiss.'

Lucy smiled. 'I hope so, too, Paul. What might it be?'

'Knowing that Mr McCloud was due here sooner or later, I've done some investigating of his background – '

'You've what?'

'I've asked some questions about Mr McCloud.'

Her face warmed. 'By what right – '

He saw her anger and was prepared to fight it. 'Not by right, by duty! Lucy, I am your attorney!'

'But I never instructed you to investigate Asher.'

'Am I to await your instructions on everything I do for you? Of course not. I see something that calls for attention and I attend to it. And now I see you bringing a virtual stranger into your house.'

'Cousin Asher is not a stranger.'

'Lucy, he most certainly is. A distant cousin whom you have not seen in fifteen years. What do you actually know of him?'

What did she know? To a degree, Paul was right. She knew that Asher's family had once been highly regarded by her own. She remembered her girlhood infatuation. They had recently exchanged a few pleasant letters. Beyond that, and a few random facts, she really knew very little.

'I know enough,' she said, feeling slightly guilty.

'I don't think so. And since you have no father, no brother, no husband to look after you – '

'I am quite capable of looking out for myself.'

'Then perhaps you will inquire into the background of this stranger whom you have invited into your house. If you prefer that someone other than I do it for you, so be it. But please, Lucy, have it done.'

Perhaps, she thought, she was being childish. She was

so delighted by Asher's arrival, delighted beyond anything she had expected, that she was reluctant to have any shadow cast on her happiness. But why should she think that Paul's information might cast a shadow?

'Very well,' she said reluctantly, 'what have you learned?'

'I have your permission to speak frankly, or must I guard my every word.'

'Please, Paul.'

'Then I am forced to tell you, Lucy, that the man's reputation has become somewhat unsavory. While it's true that he owns quite a large tobacco plantation in Virginia – '

'I know that.'

' – it is badly debt-ridden. Don't think of him as a wealthy planter, because he is not. His father mismanaged the plantation, even as my own father mismanaged ours.'

'That, Paul, is no reflection on either you or Cousin Asher.'

'Thank you, but I have yet to make my point. The point is that Mr McCloud has tried to salvage the place, it seems, by becoming something of an adventurer, and he hasn't been at all successful. He's been involved in certain obscure and apparently shady business transactions. He's a gambler, constantly running up debts. To his credit, he does pay his debts, but that isn't saving his plantation. He's bound to lose it sooner or later. He has also been involved in not one, but several rather scandalous affairs that led to pistols at ten paces. Now, God knows that no South Carolina gentleman is going to object to some honest gambling or the *code duello*. However – '

'Paul,' Lucy broke in impatiently, 'this is all terribly vague – "something of an adventurer, certain obscure business transactions." Now, what in the world does all that mean? It sounds like the meanest kind of gossip.'

'I assure you, Lucy, that my sources are impeccable.'

Miss Junella, most likely, Lucy thought, knowing Paul's aunt's propensity for gossip. She didn't want to think that this vague report carried more authority than that. 'Perhaps so, but – '

'Miss Lucy.' It was Cheney, the head driver, looking in through the doorway. 'Miss Lucy, ma'am, patrol's here.'

Ordinarily, Lucy would have welcomed an interruption to this conversation, but not by news of the patrol's presence at Sabrehill. She supported the patrol, as she was bound to do, but she preferred for it to stay as far from Sabrehill as possible. The patrolmen, largely poor whites, were hated and feared by the servants and field hands, and with good reason. Bullying Negroes was their one chance to exercise some kind of power, and they made the most of it.

'Are they after a runaway?' Lucy asked.

'Don't know, ma'am. They's awful lot of patrollers for just a runaway.'

She got up from her desk. With Paul behind her, she stepped out into the courtyard. To her surprise, there were far more than the usual half-dozen of them, all on horseback. It was an augmented patrol, obviously for some important reason.

And in the midst of them was a big barrel-chested man with gray hair and a weather-burned face. She recognized Balbo Jeppson immediately.

If Jeppson was riding with this patrol, he was leading it – whether officially or unofficially. Among his kind he always led, and glancing about, Lucy saw the thin-faced man called Skeet and another called Tucker, who were generally regarded as Jeppson's lieutenants. These were Jeppson's people, then, and no doubt many of them had been among the masked party that had killed a black man only a few weeks earlier.

Men who had heard Jeppson call her the Whore of Sabrehill.

Jeppson walked his horse forward toward her. Lucy felt rather than saw Paul move up beside her, felt rather than saw his growing tension.

Jeppson grinned, and Lucy knew he was remembering their last encounter. He grinned as if they shared a dirty secret.

'Afternoon, Miss Lucy.'

Lucy kept her voice carefully neutral. 'Good afternoon, Mr Jeppson.'

'Jeppson,' Paul said, 'if you wish to speak to Miss Lucy, you get your ass down out of that saddle and your hat off of your head.'

Jeppson grinned again as he dismounted, taking his time, and removed his hat. 'Now, Mr Devereau, sir, that ain't no way to talk in front of a lady.' He managed to give the word *lady* the faintest nasty twist.

'What do you want, Jeppson?'

'Guess you ain't heard. There's been a killing.'

'No,' Lucy said, 'we haven't heard. What happened?'

'Happened at The Roost. You know The Roost? A long day's ride from here or a bit farther.'

'We know, Jeppson,' Paul said impatiently. 'Get on with it.'

'Old Keegan, owns The Roost. Got his head beat in.'

'Do they know who did it?'

'Pretty good idea. Kitchen wench there, name of Bonni-belle something-or-other. Don't seem to have no proper name.'

'A bondwoman?'

'A slave, you mean? Naw, not exactly. Claimed to be white, and I guess she was, though a gal like that, wouldn't be surprised if there was a touch of the tar brush somewhere.' Jeppson looked directly at Lucy. 'Just a dirty little whore, if you'll excuse the expression, ma'am. Just a dirty little whore like plenty others we know, and we know some in high places, don't we, ma'am, been touched with the tar brush – '

'That's enough, Jeppson.'

Paul spoke quietly, but Jeppson's face went blank, and Lucy turned to see a small two-barreled pistol in Paul's hand. It rested there almost casually, but Lucy sensed the building fury behind Paul's unblinking eyes. And she realized again that, whatever their differences, this man would kill for her. He sometimes smiled at the aristocrats' code and said he was too poor to be able to afford it, but perhaps it was in his bones nonetheless.

And he hated Jeppson – all Jeppsons.

Lucy touched his arm. 'No, Paul.'

'I told you I'd kill him.'

'No.'

For a long moment, nobody moved. Then the grin slowly returned to Jeppson's face.

'Now, what call you got to stand around with a gun in your hand, Mr Devereau, sir?'

'Jeppson,' Paul said quietly, 'you watch everything you say. Every goddamn thing you say.'

Jeppson looked delighted. He looked around at the two dozen armed men with him, as if to invite their appreciation. He looked back at Paul.

'Hell, you ain't gonna use that.'

'Try me.'

'Mr Devereau, sir, you are threatening me illegally and most unkindly. We are doing a legal job, and my men here will be forced to defend me. If'n I give the word, sir, they will cut you down so fast – '

Paul laughed sharply. Before Jeppson could move, he stepped forward and jammed the twin barrels of his pistol up under the man's chin. 'Mr Jeppson, you just give that word. You give that word, and I shall blow your head off.'

Jeppson's grin faded.

Lucy tried to gauge the man's anger, his hatred, his foolishness. He surely realized his vulnerability. Given half an excuse, Paul would indeed blow his head off. And quite likely get away with it. Jeppson had power as a leader, and he might make this band of men do things they would not ordinarily dream of doing; but once he was dead, it was unlikely that they would be stupid enough to fire their guns to avenge him. To get away with it, they would have to kill her too. Not likely.

In any case, Jeppson evidently had no intention of dying. He stepped slowly back from Paul. Hatred was in every line of his craggy face. The pistol was no longer under his chin but still aimed directly at his head.

'You can put that pistol away, Mr Devereau, sir. Like I told you, ain't gonna be no shooting here.'

'Is that all you've got to say?'

'Didn't mean no offense. Came here to do a job. A man got murdered, a white man. And we mean to find the gal that done it. Find her and take her in and get her hung. You know we got to do that.'

'Search the plantation, you mean,' Lucy said.

'Every field, every cabin, every shack and shanty, ma'am. We got to.'

'Paul, I don't think that pistol is necessary.'

Paul slowly lowered his weapon.

And now no doubt Jeppson would want to take out his humiliation on the Sabrehill people, Lucy thought bitterly. But there was no way she could stop a search.

'Very well, do what you have to do. You may search everywhere but in the big house. You have my word that no one is hiding there.'

'Why, I thank you, ma'am.'

'But, Mr Jeppson, I want one thing clearly understood. My people are not to be abused in any way. They are not to be touched. And their belongings are to be respected. Nothing is to be broken, and no one harmed. You will

209

conduct your search as quickly as possible and be gone from Sabrehill.'

'Why, ma'am, these men wouldn't never touch a nigger, 'cept to keep him in line.' Jeppson's grin was back. ''Cause there ain't nothing in the world that white folks like better than a good nigger. Now, ain't that so?'

'But Zagreus,' Jeppson said, still grinning, 'you are one *bad* nigger.'

Some of the white men laughed, the soft knowing laughter of those who knew how to handle bad niggers, and Zag stood perfectly still, sweating more than the sun gave cause for. There was no help. Miss Lucy and Mr Paul had gone into the big house. Jebediah and Cheney stood nearby, but they could do nothing.

Jeppson moved closer to Zag and stood hunched forward, hands on hips. 'You surprised I know your name, boy? Why, I know a whole lot about you. Made a point of knowing. I remember seeing you on the road with Miss Lucy one night a while back – it was the same night that another bad nigger got hisself killed. Remember that night?'

Zag kept his eyes carefully on the ground.

Jeppson moved still closer, until Zag smelled his warm sour breath. 'I said, *remember*, boy?'

'Yes, sir.'

Jeppson nodded at Jebediah – 'I remember him from that night' – and at Cheney – 'and him too. And the next day I made me some in-quiries. And you know what I found out?'

'No, sir.'

'Oh, I think you do. I found out that you're the bad nigger that attacked a Buckridge driver that night of the raid and the house-burning. Attacked a driver, I say, and never even got whipped for it. Now, that's who you are, ain't it, Zagreus?'

Zag wanted to say *No! It weren't like that!* But he didn't dare. He said, 'Yes, sir.'

'Sure, you are. And I want to tell you something, Zagreus. You think you got away with something, but you didn't. 'Cause one day you are going to pay for what you did, boy. You are going to pay, and you are going to pay worse than any whipping you might have got. Yes, sir, you are going to pay.' Jeppson's grin widened, and his eyes almost twinkled with good humor. 'You believe me?'

'Yes, sir.' The sweat was like syrup on Zag's body.

'You see, boy, I'm what you might call . . . a nigger-watcher. Yes, sir, a nigger-watcher, that's what I am. Why, I reckon I know more different niggers on more farms and planations than any other man you'll ever meet. Know their names, know their husbands and wives, know their pickaninnies. Know 'em like Caesar used to know his legion, know every soldier by his first name. I know 'em, and I keep watch on 'em, every one. You understand?'

'Yes, sir.'

'So just you remember . . . from now on . . . I am watching you.'

Sweet Jesus, Zag thought, *he knows about Bonnibelle. He known all along. And he's going find her.*

His smile slowly vanishing, Jeppson stared at Zag for another moment. Then, apparently, satisfied, he turned to the patrol.

'Now, I guess you men know what to do. Most of you go through the field quarters. Those that was down by the river, go back there, but look through the gardens first, and don't miss nothing, not even them gazeboes. Two or three of you go through everything on the west lane, and two or three come with me along the east. When we're done, we'll meet on the road. Now, let's go.'

But if that was as far as the search went, Zag realized, Bonnibelle was safe.

Miss Lucy had given orders that the patrollers were to

be accompanied as long as they were on Sabre land. Since it was late Saturday afternoon, the field hands had returned to their quarters and could keep watch over their belongings there. Hayden arrived in time to accompany the searchers down to the river and Sabre's Landing, and Cheney went with another group toward the west outbuildings. Jebediah, Zag figured, would keep an eye on Jeppson.

As it happened, it was Jeb's house that was searched first, since it was so nearby. A small three-room building with a narrow porch, it stood at the head of the east service lane, facing the courtyard. Jeppson stomped up onto the porch, flung open the door, and walked in. He was followed by Skeet and another, younger man called Bassett. Zag and Jeb went to the open doorway and watched.

It took only a few seconds to go through the house, but when they were done, Jeppson, Skeet, and Bassett lingered in the front room. Bassett scratched his scraggly beard and looked sourly about as if he could not quite believe what he was seeing. Painted walls. Pictures. Curtains at glazed windows.

'Shee-it,' he said, 'what kind of nigger house is this?'

'Why, this is the house of a *ed*ucated nigger,' Jeppson said, 'don't you know that? Why, I thought everybody heard about what a smart, educated nigger Jebediah Hayes is.'

'Shee-it.'

'You see, Jebediah, boy, I been keeping an eye on you too.'

'Yes, sir, master, sir,' Jebediah said, flashing a broad smile, 'I sho' do 'preciate that, sir.'

Jeppson didn't seem to notice the mockery behind the slight field accent, but Zag wished Jep would stop it. It worried him.

'You 'preciate it?' Jeppson said.

'Black folks 'round here, they say Mr Jeppson, he sho' can be mean to a ba-a-ad nigger, but you a goo-o-ood nigger, ain't nobody more kind and fair than Mr Jeppson.'

The accent was getting thicker, and Zag was getting more worried.

Jeppson looked interested. 'They say that?'

'They sho' do, master, sir. They-y-y sho' do!'

'Lookee here,' Skeet interrupted, 'he even got books – books on *shelves*.'

'Books on shelves,' Bassett said indignantly, 'what's a nigger doing with books on shelves?'

'I told you,' Jeppson said, 'he's educated. You can tell for yourself how he talks almost like a white man.'

'But a nigger! Why, I ain't even got any books on shelves myself!'

'What do you care, Bassett,' Skeet said. 'You can't read.'

'*Shee-it!*'

Suddenly a book was in Bassett's hands. The cover was open, and Bassett was pulling at the pages, about to rip them out.

'That's Miss Lucy's book,' Jeb said quickly, 'they are all Miss Lucy's, none of them mine. She just lets me keep a few out here to – ah – to practice my reading, sir.'

Bassett froze. He tossed the book down on a table and stared at Jeb. Jeppson and Skeet stared, too.

'Yeah,' Jeppson said slowly, 'he sure do talk like a white man.'

Jeb smiled. 'I practice, sir. We can't learn to talk like white men if we don't practice – now, can we, sir?'

'But how come a nigger like you wants to talk like a white man?'

'Well, Mr Jeppson, sir – ' In the face of his own overweening ambition, Jeb modestly lowered his eyes. 'If I get really good at it, sir, I'm hoping Miss Lucy will take me out of the fields and make me a houseboy.'

Christ, Zag thought miserably, *he's going get us both killed! He can't NEVER stop mocking!*

But Jeppson merely looked puzzled, as if he weren't sure if he were being mocked or not. 'We're wasting time,' he said. 'Let's get out of here.'

Their next stop was the storehouse on the other side of the service lane. Jeb unlocked the door, Jeppson looked in, and they left immediately, proceeding back along the lane to the blacksmith shop. Saul, the blacksmith, hard at work, looked up resentfully from his anvil. He probably knew by now who these men were and what they were here for. Word traveled fast. Ettalee, his fifteen-year-old daughter, withdrew into a corner as if she did not wish to be seen.

The intruders marched through the shop. Jeppson threw open the door to the family quarters, and he and Skeet entered them. Bassett turned to Saul.

'We looking for that white gal you been hiding.'

'Ain't hiding nobody.'

'Don't you lie to me, nigger. We *know* you been hiding that gal!'

'No – no, I ain't – '

'If'n it ain't you, it sure is somebody here at Sabrehill, and you know about it, ain't that so?'

'I don't know.'

'If'n I say you know, then you know, and you damn well going tell. Now, where you got that white bitch hid away?'

'Master, sir, I don't know nothing about no white gal. Ain't seen no white gal, ain't heard about no white gal – '

'Who that there?' Bassett was looking at Ettalee.

'That . . . that there is my Ettalee,' Saul said hesitantly, and there was new worry in his eyes. 'That there is my little girl.'

'Don't look so little to me. 'Bout old as the gal we looking for.'

214

'Ettalee, she just a little old no-count nigger baby, sir,' Saul said quickly.

'She may be no-count, and she sure black as sin, but she sure ain't no baby. Not with a set like that.'

'Master, sir . . . ain't no white gal here.'

'Hey, Ettalee . . . wan' have some fun?'

Saul's big hand tightened on the grip of his hammer. Jeb took a step toward him and touched his forearm as if to soothe him.

'Yeah, I bet Ettalee just love doing it. Just dying for some of that white meat.' Bassett turned back to the blacksmith. 'Going tell you something, daddy. When we get that white gal, I plan to have me a real good time with her. And I'm going to be real disappointed if I don't get that good time. So if you know anything about her, if you find out anything about her, you better tell. 'Cause if I'm disappointed, you know what then?'

Saul didn't answer.

'Then I just got to come back here and have my good time with Ettalee. That's right, it's either the white gal or Ettalee. For me and some of my friends. Ettalee just going love that. All the white meat she want.'

The patrol. Feared. Hated.

On leaving the blacksmith shop, Skeet went to the carpenter shop, and Jeppson went on to the stable, followed by Jeb. Zag followed Bassett toward the coach house. Jeppson said they would meet in the big brick barn at the end of the paddock.

There were few possibilities for concealment in the ground floor of the coach house. Bassett circled the building and then went through the rooms, looking into each vehicle. When he saw the staircase Zag had built, he asked, 'What's up above?'

'Store rooms, mostly.'

'Mostly?'

'I live up there.'

He saw that Bassett intended to go up the stairs. Zag started to go first, but Bassett thrust him aside and led the way.

'Christ!'

Again, the pastered and painted walls, the pictures, the curtains at the windows. Zag was glad that there was no books in the room at the moment, not even a Bible. Bassett looked even more outraged than he had in Jeb's house.

'What's back there?' Bassett pointed to a door.

'Store rooms. Just old harnesses and the like.'

Bassett opened the door and went through the rooms. It took him a little while, because the rooms were so crowded that it was just possible that someone might devise a hiding place.

Zag remained behind; there seemed to be little point in following the white man in his search. When Bassett returned, he looked angrier than ever.

'Letting a goddamn nigger live like this . . .'

Yes, that was what was bothering Bassett. These were hardly the best slaves quarters in the South – far from it. But they were also far from the worst. And they were probably better than any that Bassett had ever had or could ever hope for.

Just poor buckra like Bonnibelle, but Christ, Zag thought, what would happen to her if this trash got his hands on her? Just what he had told Saul, probably.

Bassett seemed oddly reluctant to leave the room. He walked about it, looking into each corner, inspecting each picture on the wall, his face increasingly pinched and angry. At one moment, Zag thought he was going to sweep the bowl and pitcher off of the table, but he walked on, circling through the room again. He paused to stare at a wall.

'Plastered,' he muttered. 'Plastered and painted, by God.'

The wall was white. Bassett put one grimy hand on it. He

leaned against the wall and twisted the hand. When he removed it, there was a gray smudge on the wall.

Zag would have expected to be angry. He was not. To his surprise, he found himself smiling. This poor white bastard would always feel obliged to leave dirt behind where there had been none before. The only way he had of not feeling like the filthiest thing in the world was to dirty up a clean nigger. Nigger man might work all day long in the fields, then come in and wash up and put on something clean to feel good even if it was only last year's rags. But a Bassett, real trash, would sit around forever in his own dirt. And try to pull a nigger down into it with him.

Bassett turned from the wall.

Zag tried to wipe away the smile, but it was too late. Bassett had seen it, and, as if he knew what it meant, his anger boiled over. He came at Zag, hands up and claw-like.

'What you grinning at, nigger!'

'Nothing – nothing, sir!'

'You got nothing to grin at!'

'No, sir!'

Zag held his breath, certain that the man was about to attack. But he did not. Suddenly his face lit up as if he had found the perfect answer to Zag's smile.

'Why, you got nothing to be snotty about at all!'

'No, sir!'

'No, sir!'

'Who your master? Who your mistress? Who? Who?'

'Why, its – '

'The Whore of Sabrehill is who!' Bassett sneered the remembered phrase. 'The goddamn scarface Whore of Sabrehill!' Boots slamming, he rushed from the room, down the stairs, and out of the coach house.

Yes, sir, Zag thought, as he followed, *you got Mr Jeppson for a master, and all I got is Miss Lucy. Ain't it a shame.*

When all of the nearer outbuildings on the east side of

the big house had been searched, Skeet headed out for the gin house, accompanied by Jeb, and Zag followed Jeppson and Bassett the quarter-mile out to the field quarters. There the patrollers were going up and down the rows of cabins, running the people out into the square, asking questions, making threats, looking carefully at the lighter skins. Miss Lucy's orders that they were not to be abused and that their belongings were to be respected had little effect, and the patrollers went at their work with a kind of vicious glee. Windows were broken, dishware was smashed, clothing was tossed onto the floor and kicked out into the mud. Men and women alike were shoved brutally aside, and children were sent squalling. The longer the search went on, the greater the abuses became. This was not just a search for a fugitive; this was 'keeping the niggers in their place.'

Jeppson rode about the central square on his horse and shouted encouragement, while Zag followed. With relief, he saw that the search was almost finished. The patrollers would meet on the road then, Jeppson had said, and the danger to Bonnibelle would be past.

'You getting tired following me, boy?' Jeppson asked.

'Don't mean no harm, sir.'

'I know, you just doing what your mistress told you to do. Well, you damn well better. Now I want you to take some of us out into the fields north of here.'

The search was *not* almost finished, Zag realized, a sick feeling in the pit of his stomach, and the danger was far from past.

'. . . you hear me, boy, and you gonna make sure there ain't one single outbuilding or any other hiding place we miss. 'Cause if we miss any, boy, and I find out, I'm gonna add that to the punishment you got coming. Now, don't you forget.'

In other words, he was being asked to take Jeppson and the other patrollers to Bonnibelle.

'No, sir. I won't forget.'

'All right, let's go.'

Jeppson was rejoined by Skeet and Bassett and a couple of others, all on horseback. Together with Zag, they crossed the road that ran through the Sabre land, and they continued north, skirting fields of growing cotton. Far to the west Zag saw another small group of riders accompanied by a couple of blacks.

That reminded him: 'There's a tool shed in them trees way west over there. Ain't used now, but it's there.'

'If it's way over there,' Jeppson said, 'them others will look to it. But you tell us just the same.'

It was inevitable: they would find Bonnibelle. She would be hung, and he along with her. Twice yesterday he had visited her, and they had looked through the woods for a good hiding place. They had thought they had found one, but now it seemed impossible that anyone could ever escape Jeppson. Zag had spent half of last night with her and returned again today, trying to give her heart, trying to keep up her hopes, in spite of the miserable existence she was leading in the spider-ridden cabin. And for what? The Jeppsons, the whites – they always won in the end.

He looked for things to show the patrollers – another abandoned tool shed, a lean-to used by the field hands, even a deep stream-bed where a fugitive might lie hidden until a patrol went by. Anything to give Bonnibelle another few minutes, another half-hour.

But at last they broke through a patch of woods, and the cabin came into sight.

Beyond the cabin, less than a hundred feet, were more woods, where Bonnibelle was supposed to be safely hidden by this time. But Zag could no longer believe that, and he had an urge to run, to be anywhere else in the world when they found her. But he couldn't run. He had to keep going.

Another small group of patrollers, approaching the

cabin from the west, arrived just before them. They dismounted, kicked about in the weeds, and looked into the cabin.

'Anything?' Jeppson asked.

'Nothing but spiders,' one of them called back. 'Spiders and a couple of goddamn rattlers underneath.'

'You look underneath?'

'How you think I found out about the rattlers? Damn near got bit.'

'All right, let's get on, then. Get into them woods.' Jeppson looked down at Zag. 'Boy, is there anything in that there timber?'

'No, sir. Nothing but more snakes and skeeters.'

Jeppson laughed. 'Don't want to go in there, do you? Well, that's too bad. Just don't get bit.'

The woods quickly became junglelike, so thick in places as to be impenetrable. The horses couldn't be ridden; they had to be led. Zag hoped the searchers might soon become discouraged, but Jeppson kept goading them on. Virtually every bit of undergrowth that could be explored at all was poked and prodded and pushed aside.

'No sign of a trail anywhere,' Bassett said.

'Just you keep looking,' Jeppson commanded, 'and don't forget to look up, look up into the trees. That's an old runaway nigger trick, hiding in the trees, 'cause some people never look over their heads.'

They would find her.

But where was she?

The patrollers passed one immense thicket in which Bonnibelle might have hidden. They looked it over much more thoroughly than Zag would have expected, and she was not there. They came to a tangle of tree branches which she and Zag had considered, and again, they searched carefully. Zag knew now how foolish they had been to think that she could conceal herself in these woods.

220

Then what had happened to her?

The five white men moved on, a loosely extended line, calling back and forth to each other. Zag could only assume that Bonnibelle was somewhere ahead of them and on the run. At last they broke into a clearing where another half-dozen men were resting.

'Seen any signs?' Jeppson asked.

One of the men shook his head. 'Ain't nobody here. We been all through these woods, coming through the other way, and there ain't no fresh trails, no signs at all, 'cepting what we made. Couldn't nobody hide from us here.'

'Let's get moving, then. Ain't got much time before dark, and we got to keep moving east and meet the next patrol over on the Devereau place.

But where was Bonnibelle?

Zulie came to him in his room.

'They didn't find her?'

'No, Zulie, but – '

Zulie sighed with relief. 'She's safe, then. And you're safe. Them patrollers ain't likely to come back.'

'But, Zulie, she ain't in the cabin, she ain't in the woods, she ain't nowhere!'

Zulie looked at him as if she did not quite understand what he was saying. 'You mean she done disappeared?'

'Like a puff of smoke. I was out to the cabin and the woods with the patrollers, and they looked everywhere, all the places we thought Bonnibelle could hide, and she ain't there. Her, all her things, all just gone.'

'Oh, sweet Jesus. That means she got to be running ahead of the patrol somewhere.'

'I know that.'

'And that means they can still catch her. Most likely catch her. And if she tells them about you – '

'Maybe she won't.'

'Don't be crazy. She going be scared and maybe hurt

221

and Jesus only knows what they do to her. She going tell about you, she can't help herself.'

'Maybe it ain't that bad. Maybe she got away from them somehow.'

'Well, if she did, you better find out. Zag, if she did, you got to find her!'

'I know, I know.'

In spite of Zulie's worries, Zag's concern was far more for Bonnibelle than for himself. Was she still free? What would a man like Bassett do to her if he caught her? If she had escaped, wouldn't she be lonely and frightened? Could she survive another night alone?

The only place he could think to look for her was, once again, at the cabin or in the woods. But it was Saturday evening, a time for visiting and parties and relaxation, and he felt as if eyes were noting everything he did. He dared not start for the fields until after dark, and even then, as he moved stealthily through night-shadows, he felt as if he were being watched.

He heard her before he reached the cabin. It was no more than a whimper or perhaps a sob floating on the night air. For an instant it paralyzed him. Then he was running, running as fast as he could go, for the cabin.

'Bonnibelle!'

She was sitting on the floor, her back against a wall. Starlight through a gaping roof revealed a face wet with tears. She reached for him.

Then he was on the floor with her. He pulled her to him, their legs entangling and his arms encircling her as if to hold her protected forever.

'Bonnibelle, I been so scared for you!' She shook convulsively in his arms. He thought she must have been crying for hours. 'Bonnibelle, what happened? Where were you?'

'Under the cabin.'

'But you couldn't been. A patroller said he looked and you wasn't there.'

'I heard him say that. But he didn't look. Rattlesnakes scared him away.'

'You mean you were under there, and . . .'

Zag understood. Too late Bonnibelle had seen the patrollers coming from the west as well as from the south, and she had been unable to reach the woods. So she had taken her blankets and belongings and crawled under the cabin, down in the dirt with the spiders, taking care not to leave a trail, not to disturb the weeds that grew around the cabin. And once there, she, too, had heard the rattlers. And she had had to lie there, wanting to escape, wanting to scream, and not daring to make a move or a sound.

Zag wasn't sure that he could have done the same thing.

He held her tighter – held her, stroked her, moved his body against hers.

And suddenly he realized that he never wanted to let her go, that he could not have stood losing her. They had known each other only four days – it seemed so much longer – but that was enough. She was what he needed to complete the life that he was trying to rebuild.

'Bonni-child,' he whispered, 'ain't never going let nothing like that happen to you again. Ain't nothing ever again going hurt or harm you. I'll take care of you. I promise you. Trust me, Bonnibelle. Will you trust me?'

Her mouth was on his throat, on his cheek, on his lips. 'Yes, Zagreus. Oh, yes.'

'I'll take care of you. Don't know how yet, but I will. And you don't have to stay out here no more – late tonight, when everybody is settled down, I'll take you back again . . .'

He didn't have to say anything more. Her torn dress was open, and her nipple was hard between his fingers. Their legs still entangled, she moved rythmically against him. It seemed to him that never before in his life had he

223

wanted a woman more, and never had he been more ready.

Then there was no more thought, only the sure knowledge of what they were about to do. When he laid her back on the floor, she went willingly. He kissed her breasts and began to explore her gently, tenderly, lovingly. Almost at once she reached for him and tried to draw him to her.

Then, from somewhere outside the cabin, he heard the familiar voice of Jebediah Hayes: 'Zagreus, Zagreus, somehow I just knew . . .'

Part Three

1

He cried out.

He couldn't help it. There were dreams, now, as the fever became worse, many dreams, but he hardly knew what they were. A glimpse of Henry Brandon's terror-stricken face. A corpse struggling out of its muddy, storm-soaked grave. A dead girl like a broken, mutilated bird. The faces of strangers, shot, stabbed, garoted, who refused to stay dead. Only glimpses, but they brought cries of grief and dismay.

And he was talking. He had no idea of what he was saying or trying to say, but he was talking, and he *must not* talk, or the game was up, it was over, he was a hanged man. He *tried not to talk*, and in the very effort once again cried out.

There were some moments more lucid than others.

'Zulie . . . Zulie, please . . . where are you?'

'It's all right. I'm right here, Mr McCloud, sir.'

'Zulie, help me.'

'Why, course Zulie help you. Zulie making you well. Now, don't you fret.'

'Don't go away.'

'No, no, Zulie staying right here.'

But Zulie did go away, and then there was a houseboy called Irish looking after him, and he felt betrayed. Once or twice Leila looked in on him. Lucy visited his bedside repeatedly.

A cool hand on his forehead.

'He's still so hot.'

'Hotter'n ever.'

'Irish, you've got to keep bathing him.'

'Oh, I do. Get him wet, then step away quick so I don't breathe his miasma, just like you told me. But I hardly get him wet when he's all hot again, and I wet him some more.'

'Good. And if he gets any hotter, if there's any turn for the worse, call Zulie right away. Then let me know.'

Zulie. Yes, it was Zulie he wanted. He tried to call to her, but he wasn't sure that what he said made sense.

And he must not talk.

'Cousin Ash . . .'

'Yes . . .'

'Do you know where you are?'

He was bewildered to find that he had no idea. 'No . . . I . . .'

'You're at Sabrehill. We're taking care of you, and you're going to be all right.'

Not if she found out. Not if she knew.

'Zulie . . .'

'Yes, Mr McCloud, sir?'

So she was with him again. A light seemed to turn on in his mind, and suddenly he knew clearly where he was; he was in the downstairs bed chamber at Sabrehill, and it was night again. Zulie, half-hidden in shadows, was sitting in a chair in a far corner of the room. They were alone.

'Zulie, come here.'

She obeyed. She arose from the chair and walked toward him, coming into the light. But she came slowly, her arms crossed under her full breasts, moving with arrogant grace, as if to demonstrate his dependence on her. And suddenly, so weak and all but naked, he felt like a sacrifice laid out on some pagan altar.

That brought it back: the anger. To be so sick, so out of control . . !

Perhaps she saw it. 'Can I help you, Mr McCloud? Time I wet you down some more?'

He shook his head. 'What have I been saying, Zulie? What have I been talking about?'

Her rich brown eyes widened with something that could have been surprise or concern or amusement. 'Why, you ain't been saying nothing, Mr McCloud, sir. You been sleeping.'

'I've been talking. I know I have. The fever made me talk.'

'Mr McCloud, honey, 'bout the only talking you done was jabber-jabber, didn't mean nothing. Just jabber-jabber, with hardly no real words.'

He wasn't sure he could believe her. 'If I said anything strange, that was just the fever talking.'

'I understand that, Mr McCloud. Sometimes fever do make a body say crazy things.'

'Whatever I said . . . don't tell . . . anybody.'

'But you didn't say *nothing*, Mr McCloud! Just jabber-jabber, that's all.'

He wanted to weep from gratitude. 'Zulie, you are a good girl.'

She sat down on the edge of his bed. 'Now this nice master going let me put more cool water on him.'

He knew the wet cloths were necessary, but he didn't like them. At times, as now, they made him feel deeply nauseous – sick to the very soul, if there were such a thing. Then they made him shiver, and at the same time he felt the heat of the fever beneath them.

The heat of hell.

He was going to die.

The knowledge came as a stunning revelation. It was the first time in his life that he had truly known that his death was imminent. He had long ago discovered the fragility of all life, including his own; he had watched it, studied it, observed it. All death held a fascination, in different measures, and he had even meditated on his own

229

death, to come at some future date. But now at last he had arrived at the future. At the precipice.

He was going to die.

That was why his dreams brought not only terror but grief and dismay: he was now joining all those canceled-out lives, lives that – because the past was a fiction – *now*, in his view, had never really existed.

Wiped out. A fading rumor. Oblivion.

'Zulie,' he heard himself saying, 'hold my hand. Please. Hold my hand. And for God's sake . . . don't let go!'

She seemed to understand. One of her hands gripped his tightly while her other continued to bathe his face. 'Sure, I hold your hand, Mr McCloud,' she said, and he thought she sounded almost happy. 'Going hold your hand and ain't never, never going let you go . . .'

As Zag led the girl out of the cabin, she clung to his arm as if it were all that kept her from dying, and he could feel her tremble.

'Zagreus,' Jeb said, 'I just knew you were up to something, the way you've been running around like a chicken with its head cut off.'

Zag couldn't see Jeb's face under the shadowing brim of his hat, but his voice was quiet, gentle, even sad – almost as if he knew he was looking at death-to-come. And Zag felt now that, even having escaped the patrol, it had to end this way. There was no escaping the watchful eye of Jebediah Hayes.

'She's the girl they were looking for, isn't she, Zagreus? The girl they say killed Mr Keegan. How did you get mixed up with her?'

'I met her at that place they call The Roost. Jebediah, you don't know what all happened to this here gal, how that Mr Keegan treated her!'

'Oh, I can guess. I've heard about The Roost and Mr

Lacy Keegan. Among white folks, they're notorious. But it's still a murder you've got yourself mixed up in this time, Zagreus. Not just a brawl with a black driver, but the killing of a white man. How did you come to bring the girl back here?'

'I had to. I had to take her some place, and there just weren't no other. I had to hide her somehow!'

'Why you?'

The question left Zag oddly breathless. Why him indeed? Because chance had taken him to The Roost? Because Bonnibelle had blackmailed him into helping her escape? The random chance and the desperate blackmail were threatening his life now, but they were the very things that had brought love to him again and given his life new meaning.

He could only say: 'I don't know, Jebediah. I only know I had to try.'

Jebediah sighed and shook his head. 'Zagreus, there are only two kinds of people in this world, villains and fools. For what it's worth, you're a fool.'

'Oh, hell, I always known that.' Zag wanted to weep. He pulled his arm free of Bonnibelle's grip and wrapped it around her shoulders, holding her close.

'Well, let's get going Zagreus. I've got to take you both to Miss Lucy.'

'Jebediah, no! The patrol done passed by, and they ain't coming back. I can hide her. I can keep her safe and take care of her.'

It was a last desperate attempt, a futile attempt, and Jeb shook his head, as Zag had known he would. 'No use, you couldn't do it. Sooner or later, it would be found out.'

'But Jebediah – '

'We've got to go to Miss Lucy. No choice.'

They started the walk back toward the big house. Zag and Bonnibelle led the way, with Jeb following a few

231

yards behind. Zag had made the journey many times lately with his heart filled with unnamed wild hopes, but now he felt as if he were walking toward a gallows. At his side, Bonnibelle clung to his waist with one arm and to her bundle and tin box with the other. The little sounds that came from her throat reminded Zag of those a rabbit sometimes made when caught in a snare: the sounds of panic. Yes, it was a gallows they were walking toward, and she knew it.

He tried to comfort her with soft words – 'Now, don't you worry. Everything going be all right' – but she didn't seem to hear him, and he wondered angrily what the hell could he *do*? Start running with Bonnibelle when they passed through the darkness of a patch of woods? Turn on Jebediah and hold him, beat him down, kill him, while Bonnibelle ran? He knew that neither he nor Bonnibelle had a chance.

'Listen to me, Jebediah, you could help us – '

'I'm helping you the only way I know, Zagreus. If you've got a hope in the world, it's this way.'

A slim hope, but maybe it was there if Jebediah said so. Jebediah had never lied to him, had always been honest and fair with him. He had to cling to that.

They crossed the main road and entered the open gateway. On the rise ahead of them the big two-and-a-half story brick mansion with its wide cupola could hardly be seen in the night, except for a light flickering dimly in the passage. They walked toward that light – from under the oaks, it was like the light at the end of a dark tunnel.

When they reached the courtyard, Zag saw that there was no light in the office. A few people stood by the kitchen house door, where Momma Lucinda was evidently still at work; they glanced around without interest and returned to their conversation. Zag, Bonnibelle, and Jeb went on by them, scarcely noticed, to the big house.

232

Jeb reached in the open doorway, banged the knocker, and called out: 'Miss Lucy?'

'In here, Jebediah,' Miss Lucy's voice came back to them. 'In the library.'

Jebediah led the way through the passage and the dining room into the library in the west wing of the house. Miss Lucy was speaking to Leila, the housekeeper, and she turned to say something to Jeb.

She saw Zag and the girl.

Her eyes widened, and for a moment she appeared stunned. Then, almost at once, she seemed to understand what the situation was. Her eyes went wild, and a hand went to her cheek. She seemed to be holding her breath. Her eyes went to Jeb and steadied, and she began to breathe again.

'Yes, Miss Lucy,' Jeb said, 'it's her. The girl the patrol was looking for.'

Leila, who had looked confused, murmured, 'Oh, my sweet savior.'

'But how did she get here?' Miss Lucy asked. 'Was it Zagreus? Did Zagreus bring her?'

'I'm afraid he did.'

'But, my God, does he realize what he's done?'

'I think his main concern is helping the girl, Miss Lucy. You can see, she's little more than a child.'

Miss Lucy looked at Bonnibelle, looked at her with hard blue eyes that were pitiless and searching, and Zag realized she was seeing someone far different from the girl he knew. All she was seeing was the little swamp-rat girl, filthy with the dirt from under the cabin, her dress ripped open, clinging to her bundle and tin box. A little white trash girl that no lady, such as herself, would knowingly have allowed through her door.

'She needed help, ma'am,' he said. 'I had to help her.'

Those implacable blue eyes shifted to him.

233

'Where did you meet her?'

'At The Roost, ma'am.'

'Then you were there the night that that Keegan person died?'

'Yes, ma'am.'

'And it's true that this girl killed him?'

Zag looked desperately for a convincing lie. 'It was an accident. He fell down, fell down something awful – '

'The girl told you this?'

'No, ma'am, I saw – I saw – '

'He didn't fall down, Zagreus, he had his head beaten in.'

Miss Lucy stated the words flatly, a flat contradiction, her eyes still hard on him, and Zag knew he could not lie to her. She would see through anything false that he said. But still he had to try to protect Bonnibelle, even as Miss Lucy had not long ago fought to protect him.

'Miss Lucy, it ain't her fault. She never wanted to hurt nobody. She's just a no-count little gal, her daddy sold her to Mr Keegan when she wasn't much more than a pickaninny. And, Miss Lucy, he done terrible things to her ever since. I don't dare tell a lady the things he done to her. He worked her and whipped her and whored her so bad, he was worse than any bad overseer. He was worse than that old Mr Turnage who was here, and if you know what Mr Turnage done to Zulie and Leila – '

He broke off. Leila had stiffened, and Miss Lucy looked as if he had thrown something filthy in her face. The scar down the right side of her face was vivid. She knew as well as anyone at Sabrehill the kind of man Mr Turnage had been. But that was part of the buried past, and by some unwritten law, a tacit understanding between servant and mistress, his name was never mentioned in her presence. She had never requested this; it was simply assumed. But in the heat of the moment, he had forgotten.

Miss Lucy turned away from him. She closed the door to the hallway between the library and the downstairs bedchamber – the same hallway in which Zulie now had a bed. As if this were a signal, Leila closed the door to the dining room. Miss Lucy then crossed the room and seated herself in a comfortable chair.

'Zagreus,' she said, 'I think you had better tell me all about it. And I think that for your own sake, and possibly this girl's as well, you had better tell me the truth. The exact truth, Zagreus, omitting nothing.'

When Zagreus had finished his story, Lucy sat weary and unmoving and wondered how much he had added or omitted or distorted. He looked as if he wanted to go down on his knees and beg for help, and the girl had, in fact, slumped to the floor, where she clung to his leg like a half-mad supplicant. Leila had slumped into a chair, and Jebediah leaned back against a door, his arms folded over his chest.

Lucy had dug at an occasional point when she had felt that Zagreus was not telling all, but she felt that his story was in the main accurate. He had been caught out in the storm, the same storm they had had that night at Sabrehill. He had been directed to The Roost. If anyone had known he was there, it would have been suspected that he and this – this Bonnibelle had fled together, but Jeppson had said nothing about a Negro. The girl had killed that wretched Keegan and forced Zagreus to help her escape. Forced him – that was one of the points that Lucy had had to dig for. And far from resenting the blackmail Zagreus seemed utterly determined to help the girl.

'Miss Lucy, you know what they'll most likely do to her if they catch her – a poor servant girl, no family, nobody to protect her!'

'Yes, and I know what they'll most likely do to you – if

235

not hang you along with her, then whip you until you wish they had.'

She regretted her careless words. The girl was already so clearly terrified.

But what should she do?

The most sensible thing she could do, she supposed, was to call for the law. She could hire Paul and any number of other lawyers to defend Zagreus – and Bonnibelle, too, for that matter. Money was not a problem, and these two did, after all, have the right on their side, whatever mistakes they had made.

But The Right, she thought bitterly, when had The Right started being such a potent force for good?

Certainly blacks and poor whites had been given fair trials and justice many times – it would be foolish to deny it – but how often had they not? How often had they been hung by hysterical courts on but the flimsiest of evidence?

And a murder case where a black man undoubtedly aided a *white woman*? Black and white, lovers no doubt, kill a *white man*?

Perhaps she was wrong, but she could not believe that either of them had the slightest chance. And if Jeppson and his people were to get their hands on them . . .

Still. Zagreus was a good boy, but what did she *really* know about the essential innocence of the girl? She believed the girl had probably been justified, but . . .

She suddenly realized that it was in the girl that she believed most of all. She reached up and felt the scar on her cheek. She thought of other scars she bore that no one would ever see. She thought of the blows she had born at a man's hands and how she had been driven to reach for the haft of the knife.

The Whore of The Roost and the Whore of Sabrehill, she thought wryly. They came from different worlds, as

236

distant as black and white; yet they were sisters, though this child would never know it.

But what could she do, what could she do?

Suddenly the girl, still on the floor and clinging to Zagreus's leg, broke down completely. Lucy knew she should have seen it coming, but she had been too busy with her own thoughts. Bonnibelle had been clinging to Zagreus and weeping ever since they had entered the room. She had looked about with the eyes of a terrified animal, and now the eyes were wide and blank, and the sounds that came from her throat were animal, too – the rapid bleating of a lamb that sensed its coming slaughter.

'Now, you stop that, you silly girl!'

Lucy was out of her chair in an instant. Leaning down, she slapped Bonnibelle with all her strength. Then she was on her own knees, holding Bonnibelle's shoulders and shaking her.

'I said, stop that! Nobody is going to hurt you, you silly girl, we're all here to help you! Now, you stop acting like a baby! Stop it, I say!'

The bleating stopped. The girl's eyes wavered as if seeking a focus, then found Lucy.

'Now, do you think you can get to your feet, go sit down, and start acting like a lady?'

The girl nodded.

'Then do it! Zagreus, help her.'

The girl's face crumpled, and she began to bawl again, but she struggled valiantly to hold the noise down. As Lucy and Zagreus each took her by an arm and helped her to her feet, she continued to cling to her possessions as a child might to a pair of dolls. They marched her to a sofa and sat her down, Zagreus beside her, and Lucy returned to her chair.

'Now,' she said, 'I seem to have committed us to helping this girl.'

237

'Godamighty!' Leila looked appalled.

'Well, what would you have me do, Leila?' Lucy snapped. 'Take her out behind the barn and put her out of her misery?'

'Hell, I don't know. I ain't no answer person, Miss Lucy. But I sure as hell got some good questions.'

'Very well, ask them.'

Leila turned to Zagreus. 'Just how the hell did *you* expect to help the girl? You ain't been too clear about that.'

'Just hide her from the patrol, like we did,' Zagreus said miserably. 'Then bring her back to my room at night and hide her some more. Ain't nobody ever goes up there without my permission – '

'Miss Lucy,' Leila interrupted angrily, 'this gooberhead got gals in rut trotting up there night and day. He couldn't never kept her hidden up there!'

'All right,' Lucy said, 'someone would have found out. But even if no one had – what then, Zagreus?'

'Would have kept her up there. Brought food to her. Kept her there till Mr Keegan was all forgot. Then one night late, when . . .' Zagreus hesitated. '. . . when she want to go, I figure I'd sneak her away from Sabrehill and take her to Riverboro or some place. She got a little money, maybe she can ride a coach north.'

'That – that is just – just plain gooberhead foolishness!' Leila sputtered.

'Not entirely,' Lucy said. 'Jebediah, what do you think?'

Jebediah was still leaning against the door, a little smile on his face. Now he looked at Zagreus with a certain fond amusement. 'Our gallant's plans do seem a little vague,' he said, 'but not altogether unworkable. And now that we know about the girl, there's no need for him to "sneak her away" past us. That can make matters easier.'

238

'How?' Leila demanded. 'Just exactly how?'

'Well, for example, if we keep the girl hidden until Miss Lucy decides to visit Charleston, she can go along as a member of the party. Just a recently arrived visitor, as far as any of the servants are concerned.'

'That trash?' Leila asked, unbelieving. 'A visitor at Sabrehill?'

Jebediah ignored the objection. 'And then, once in Charleston, Miss Lucy can put her on a boat north, and she can start life over again with a new identity.'

'I could do that,' Lucy agreed. 'I might even be able to find her employment with one of my northern friends.' She observed Zagreus's arm tightening around Bonnibelle's shoulder. It struck her as less a gesture of hope than one of reluctance to let the girl go. Well, all things considered, she wasn't too surprised.

'Then the question is,' Jebediah went on, 'how to keep word from getting about that we have a white girl here, a white girl who appeared just about the time the patrol was looking for one. If our people find out . . . well, you can be sure that the entire countryside will soon know. It's not a secret they could keep even if they wanted to.'

'We'll just have to keep her hidden.'

'And how in the world you gonna do that?' Leila asked. 'Just where you think you're gonna put her?'

Yes, where? Obviously Bonnibelle could not continue to live in some old wreck of a cabin out in the fields – Zagreus had been right about that. Aside from the discomfort, some field hand, some wanderer, would see her sooner or later and become curious. And Leila was right in saying that the girl would soon be discovered if she stayed in Zagreus's quarters. Could she be concealed in some high room of the mansion or tucked away in some cellar? It seemed a poor idea. Even if Bonnibelle could stand the confinement, she would be seen at a window, or heard, or someone would notice strange goings-on.

Then where, where . . .?

'I take it, Leila, that you have no suggestions?'

'I say don't hide her at all.' Leila sounded almost angry. 'I say put her right back in a carriage with Zagreus and send them both back to Charleston. Let him put her on a boat north, and let that be the end of it!'

'She can't travel like that now, she'd be noticed – ' Lucy broke off. She thought she had the answer, or at least a part of it. It now seemed quite obvious.

'She traveled here, didn't she?' Leila asked. 'She pretended to be Genevra, and she can go on being Genevra till she gets to Charleston.'

'No,' Jeb said. 'She and Zag were just lucky they didn't meet someone who knew her. A lot of people who saw her at The Roost are going to have their eyes open for her for some time to come, and she isn't going to be able to fool them that she's some unknown colored girl. They'll know she's white.'

'On the other hand,' Lucy said, 'nobody *here* knows she's white. Nobody but us. And Zulie, of course.'

The others stared at her.

What was the phrase that Jeppson had used? A touch of that tar brush. It was all that was needed to turn a white girl into a black – and a slave. If Bonnibelle were to be presented to the people of Sabrehill as a slave, it would be assumed that she had that touch, that she was black, no matter how light her skin. How could it be otherwise? One heard of an occasional black who passed as a white, but who ever heard of a white trying to pass as a black?

Leila's eyes widened. 'You gonna keep her here as a *nigger* gal?'

'Why not? In a few weeks, a month or two, the excitement over Mr Keegan's death will have died down.

240

No one will be looking for the girl or ever expect to see her. Then perhaps I'll make a trip to Charleston. We can tuck Bonnibelle into a covered wagon, and she'll never be seen.'

'But if you're wrong – if you're stopped and searched –'

'Not likely, and I'll just have to take that chance.' Lucy crossed the room to the sofa where Zag and Bonnibelle sat. 'Bonnibelle, no one has consulted you about this. Would you mind continuing as a – a Negress a little longer?'

The girl had quit sobbing, and now she merely sniffled. 'Reckon not,' she said, her first words since entering the room. 'Like Zagreus says, what I want to be, a live nigger or a dead white gal?'

'Zagreus is an intelligent young man.' Lucy looked at the others. 'Does anyone see any objection?'

Leila shook her head as if to clear a clouded and unbelieving mind, but Jeb looked pleased. 'It seems like a perfect means of concealment. She's just one of us, one of the people of Sabrehill. No one here will question that, and no one from away from Sabrehill is likely to notice her.'

'Then we're agreed. Bonnibelle is simply one of our people, newly arrived. But we still haven't decided exactly how she got here and why.'

'*Why* she is here,' Leila said, 'is because damn fool Zagreus *want* her here. That's why!'

'Very good, Leila!' Lucy said with mock amazement. 'And here you told us you had no answers. You're right, of course – that is exactly why Bonnibelle is here. Because Zagreus has asked that she be allowed to be here with him. Zagreus, is this agreeable to you?'

'Miss Lucy, ma'am,' Zag said, 'I'll do or say anything you want. Anything!'

Jebediah was right, Lucy thought: Zagreus's concern

241

was for the girl, whatever the danger to himself. He might well be in love with her, whether he realized it or not.

'Then say that Bonnibelle is your girl from Charleston. I seem to remember from our trips to Charleston in the past that you had quite a few girls there.'

'Oh, yes, ma'am,' Zag said quickly. 'I could say that this is Albinia – 'cause none our people ever saw Albinia. All they know is, she's a light-skin gal just like this one, that I cotton to a lot.'

'*Very* good! Bonnibelle, can you remember that your name is Albinia from now on?'

'Yes, ma'am. I like that name, ma'am.' The girl was beginning to look alert and aware.

'You'll probably be called Binnie for short, and that's close to Bonnie.'

'Yes, ma'am. I like that, too.'

'And now what I suspect will be the hard question. Just how has it come about that Albinia is here with us?'

The room was silent. Lucy went back to her chair and sat down.

'No suggestions?'

'Zag stole her and brought her back with him,' Leila said after a moment. 'Been trying to keep her hidden ever since.'

'Not likely,' Jebediah said.

'It's exactly what happened!'

'No. Bonnibelle was a fugitive he planned to hide just long enough so she could escape. But Albinia, if he stole her, must be someone he cares for, someone he wants to live with. He can't keep her hidden forever, and he's smart enough to know that. No one would ever expect Zagreus to do such a thing. So that can't be what happened.'

'I suppose Mr Paul Devereau might help us with this,' Lucy said. 'Maybe he would say that he made the purchase of Albinia for me and brought her here.'

242

'Miss Lucy,' Jebediah said, 'I suggest that you keep Mr Devereau out of this if at all possible. The fewer people that know, the better. If it turns out that you need papers for Albinia and he can help you, then tell him. But right now all you need is some kind of tale for the servants and the hands.'

'All right.' Lucy took a deep breath. 'Here's what happened. As soon as Zagreus reached Charleston on this trip, he looked for his Albinia and found her. And he found that he cared for her as much as ever, or even more. But within a week she was sold to a trader who was preparing a coffle for the up country. Zagreus got back here as soon as possible, and ever since then he has been hounding me to buy the girl. Fortunately, the coffle was coming this way, as so many of them do, which made it easier. But I would probably have bought the girl anyway, because Zagreus was so persistent. Zagreus, how does that sound.'

'Why, it could happen just like that, ma'am.'

'Only trouble is,' Leila said sceptically, 'the coffle didn't get here tonight. The coffle got here *last* night, and it left this morning. So what's this here Al*bin*ia been doing all this time that none of us even seen her?'

'Well, now,' Lucy said, 'Albinia has had a long and tiring trip, and what's more, it's been some days since she last saw Zagreus. If you'll stop and think about it for a moment, Leila, I think you'll know what she's been doing.'

'Oh.'

'One thing more,' Jebediah said. 'I don't think you'd buy Binnie for Zagreus unless they were pledged to each other. So unless you want to fool people with a false wedding – and I don't think it's necessary to do it – it would be best to pretend that they already jumped over the broomstick in Charleston.'

243

'Albinia?' Lucy watched the girl's reaction carefully. For a sandhiller girl, even one in Bonnibelle's – Albinia's – predicament, this was surely an offensive suggestion. But the girl merely shrugged.

'If I'm gonna pretend I'm a nigger, I don't see no harm pretending I'm married to one.'

'Good. And that's all right with you, Zagreus?'

'Course, Miss Lucy.'

'Then you'll have to appear to live together. You need not actually, of course, but – Zagreus, can you clean out at least part of the room next to yours? to make room for Albinia?'

'I can clean it all out.'

'Do whatever is necessary. Now, a few more details . . .'

As they developed a background for Albinia, Lucy continued to watch the girl carefully. Now that her fear was diminishing, she seemed to have a reasonably quick and ready mind, and though she was quite uneducated, she was not altogether ignorant. That was all to the good. If the girl had been a total fool, the situation would have been impossible.

'And now a warning to each of you. Albinia . . .'

'Yes, ma'am.'

'I know that, whatever you may say, you must resent having to pretend to be black.'

'Well – I – '

'But for now you must forget that you were ever white. If you are to succeed in this masquerade – and save your own life – you must think of yourself as simply one of the people of Sabrehill. Be with them, be one of them. Never let them guess that you're anything else, never act as if you're harboring a secret. You have no secrets, Albinia. From now on, you are simply Albinia of Sabrehill.'

'Yes, ma'am.'

'And Zagreus. However you got into this predicament, it's clear that you are fond of Albinia. Isn't that true?'

'Why, yes, ma'am.'

'But you must not allow yourself to become too fond. Always remember that sometime soon, in a month or two, Albinia will be leaving. We'll let it be known then that you two haven't been getting along well and that I'm sending Albinia back to Charleston. The marriage will be dissolved.' There was no problem in this, since slave marriages had no legal standing. Lucy added, 'It might be well if after a week or two you and Albinia made a show of beginning to quarrel.'

Zagreus nodded slowly and reluctantly, and his 'Yes, ma'am' could barely be heard.

'Now you and Albinia may leave, and for goodness sake, get her cleaned up. I'll send Zulie out in a few minutes with a clean dress. Then I'm sure you'll want to have your Saturday night with the others. Zagreus, you know the way out.'

When the pair had left the room, Jebediah quietly closed the door behind them. Without waiting for an invitation, he sat down.

'You know, of course,' Lucy said to him after a moment, 'that Leila is quite right. It's extremely foolish to try to hide that girl.'

'Of course.'

'Fortunately, she's no fool, but there's still a good chance that she'll give our game away. Or Zagreus, who's no fool either, will nevertheless make a mistake. He'll love the girl too much and do something wrong or say the wrong thing.'

'I know that.'

'But what else can I do? Let the poor girl hang? Let Zagreus hang with her? If I were a Callie Buckridge or an Adamina Kimbrough, I suppose I'd do precisely that. But

I'm not a Callie or an Adamina.' She touched the scar on her cheek. 'Nor do I wish to be.'

Smiling, Leila reached over and touched Lucy's arm. 'Don't you worry, Lucy-child. We all been through lots worse than this. We gonna be all right.'

Gratefully, Lucy returned the touch. 'yes, Leila,' she said. 'Somehow, we're going to be all right.'

It was one of the great evenings of his life. He could conquer giants. He could defeat dragons.

'I told you I'd take care of you,' he said as he led her toward the coach house. 'I told you I wouldn't let nothing harm you.'

'I know, I know!' Clinging to his arm, her head pressed to his shoulder, she sang the words.

'Miss Lucy and me, we get along fine. Why, we're real good friends.'

'She is the most *won-n-n*derful lady!'

'I told you. Nothing to worry about.'

Back in his room, remembering those last moments in the cabin, he wanted her again. Never in his life had he thought to touch a white girl, never would he have dared, but in those moments there had been no difference of black and white between them. There had only been the two of them, his Bonnibelle and himself.

Now she was his Albinia.

She would leave in a month or two, Miss Lucy had said, and he must never forget that. But he wanted to forget. He wanted to believe that that time would never come. Somehow he would find a way to keep her.

'Now, you just turn your back,' she said, 'and let me wash up.'

But he did not wish to turn his back. He wanted to help her out of the torn and dirty dress. He wanted to wash her himself, wash her as tenderly and gently as he would a

246

child. Bathe the young breasts and the nipples he had touched, bathe the curve of belly, the thighs . . .

Aroused, he did at last turn away from her. The moment when he could have had her had passed. But if he were patient, it would come again. It had to come again.

Zulie arrived with one of Leila's old dresses. It was a castoff, yet it was by far the finest that Bonnibelle – no, Albinia, Zag reminded himself – had ever had, and she could hardly believe that it was really to be hers. 'You like it so much,' Zulie said, 'you better take care of it. I'll get you a couple old shifts for work in a day or two. Get you new shoes, too, but you best go barefoot like most us women folk do to save 'em.'

New clothes, new shoes. Albinia looked dazed and unbelieving one minute and half-mad with delight the next, and her delight gave Zag his greatest happiness in years.

When she was ready, he took her out to the field quarters. As usual on Saturday nights, the quarters were feverish with activity. A number of parties were in progress, and Zag took Albinia from cabin to cabin.

'Why, come on in, you two . . .'

'*You're* Albinia from Charleston? Why, we heard all 'bout you . . .'

'Zag, you dog, how you get mistress to let you keep her? . . .'

'*Ain't* she *li-i-ight?* . . .'

'Welcome to Sabrehill, Binnie. Zag ain't bad as he looks . . .'

'Where you be working, honey? I plow your patch anytime . . .'

One by one she met them. Luther, Hayden, Irish, Orion, Paris, Cawly, Wayland, Hannibal, Solon, Rameses. Momma Lucinda, Isa, Maybelle, Olympia, the

Coffey sisters, a wondering Rolanda, an astonished Vidette. And more – more names than she could remember, a small army of Sabrehill people greeting her, staring at her, flirting with her, laughing with her, approving and disapproving of her, and – in the main – making her feel welcome.

'Hope you like Sabrehill, Binnie. Hope it's better'n your last place.'

Her last place . . . The Roost . . . where she had been white and free . . .

But she must not think of that. She was Albinia now, Albinia Sabrehill – *What a grand name!* she thought with a thrill of delight – and with Zagreus she went from cabin to cabin, having a sip of corn liquor here and there, listening to the fiddles and the drums, and chatting with Zag's old friends. She clung to his arm, never for a minute letting him go.

At last the parties ended, the lights began to go out, and he led her, weary and stumbling, back along the path that took them to the east lane and the coach house. Laughing, staggering, they mounted the stairs. And when they were once again back in his room and the trapdoor was shut, Zag felt a deep inner trembling, as if this were the first time he had ever been alone with a woman.

'Want some light?' he asked.

Albinia sat down on the far side of the moonlit bed. 'Ain't no need.'

'Hope you enjoyed yourself, Binnie, honey.'

'Oh, I enjoyed myself just grand. I can't think of another day when I laughed and cried so much and been so scared and so happy.'

'Now, we ain't gonna talk about tears and scares no more, Binnie. We left all that with Bonnibelle, and she's far away.'

'I'm sorry. I forgot.'

248

'Tomorrow I'll start fixing up the next room for you. Tonight you use the bed, and I'll make a pallet on the floor.'

'Now, why do that? It'll just get hard for you again, same as the last time, and you'll have to get up on the bed after I'm asleep.' Albinia lifted her bare feet up onto the bed and stretched out. 'Come on, there's plenty of room for both of us.'

It was what Zag wanted to hear. Sitting on the edge of the bed, he pulled off his boots and his shirt, and he stretched out beside Albinia. The trembling sensation within him became stronger. He raised up on one elbow, the better to see Albinia in the moonlight.

She smiled at him.

He touched her cheek. 'Binnie, out there at the cabin . . . before Jebediah found us . . .'

He felt her stiffen, sensed it through some faint shaking in the bed, and he saw dismay in her eyes.

'Is that what you want?' she asked.

'Don't you?' he was confused. 'I thought that you . . .'

Suddenly she smiled brightly, much too brightly, and her eyes glistened so in the moonlight that there might have been tears welling up in them. 'Oh, hell,' she said, 'why not? Besides, I never done it with a nigger.'

It was like having Cheney hit him squarely between the eyes. *She never done it with a nigger.* Zag fell back on the bed, stunned.

In spite of all the pretense, then, she was still white . . . and he was just a nigger.

And she was willing to pay him off for his help. Like a whore.

'Zagreus?' She sat up beside him. 'What's the matter, Zagreus? I said I was willing.'

'Nothing's the matter, Binnie. I just thought you felt something for me, is all.'

'But I do! Why, you are the best friend I got in all the world!'

'Yes,' Zag said dryly, 'and you "never done it with a nigger."'

Her head sank down on his chest. 'I'm sorry,' she said, her voice muffled. 'I forgot I'm a nigger too.'

'That ain't what you forgot.'

'I don't understand.' She raised her head to look at him, and she sounded genuinely puzzled. 'Did I hurt you some way, Zagreus? I didn't mean to hurt you.'

He tried again. 'I said, I thought you felt something for me. I thought you felt something for me out at the cabin tonight, before Jebediah come along. I thought . . . we sort of . . . found each other.'

She tore herself away from him. She threw herself violently from him, to sit on the edge of the bed, her head hanging down.

He waited.

'I just don't feel that way right now,' she said slowly. 'I can't help it if I don't feel that way right now, can I?'

'No, Binnie, I reckon you can't.'

'Do you want to know something, Zagreus? What happened out at the cabin – that really scared me.'

'Why? 'Cause I'm . . . a nigger?'

She looked around at him in surprise. 'No! It scared me 'cause I never felt nothing like that with a man since I don't know when. Felt a little that way when I was first at The Roost and saw some fellers that come there. But then Mr Keegan put 'em on me, and I couldn't stand 'em anymore. Got so I wished to God I'd never seen another man in my life. Never could understand how Mrs Keegan *liked* it with men, for God's sake! So, Zagreus, when that happened to me with you . . . when we were out at the cabin this evening . . .' Binnie shook her head, and Zag realized that she was on the verge of tears. 'Zagreus, I found that *very upsetting!*'

250

Something within Zagreus began to tremble again, began to tremble and to sing. He reached up and stroked Binnie's shoulder.

'Guess I can't blame you for that.'

'I'm sorry, Zagreus.'

'No need to be. The important thing is, what happened . . . would you like to have it happen again?'

'I don't know. Maybe. But not now!'

'No, Binnie-child, not now.'

The tears began to flow. 'I don't know if you thought about it, Zagreus, but so much has happened . . . this has been one *hell* of a long day!'

'I know, honey, I know.' He pulled Binnie down on the bed beside him, his arm around her. 'Now, why don't you just curl up with me here and get yourself a nice long rest.'

She was still weeping in his arms when he fell asleep, smiling.

2

This time when she awakened she knew there would be no more danger and pain. All that was behind her; it had no part in her life. It had been part of the life of Bonnibelle, yes, but not of Albinia, the light-skinned girl of color who had been brought to Sabrehill from Charleston to be the wife of Zagreus. Albinia awakened smiling. She rolled over on the bed and looked at the sleeping Zagreus and loved him.

Her stomach gurled loudly, and she prodded Zagreus. 'Hey, wake up! Your Albinia, she starving to death!'

Perhaps he hadn't been sleeping after all, for he suddenly reached out and grabbed her, and they wrestled laughing on the bed. She quickly disengaged herself, fearful of bringing on his need. She loved him, but she wasn't ready for that yet.

'Zagreus, durn it, let's find us some food!'

They had slept late. They found the service lane full of hot sunlight and Sunday morning laziness. As they walked toward the courtyard and the big-house kitchen, Albinia greeted new acquaintances as if they were old friends. 'Morning, Hayden . . . Hey, there, Ettalee!'

At the kitchen, Momma Lucinda was cross with them. 'You come too late for breakfast and too soon for Sunday dinner. Don't know as we got anything for you to eat at all.' But food was found, even if it was only some warmed over grits and bacon. Zag explained to Albinia that, as on most plantations, each family received rations, which it could cook for itself if it wished. But most single people, and some families, found it more convenient to contribute

252

their rations to a communal kitchen. Since he lived close to the big house, he found it convenient to eat at the big-house kitchen, and besides you got by far the best food there.

After breakfast – 'Now, you two wash them dishes! Don't you just leave 'em laying there!' – they returned to the coach house. While Zag turned his back, Albinia put on her old torn dress, contriving to fasten it closed somewhat with pieces of string and her broach, and she and Zag went to work cleaning out the next room. Dozens of pieces of dusty harness hung from the rafters and lay heaped on the floor, and Zag insisted that every last piece must be crowded into another room. When he got done, he said, this room would be as clean and neat and pretty as his own. Her home would be the finest, outside the big house, on the entire planation.

He seemed to forget that she would be here only a short while.

They paused in their work only for Sunday dinner. Zag sent Albinia to the kitchen, where Momma Lucinda heaped two plates much too high with food in honor of Albinia's arrival. 'Now, *that* plate is yours,' she said, pointing to the one with the choicer morsels of chicken. 'and don't you go letting that greedy Zagreus get at it!'

Their dinner finished, they went back to work on Albinia's room, but before long they were interrupted by Vidette and Rolanda, who yelled from below and, with Zag's permission, stuck their heads up through the trap-door.

'What you want?' Zag asked. 'You stay here, you got to help work.'

'Thought Binnie maybe like to come swimming with us,' Vidette said.

'Yeah,' Rolanda said, 'Sunday afternoon ain't no time for work.'

'Well . . .'

Binnie hoped Zag would say *no*. From what she had gathered in the field quarters last night, Vidette and Rolanda were among the 'gals in rut' that Miss Leila said Zag had 'trotting up day and night,' and she didn't want Zag hanging around them. Or them hanging around him.

'Well, I guess we done enough for today. Wouldn't hurt none if we go swim – '

'Oh, not *ye-e-ew!*' Rolanda said, with a disdainful wave of her hand. 'We don't want *ye-e-ew*, it's Albinia we wants to come with us!'

'Well . . .' Zag did not look too happy with the idea of Albinia going off with the girls, but he managed a smile. 'If you want to, Binnie . . .'

Suddenly Albinia wanted to, she wanted to very much – as long as Zag didn't come along. She was intensely curious about these girls who were always 'trotting up' to Zag's room – but no more! – and she was eager to engage in any activity which might make her more a part of Sabrehill.

'I'd sure like to,' she said. 'I got so much dirt and grime on me, I can't hardly stand it no more.'

'Then you go on with these here ladies,' Zag said, giving her a little pat on the rump, 'and you and me, maybe we swim later.'

Vidette and Rolanda led her out the west service lane, past the big-house quarters, to a distant line of trees that followed a stream, then up the stream until they came to a satisfactory pond. On their way, they passed a couple of swimming parties, as well as two or three solitary couples, and it was clear that Vidette and Rolanda did not intend to share Albinia's company with anyone else. They were as curious about her as she was about them.

After looking about carefully for snakes, they slipped into the water, their dresses still on. The slow-moving stream, thigh deep, was warm but pleasant, and Albinia knelt to let it wash the dust and sweat away from her body.

They chatted. Vidette told her some of the gossip of Sabrehill. Rolanda commented that Binnie didn't talk much like some Charleston people who visited Sabrehill – 'real fast with funny sounding words' – and Albinia answered that, well, she hadn't been there very long. She was lackadaisical and vague when they questioned her about her past, as if the subject really didn't interest her.

She soon realized that they were intensely curious about the lightness of her skin. Her face, her arms, her calves were all tanned, but the torn dress gave clues to the whiteness of her body. When Vidette and Rolanda decided to swim 'skinny' and pulled off their dresses, she reluctantly agreed to do the same, and tossed her dress with theirs onto the bank of the stream.

'My, ain't she *white!*' Rolanda said. 'Got some light-skin people at Sabrehill, but reckon ain't more'n three or four anywheres near her.'

'Reckon she's near as white as Miss Lucy.'

'Honey, you *sure* you is a nigger gal?'

Albinia felt an instant of anxiety. Never in her life, until the last few days, had she dreamed that she would want to be looked on as black. Her whiteness, as distinguished from black, was her pride, and very nearly her only pride. But now it was a threat.

She looked at the other two young women in a new way. Vidette: smoothly brown, quick-eyed, sleek-bodied, and undeniably pretty. Rolanda: also pretty, Albinia supposed, but in a different way – much darker, almost black; lazy, sensuous, slow eyes; a thin, hard-muscled body. Fancy goods, Albinia decided, both of them. And they made her feel not fancy at all. She knew that ladies often prided themselves on the milky whiteness of their skin, but Vidette and Rolanda made her feel plumb blanched out, and she wondered how Zagreus could possibly prefer a poor piece of goods like her. Even if she were white.

But I ain't white, she reminded herself. And maybe with *my dress off like this, I'll darken up some.*

They finally got around to the topic of common interest, the true reason for this swim together.

'Sure was a surprise when Zag got hisself a wife from Charleston,' Vidette said. 'Last thing in the world we expect is Zag get hisself a wife.'

'Truth is,' Rolanda said, 'Vidette sorta had her cap set for Zag herself.'

'Oh, shut your mouth, gal.' Vidette splashed Rolanda. 'Anybody got her cap set, it were you!'

'Oh, I like Zag, I like Zag a lot. But truth is I need a younger man, can give me more what I need.'

'Truth is, truth is! Truth is you is just a bit jealous 'cause Zag is 'bout the best you ever had, and he went and got hisself this little gal 'stead of you.'

'Oh, I don't know. He ain't the only cock in the hen house. What if I told you I have been having me some real fine times with Mr Jebediah Hayes?'

'*Truth is*, gal, you ain't had none of Mr Jeb since last summer, when he was banging everything in sight. Truth is, if Mr Jeb is doing that nice thing to anybody, I figure it's Miss Lucy.'

'Miss Lucy!' Albinia wasn't at all sure she understood correctly. Somehow the idea of Miss Lucy bedding with anyone at all, let alone a man who was black and a mere foreman, was beyond her. *Miss Lucy?*

'Why, sure 'nough Miss Lucy, honey,' Vidette said. 'You think she don't need her pleasuring same as the rest of us?'

Albinia hardly knew what to answer. Since the previous

evening, Miss Lucy had been the most wonderful woman in the world to her. Together with Zagreus, Miss Lucy was her savior. She would have done anything in the world for Miss Lucy, she now realized, and it seemed impossible that such a woman might have the same hungers as a Dora Keegan or a Vidette or a Rolanda.

And yet . . . and yet . . .

Rolanda screamed.

Vidette started to scream, but it turned into a burst of wild laughter, and Albinia turned to look where she was pointing. There, peeking through the brush, was the houseboy they called Irish, and it was impossible to know how long he had been watching them. Now the brush parted, and Irish, as naked as they, came bursting out, and with an Indian whoop he dashed splashing and spraying into the stream with them.

'Get your dress,' Vidette screamed to Albinia, 'get your dress!'

'Never mind your dress,' Rolanda yelled. '*Get Irish!*'

Then she was climbing Irish's back and pounding his head and shoulders. Vidette followed her lead, and threw herself at Irish.

'Get him, get him!'

'Push him under!'

'Drown him!'

Water flew. Irish twisted and turned, but Rolanda clung to his back, and Vidette tried to pull him down. Then Albinia was on him, too, the four of them struggling, screaming, laughing.

'Get him down! Get him under!'

'Don't let him get away!'

'Bye-bye, Irish!'

'Blub, blub, blub, Irish!'

'*Blub!*'

At last they let him go, and Irish pretended to float

257

away, drowned. Laughing, Albinia and Vidette climed out of the water, pulled on their dresses, and started to walk downstream.

''Bout a year ago,' Vidette said, 'Irish found the Coffey sisters swimming skinny with a feller, and he stole all their clothes. They had to run all the way home jay-bird naked with everybody hooting and hollering after them.' She paused and looked back. 'Oh-oh.'

Suddenly Albinia realized that Rolanda was no longer with them. Following Vidette's gaze back between trees and underbrush, she saw that Rolanda was still in the pond with Irish, the two of them wrestling playfully, and it was obvious that Irish was by no means ready to quit.

'Looks like Rolanda gonna have herself something nice,' Vidette said. An impish smile played over her face. 'Want to sneak back and watch?'

'No.'

Albinia felt that she had had enough of that sort of thing to last her for a lifetime. Had had it and hated it. Yet now she felt a little shock at the suggestion – and a little excitement.

She looked curiously at Vidette as they continued along the stream. 'You really do like it, don't you?'

'Like what?'

'Pleasuring.'

Vidette was surprised. 'Well, don't you?'

Albinia sensed that she had made a mistake. 'Yes, of course! Of course I do!'

'I should think so, with a real pleasuring kind of feller like Zag. If there wasn't no pleasure in pleasuring, a body wouldn't pleasure.'

'Guess not.'

And yet this simple, uncomplicated approach to pleasure seemed strange to Albinia. The sullen, angry blacks of The Roost had shown no sign of pleasure in their lives, and the pleasure of the whites had always had a vicious-ness in it that made it a torture for her. Of course, not all of the people of Sabrehill were as casually promiscuous as Vidette and Rolanda apparently were; she had met some last night who had seemed quite straight-laced. But generally, in the idle talk of courting and mating, and in the casual flirtations openly carried on, she had sensed a reluctance to make pleasure a reason for pain and guilt. *Just be kind*, the attitude seemed to be; *we all got troubles enough without making more.*

Albinia Sabrehill had a feeling that her life was going to be far different from that of Bonnibelle Calhoun.

By evening she had a bed of her own in the newly cleared-out room. 'It ain't much,' Zag said, 'but it ain't so bad neither, and I get a chance, I make you a better one.'

'It's grand. I never had my own bed before.'

'Never?'

'We were little, I slept with the others. And all them years at you-know-where, I slept on the floor of the kitchen.'

'Well, honey, you got your own bed now. And you get lonely, you just remember I'm in my bed, going plumb crazy waiting for you to walk through that door and climb into it with me.'

She spent some time that evening on his bed, curled up in his arms and telling of her adventures while away from him. He did not seem as amused as she was by the incident with Irish, and she felt his arms tighten around her.

'Irish ain't bad,' he said. 'I like Irish, but sometime he goes *lee*dle bit too far. He give you any trouble, you come to me.'

She understood. These arms were a haven. Sabrehill was a big world, a much bigger world in some ways than The Roost, and it interested and excited her. She wanted

259

to explore it. But if it became too much for her, there were always these arms to return to.

They were up at dawn the next morning, awakened by shouts and a pounding on the underside of Zag's trapdoor. Awareness of the new day spread like ripples crisscrossing in a pond, as each servant made sure that his neighbor was awake. Binnie hurriedly pulled on one of the new work shifts that Zulie had given her the evening before, and, with Zag, went to the kitchen for breakfast. They ate on the steps of a little cottage not far from the kitchen with some of her new friends – Irish, Isa, Isa's husband Wayland. They had hardly finished when Mr Jeb approached them.

'I see you're meeting the right people, Albinia,' he said, 'because you're going to be working with Isa. She needs help in the kitchen garden. Have you ever gardened before?'

'Not much. But I can learn.'

'I'm sure you can. Isa will tell you what to do.'

They went to work right after breakfast. 'My pa's the gardener, you know,' Isa explained, 'and he's sick. And Wayland, he's real busy with his pa in the blacksmith shop, so I really need help. Now, what we got to do today is weed, and we can't do it all, so we do peas and beans and carrots and turnips, just them rows. It's enough to keep us busy all day unless we work real hard. We work hard, we can quit early. But we got to finish or my pa and Mr Jeb, they going be mad. But don't worry. We get it done.'

Whenever possible, Binnie learned, Mr Jeb liked to use the task system rather than the gang system. It gave the worker an incentive to work quickly and well, thus making free time for himself.

Weeding was hard on the back and the knees, but Isa, an attractive twenty-year-old, was a chattery, cheerful co-worker who liked to sing and gossip, her hands rarely ceasing to move, and Binnie found the morning passing quickly and pleasantly.

'Want to get done early so I can spend a little time on my own garden,' she said. 'Me and Wayland, we got our own patch, 'cause Wayland, he do like succotash like nobody you ever seen. We eat from the big-house kitchen, but sometimes I just got to cook up an extra mess of my special succotash for Wayland to eat till he groan. The way that boy eat . . .'

Binnie decided that she and Zagreus were going to have a garden patch of their own – and then remembered that before long she would be leaving.

And where would she go?, she thought with sudden fright. What would happen to her?

'Hey, look at that Hayden, top of the spinning house!' Isa said with a laugh. 'Ain't he something?'

Hayden was indeed on top of the spinning house, striding along the ridge and kneeling down to bang away with a hammer.

'Don't know why that Hayden ain't married,' Isa went on. 'Used to be a driver, but Mr Jeb said too fast with a whip. But he's a real hard worker, always in the blacksmith shop with Wayland's pa or in the carpenter shop or helping Zag. Bound and determined he ain't gonna be no common field hand. And he is *so* good-looking, and with that snoozy beddy-time voice! Weren't for Wayland, he could park his brogans under my bed anytime!'

Binnie was a little surprised at Isa's words, even a little shocked. On reflection, she had to admit it was true: Hayden was an attractive man. But – this not being The Roost – did one *say* such a thing?

'What if Wayland heard you say that?'

Isa waved an indifferent hand. 'Aw, it don't mean nothing. You think Wayland don't notice pretty girls? He stop, I sure ain't gonna have much fun in bed. Also, besides, you want to live somewhere where they ain't nothing by ugly people? Me, I like to look at pretty people, and I don't aim to stop!'

Binnie looked at Hayden again, as he continued to hammer away on the roof of the spinning house. She figured that he must be twice as old as she was, maybe even older than that. Older than Zagreus. But – yes once again – he was an attractive man.

Something warmed in Binnie. She dimly realized what was happening to her: for the first time in years, perhaps for the first time in her life, she was beginning to recognize beauty. At The Roost beauty had been a threat. If she had recognized it, if she had allowed her eyes to rest on it, it would turn on her and abuse her. But not here at Sabrehill. At Sabrehill, with Zagreus and Miss Lucy, she was safe.

The morning went quickly. Wayland and his sister, Ettalee, came over from the blacksmith shop to chat for a few minutes. Binnie decided that Wayland was handsome and allowed her eyes to feast on him – until Isa noticed and burst out laughing. Later Irish came by to implore them both to run away with him to Canada, where they would become immeasurably rich and live a life of love for a hundred years to come. He kept it up until Momma Lucinda came and got him, telling him to 'get yourself back where you belong, you lazy no-good . . .'

They worked so hard and steadily that, when the hottest part of the day came, they were almost done. When the kitchen bell rang, Binnie was willing to eat quickly and go right on working, but Isa said, no, that was how people got sick from the sun, and they must stop for at least two hours. Wayland was coming to meet her, she said, and why didn't Binnie got get Zag, and they would all eat together and go for a swim? Binnie agreed.

Hayden was in the carpenter shop when she passed it. She saw him look at her, then heard his footsteps behind her.

'Binnie, honey . . .'

She was in the coach house, her foot on the stairs to Zag's room, when Hayden spoke. What had Isa called his voice? Snoozy bed-timey? She supposed it was – it was low and soft.

She turned to him. 'Looking for Zagreus.'

'He ain't here. Miss Lucy come by just now, told him to take her over to the Devereau place. So he ain't going be back for some time.'

Hayden took three short slow steps toward her. He seemed to be approaching her with caution, and that in itself set off an obscure alarm within her. But he wouldn't hurt her, she assured herself, nobody here at Sabrehill would hurt her. And Isa was right: he was in his way a handsome man.

. . . he could park his brogans under my bed anytime!

'You want something, Hayden?'

'Just thought I'd tell you about Zag.'

'Well, thank you.'

As she started up the stairs again, she heard Hayden quietly stepping closer. He stopped the instant she looked around.

'Was there something else?'

'Zag wants some shelves put in. Figure on helping him. Got to look around the room, see how they best go.'

'But Zag don't allow nobody in his room when he ain't here.'

'Oh, I know that,' Hayden said smoothly, softly, 'but *you* here.' He smiled reassuringly at her. 'Come on, let me see how I'm going make them shelves for my friend Zag.'

'Well, I don't know . . .'

'And you and me get better 'quainted. Ought to get 'quainted with my good friend's woman, that's only right.'

He seemed very friendly, and there was something about him that made her feel warm, but the faint alarm remained. Should she allow him to come up for a few minutes, just long enough to decide on the shelves? Of course, she must not allow him to find out about the second bed in the other room, but she could probably manage that.

She smiled at him.

He smiled back, and she felt her face flush.

'Come on, Binnie, honey.'

'Well . . .'

She didn't really want to say *yes*. Somehow she knew it would be the wrong thing to do, but she didn't know how to refuse Hayden. And after all, she thought, what harm would there be? Just a few minutes up in the room . . .

'Hayden,' Zagreus said.

To her relief, he was standing in the doorway, and a decision was no longer necessary.

'You want something, Hayden?'

'You said something about wanting some shelves. Thought I'd – '

'Just you stay out of my quarters, boy. You stay out of mine, I stay out of yours.'

'Well, Binnie here – '

'Binnie don't know everything you and me know. Now, *out!*'

Hayden shrugged. 'Why, sure Zag. Didn't mean no harm.' He stepped off of the stairs and sauntered away.

'He told me you took Miss Lucy some place,' Binnie said. She didn't know why, but she felt slightly guilty. 'Told me you wouldn't be back for a time, and said he was going make some shelves for you.'

'I was supposed to drive Miss Lucy, but she changed her

264

mind. And I guess he just might help me with those shelves. Old Hayden, he sure do like to be helpful. But I don't want him or nobody else 'cept you in my room when I'm gone. And not you and him together.'

The guilt faded, and Binnie impulsively threw her arms around Zag's waist. 'You sure do take care of me,' she said, hugging him. 'You sure, sure do!'

'Yes, Binni-child,' he said, stroking her hair, 'I sure, sure do.'

He was home and safety to her. She couldn't always be with him, and she knew that in the days to come she would explore her new life in ever-widening circles. But he would always be there, warm and waiting, when at last she was ready to return.

3

He was not dead.

Mind and body, he was weak, hardly awake, hardly existent, but suddenly he was looking across the room through the morning light, and his very first thought was, *I live*.

He knew he had been to the precipice. He thought that perhaps he had even been over it, sinking down through some fiery hell into eternal oblivion. Yet he lived.

His second thought was, *Zulie*.

He knew somehow that it was because of Zulie that he was here. He had been over the precipice, but she had caught him. She had caught him up in her arms like a dark angel and had borne him back to the land of the living. And his life would never again be quite the same.

Zulie. He moved his head weakly on his pillow, looking for her, wanting her. Without her, he could not feel completely safe even yet. He tried to call her name aloud and found that he could barely whisper.

He might have drifted off, but consciousness was such a precarious thing that he could hardly tell. It was in this state that so many visions, such horrors, had come to him, but now the visions and the horrors were over. When he opened his eyes, he was simply in a bed chamber, and the world was real and common and ordinary and sunlit. Once again he was safe.

'Oh, so you're awake.'

It was Lucy standing at his bedside. He had not seen her enter the room. She smiled at him. Even now, close to mindless, he realized that she was making no attempt to turn the scarred side of her face away from him. That reminded him of the kind of woman she was: not the kind to hide such a mark. Others might show you beauty and let you discover a scar. Cousin Lucy would flaunt the scar and let you discover the beauty.

The thought helped to bring him further awake, and he returned her smile, feeling a kind of warmth that was strange to him.

'I think,' he whispered, 'that I am alive.'

'You are, and you're going to remain alive for a very long time to come. But you have been extremely sick.'

'I seem to recall promising you that I would survive, but I believe I was given a considerable amount of help.'

'We did try to help. Someone was with you night and day.'

'My fever is gone?'

Lucy put a light cool hand on his forehead. 'It does seem to be. But you're far from being well, Cousin Ash, and we're getting into the sickly season. You could easily contract another fever, or something as bad, if you don't regain your strength. You are going to remain in bed for some days to come, and that, sir, is an order.'

'Dear Cousin!' A sound like the ghost of a laugh rattled out of Ash. 'I don't think I could stand up if my life depended on it.'

The cool hand stroked his forehead. 'We'll get you well as quickly as possible.'

She left the room, and he closed his eyes. He seemed to float, but unfevered and comfortable, and he might have slept a little. He was vaguely aware of Irish, the houseboy, coming and going, and then Lucy was back.

'Who's been taking care of me?' he asked, his voice stronger now. 'Tell me about them.'

'Well, I've helped a little, and so has Leila, my house-keeper, and Momma Lucinda, our cook. But her son,

267

Irish, has done more for you than we have, and Zulie has done the most of all. In fact, Zulie has been in charge of you.'

Zulie. That was who he wanted to hear about. 'Tell me about Zulie.'

'She works in the laundry most of the time, and she helps with the sick. She's also a conjurewoman.'

'A *what?*'

'A conjurewoman, a witch, a – what's the word? – a voodoo *mamaloi*. I'm sure she's been working all kinds of potent magic on you. And obviously to good effect.'

Was she serious? She seemed amused by his consternation. Of course, he didn't believe in voodoo or hoodoo or obeah, he didn't believe in any such pagan nonsense, any more than he believed in a Christian god. But it gave him an odd feeling to think that a witch might have been working her spells on him.

'I thought you people down this way didn't allow voodoo on your plantations. I've heard of niggers being killed for using voodoo.'

'Most planters around here do make a show of stamping it out, but you know how every old woman has her two or three spells. And a place this big always has its few people who are specially known for magic and potions and the like. Now, you count yourself lucky, Cousin Ash, because Zulie is supposed to be one of our very best.'

'Ringing the necks of chickens to the beat of voodoo drums? All that sort of thing?'

Lucy laughed. 'I don't think Zulie does much in the way of rituals, but when it comes to magic, I'm sure she'll be glad to put a badmouth on your enemy or a love spell on your lady friend. Don't hesitate to ask her.'

'I won't.' The odd, nervous feeling refused to go away. 'This voodoo business doesn't bother you at all?'

'No, why should it? My father encountered it in both

Charleston and New Orleans, and he told me something about it. He saw no harm in it.'

'And so I have fallen into the hands of witch women.'

'And aren't you fortunate! Because whether it's her spells or her herb remedies, Zulie is just about the best healer we have here. And she's going to go right on helping you to get well.'

After Irish had fed him a bowl of broth and assisted him with the indignities of the chamber pot, Ash went back to sleep. He fell asleep suddenly, slept deeply and dreamlessly, and when he awakened, he sensed that it was another day.

'Zulie . . .'

'Yes, Mr Ash?'

He didn't know why he had spoken her name, but he looked around to find her standing by his bed. She smiled down at him.

'You been looking after me, Zulie?'

'Sure have, Mr Ash, all the time. Got me a bed in the hall so I can sleep days when Irish is with you. I been up with you nights.'

'You don't have to do that anymore.'

'That's right, now the fever's gone, I can get me a good night's sleep. But I'll go on sleeping in the hall, and you call me anytime you want.'

She was truly a handsome wench, he thought, the damnedest, handsomest wench he had ever seen. No, not handsome – beautiful. Even a man just back from the grave could see that. Without thinking, he reached for her hand, and her fingers laced with his.

'I thank you, Zulie.'

'No need, master.'

Her long brown fingers, so strong, tightened on his, then loosened and slipped away, and she left the room.

When she returned a few minutes later, she had a bowl

of warm broth. He suspected he had been living on broths and teas for the last few days, though he only barely remembered. Zulie helped him to sit up in bed, and, sitting beside him, she spoon-fed him.

'I can do it myself.'

'No, master, no. Just let Zulie. Now, be a nice master, do like Zulie tell you.'

Her use of the word *master*, subtly mocking, somehow provocative, made him laugh, and she laughed along with him, as if she had managed to please a child.

When he had finished eating, Zulie brought shaving equipment. She made clear that *she* was going to whack off his whiskers, and not he, and he looked at the wicked edge with some trepidation until he saw how expertly she stropped it. She heaped hot lather on his face, and, without leaving a single scratch, proceeded to scrape it all off again.

She made him take off his nightshirt. As impersonally as if he had been a small child, she wiped him down with a cool wet cloth, and she pulled a fresh shirt over his head. In spite of his profound weakness, by the time she was finished with him he felt much better.

'Zulie . . .'

'Once again his fingers caught hers, and she sat down beside him.

'Yes, sir, Mr Ash.'

'Don't go away.'

'Not if you don't want me to, Mr Ash.'

'Miss Lucy says you've probably been working magic on me.'

Zulie laughed. 'Magic?'

'Spells. She says you're a witch. A conjurewoman.'

'Now, why in the world she say that?'

'You been putting spells on me, Zulie?'

'Why, course I have. Lots of spells to make you well.'

270

'She says you can put a curse on my enemies for me and a love spell on a woman.'

'You want me to make a spell for you, Mr Ash?'

'How would you do it?'

Zulie shrugged, and Ash watched the movement of her body under the thin dress, the tilt of her head, the play of the smile on her lips. Every movement she mads fascinated him. 'How, Zulie?'

'Well, curse is easy, least if your enemy is nearby. Like you can spit in his food and stir it up and say, "God damn son of a bitch!" Spit is good for a curse. Good for a love spell, but best for a curse.'

'And how do you make a love spell?'

Zulie smiled and squeezed his hand. 'Who you going love spell?'

'Just tell me how.'

'Love spell. All right. Thing is, you got put her with you and you with her. So one thing you can do is take something from your woman and wear it close to you. Like a ribbon or a thread or some of her hair. Say love words, and wear it close to your skin. Witch spell words are best, but you just say what you want. And another thing you can do, you take some food, little bit of bacon maybe, and put it in your shoe or your clothes for a few days, then cook it in your lady's food. That puts you with her and her with you, and you got a fine love spell.'

'I'll have to try it.'

'Who you aim to try it on?'

'Maybe I'll try it on you.'

Zulie laughed again. She seemed delighted, and he wanted to sit up and hold her and laugh with her.

'I got to clean up this here shaving mess, Mr Ash.'

'But you'll come back right away?'

'I'll come back and sit with you,' Zulie promised.

'We'll talk about Charleston.'

He couldn't take his eyes off of her as she moved about the room, straightening and cleaning up, and carrying the 'shaving mess' away. He thought of other women, both black and white, he had known. Only a few days earlier he would have said that a mere woman was only half-human and that a black was hardly human at all. And Zulie was both a woman and a black. But she was different, somehow. Different. Perhaps it was just that she had drawn him back from that dark pit of oblivion, but she was different.

And watching her move about the room on silent bare feet – tall, broad-shouldered, strong, the small beautiful head bound up in a yellow kerchief – he wanted her.

Weak as he was, he wanted her as much as he had ever wanted any woman.

'Zulie,' he said, 'did you put one of your love spells on me?'

She flashed him a wide smile. 'Why, course, master. Zulie *do* want her master to love her.'

He could almost believe her.

By God, he thought, *before I'm through here, I'm going to have her!*

But sanity made its claim. He must do nothing, absolutely nothing, to endanger his plans. The sudden onslaught of fever had been bad enough. It had meant no trip to Georgia and no further 'business' to fill his purse before coming here – he had been forced to arrive a poorer man than he had planned. But he had sensed that the fever was going to be a bad one, and Sabrehill had been nearby – Sabrehill, where he had been sure he would be well cared for.

And he had been. He had survived the fever. And he must not now risk everything, he told himself toughly, on a passing lech for a mere nigger wench.

272

Not if he wanted Sabrehill for his own.

My God, she thought, *I am acting like a foolish school girl!*

She couldn't help it. Suddenly everything was all right again, and she was happier than she had been in months or even years. Asher was here, and he would soon be well and strong again, and Sabrehill's troubles would be over.

And that was a foolish thought, she knew – that, this side of death, troubles could be over. There would always be troubles, and life would be a bore if there were no problems to be solved. But still it was the way she felt. Asher was here.

She couldn't keep her mind off of him, not even when she should have been going over her accounts, not when she should have been inspecting a field or listening to Jebediah's reports. He was always in her thoughts, not as the drawn and wasted man who lay in the downstairs bedchamber right now, but as the healthy and magnetically handsome boy he had been and as the man he would become when he was well again. More often than she should have, she visited the bedchamber, and she envied Zulie who spent most of her hours there – poor Zulie, who must be so bored, tending to a single patient.

Or perhaps not always so bored: occasionally there was quiet laughter from the bedchamber . . .

Lucy wondered, *Might I be in love with Asher?*

No. Of course not. It had only been a random thought. She was highly attracted to him, just as she had been in her girlhood, but an attraction was not necessarily the equivalent of love. And Lucy had long ago concluded that it was very unlikely that she would ever love again.

But, then, a year ago she had thought it impossible that she would even be attracted to a man.

Once the fever had been broken, it seemed to her that she could see Asher growing stronger by the day and almost by the hour. The blue eyes lost their haunted look, and the voice rapidly grew steadier.

'Lucy, you're looking lovelier than ever today.'

'Thank you, Ash, but I'm a rather battered and scratched up old woman . . .'

Nevertheless, he brought a blush to her face and, to her body, a tingling stab of desire.

On Saturday evening, his ninth day at Sabrehill, Asher donned a robe and slippers and joined her for supper. He was unsteady on his feet, but he seemed to glow with life.

'I remember distinctly, Lucy, that when we danced, you did your best to make things difficult for me. Whenever possible, you stepped on my toes. You tried to trip me up, you all but kicked me. I could not understand why you *hated* me so!'

'Hated you, what nonsense. You know perfectly well that I was only trying to get your attention.'

'But you *had* my attention! It was I who was trying to get *your* attention!'

'You did no such thing. When did you ever try?'

'Lucy, you are as obtuse or as stubborn as you ever were – '

'I am not!'

'Why do you think I engaged in those shooting matches and dangled my prizes before your indifferent eyes?'

'*Your* eyes were indifferent – you never even looked at me!'

'And why do you think I damned near killed a good horse racing Paul Devereau, if not to impress you? And everything failed, all my efforts. Cruel Lucy! Wretched McCloud!'

He made her feel fifteen again. Fifteen and unscarred and under the illusion of love. Yes, she knew it was only an illusion, but still . . .

They ended the evening in the library, sipping brandy

and talking of old times. She avoided the bad years, for there was still much that she dared not look back on, but Ash could almost make her forget that those times had existed. The worst of the past was dead, and what remained was a treasure they shared, and there was still more treasure to come.

At last she saw by his eyes that he was tired, and she reluctantly insisted that he return to his bed. 'No more tonight, Ash. There's tomorrow . . .'

She led him out of the library, past Zulie's bed in the corner hallway, and into his bedchamber. With irritation, she saw that Zulie was there, her face inscrutable, as if she had been waiting. But Zulie slipped out into the passage as Ash took Lucy's shoulders and turned her to face him. His head moved to one side. He kissed her first on the left cheek and then, as if the scar were not there, on the right, and for an instant she thought he was going to kiss her on the mouth.

'As long as you've promised there's a tomorrow,' he murmured.

'I promise.'

If he had kissed her on the mouth then, she didn't know what might have happened. But instead his lips touched her forehead and he bade her good night. Feeling warm and bruised and more than a little drunk, she went out into the passage. Zulie was nowhere to be seen, and Lucy was just as glad. At that moment, she didn't want anyone to see her. Not Zulie, not Leila, not Jebediah.

I'm a fool, she thought. *I am thirty years old and as foolish as I was at fifteen. Thirty years old and made giddy as a school girl by a man – yes, Paul is right – by a man I hardly know.*

Slowly she mounted the steps that led to her lonely bedroom.

* * *

275

'You putting a love spell on her?'

Asher was just tossing his robe aside, preparatory to climbing into bed, when he heard Zulie speak. He turned to see her standing at the same doorway through which he and Lucy had entered the room.

'You been standing out there listening?'

'Saw her go up the stairs. Saw how she looked. She didn't see me.'

Only rarely did he see Zulie without a smile; she chattered and joked and laughed with him. Tonight for the first time she looked sullen. She stood legs apart, arms crossed under her full, pointed breasts, head held high. And there was a resentful glitter in her eyes. By God, Asher thought, she was one insolent nigger. No, not insolent – arrogant.

And he wanted her.

'Now, why would I put a spell on her when you're putting one on me? Why would I want to?'

'Maybe you got your reasons.'

Asher laughed. 'Maybe I do. How's your spell on me coming along?'

Zulie barely smiled. Her eyes narrowed, and the tip of her tongue moved along her lips.

'I guess,' she said at last, 'you know that better'n me.'

In that instant he realized that she was his. She was actually jealous of Lucy, and he could have her any time he wished, possessing her as completely as he ever had any woman. He could have her now.

But he did not dare – yet.

Too much was at stake – a plantation, a fortune, an entire future. He must do nothing, absolutely nothing, that might risk that.

Nothing? No matter how tempting the challenge?

Nothing, he told himself harshly.

'Yes, I guess I do know better than you,' he said, his

276

voice catching in his throat. He tried to smile back at her. 'We'll talk about it another time. Good night, Zulie.'

'Good night . . . master.'

She went back out into the hallway. Asher put out the light. He tried not to think of her being out there, only a few feet away from him, lying in her bed.

The next afternoon, Sunday, Paul Devereau came to dinner. The meeting between him and Asher was one Lucy had looked forward to with mixed feelings – largely amusement, with a small measure of dread. Paul had made it clear that he disapproved of Asher, but it would be convenient if the two men got along together.

They began the afternoon with dry sherry on the piazza. At first, of course, the men were 'Mr McCloud' and 'Mr Devereau' to each other; she was 'Miss Lucy' to Paul and 'Cousin Lucy' to Asher, but Paul quickly followed Asher's lead and began to call her 'Cousin.' 'But you must stop being so formal,' Lucy said, 'because we are all old friends, and there are no strangers here with us. We are Paul and Ash and Lucy. Or – ' she turned to Asher – 'do you still hate being called by that name?'

'Oh, no,' Asher laughed, 'it will do – Asher, or Ash if you like.' He explained to Paul: 'I was once told that "Asher" meant "Happy" or "Lucky." "Happy" seemed fatuous to me, and "Lucky" – well, I liked to think I made my own luck, that I owed nothing to the gods or to chance. I've grown a bit older and perhaps a little wiser since then.'

'Asher Quinlan McCloud,' Lucy said. 'You may remember, Paul, he preferred to be called Quinn.'

'Oh,' Asher laughed again, 'I haven't been called that in years.'

The dinner went well, and Lucy was flattered to detect a subtle rivalry between the two men to determine who was the primary male on the premises. Was Asher, the nearer cousin, more at home, and Paul more the guest? Or was Paul, the older friend, more at home, and Asher the guest? Paul asserted himself as the polished gentleman, totally in command of any situation and certainly of this one. Asher countered with a certain smiling, boyish awkwardness which invited Paul to make himself at home. Lucy didn't bother to suppress her smiles.

'And how long do you expect to be with us, Asher?' Paul asked later, as they were having brandy in the cool of the passage.

'Well, you know that Lucy has been having difficulties with certain of her neighbors.'

'Indeed I do.'

'I can hardly stay forever, of course, but I imagine I'll be here as long as I'm needed.'

'But won't you find that inconvenient? I've never thought absentee ownership of a plantation was very efficient.'

Asher shrugged. 'I agree completely. And the fact is that my own place is very large and inefficient.'

'Well, then – '

'Fortunately, I have good overseers, but for years the place was ill-managed. Our staple is tobacco, and you know how hard that is on the soil. Too much of my soil is worn out. Now, I'm sure it can be revived by some of the new scientific methods, but that takes time. And money. And I have very little of either.'

'Can't you borrow against part of your land?' Paul asked.

'Are you a businessman, Paul?'

'No, not really.'

'Neither was my father, and neither am I. My father tried borrowing against the land, and he only increased his debts. I've gone into trade in various ways, and I've even made a little money, but only enough to keep my head above water. Let's face it, Paul, trade just isn't a gentleman's game. Maybe it was for a few very special people twenty-five or thirty years ago, but most of us merely lower ourselves in the eyes of our neighbors when we go into trade. Can't blame them either, all that cut-throat haggling and scheming. Trade is for the goddamn Yankees and the Jews, and I personally prefer the Jews.'

'What do you plan to do, then?'

Asher sighed. 'Let's face it, Paul, in our world a man must have either land or a profession. You're fortunate, you have both. Me, I'm just a simple farm boy, and if I ain't got land, I ain't got nothing. But I'm going to have to sell. I'm going to have to sell lock, stock, and barrel to someone who can rebuild my place – I have some potential buyers – but I'm going to wring every last cent, farthing, and doubloon I can out of it. Then I'm going to start again, but this time it'll be cotton.

'And that's one reason I don't mind being away from home for a lengthy time. I want to look around, find myself a new piece of land. It won't be anything as big as my Virginia place, but on the other hand, your land down here is much richer, and cotton doesn't wear it out as fast.'

'Cotton market's been poor since 'nineteen, though,' Paul said. 'Have you thought about going into rice?'

'Thought about it, yes, but it doesn't look to me like rice is all that much better. And, Paul, I figure cotton to get *much* better. I figure, whether you people know it or not, you're still building a cotton kingdom, and it's spreading west fast. If I don't find what I want here, I'll go out to Mississippi or Alabama. There's flush times ahead in Mississippi and Alabama.'

Somehow, just listening to Asher talk excited Lucy. Paul had been so suspicious of him, as if there were something disreputable about him and he might pull some

279

shabby trick. And now he was talking so openly and frankly about his problems, about the failure of his plantation and about his too-small success in trade. And he was talking bravely, too, looking not to the failures of the past but to the bright successes of the future.

Still, it must hurt him terribly to give up his home, the Castle. She knew how she would feel if ever she lost Sabrehill.

'Ash,' she said impulsively, 'isn't there some way I can help?'

'Help, Lucy?'

'I know you must have tried hard to save your plantation, and you wouldn't have done it if it weren't important to you.'

'Well, of course, it's important. As I said – '

'If it's money you need, money to buy time to improve your land – '

For one split second she saw a stricken look on Paul's face, and Asher stared at her. Then Asher laughed and shook his head.

'Thank you, Lucy, but you wouldn't want to do that.'

'But I have money – '

'Paul, please convince our dear cousin that I could not possibly accept money from her.'

'But I was thinking of it as an investment,' Lucy said, 'a perfectly legitimate investment.'

'Objectively, a poor one, I'm afraid,' Paul said, managing a smile. 'I'm sure Asher would agree to that.'

'I certainly would. When there's plenty of good land out west, why put your money into poor?'

'If that's true,' Lucy said, 'how do you expect to find a buyer?'

'Simple. There are Virginians who would never dream of leaving the land of their Founding fathers, and my neighbors would dearly love to expand their holdings. I may not be much of a businessman, Lucy; but believe me, before long I'll have them bidding against each other.'

And no doubt, Lucy thought, that would generate more unfair talk about Asher being 'something of an adventurer' involved in 'shady business transactions'. Whatever Paul might think, the truth seemed to be that he was a very resourceful man, in spite of his business failures. His only fault was that he had been caught land-poor, which was hardly his *fault* at all, and as a planter with new land, he would probably be a great success . . .

. . . the kind of man who, if ever she were to marry again, would make a fine master for Sabrehill.

The day waned. The three of them wandered together through the large formal gardens that flanked the house. Lucy helped Asher to renew his acquaintanceship with Sabrehill by pointing out various features – the twin gazebos in the gardens, the little guest houses to the west. They walked down to Sabre's Landing on the river. Because it brought back tragic memories, Lucy had not visited it in months, but now she found it calm and peaceful, a beautiful place from which to view the broad expanse of dark water.

The subtle fencing between the two men seemed to have ended, the rivalry to have vanished. They were at ease with each other, enjoyed each other's company. At Lucy's urging, Paul stayed for supper, and it was quite dark when at last she let him go.

She and Asher walked up and down the service lanes together, her hand in his in the darkness.

Then at last it was time to part.

He kissed her on the mouth this time. He kissed her as they stood in the dark of the passage. Nothing was said. He kissed her on each cheek, as he had before, and then his arms went around her shoulders, and his mouth came down on hers.

281

It was a most improper thing to do . . .

She at last freed herself of his embrace, freed herself carefully, gently, but with firm insistence. She knew she must be wise, she must not let this go on. He tried to draw her back into his arms again, but she would not allow that. Her heart was thumping too hard, and her head was swimming. She touched her fingers to his lips and turned away.

Once again up the stairs, up to the lonely bedroom, up to the lonely bed . . .

Asher did not move as she mounted the steps. Once she stopped, and he thought she whispered good night. He said nothing, but watched her, a shadow on the staircase, until she had disappeared.

He went to the bedchamber. He lit a lamp and began to get ready for bed.

It was going very well, he thought. Far better, in fact, than he could ever have expected. He had planned to have more money in his pocket, enough to pretend to some wealth, but it seemed that that was not necessary at all. And a good thing. Mr Devereau had his suspicions, and Asher remembered Paul's Auntie Junella quite well. It seemed that the old bitch was visiting Paul right now, and no doubt she had given him an earful. Of the truth.

But not enough of the truth.

Nobody ever was going to know the full truth.

He thought about the good-night kisses in the passage. They had answered any last question he might have as to Lucy's attraction to him. She would be his, without a doubt, if only he were careful. And if she was his, Sabrehill would in effect he his too.

As he climbed into the bed, he wondered about the scar on Lucy's face, the long line past her temple down her right cheek to her jawbone. He had no idea of how she had got it, and of course he could never ask. It could have been worse, of course – he had seen cuts on the cheek that paralyzed one side of the face. Lucy didn't have that. Still, it was too bad. Except for the scar, she was a beautiful woman, and he felt sorry for her, somehow touched . . .

He broke off his thoughts in disgust. What did he mean, sorry for her? He wasn't in love with the bitch. She was only a woman, after all, and not half the woman the nigger wench was. Not half the woman Zulie was.

Zulie . . .

Asleep now in the hallway between this room and the library . . .

He had to put her out of his mind. If he let her into his mind now, if his mind got to working on her, if he started seeing her in his mind, he would never sleep.

He put out the lamp.

He couldn't have been asleep for long. He awakened too easily, too quickly, without transition from one state to the other.

He knew someone was in the room with him, he knew it even before he opened his eyes, and with the knowledge came two questions: who was it, and where was his pistol?

Panic touched him, but almost at once he realized that his visitor might not be an enemy. Years had prepared him for the moment when an enemy might catch up with him in the night, but he didn't expect that here, not at Sabrehill.

No, this was no enemy.

Very slowly he opened his eyes. She was sitting on the edge of his bed, that was what had awakened him, and for an instant he thought it might be Lucy, but of course it was not. It couldn't possibly be.

He sat up, moved up in the bed. On impulse, he threw off his nightshirt. He didn't know why, it was the wrong thing to do, absolutely the wrong thing, but he did it.

He leaned over to the table and lit the lamp.

As always, she wore only an old cotton dress, clean but plain and gray and often repaired, and she was barefoot. Her kerchief tonight was white and blue and yellow and red, a delicately flowered kerchief, and it appeared to be silk. It had to have been expensive, and he wondered vaguely how she had come by such a thing.

'Zulie . . .'

'You want Zulie come here to you,' she whispered. Her lips trembled slightly as she tried to smile, but she seemed frightened. 'You want Zulie . . .'

What could he answer? Of course he wanted her, and they both knew it. He had just pulled off his nightshirt, and he was naked under the single sheet that covered his thighs. But this wasn't the time – they might be heard. He tried to speak, but the words – he didn't know what they would be – stuck in his throat.

Her gaze moved over him. She seemed to see through the sheet, and he felt the abrupt quickening of his flesh.

She knew. Her eyes went to his again.

'You like to look at your Zulie, master?'

'Zulie, you're . . . you're beautiful.'

But that wasn't what she was asking.

'You like to look?'

Again he tried to speak but couldn't. He might as well have had a mouthful of sand.

But she knew the answer.

She reached down and took the ragged hem of her dress. Unhurriedly she drew it up to show him long brown thighs pressed tightly together. Black pelt came into view. She raised her hip from the bed briefly to pull her skirt from under it, and he saw that she had something tied around her waist. Then the dress was rising from full, hard-nippled breasts and sailing over Zulie's head and down to the floor.

She sat on the edge of the bed as naked as he. No, not quite as naked; she still had the bright kerchief on her head, and slanted across her belly was a rawhide string. As he stared at her, she lay across the bed on one elbow and relaxed her clinched thighs. They moved apart, and she arched toward him as if to show him all that she was offering.

'Master,' she whispered, 'you want?'

He reached for her. But somehow she eluded his grasp. She was off of the bed and away from him, and she ripped away the sheet that was his last covering. Then she returned, sliding a knee onto the bed toward him, and again she arched toward him, and this time waited for his touch.

Then he saw why she wore the rawhide string. Dangling from it, hanging now against her thighs, was a long knife in a soft leather sheath.

For an instant he could hardly believe what he was seeing. Somehow, he couldn't have said why, it made his excitement almost unbearable. He no longer had any thought of where he was or what the risk might be. He knew only that he was about to take this naked wench, this beautiful black bitch who wore a knife dangling before her bare legs.

This time, when he reached for her, she came to him.

She was not, Lucy assured herself as she lay in her lonely bed, in love with him. She liked him, she liked him very much. She was attracted to him. He amused her, and she respected him. But she did not love him . . . she only wanted him.

And why the hell had he had to kiss her in that way?

She did not flatter herself that he was in love with her. They were congenial, but after all, they had had only a few days together, and what was a mere kiss to him?

285

He could have no idea of how it would affect her. Could he?

She was even willing to concede that there might be some truth in Paul's view that Ash's presence here was self-serving. But was that really so terrible? He needed money or a plantation or both, and she had both. She needed a man for Sabrehill. And, yes, she needed a man for herself.

And there was nothing wrong with that, either. Perhaps it was unladylike, but she remembered her father saying of his daughters, *I never tried to make ladies out of you girls. I raised you like frontier farm girls and let you run wild and unchaperoned in a way that was disgraceful, and figured you'd grow up to be real women and WIVES God damn it!*

Real women and wives.

Yes, she and Ash needed each other, they were convenient for each other, and marriages were arranged on the basis of convenience all the time. All the best marriages were, in fact. Young men weighed the probable dowry quite nicely before contriving to fall in love, and silly girls took into consideration much more than the breadth of a man's shoulders. It was the way of the world.

It hadn't always been her way, but . . . yes, it was the way the world worked.

A sudden vision of Ash came to her, Ash in his bed only a few feet away from her, in the room immediately below, and she groaned and rolled over. She simply must not think about him, she decided. All she had to do was put him out of her mind. It shouldn't be difficult. After all, only a few months ago she had thought she would never be aroused by a man again. No, not a few months ago – a few weeks, a few days. She had been physically and spiritually so beaten, mauled, scarred, that she wanted never again even to think of love. If it hadn't been for her

286

duties at Sabrehill, she would willingly have entered a convent and forgotten that there was such a thing as the male sex.

But now . . .

She rolled over again. This was so silly. The more she tried *not* to think about Ash, the more she *did* think about Ash – and how was she *ever* going to get to sleep! She tried to think of some forbidden words that would help give vent to her frustrations. *Oh, shit, shit, shit –*

No. That was a silly, childish game, and she knew it wouldn't help at all. She laughed aloud at her childishness. But just the same, she kept seeing Ash down there in the room below, she kept seeing a handsome, graceful, still-young man, slender, lean-muscled, strong – and, *yes*, damn it!, so truly male!

'*Oh, this is stupid!*'

She flounced out of bed. Sleep was a thousand miles away. In the dark, she found a robe and pulled it on, and she paced the room like a caged animal. 'Now, just calm down, damn it,' she growled softly between clenched teeth, 'just *calm – your – self – down!*'

What she had to do, she knew, was make a clear-minded attempt at thinking this situation through. First of all, they were two people without husband or wife. Adults. Who were, it seemed, not only compatible but attracted to each other. Each had certain practical needs, certain requirements, which the other could supply. And it was entirely possible that in time love would come – that sort of thing did happen. She thought it very likely that there would be love between herself and Ash.

But juvenile infatuation was hardly necessary. The necessary qualities were respect and attraction and enjoyment. And unless she were very much mistaken Ash had those feelings for her, just as she had them for him.

There. She was thinking in a logical, clear-minded

fashion. The thing to do was to talk the whole matter over quite openly with Ash. Talk it over in a calm, businesslike way. Be reasonable. Assure him that he would have all the privileges of a husband – that she *wanted* him to have them. She would be *proud* to bear his children, she *wanted* to have children, and the sooner the better. Just talk to him and let him know, nobody was committed to anything if they just talked –

They could do it right now. It wasn't really very late yet, and Ash might be as sleepless as she. In any case, it wouldn't hurt to awaken him. She would go downstairs through the passage rather than using the small hallway, and that way she would avoid disturbing Zulie. She would wake him up, and they would talk together, and –

'Oh, my God!' She leaned against a bedpost and embraced it. What in the world was she thinking? If she went downstairs, dressed like this, in the middle of the night, he would think she had come for just one thing.

And wouldn't he be right?

Why did she lie to herself? She despised people who lied to themselves. She was no dewy-eyed virgin who wasn't yet quite sure what a man and a woman did when they were alone together in a bedroom. She was a thirty-year-old widow who for a very long time had been deprived. And downstairs there was a decent, attractive, virile male who quite likely felt the same way.

She liked him. She wanted him.

So go downstairs, damn it, she thought – and it was all so ridiculous that she had to laugh out loud. *Go downstairs and see what happens, and if he accommodates you,* THEN *maybe you can get some sleep!*

She laughed again, but it was laughter close to tears.

'Lucy? Miss Lucy, are you all right?'

'What . . .?' It was Leila, standing in the open doorway. 'What is it, Leila?'

'I said, are you all right?'

'Why yes . . . yes, I'm all right.'

'I heard you, sound like you was crying.'

'Not really. A little private problem. Childish, really, nothing to worry about.'

'If you want me to stay with you . . .'

'No. It was just a . . . a dream. I'm sorry I disturbed you.'

'That's all right. Well . . .'

'Good night, Leila.'

'Night, Miss Lucy.'

Lucy climbed back into her bed.

Well, she couldn't go downstairs now. Leila would lie awake for a time, Leila would sleep lightly in case she was needed, Leila would know. Faithful Leila.

Oh, *Ga-a-awd*, faithful Leila!

Lucy laughed, sobbed, bit her pillow. Eventually she found the means to go to sleep.

She knew he was no longer asleep. He lay against her, one leg thrown over hers, his face to her cheek. His hand moved over her waist, the knife gone now, and up to her breast and then to her head. His fingers tightened against her skull.

It had all gone wrong, she thought. It was as if the *loas*, the gods, were playing with her. Perhaps they were angry because it was so long since she had performed any of the ceremonies – Taking the Name, Washing the Head, Placing the Soul. In any case, her mother had warned her, and Zagreus had reminded her, that magic could turn against the very witch who made use of it.

But didn't she have the right to place curses? After all she had suffered . . . Oh, she had been happy enough at Sabrehill as a child, she supposed, but after Mr Turnage came – that was a different matter. He had become worse

289

with each passing year. And the Sabrehill masters had *allowed* the things he had done to her and her brothers and so many others. They *deserved* the deadly curses she had put on them.

But had she gone too far? Was that why the gods were playing with her?

She had told Zag: she was going to spell the whites, badmouth them, bring trouble to Sabrehill. And in due course the trouble had come. But never had she dreamed that Zagreus himself would bring it. How could she possibly have known that he would bring a white wench to Sabrehill, a wench who might well get him killed? So far, they had been lucky – but for how much longer? The girl had brought the scent of death and destruction with her, and to Zulie it still hung heavy in the air.

Something bad, very bad, was going to happen.

And then there was Mr Ash, the white man in whose bed she now lay and whose hand now strayed from her head down to her breast. The very moment she had first seen him, she had known that he was more of the trouble she had asked for, trouble for Sabrehill. The gods gave her knowledge of such things. And she had had such an inspiration, surely given to her by the gods: Miss Lucy was obviously entranced by Mr Ash, whether she knew it or not; but she, Zulie, would take him from her. She would enchant him and take him away from Miss Lucy, and how the white bitch would suffer! Scorned for a black conjure-woman! Mr Ash would buy his Zulie, steal her, do anything he had to do to get her away from Miss Lucy and take her to Charleston. And *he*, not she, would be the slave.

But the gods had tricked her.

Oh, her magic had worked all right, her magic had worked beautifully. He had known as well as she that this was to be the night, and he had tossed off his shirt before

290

either of them had said a word, before he had even lit the lamp. The moment they were naked together, he had reached for her, but she had held him off. She had shown him that she was stronger. She had teased him, played with him, maddened him before allowing him to take her. Only when at last they were sprawled half off of the bed and she had him in the tight grip of her body had she rewarded him with any illusion that he commanded her. Then, tearing at him with her nails, she had panted *Master, oh master, oh love Zulie, oh love me* as if each long, hard thrust were driving her mindless with pleasure. And he had been no harder to fool than any black lover. *Oh, master, master, please, love . . .*

But something had happened.

It was as if he had seen through her. It was as if the gods had whispered her secret into his ear.

Suddenly he had withdrawn from her. He had looked angrily down at her. While she had gazed back at him with astonishment he had evaded her attempts to regain him, and only when she had begged him – *Master! Please! Oh, please, master!* – had he taken her again.

And then he had truly driven her out of her mind. In the next few hours, he had thrown her about the bed, stroked her, kissed her, tasted her, explored every inch of her body. He had taken her repeatedly, only to leave her in agony and then take her again. He had perhaps three or four times found his release; her own moments had gone uncounted.

And now, near dawn, he was beginning again. She didn't resist, didn't want to resist, as he blew on the coals and rebuilt the fire. 'Take me, master, take me,' she murmured as she fondled him, and she led him where he wanted to go. But she knew now that what she felt for him did not begin and end with mere pleasure. This was a man she had spent every waking hour with for several days.

This was a man she had nursed back from near-death, a man to whom she had confided some of her most secret dreams. (And why hadn't she guessed then what the gods had in store for her?) In some strange manner he had become dear to her.

More than that. She loved him.

Yes, that was the prank of the gods. The knowledge welled up in her startlingly, almost frighteningly. She had become the victim of her own spells. Aside from her brothers, this white man was possibly the only man she had ever truly loved. And why, oh why, did it have to be him?

She had the glimpse of an answer then, a fleeting thought of Zagreus and the danger he was in.

But it passed. Her master was between her thighs once more, joining with her, and that was the only thing that mattered. She thought only of love.

4

For their first few days together, Binnie stayed as close to Zag as possible. It was she who awakened him in the morning, even before the first shout from the lane. They ate their breakfast together and stayed together until the last possible moment before going their separate ways to work. During the day, Zag would try to steal a few minutes to visit Binnie in the kitchen garden, or Binnie would steal a quarter-hour to visit him in the stable. At midday, if it wasn't raining, they would eat hurriedly and go off for a cooling swim together. In the evening, after supper together, they would retire to his room, where he tried to teach her letters and numbers and read aloud to her to improve his own skills.

And increasingly, Zag found this situation maddening. He loved the girl. He wanted her. And they had to give the appearance of being young lovers. But he hardly dared touch Binnie as she lay sprawled lazily across his bed each evening, for she would instantly become tense and skittish, almost as if he frightened her. And he certainly had no intention of forcing himself on the girl. He could only wait for that moment in the cabin to repeat itself.

There were times when he suspected Binnie of purposely tormenting him, or perhaps of testing his forebearance. Her 'swamp rat' aspect was rapidly disappearing, and Zag could see her plumping out almost from day to day. Hips were rounding, legs were growing sleeker, and eyes were no longer so large in cavernous sockets. Binnie had had a certain attraction for Zag from the first, and it was certainly not growing less. And how was he to keep his eyes on the printed page as he read and off of that half-open dress and those long bare legs?

Nights were bad. He told Zulie: 'There she is on *her* side of the wall, and here I is – am – on *my* side of the wall, and ain't neither of us getting *nothing*!'

Zulie grinned. 'You remind me of certain other fine gentleman ain't getting nothing neither – yet. Want me to put a spell on her?'

'No. Never needed no spells to get me a gal, and I ain't starting now.'

Twice he woke up in the night to find her in bed with him. She had had nightmares, she said. Zag stifled his groans.

One day when Binnie wasn't around, the Coffey sisters signaled their willingness to 'take a little walk' with him. He was briefly tempted. A couple of hours with the Coffey sisters could have wiped out a considerable amount of frustration. However, such an episode could never have been kept a secret. The sisters would inevitably have bragged that they had taken Zag away from his woman, and the incident would have reflected badly on Binnie. He was forced to decline the opportunity.

The day came when Zag began to see less of Binnie, but that only increased his frustrations and anxieties. On that day he found that she was again going swimming with Vidette and Rolanda, and again he was not invited. Thereafter, Binnie spent an increasing amount of time with the other two young women and their friends, and, for the first time since Cissie's death, Zag found himself becoming moralistic and disapproving.

'Why you have to be with them all the time?' he asked. 'You supposed to be a married woman, whyn't you *be* with married women?'

Binnie looked confused. 'But I *do* be with married

women. I'm in the kitchen garden with Isa all day long. And Maybelle, she's one of my best friends, she's married. Thought you liked Vidette and Rolanda.'

'Well, I do. But they ain't settled down yet. You, you supposed to be settled down with me, and it don't look good, you being with them so much. What you *do* with them, anyway?'

There was no doubt about it, Binnie blushed. And the blush seemed to confirm Zag's darker suspicions. Nobody at Sabrehill knew better than he what those girls' major interest in life was, and if they weren't doing something about it, they were usually talking about it.

'You been swimming naked with that damn Irish again?'

'No!' Binnie looked so surprised that he believed her.

'Then what you *do* with them?'

Still rosy-cheeked, she looked away from him. 'We just . . . talk a little . . . fool around a little.'

'Talk about what?'

'You,' Binnie said hesitantly. 'And Irish. And Solon. And Hannibal and others.'

'What about us?'

'You know. What you all are like. The things you like to do. What it's like with you. Only I just pretend, 'cause I don't really know.'

Zag was indignant. 'If you're talking about what I think you're talking about, how come you want to talk about *that?*'

For the first time, Binnie looked at him with something like defiance on her face. 'I already told you, all my life men never done nothing but hurt me. Never got no pleasure at all except by myself, and never did see how Mrs Keegan could stand men. You want me to go on being like that the rest of my life?'

'No, Binnie, course not.'

Her eyes dropped from his. 'Vidette and Rolanda, they ain't like that. Isa ain't like that, nor Maybelle. Isa, she gets feeling so good just telling me about Wayland, she's got to run off and find him. Don't know why I shouldn't be like that too. I got a right, ain't I?'

'Course you got a right.'

'So I'm trying to find out, is all. They know how, and they like to talk about it, and I'm trying to find out.'

'Binnie there is two real old sayings.'

'What?'

'"Talk is cheap" – and "*Practice* makes perfect!"'

To his surprise, she burst out laughing.

Nevertheless, as the days turned into weeks, there was still no practice. At least there was none as far as Zag was concerned. From time to time he wondered about Irish, Solon, Hannibal, and others. As Binnie came to feel more secure at Sabrehill, she began to spread her circle of friendships, and it was by no means confined to women. She was leaning to twitch her newly rounded tail in a most becoming way, Zag noted, and she was not at all taken aback by the admiring glances she drew.

'Man,' Irish sighed indiscreetly, 'got to hand it to you, Zag, your woman really got a sweet little ass,' and Zag damn near pounded his teeth in. 'Hey, didn't mean nothing, Zag!' he said in alarm as he saw the raised fist. 'Didn't mean no harm!'

'Just you watch your goddamn mouth, boy!'

Afterwards, he had a word with Binnie.

'Why, Irish ain't a bad boy, but I would have busted his head. Don't you know what you do to a man, you stick your butt out at him like that and smile over your shoulder at him so? Don't you know you're just asking him to jump on you, Binnie?'

She looked bewildered. 'Ain't nobody tried to jump on me yet.'

'Ain't for lack of wanting. Binnie, how come you *do* like you do?'

'I just want everybody to like me.'

'You ain't got no problem there. You ain't even building up to that problem.'

'Nobody ever liked me before, 'cept maybe the cook at . . .' She hesitated over the forbidden words. ' . . .at The Roost, and she died. Mr and Mrs Keegan, they didn't like me. The men they put on me, they never liked me. Just liked to hit me and slap me and do what they done to me like they hated me. You was about the only man I ever met that I really liked.'

'Ah, Binnie . . .'

She had him warming to her, almost regretting his words, but then she had to spoil it. 'It's just kind of nice,' she said, 'to know there's other nice men besides you.'

'Oh, thank you! Thank you very much!'

She honestly did not seem to realize what a tease to men she was. It was beyond her to believe that she could be all that attractive to them. She reveled in their attentions, partly because she thought she could have no real importance to them, and therefore her little flirtations were perfectly safe. And, after all, everybody knew that she was (supposedly) Zag's woman and unavailable.

Zag finally persuaded her that it did not look good *for him* if she appeared to be having too good a time with other men. It looked as if she might be stepping out on him, or contemplating doing so. It looked as if he weren't satisfying her. 'Suppose you started hearing that I was getting my fun from Rolanda?' he asked. 'Suppose you heard, "That Zag, maybe he married now, but he sure got plenty of the stuff to spare for the other gals. Sure don't seem like that Binnie got what it takes to satisfy old Zag." Now, how that going to make you feel?'

Binnie got the point. She promised that she would be

more careful in her relationships with other men. She would never allow them to conclude that her heart, or tail, belonged to anyone but Zag.

Still, Zag noted a day or two later, the men tended to gather around Binnie whenever she was away from the coach house. And still their eyes followed her as she walked along the service lanes.

The fact was that, however she behaved, the swamp rat had in less than a month metamorphosed into quite a charming little titmouse.

Chickadee? nuthatch? peckerwood?

And Zag continued to suffer. There were times, when Binnie disappeared for an hour or two in the evening, that he almost wished she would not come back. In the morning it would be clear that she had gone off to another man to get laid, and he would be done with her. He could tell Miss Lucy that they had had their official quarrel, and please, please, send the wench off to Charleston.

But of course he did not really want that. He wanted Binnie to forget that she had ever planned to leave; he wanted Miss Lucy to forget that she had ever planned to send the girl away. He wanted to make her his, and keep her here at Sabrehill, his forever.

On a Saturday morning one month after he had brought Binnie to Sabrehill, Zag decided he could stand the situation no longer.

It was a special day not only because Saturdays were short workdays but also because Miss Lucy was to give a big party that evening for her guest, Mr McCloud. Saturday night parties were traditional in the field quarters, but they became very special occasions whenever a big party was also held in the big house. There had been no such occasions for a year, not even at Christmas, and so anticipation ran high. At the last truly big party, many recalled, there had occurred the celebrated battle between

298

Mr Jeb and Cheney, the driver. Maybe there would be similar excitement tonight.

Zag and Binnie arose, as usual, shortly after dawn and went to the big-house kitchen to eat. Zulie soon joined them. She came not from her house in the field quarters but from one of the little guest houses out beyond the west gardens. Mr McCloud, as all the house servants knew, had moved into one of those little houses about three weeks ago, and they probably also knew that Zulie was his woman and slept with him every night. She hardly tried to hide the fact.

Well, Zag thought wryly, that meant that at least one member of the family was getting what she needed.

When Binnie had finished her breakfast, she drifted away from Zag and Zulie, crossing the west service lane to the gardener's cottage, where Isa and Wayland were sitting on the steps. Before long Hannibal and Rameses joined them. Their admiration of Binnie was obvious, and Binnie giggled audibly at whatever jokes they were making.

'You going to put up with that?' Zulie asked.

'Don't mean nothing.'

Zulie looked at him as if he were a fool. 'You ain't taking care of her right, are you?'

'That ain't nobody's business.'

'Zag, when a gal got a little something to spare and don't quite know what to do with it, them boys know it. And they're willing to teach her. Now, I know you like that gal, Zag, and she is going to make you feel mighty bad, you don't whip her ass into line. You going to have to bust some heads.'

Maybe, Zag thought, Zulie was right. Maybe he was losing Binnie. Maybe what she needed was a strong hand, a much stronger hand than he had given her thus far.

He worried about the matter through half of the

morning, until at last he decided he had to see Binnie. He had to see her if only at a distance to know what she was doing. He left the stable and walked toward the courtyard. From there he could see through the oaks and across open land to the kitchen garden.

Binnie and Isa were not alone.

They were on their knees, working in the garden, as was proper. Standing nearby, apparently talking to them, were three young men. One was Irish, and the others were Cawly and Solon, Zag thought, though it was hard to tell at that distance.

Zag knew that the anger he felt sprang from jealousy. He knew he had only slight reason for criticizing Binnie. But Zulie's words echoed in his mind: *When a gal got a little something to spare and don't quite know what to do with it, them boys know it. And they're willing to teach her . . .*

Maybe Wayland didn't mind other men fooling around with his wife, but Zag, by God, felt differently.

He made a beeline for the kitchen garden, straight for Binnie, striding long and fast.

It was odd what happened then. Irish, Cawly, and Solon seemed to sense his approach even before they saw him, or perhaps it was just that Isa said something like 'Here come Zag.' They fell silent; they stood awkwardly. Zag kept on striding, and they stepped back from Binnie and Isa. *Aw, shit . . . trouble coming . . . goddammit . . .* And still Zag kept coming, his anger building.

Zag felt as if the whole world were watching, and maybe part of it was, because there was a sudden yell from Momma Lucinda in the courtyard – Momma Lucinda, who had a feeling for trouble. 'Irish, what you doing out there! You get back here where you're needed, you hear me? You get back here right now!'

'Coming, Momma!' Irish moved off at a trot.

'And Cawly, Solon, what you pestering them gals for! You get back to work, or I'm sending for Mr Jeb right now! You hear me? Right now!'

Cawly and Solon moved reluctantly off.

Zag didn't even bother to look at them. He looked only at Binnie, kneeling in the dirt at his feet, and he saw that she was worried, even scared – scared just by the unsmiling look on his face and the way he had come walking. Out of the corner of his eye, he saw Isa get up and move away toward the far end of the garden.

He dropped to his knees in front of Binnie, so close that the insides of his knees touched the outsides of hers. He didn't touch her in any other way, but he looked so directly into her eyes that it was almost a kind of touch.

'Binnie,' he said, 'whose woman are you?'

'Yours, Zag.' Her voice was little more than a whisper.

He knew exactly what he intended to say. He meant to say, *Then for the love of God, Binnie,* BE *my woman! You know you can, you know how it was that night in the cabin, you know it can be that way again! Now, I am sick and tired of watching you blink your eyes at other men and go off to play Tickle My Fancy with them gals! I been mighty patient with you, but if you are my woman, God damn it, I want what's coming to me!*

But somehow it didn't come out that way.

'I just want you to know,' he heard himself saying gently, 'that if you don't want it that way, it don't have to be that way. I like you, Binnie, and I think you like me, but there ain't no law says you got to be my woman. You don't want to be, I ain't going to hurt you, ain't going to do nothing. Ain't going to tell Miss Lucy to send you to Charleston if you don't want to go, nothing like that. Just going to ask you, go live some place else, and you and me, we still be real good friends.'

He watched as the tears gathered in her eyes. Her

301

brow pinched as if she were in pain. Her mouth quivered.

'Don't you want me no more, Zag?' she asked, her voice breaking.

'*Want you!*' Zag thought he was going to explode. 'Woman, you have been driving me out of my mind for wanting you! Night and day, out of my mind! You have got to *know* how much I want you!'

Slowly the brow smoothed, a smile steadied the mouth.

'Really, Zagreus?'

'You have got to *know!*'

'That much?'

'*More!*'

The eyes closed. Binnie leaned forward until her forehead rested on Zag's shoulder.

'I want you too,' she whispered.

He could hardly believe it. '*Really?*'

'Yes. Been thinking about it for a long time. What it would be like.'

'So have I!'

'Tonight, Zagreus. After the party.'

'Tonight . . .'

They kissed then, and he knew from the kiss that she meant what she said, that she was ready at last, that tonight would truly be their long awaited wedding night.

They felt so good that they had to laugh, and they kissed again, still kneeling there in the garden. Then, as Binnie looked over Zag's shoulder, he saw a little frown come onto her face.

'Zagreus, who is that?'

Zag looked around to see the man coming out of the big house.

'That's Mr McCloud, the white master Zulie been messing around with. Him that Miss Lucy is giving the party tonight.' The frown didn't go away. 'Why? Ain't you seen him before?'

302

'Once or twice. Not close.'

That wasn't surprising. There was no reason for Binnie to have seen the man any closer than this. Most of the Sabrehill people had never seen him at all, and, until the party had been announced, a great many had been unaware that Miss Lucy even had a guest. The information had held no interest for them.

They watched as Mr McCloud headed for the east service lane.

'I better get back,' Zag said. 'He's going to want a horse, and I don't know as anybody's there to get it for him.'

'I don't like him, Zagreus.'

Zag was surprised by Binnie's seriousness. 'Now, why you say that? When you just told me you ain't even seen him up close?'

'I don't know. I just don't like him.'

'I got to go.'

'Kiss me once more.'

He kissed her again. She was his now, and tonight she would be truly his. Forever.

He had it all in the palm of his hand, that was what it amounted to. He had it all in the palm of his hand, and tonight, if all went well, he would close his fingers. Sabrehill would be his, and by God, he would never let go.

As Ash walked toward the stable, he felt as if he once again were in complete control of himself and the entire world around him. There had been a time when he'd had the fool idea that he was going to die and be dragged off screaming into oblivion. Then he had thought he was going to ruin everything through his need for the nigger wench. But he had been wrong, as wrong as he now was right.

That damned lazy Zagreus wasn't in the stable when Ash got there, and neither were his damned lazy brothers, but Hayden quickly appeared from the carpenter shop and saddled a horse. Sly nigger, that Hayden. Had a sly way of letting a white man know he was *his* nigger, Asher's, and not the goddamn Miss Lucy's. Figured that was where his best chances lay. Well, let the stupid bastard think so – he might prove useful.

Now to locate Harpe.

Of course, if he were lucky, Harpe would never show up. He'd have gone off somewhere and got his head blown off, and Asher would never see him again. Harpe had served his purpose, and from now on he could only be a threat, a danger.

Ash patted his pocket as he rode toward Riverboro – the pocket that held the small two-barreled pistol. There was always the possibility . . .

Only a slim one, though. It was amazing, when you came to think about it, how seldom Harpe ever turned his back on another man. Without seeming to, he rarely turned away even from Ash, who by now more or less rated as his best friend. Ash remembered how they had met. They had been shooting craps some years back in a Savannah tavern, and Ash had gone broke. Harpe, rather amazingly, extended credit to him, a perfect stranger, and Ash lost another three hundred dollars. How was he to pay it? Why that was simple enough, Harpe explained – they would simply follow the heaviest winner in the game, who was obviously a dishonest man, and take their money back, together with interest. Ash could then pay the three hundred dollars from his share.

Harpe had sized Ash up shrewdly. They followed their man out of Savannah, killed him on a lonely road, and took his money. And not once, Ash soon realized, had either of them turned his back on the other.

It had been the beginning of a profitable partnership, but Ash had no wish to spend the rest of his life guarding his back. And when Cousin Lucy became disillusioned, as was bound to happen, found that she had a sympathetic Mr Harpe on the premises . . .

Ash had no intention of allowing himself to be displaced.

Harpe was in Riverboro, just as he had promised he would be. 'Four weeks,' he had said. 'Look for me in four weeks.' And the man was nothing if not reliable. Ash had told him to stay away while he was courting Cousin Lucy, and the man had done so, but the four weeks were over.

Harpe was sitting at a table in a tavern. Ash barely glanced in the door. He immediately mounted his horse and rode unhurriedly out of town. He didn't have to worry about having his back turned to Harpe at present. He was Harpe's good fortune.

He had become fairly well acquainted with the area, and he waited in a grove of trees near a seldom used trail. Before long he heard Harpe's loud off-key whistling, and he toyed with the idea of an ambush. He didn't like the idea of trying one with such a small weapon as he was carrying, but Harpe certainly didn't seem to be on his guard.

After a few minutes Harpe rode into the grove.

'You sure as hell make a lot of noise.'

'Man who whistles his fool head off ain't got nothing to hide, Asher. You ought to know that.'

Ash grinned. 'Welcome to Riverboro.'

'You wasn't so friendly back there at the tavern. Wasn't friendly at all. You was supposed to come in and say good morning to your old friend Robert Burnwell. You was supposed to make me feel right at home, maybe even invite me out to Sabrehill. Now, how come you was so unfriendly to your old friend Robert Burnwell?'

No, Harpe was not only not off his guard, he was

suspicious and even a little angry. Well, Ash could match anger for anger.

'Because I didn't recognize my old friend Robert Burnwell in that goddamn mustache! And God damn it, I thought I told you to cut it off!'

That set the man back in his saddle. Good. Now maybe he remembered who was the general in this army.

'Well, I thought about it,' Harpe said, fingering the long blond strands, 'but I surely hated to part with it. And since it ain't black no more, and you ain't got your beard, I figure ain't nobody going to look at us and say, "there's that nice Mr Harpe and Mr Quinn."'

'Christ, and I was thinking earlier how reliable you were.'

Harpe sighed. 'Asher, simmer down. I been here most of three days now and ain't had a bit of trouble. You met Buckridge yet?'

'No.'

'Well, I have. Met him, drank with him, looked him straight in the eye, and he hadn't no idea who I was.'

'Did you mention my name?'

'Your name never even come up.'

'Just as well, maybe. Now tell me how it all looks from where you sit.'

'It looks pretty good, Asher. That last raid we pulled around here, the one on the Buckridge place, that really got folks stirred up. They still can't talk about nothing except how important it is to crack down on the niggers. And, just like you figured, they still talk about how that damn fool Miss Lucy was trying to run Sabrehill without even a single white man on the place. If they were hard on her before she even wrote to you, we sure made it a hell of a lot worse for her, and I don't know what they mightn't have done to her if you hadn't come along. Maybe it's just as well you got sick and went to Sabrehill when you did.'

'It is.' Asher now wondered if their raids had even been necessary, except, of course, that they had needed the money. 'What else?'

'Nothing much. I'm just honest Robert Burnwell, looking for some land to buy and maybe an overseer's job and sure as hell a game of cards. Your last name was mentioned during a card game last night, by the way, so I had to mention that I knew a McCloud, but it never went any further than that.' Harpe frowned. 'The real bad medicine around here is a man called Balbo Jeppson. Heard of him?'

'A nigger-hater. Farmer. Leads a lynch mob when he isn't riding the patrol.'

'That's him. I'm getting to know Balbo real good, real cozy like. 'Cause he's the kind of bastard that likes to sniff out trouble, and if he once looks at me sideways, I'm going to blow his fucking brains out.'

Ash laughed. 'Hell, do it anyway. Not many around here will miss him from what I hear.'

'Maybe I will. How's it look from where you are?'

'Couldn't be better. Cousin Lucy is ripe for a man. She may look like a chipped iceberg, but I got her damned drawers on fire.'

'Well, good!'

'People around here like me. She's giving a party for me tonight. After it's over, maybe Miss Lucy and I will come to an understanding.'

Harpe looked pleased. 'Say, maybe I could help! Come around after dark and shoot the place up a little bit, then you come out, guns blazing, like you was driving the raiders off single-handed – '

'No, God damn it, you just stay away from Sabrehill and from me until I tell you!' Sometimes the man was infuriating. 'Harpe, is that your idea of how to get a woman's pants off? To spoil a big party she's been planning for weeks?'

'Well, I just thought – '

'Leave the thinking to me.'

'All right,' Harpe said good-naturedly, 'you're the boss.'

'You're damn right I am. Now give me five minutes to get away from here.'

As Ash started off, he noted how carefully Harpe kept his back protected.

'Oh, Mr McCloud.'

Ash reined up. 'Yes, Mr Burnwell?'

'Ain't nothing going wrong, is there?'

'Of course not. Why should there be?'

'No reason.' Harpe hesitated. 'It's just that I'm fifty years old and getting a little old for running around shoving a pistol in people's faces. I ain't asking half for helping you with this, but I sure look forward to what you promised. An overseer's job, with good pay, and with a nice house, and a sweet little black girl who kind of likes me to look after me for the rest of my days. That's what you promised, McCloud, and I sure as hell look forward to collecting.'

Harpe had spoken reasonably, even meekly, yet it seemed to Ash that there was a hint of threat in his final words. And once again he had the feeling that Harpe had never been quite the follower he had pretended to be.

Ash forced a grin. 'Nothing's going wrong. You'll get everything I promised. When I hooked up with you, I got me a damn good man.'

'A hell of a man.'

A hell of a good dead man!

5

He held his hand palm up. Looking at the palm, he slowly closed his fingers.

Tonight. After the party. Carriages were already rolling up to the mansion, and he had to get over there. But first he had to make Zulie understand.

'Zulie,' he said, 'tonight I am going to ask Miss Lucy to marry me.'

Her eyes showing pain, she gazed steadily at him from the bed where he had refused to join her. She was silent for so long that he thought she was not going to answer. Then suddenly she was on her knees on the bed.

'You don't want to marry her, you don't!'

'Honey, I've got no choice – '

'Tell her you want to buy me. *Make* her sell me. I beg her, she ain't going to make me stay here. We can go to Charleston, find us a house – '

'Zulie, I thought you understood! Get it into your head, honey child, that I don't have that much money, I don't have nearly enough to live the way I like. All I've got is a hell of a lot of worn-out land up in Virginia. Now, I have *got* to marry Miss Lucy. And I've got to have her trusting me enough that I can get some control of Sabrehill. That goddamn lawyer, Paul Devereau, is going to fight that, but I'm going to have me Miss Lucy, and I'm going to have me Sabrehill, and that's that!'

It was strange how frankly he talked to her. He had never thought he would talk so frankly to any woman, not even a wife, and certainly not a black mistress. But Zulie . . . Zulie was different.

'I tell Miss Lucy about you and me pleasuring every night, she might feel different about you.'

The threat was startling. 'If you did that . . . and she did feel different . . . I'd have to kill you.'

'Think you could?'

Could he? Yes, probably. And know for the rest of his life that he had cut his own heart out.

He sat on the bed, put an arm around her shoulders, and pulled her to him. 'Listen, black lady, it's going to be all right. My marrying Miss Lucy, all that means is that you and I are going to have money. And we're going to live in Charleston most of the year, just the way you want. We'll find a nice house for you and your brothers, servants quarters right near Miss Lucy's Lynch Street place. That way I'll get a chance to drop by and see you 'most every day. And we're going to live good, you and me, for the rest of our lives. Now' don't you see why I've got to marry Miss Lucy? Don't you understand?'

She didn't answer. She closed her eyes and rubbed her head against his shoulder. 'You love your Zulie?'

Did he? He supposed he did, insofar as he believed in such a thing as love. All he really knew was that he had formed some kind of partnership with this woman, a pact that went even beyond the pleasures they shared, and he didn't want ever to lose her.

'Haven't I said so? You're damn right, I love my Zulie.'

'Then how come you don't want to do nothing? 'Cause you figure Miss Lucy about ready to hop into bed with you, ain't that right? Saving it all for her.'

Ash laughed. 'All right, I won't lie to you. First chance I get, I'm going to pleasure hell out of that lady. Sooner I get her knocked up, the better for both you and me. A son, *my* son, the heir to Sabrehill – that's going to be my hold on Miss Lucy.'

Zulie continued to rub her head against his shoulder.

With one hand she brought his head down until their lips touched. 'And this is going to be my hold on you,' she whispered, and as her tongue speared into his mouth, her other hand caught his and brought it up under her skirt. He was caught instantly in a rush of desire.

'You bitch!' he growled as he pulled away from her. 'You damn teasing bitch!'

'Now, you be careful what you say when you doing it to her,' Zulie said triumphantly. 'You be careful you don't say Zulie's name!'

Ash went to the door. 'No chance. You want to stay here, bitch, maybe when I get back there'll be a little left over for you.'

'No chance!' Zulie called after him as he left the room and the house. 'Leaving here and ain't coming back till you come begging!'

But she knew she would come back.

She lay down on the bed and stared at the ceiling. She would leave soon and look for Zagreus; perhaps she would find some comfort in being with him. But she would always come back. She would return later in the evening, and if Asher never appeared, she would spend the whole night in angry grieving jealousy over his infidelity. But she would always do as he wanted, would always return to him.

And what good were all her voodoo curses?

They had him working his ass off.

There hadn't been a party like this at Sabrehill in years; the guests kept pouring in. The ones who lived closest, such as the Devereaux and the Kimbroughs, came latest and would leave as soon as the party was over. But those who came greater distances started arriving in the late afternoon, and they wouldn't be leaving until after breakfast, or even dinner, the next day. And caring for their

311

horses and carriages was just part of Zag's work. Every-one, it seemed, had errands to be run and luggage to be carried and ever manner of task to be performed.

'Zag, this damn harness started coming apart on the way over here. Suppose you could fix it before we start back tonight?'

'Hey, boy, look at that wheel, it's damn near off. Now, you find someone who can take care of that and get it fixed, huh?'

'Hey, boy, over here! Move your lazy tail . . .'

I'll move your lazy tail!

Most of the big house bedrooms and two or three of the guest houses were filled up, and everybody, everybody it seemed, wanted something done. Zag had hoped that, once all the guests had arrived and settled in, he would be able to spend a little time at the field quarters party. But the evening was almost half over, and he was beginning to doubt that he would have the chance.

He had managed to find two minutes of peace in the stable, talking to Zulie, when Binnie appeared, 'When you coming?' she asked excitedly. 'You going to miss everything!'

She had never looked prettier, it seemed to him. She was barefoot, and the only thing special she wore for this great occasion was a yellow kerchief borrowed from Zulie and her own ivory and silver pin, but to Zag she looked absolutely beautiful. He enfolded her in an arm and pulled her to his side.

'They keeping me awful busy,' he explained, 'and I don't know if I can come. But I'll try to come real soon.'

She danced up and down in the curve of his arm. 'But you got to come, Zagreus! Listen, you can hear the music clear from here, almost loud as from the big house. Zagreus, I never known there was such parties, I never been to anything like this in my life! Zulie, tell him he's got to come.'

Zulie smiled and shrugged. 'He will if he can.'

Zag pulled Binnie closer and nuzzled her. It was then that he smelled her breath and realized what caused some of the flush in her cheeks.

'You just have yourself a good time, you hear me? And then later . . .'

She smiled and nodded. She closed her eyes. 'Later,' she whispered.

''Cause I love you,' he said, and Zulie drifted away from them. ''Cause I love you, and I want you so bad.'

Her laugh was tender. 'No more'n I love and want you. Zagreus is my man, going to take care of his baby.'

Zag pushed her away and swatted her rump. 'But don't you drink too much of that stuff,' he warned happily, ''cause I want me a *live* one tonight!'

'Don't *you* drink too much of that stuff, Zagreus Sabrehill! You think *I* don't want a live one? I know what too much of that stuff will do to a man!'

'Not me, honeychild. Tonight, I am *inn – egg – zausti-ble!*'

He might have expatiated a bit on his powers, but at that moment he heard a carriage rattling in the lane and the voice of Royal Buckridge calling for him, so he said 'Oh, shit' and 'I'll be out to the party soon's I can, honey.' He ignored Mr Royal's calls while he watched Binnie head back for the field quarters, watched her while he felt the pain of his love for her. It seemed to make a great sweet ache in him that he didn't want ever to go away.

Then, vaguely worried, he turned to Zulie.

'Whyn't you go along with her?' he suggested. 'Kind of look after her for a while till I get out there.'

Without a word, Zulie followed after Binnie.

* * *

313

There was no doubt about it, Ash thought, Lucy's party was an absolute success. And by extension, since the party was for him, *he* was an absolute success. He had met a number of these people before and gotten along fine with them, but tonight nailed it down. He had jollied the men and flattered their women, and they *wanted* him to be the master of Sabrehill.

Nothing of the sort was said aloud, of course; that would have been most unpolitic and indiscreet. But everybody subtly made it clear that he was most welcome as the male guiding force at Sabrehill. As Lucy's cousin, and the only white male on the plantation, he was somewhat regarded as the man of the house and Lucy's protector.

Lucy, he saw, was in her glory and clearly enjoying this triumph. She hurried from guest to guest, she introduced people, she served refreshments, she kept the musicians churning away in the ballroom. She still wore the black of a widow, but with a bit of white lace now, and with a well-scooped neckline in honor of the occasion.

And, he saw, she was beautiful. He didn't know how that could possibly be, when she had that hideous scar down one side of her face, but it was simply and literally true. The scar even seemed in some mysterious way to enhance the beauty or at least to call attention to it. That was no simpering little girl's face; that, by God, was a face to remember, and if it hadn't been for Zulie . . .

Ah, hell, he thought; he'd had a drink too many. The important thing was that, when it came to seducing the bitch, he wouldn't have to put a bag over her head or turn out the damn light.

'Mr Owen Buckridge,' Irish announced loudly. 'Mr Royal Buckridge.'

Ash was in the south parlor when he heard the names, and he froze for a moment. So they were here – two of the

314

three living Buckridges who had seen him during the raid. Well, he had to meet them sooner or later, and he'd never thought there was much risk, or he wouldn't have played it the way he had.

When he stepped out into the passage, Lucy was already greeting the Buckridge men. He recognized them instantly, but he was struck by how much the older man had changed. His face was thin and lined, the eyes hollow and haunted and even a little mad.

'Callie didn't feel up to it, you understand,' he was saying.

'Why, of course I understand, Mr Buckridge.'

'And we won't stay but a minute. We just wanted to pay our respects and meet your cousin, Mr McCloud.'

'I'm so glad you came. Asher . . .'

Ash stepped forward. Lucy performed the introductions, and Ash shook each man's hand. Owen Buckridge's feverish eyes hung unwaveringly on Ash's, and a small futile smile played over his lips.

'Seems to me we met before,' he said. 'Didn't you and your folks visit down here a long time ago?'

'Yes sir, we did, quite a long time ago, and I think we did meet. But it's a pleasure to do so again.'

'Oh, our pleasure, our pleasure! You don't know how good it is to know that our Miss Lucy here has a good man looking after her. We all hope you'll be here for a long time, sir, a long, long time.'

'As long,' Ash promised, 'as Miss Lucy can stand my rather dull presence.'

Lucy cleared her throat and spoke quickly. 'I'm almost afraid to ask, but . . . I don't suppose . . . there's been any news . . .'

Owen Buckridge looked at the floor and shook his head. 'Not a damn thing, Miss Lucy, not a single goddamn thing.'

315

'Pa's got the idea in his head now it was Adaba,' Royal Buckridge said.

Ah-dah-bah. A strange word. Owen Buckridge saw the puzzled look on Ash's face.

'Gullah,' he said. 'Or somebody told me it was Yoruba. It means the Brown Dove. He's a goddamn maroon that should have been killed off years ago. They say he's sent more niggers to Canada than any Quaker abolitionist you ever met. Lures 'em away, steals 'em away, then sends 'em north.'

'But he didn't take any of your Negro people, did he, Mr Buckridge?' Lucy asked. 'I thought he only took – '

'Don't make no difference. Any nigger that would steal other niggers would steal silver too and kill a man's daughter and burn his house down.' Owen Buckridge's face reddened and his voice shook. 'I don't know of anybody but that damn Adaba who could have disappeared the way those marauders did. And someday, somehow, I'm going to get my hands on him, and I'll tell you now that he ain't going to die fast.'

But this was marvelous, Ash thought. Here was old Buckridge staring at one of his daughter's killers – legally Ash was as guilty as Harpe – and blaming it on some damn maroon known as the Brown Dove. The whole business could not possibly have worked out more beautifully.

'I hope to God you do get him, sir,' he said fervently. 'I've heard the whole story of what happened, and I hope to God you do get him.'

'Thank you, sir,' Owen Buckridge said. 'Thank you.'

She accepted a drink from Luther's jug. She liked Luther even if he did keep trying to feel her tits, but tonight she liked the whole world. Zulie took a drink from the jug, and Luther handed it back to Binnie, but Zulie said,

'Don't give her no more. I got an idea she ain't used to it.'
Binnie said, 'Oh, I'm all right,' and took a sip anyway.

Never before in her life had she had such fun. Nothing like this had ever occurred in the field quarters of The Roost, and there had been other pleasant Saturday nights here at Sabrehill, four of them to be exact, and Wednesday evenings the younger people tended to have some fun, because you couldn't hold them down, but never, ever, had there been anything like this.

Oh, Zagreus, she thought, *how can you bear to miss it!*

Most Saturday nights there were just a lot of little parties. People wandered from house to house, they gathered around the steps and chatted, they listened to a fiddle here and a banjo there. But tonight everyone was *out!* The central square of the quarters was lit by torches, and the crowd milled through it, shouting, singing, laughing. Children ran about with no thought of bedtime. Boys chased squealing girls. There were good things to eat, candies and fruits, and jugs were passed about as if they belonged to whoever wanted a drink.

The dancing was mostly at the north side of the square. There everyone who could play an instrument – fiddles, banjos, drums, gourds, bones, even washing sticks – had gathered, and the music might die down occasionally, but it hardly ever stopped. At times there might be thirty or forty or more people dancing, while others stood around and watched. Then suddenly, as if on signal, there might be only a single couple in the middle of a big open circle, while everybody else clapped and cheered them on. Once it was Rolanda and Cawly. Everybody *knew* how Cawly had been trying for weeks to get under Rolanda's skirt, and they all laughed and cheered their heads off when they saw how the dancing Rolanda was just teasing that poor boy right out of his mind. In all her born days Binnie had never seen anything so funny, and she laughed till she cried.

After that, she had to dance too. She just *had* to! Of course, she didn't know how, she hadn't even tried since she was about six years old, but that didn't seem to matter. She had another drink from Luther's jug, and then all she had to do was listen to the music and watch the others. She danced with Luther, she danced with Irish and Solon and Rameses, she danced alone. She danced wildly, she danced wantonly, she danced in a frenzy of joy.

Oh, Zagreus, come out and dance with me now!

She had to see him. Her heart was warm for him, her heart was warm for the world. Without even thinking about it, she knew that this *was* her world, the one place where she had ever been happy, and Zagreus stood squarely at its center. His magic, and Miss Lucy's, had given it to her. She hurried through the darknes between the field quarters and the stable to find him.

'Oh, Zagreus, can't you come yet?'

''Fraid not,' Zag said, looking worried. 'It's getting late, and people are going to be leaving soon, all wanting their horses and carriages at once. Some left already.'

'But I want to dance with you, you got to dance with me, Zagreus!'

She was happy, and she knew it was her happiness that made him laugh. 'I'll try to get out there soon as possible. Party out there going to last a lot longer than in the big house, I reckon.' His worried look came back. 'Binnie, you feeling all right?'

'Course, I feel all right! But I want to dance some more, want to dance with you!'

'All right, you go dance. But I tell you what. I'm not out there real soon, you come back for me. Then when I'm done here, we'll go to the party together.'

'Good! I will! I'll come get you!'

'You do that. And you tell Zulie I said to see you get a real good time.'

318

But Zulie was nowhere to be seen when Binnie returned to the field quarters, and Binnie didn't need her to have a good time, anyway. Rameses and Solon and Hannibal were there, and Rolanda and Vidette and Isa, and plenty of others. The music was still playing, and she no longer had to watch the others to learn how to dance; she knew how, she felt she had known all of her life.

She danced. She danced and laughed, shouted and sang, in the flickering torch light, until she found herself stumbling almost exhausted into the outlying shadows. Someone caught her elbow and kept her from falling.

'Hey, now, little girl . . .', It was Hayden. Kindly Hayden, thoughtful Hayden. Zagreus didn't seem to like him much, but if Zag were here now, on this most wonderful of evenings, he would understand that Hayden wasn't really so bad, not so bad at all.

'Been watching you dance, little girl, and you just about the best there is at Sabrehill.'

Binnie giggled, pleased. 'No. Don't hardly know how.'

'Oh, that ain't true! Don't know when I last seen a gal dance like that. You must be plumb wore out. Here, have a swallow from my jug.'

Binnie gratefully took a sip. It tore at her throat and took her breath away, but her stomach was already so warmed by liquor that she hardly felt it go down.

'That good, Binnie?'

'Mm! Thank you, Hayden.'

'Anything for my friend Zag's woman. Want some more?'

'Not right now.'

They were walking somewhere. She wasn't quite sure where, except that it was away from the party and into the shadows. But that was all right, because they were going toward Zagreus, and she had to go get Zagreus very soon now.

'Yes, ma'am, anything at all for my friend Zag's woman. He sure lucky to find a woman like you, Binnie. He sure lucky.'

'Reckon I'm luckier.'

'Hm-mm. No, you ain't. And you want to know why?'

'Why ain't I?'

Hayden sighed. ''Cause you is so much woman, don't you know that, Binnie?'

'Don't know what you talking about.'

'You *real* woman. Ain't often a man find a woman like you.'

Binnie tried to suppress a smile. 'You sure got a lot of sweet talk, Hayden.'

'Ain't sweet-talking you. It's the Lord's truth. Even if Rolanda and Vidette don't tell me, I know sure. Can tell from the way you dance.'

'*How* you tell from that?'

''Cause you dance like so much woman, ain't no man enough for you, that's how. Not Zag, maybe not even Zag and me both. Just too much woman for all us to take care of.'

For some reason, that made Binnie almost double up with laughter, and Hayden had to grab her around the waist to keep her from falling. She, Bonnibelle – *no, no, Albinia!* – was too much woman for all of them to take care of!

'Tell you something, Hayden.'

'Tell me what, honey?'

'Maybe – maybe Zagreus is too much man for me.'

'Oh, can't hardly believe that, sweetie.'

'Why, that boy wants me so ba-a-ad . . .' *Shutupshutup-shutupshutup!* She was talking too much, and she knew it.

'He want you so bad?'

'Yes.'

'Well, that don't mean nothing. Question is, do he want

320

you enough? Can he give you all you *need*, Binnie honey, all you *need*?'

''Course he can.'

Hayden ignored her answer. ''Cause a gal got a right to get all she need, don't she? Ain't her fault a man can't give her enough. She got a right, same as any man, ain't that so?'

'I reckon.' Binnie was not at all certain what she was agreeing to. Everything was warm and fuzzy here in the dark.

'And when you go back to your quarters with Zag tonight, you going to want your pleasure, ain't you? You got a *right* to your pleasure, ain't you?'

'. . . Reckon.'

'Now, tell the truth, honey. You going get all you want from Zag tonight? You going get all you *need*? Any one man going to be able give you all you need tonight, or you going need so-o-o much . . .'

Then it came to her in a rush, breathtakingly. The thought she had been trying to evade throughout the evening. Abruptly she was sober, the night air filled her lungs, and the stars were clear in the sky.

This was the night she had promised Zagreus, the night she herself had looked forward to for so long. This was the night in which she would try to recapture that moment she had had with Zagreus four weeks ago in the cabin. It was the night she had tried so hard to prepare herself for, talking to the other girls, 'fooling around' with them, dreaming, as she lay alone in her bed, of what it would be like.

Trying to overcome the long years of abuse by men . . . the years in which she had had to lock away in herself any natural feelings that she might have had for them . . .

But how could she ever be what Zagreus wanted her to be? How could she ever be what she herself wanted to be?

To *give herself?* And actually to *take* pleasure from a man? The hours spent with Vidette and Rolanda, trying to learn their secrets, meant nothing, or so it seemed to Binnie now. No matter how dear Zagreus was to her, she saw nothing ahead in the night for him but bitter disillusionment – and for herself as well.

I ain't no kind of woman, she thought, *I ain't, I ain't! Can't never be like Isa or Vidette, can't never!*

It came to this, she dimly recognized: a great many men had made use of her body; but where Zagreus was concerned, she was still a virgin. And frightened.

'Hayden,' she said, trying to steady her voice, 'you think I could have another swallow from that jug of yours?'

The last of the guests had either departed from Sabrehill or gone to their rooms. The maids would not clean the house until morning. Most of the lights had been put out. And Lucy, watching Ash pour brandy, could not think when she had last felt so happy, so alive.

'They've never seen such a party at this time of year,' she said, taking the glass Ash offered her, 'at least not often. Some came all the way from Sullivan's Island just to meet you, you know.'

'I thank you, Cousin Lucy,' Ash said, touching his glass to hers. 'I have been signally honored.'

They usually ended the day like this. When they were at last alone in the office or the library, Ash would pour a drink for each of them, and they would sit and talk quietly for a time. Then Ash would rise to depart, and if it were convenient, if she were near him, his lips could brush hers. No more than that. And he would leave.

He sat down now with her on a sofa. It was something he rarely did – they usually sat apart – and she became acutely aware of his physical nearness. *Blue eyes,* she thought, *we both have blue eyes.* It was a silly thought, perhaps, but she had been inclined toward silly thoughts lately.

'Lucy, there's something I've been meaning to speak to you about. I've been here a month now . . .'

He let the words drift off. Lucy had to steady her brandy glass with both hands.

'You don't know how helpful you've been, Ash. I knew so little about managing a plantation when I took charge of Sabrehill. Most of what Mr Jeb and I knew when you arrived, we'd had to figure out on our own. You've taught us so much.'

Ash shook his head. 'Cotton's not really my crop, not yet. I've learned a few things myself. And you've done a magnificent job here . . .'

Again he let the words drift off, and Lucy found herself waiting almost fearfully for him to continue.

'Lucy, I've been here a month now . . . and I think it's about time I left.'

Whatever she had expected to hear, this was not it. 'Why, Cousin Ash,' she said with false cheerfulness, 'a month isn't a long time, not when you've come all the way from Virginia. Paul's Aunt Junella has been here over two months, and I expect you to stay at least as long as she does. Why, if you were to leave now, I'd think there was something wrong with my hospitality. Now, I'm not going to hear any more about your leaving – '

'Lucy, Lucy.'

His hand took hers, holding the glass. She was saying too much and talking too rapidly, and she allowed him to silence her.

'I really think it's time, Lucy.'

'But why?'

He put his arm on the back of the sofa behind her shoulders. He faced her, but shook his head as if he did not really wish to answer.

'Lucy . . .'

'If you *have* to be somewhere else . . . if there's . . . someone . . .'

'No. It's nothing like that.'

'Then – '

'For God's sake, Lucy!' He had set his glass aside. Now he took hers and put it by his. 'For God's sake, how do you think I feel! These last weeks have been the best of my life. But I have nothing to offer a woman like you. All I have is a rundown plantation that I'm going to sell, and I can't expect you to see any possibilities in a – in a man like me!'

Lucy felt as if her heart were opening up. 'Are you trying to say . . .?'

'I'm trying to say that I love you. I think I must have loved you since that moment when I damn near fell off of my horse and into your arms. Or maybe since I was just a young buck and you were a fifteen-year-old girl. But how can I ever ask you to marry me?'

Her impulse was to say *Ask me!* But that would be to commit herself. And some life-saving caution made her hold back.

'I don't know what to say, Ash.'

'You don't have to say anything.' There was bitterness in his voice.

'I don't know that I love you. Certainly I'm drawn to you. More than to any other man I've known in years.'

'But I am an impoverished Virginia aristocrat, and you are a very rich South Carolina lady. There is nothing more to be said.'

'I don't know that that's true. It may sound immodest, but I think now that I may very well marry again one day. And my husband may very well have no more wealth than you, or even less. The important thing will be – '

'Lucy, you're making this very difficult for me.'

'I'm sorry, I don't mean to.' She found her voice shaking. 'I only mean that you're wrong to disqualify yourself with any woman merely on the grounds of lacking money. After all, there are other things that are far more important.'

'Are you saying that you would accept me?'

'No,' Lucy said quickly, 'no, I don't know that I would. Not without a great deal of thought – '

'Oh, to hell with it.'

Ash looked away, and for an instant Lucy thought he was going to leave her. He would hurry from the room, and in the morning he would be gone. But just as quickly, he turned back to her, and his face moved toward hers. His arm slipped from the back of the sofa down around her shoulders, and their lips met. They didn't move from the sofa, but she felt as if she were being carried away. A hand slid from her shoulder down her side to her hip and seemed to lift her. The hand stroked her as the mouth worked on hers, and she found her mouth working back. Their tongues met. Hers pressed against his, pressed between his teeth, stabbed into his mouth. The hand moved to her breast . . .

'Oh, Christ, Lucy,' Ash moaned as his mouth pulled from hers and moved over her face. 'You say you may marry a man with less than me – well, I'm damned if I'm going to lose you to any such nameless, faceless bastard. I'm damned, and propriety be damned, I want you, and I want to marry you. Marry me, Lucy. Please marry me.'

'Ash . . .'

'Please!'

'I told you . . . I must think . . . and I can't think now.'

No, she couldn't think, because the mouth was on hers again, the hand was moving over her, she was floating, warmly floating, her dress was off on her shoulder, her breast was bare, their tongues were mating, her flesh under his fingers was hard and erect as his, she wanted him . . .

'No, Ash . . .'

Her head swimming, her sight blurred, she pulled away from him. Another moment, and he could have done as he pleased with her. The downstairs bed chamber was the one empty one in the house, and it had been so long for her, and they could go in there and no one would ever know, and . . .

But she must not even think about that. She covered her breast. Shaking her head, she tried desperately to clear it.

'No more, Ash. Please.'

'I'm sorry. But the thought of you with another man . . . You must marry me, Lucy.'

'I don't know, I don't know.'

'I shall ask you again tomorrow. I shall ask you every day that I'm here. But I can't bear to stay here much longer and not know your answer.'

'I understand, Ash.'

'Then give me your answer soon. Tomorrow.'

'I . . . I'll try, Ash.'

'Tomorrow!'

She found herself nodding. 'Tomorrow.'

He stood up. He helped her to her feet, and she swayed, still half-mindless. When he kissed her this time, he was gentle.

'I tell you again, Lucy, that I love you. Sleep with the thought that I love you.'

'I shall. Go now.'

'And tomorrow . . .'

'We'll talk again tomorrow. After the guests have left and we can be alone.'

'Good night, my love.'

He kissed her once more, then, and left her.

She had so much to think about, so much to consider. But she thought she already knew what her answer would be.

Where the hell was she, Zag wondered angrily, as he walked about the darkening square of the field quarters, where the hell was she? She had promised to return to the stable, but he had waited in vain. And Zulie, who was supposed to look after her, was nowhere to be seen. And now the torches were burning out, and people were beginning to scatter to their houses, and the party was coming to an end.

So where the hell was she?

The moon dipped in the sky, and the world spun like a carousel, and Binnie rocked with laughter as she ducked away from Hayden.

'Now, Hayden, don't you do that no more!'

'Honey child, you know you like it.'

'Now, no more, Hayden, no more!'

'Want another swallow?'

'Just one. One last little sip.'

She took the jug, and as Hayden tried to move in close to her, she turned her back on him. But of course that didn't stop Hayden. He simply moved up close behind her, and, as she raised the jug to her mouth, he reached around her and put his hand into her dress again to fondle her breasts. She giggled, and liquor ran down her chin.

'You know you like it,' Hayden whispered into her ear, 'you know you do.'

It was true. She did like it, and so she allowed Hayden to continue caressing her while she sipped from the jug. She liked the way he was pressing against her rump and the way his breath in her ear made her shiver, and she could not imagine why she had been so nervous earlier in

327

the evening at the thought of what was to come with Zagreus. There was nothing to be afraid of, she realized now, absolutely nothing.

Once again she slipped away from Hayden, and once again – *whoooo-eeee!* – the world spun. The jug was empty, and she tossed it aside.

'Binnie, honey, where you going?'

'Got to find Zagreus.'

'Now, why you in such a hurry to find Zagreus?'

Binnie giggled. 'You know why. 'Cause he is my-y-y ma-a-an!'

She seemed to have been running, and arms embraced her from the rear again as she stumbled.

'But you know you need more than just one man.'

'No, I don't. Just need my Zagreus.' The hand entered the front of her dress again, but her struggle against it was weak, and her giggles seemed to weaken her further. It occurred to her that if Hayden had not started fooling around with her like this, she might still be nervous about Zagreus. And so, since he wasn't really hurting her . . .

'Why, he ain't enough for you, Binnie,' Hayden crooned. 'You know he ain't enough for you.'

'He sure is, Hayden, and if you don't let me go . . .'

''Sides, if he's off pleasuring other gals, gals like the Coffrey sisters and Rolanda – '

'He ain't!' The thought froze Binnie for an instant.

'Honey, I only meant he done it before, he had lots of fun with them gals, and don't that give you the right to have some fun too?'

Binnie thawed and leaned back giggling against Hayden. Of course she had the right to have a little fun. Wasn't no harm. She hardly even cared if Zag was off spreading one of them gals right now. What was the harm? Plenty of fun for everybody.

'Fun for e'body,' she said.

'Why, sure, honey.'

The hand went from one breast to the other, stroking, probing, drawing.

'Hay'n, I getting drung-ger?'

'Why, no. Cause you ain't drinking no more. You just had a little. No harm in that.'

'Got find Zag.'

'He said for you to wait here with me.'

'Zag said that?'

'He sure did.'

'. . . Oh.'

She relaxed to accept the warm caressing hand. She felt thoroughly aroused and yet almost asleep. Her eyes wanted to fall closed, and even when she opened them, she could hardly see. Why, why, she wondered, had the night become so dark?

She had no idea of how much time passed before she felt the hand on her bare buttock.

'Hay'n, don' do tha'.'

'Now, honey, ain't no harm, is there?'

'No, but – '

'And you know you like it, it so nice, and ain't no harm . . .'

No, there was no harm, and she did like it, and she had never felt like this with a man before. She even liked it when he slid his hand between her thighs, but then it became so good it was almost unbearable.

'Hay'n . . . no . . . no more . . . no more . . .'

She swung about, trying to escape his touch, but that only aroused her further. Yet she must have escaped him somehow, for she found herself running in the dark, and it was like running blindfolded.

'Zagreus . . . Za' . . . Za' . . .'

He was somewhere. He was waiting for her. She had to find him.

But she ran straight into Hayden's arms.

This time he lifted the front of her dress to stroke her, and she spread her thighs for him, pressing herself into his hand.

'Za'!' she panted, 'Za'! Don' stop!'

'Don't worry, honey, ain't going to stop.'

'Za'! Za'!'

But he did stop, against her protests, as he sat her down on the ground and drew her dress up to her armpits. As he laid her back on the ground, she saw that he was Hayden, still Hayden, but that hardly seemed to matter.

'You gon' do me, Hay'n?'

'Yeh, honey, going to do you real good.'

That was all right. No harm. Just Hayden, their good friend Hayden. Binnie giggled. Zagreus was probably off doing Vidette or some other gal right now.

Hayden was now so close to her that she could see him clearly in spite of the extraordinary darkness of the night. He had tossed off his shirt, and now he lowered his pants, and he was ready for her, oh, yes, he was. He nuzzled her breasts and stroked her some more, and then knelt between her spread thighs.

No harm, she thought as he tried to enter her, and she lifted herself and reached to help him. *No harm, Zagreus won't mind* –

It was then that she realized.

For the second time that evening she experienced a moment of abrupt sobriety and utter clarity. With horror she watched herself being taken and knew that Zagreus was waiting for her and that she was betraying him and that Hayden was no different from the nameless dozens or hundreds of other men who had thrown themselves on her, drunk or sober, and used her for their whore. And everything she had ever dreamed of, everything she had

330

found at Sabrehill, thanks to Zagreus and Miss Lucy, she was throwing away.

Something like a scream, a cry, a wail came from her throat. Before Hayden could go farther, she pulled away from him. On her back she tried to scramble out from under him.

'Hey, now honey – '

'No Hayden, no!'

'Now, sweet baby – '

'No, Hayden, I don't want to!'

'Well, God damn, sweet ass, it's too late for that now!'

She fought him as he tried to hold her down and take her. She screamed, but the only answer was Hayden's curses and, from somewhere close by, male laughter. Hayden grabbed her wrists as she tried to push him away, and when she bit his hand, he slapped her – blows that brought exploding lights to her head.

'Now, God damn,' Hayden swore, 'you ain't going to do like this to me! You know what we been doing, and you going to give me what I want! You hear me, Binnie, you going to give me what I want! You hear me, Binnie, you going to spread!'

He slapped her twice more, and the blows seemed to take the last of her strength. She thought he might kill her if she didn't yield to him. She gave one last long wail of despair and lay still.

Zag knew something was wrong, badly wrong, even before he heard the scream. He knew it with his mind, he somehow knew it even in his bones. Binnie might have strayed off for a time, she might have been slow to return to the stable, but, unless something were badly wrong, she would never have disappeared like this.

He had looked all about the square. He had asked questions. He had tried to believe that Binnie had gone off somewhere with Zulie, that the two of them might be visiting someone in one of the cabins. But he simply knew that that wasn't true. Zulie had no doubt gone off to meet her goddamn white lover, and Binnie had disappeared.

Then came the scream.

It was unrecognizable as Binnie's voice, yet he knew it was she. It came from a considerable distance – from beyond the far, east side of the quarters – and as he ran toward it, it was repeated.

He had the feeling of running in a dream, of running endlessly and getting nowhere. Others had also heard the screams and were running with him. There were more cries. Then he was running between the ranks of cabins. He pushed through a group of people, and at last he could see clearly into the moonlit field beyond.

'. . . ain't going to do like this to me! You know what we been doing, and you going to give me what I want! You hear me, Binnie, you going to spread!'

Zag saw Hayden's big hand come down twice; he heard the blows. Then, as Hayden tried to mount the naked Binnie, he found himself running again, running with all his furious strength, running like a charging, maddened bull.

He meant to kick Hayden off of Binnie. He meant to give him one hard kick to the jaw, a blow that would probably mean one less slave at Sabrehill.

But Hayden heard him coming. He looked up from Binnie and raised his arms protectively. Zag's oncoming boot hit his shoulder like a battering ram and sent him sprawling.

Zag looked down at Binnie. Sobbing, she rolled over, trying to hide her nakedness. Vidette hurried to her and helped her get her dress down over her body. Zag didn't know how long he stared at her.

There was laughter around them. A crowd was quickly

332

gathering. There were sounds of indignation, too, but far more laughter. 'God damn, man,' he heard Hayden say, 'you got no call kicking me like that.'

'Don't I?'

'Hell, no. You can't keep her, that ain't my fault. I wouldn't touched her, she didn't keep teasing me on. She just plain asked for it.'

From somewhere behind Zag, Cawly said, 'That sure right. Luther and me, we was watching 'em.' He made his voice a falsetto in imitation of Binnie. '"Ah! Don't stop, honey! Ah! Ah! That do feel good! Oh, don't stop! You gon' do me, honey? You gon' put that big thing in me, honey? Oh, it so big! Ah! Ah! Do me real good, honey!"'

Still on the ground, Binnie started vomiting, while Vidette held her head. *Drunk*, Zag thought dully. *Drunk as hell*.

'"Ah! Oh, honey! Oh, it going in now! Ah! Ah! Oh, Hayden, don't stop!"'

Zag turned to Cawly.

He smiled.

The distance was good, and Cawly never saw it coming. It picked him up off the ground, and there was a snapping sound, and for one painful instant Zag thought it was his own right hand. Then Cawly was on his back on the ground, and, feeling his hand, Zag was reasonably certain it would be all right in a few days.

'Better see Zulie about that jaw,' Zag said. 'Tell her could be it broke.'

Then Hayden was on him.

Zag had half-expected it, had even half-invited it by turning his back. Hayden would figure that Zag would want to settle matters between them here and now. If Zag had hit Cawly for a comparatively minor offense, surely Hayden was next in line.

Zag took the blow on a shoulder. It sent him staggering

333

sideways, and another blow, to the chest, sent him to the ground. He found himself looking up at a towering Hayden and at the night sky.

'You got a idea about taking me, skinny fellow,' Hayden said, 'you just forget. 'Cause I had you under my whip many a time, and I take you apart.'

That was it, of course: the resentment at losing his whip and at finding his former victim with status above him. Zag was the one with foreman rank now and Hayden the common laborer. Zag had been right to distrust the man's friendship. Hayden would have done anything to assert himself over Zag – take his woman or his job, or, now, beat him to the ground.

Zag rubbed his sore shoulder with one hand; the other hand he extended toward Hayden. 'All right, you hit me down, now help me up.'

Hayden took the extended hand and pulled on it. He was wary; he knew Zag might be trying to trick him. But he wasn't wary enough or fast enough. Zag, instead of drawing his hand back from his shoulder and then slamming it forward, struck backhanded, a hammering blow with the bottom of his fist that drove Hayden's head around. He then drove his other fist deep into Hayden's guts, a satisfying blow that drew a cry of pain and rage from Hayden and doubled him up. And as Hayden's head went down, Zag's knee came up. The nose smashed, and blood poured from it as the head came up again. Zag shot his aching hand at the jaw, and Hayden went down as solidly as Cawly had.

'You got a idea about getting away from me, fat boy,' Zag said, 'you just forget. 'Cause I know you from way back, and it's time I butchered me a pig.'

He helped Hayden up and knocked him down again. It was easy, almost too easy. He was a good eight or nine years younger than Hayden, but Hayden was by far the heavier, the bigger boned, the bigger muscled. The wise money would have been on Hayden. But Zag felt just as he had on the day he had whipped Luther – cold and deadly and primed to kill.

He lifted Hayden to his feet again and tried not to knock him down. He wanted to tear and slash and cut with his fists, he wanted to make the man ache and bleed from a hundred places, but it was no use. He couldn't restrain the power of his fists sufficiently, and the man faded too fast.

Finally he muttered, 'Oh, shit. Go to sleep, Hayden,' and put him on the ground one final time. Hayden lay without moving.

It was only then that Zag was really aware of the crowd that had gathered around. He saw that Vidette had got the sobbing, drunken Binnie to her feet. For a brief moment he felt sorry for her, but he had no illusion that Hayden had acted without encouragement.

'She's your friend, you take care of her,' he told Vidette. 'Woman wants another bed, she ain't my woman. Just keep her away from me.'

Binnie's sobs faded behind him as he walked away. He felt less grieved than stunned. He had loved the girl, and – how did he know? – maybe he still did. He had been rebuilding his life, and he had thought he was helping her to rebuild hers. Two broken, trash-heap people making something good and sweet and whole and wonderful together.

Well, that was all over now.

To hell with it.

6

Sunday morning was hectic. Lucy still had two dozen
guests to feed, which meant turning the ballroom into a
dining hall, even though it seemed impossible to get
everybody to the table at the same time. Fortunately,
Jebediah was willing to help, and no one else could have
been a better butler. But Irish, who insisted that he was
the butler and not a houseboy, was miffed at being
superseded, and Olympia and Maybelle were too busy
gossiping to keep their minds on their work, and Vidette
was feuding with the Coffey sisters in the kitchen, and . . .

Hectic!

Nevertheless, Lucy seemed to float through the morning, managing deftly, and her only fear was that she
might make herself ridiculous by suddenly bursting out
into song.

She had a decision make. It was a terribly important
decision, one that could be a turning point in her life and a
turning point for Sabrehill and everyone who lived there.
And yet it didn't weigh on her. Though she had stayed
awake half the night thinking about it, she had not
agonized over it. No, it would be truer to say that she had
savored it.

Which suggested, though she didn't want to admit it to
herself, that she had already made up her mind.

But she couldn't *really* make the decision, it seemed to
her, until she had talked to someone about it. Ordinarily
she might have appealed to a parent or an older brother,
but she had none. She already knew what old friends such
as the Kimbroughs and the Buckridges would say: they

liked Asher and were determined to see her married. There was no objective help there. And Paul Devereau was just as prejudiced in the other direction.

That left Jebediah Hayes and Leila and Momma Lucinda.

Jebediah was certainly one of the best friends she had ever had, and his future might be very strongly affected by her decision. Quite likely he would want his freedom, which, of course, was his for the asking. She would definitely have to speak to him. But he was, after all, a man, and she wanted first of all to speak to another woman.

That left Leila and Momma Lucinda.

But Momma Lucinda was busy out in the kitchen house, while Lucy was constantly encountering her housekeeper. And so it was to Leila that she whispered a request to meet in Lucy's bedroom as soon as possible after breakfast had been served.

Odd about Leila. A year ago, Lucy remembered as she waited in her bedroom, she had regarded the beautiful little Negro girl as perhaps the most useless of all the house maids. Beautiful, yes, but useless, sluttish, and quite unintelligent. But adversity made strange allies, and they had become friends of a sort in spite of themselves. She had soon discovered that Leila was far from stupid and was like herself, a fighter and a survivor. And when it became apparent that Lucy needed a housekeeper, she had asked for the job, she had begged for it, she had demanded it, she had fought for it, she had *taken* it in spite of Lucy's misgivings – and she had performed it magnificently.

Now Lucy felt almost as close to her as she did to Jebediah and Momma Lucinda.

Leila was frowning slightly as she entered the room, as if she understood the gravity of this meeting; and, indeed, she might very well have had a suspicion of what was to come, since she had been watching Lucy and Asher these past weeks.

'Yes, ma'am? You want to see me?'

'I need your help, Leila. You see, I . . . I have an important decision to make, and . . . and I need advice.'

'Yes, ma'am.' Leila didn't seem very impressed or even very interested. Still frowning rather sullenly, she looked out the window toward the river.

'Leila, I know you're very busy, and I'm sorry I interrupted your work, but you see, this *is* important, it's a decision that . . . that may affect all of us.'

Reluctantly, Leila drew her gaze from the window back to Lucy, but her expression didn't change.

Lucy decided to come right out with it: 'You see, Mr Ash has asked me to marry him.'

Leila didn't bat an eye.

'You're not surprised?'

'Anybody with half a head could see that coming.'

'It might be the best thing for Sabrehill if I accepted him. You know how our neighbors disapprove of there not being a white man here, not even as overseer. And since Mr Ash plans to sell his plantation in Virginia – '

'Miss Lucy, you love that man?'

Lucy couldn't help but hear the faint sneer behind the words *that man*, and it kept her from answering for a moment.

'I don't know,' she said slowly. 'Perhaps not, but I find him very attractive, and I could certainly learn to love him.'

'Love him no matter what?'

'I think so.'

Leila shrugged and turned toward the door. 'Up to you.'

Lucy was baffled by the younger woman's attitude. She

338

might have expected almost any other reaction: worry at having her position endangered by a new master; happiness at her mistress's finding a husband and lover. But she could not understand this so-sullen apparent indifference.

'Wait,' she cried. 'Leila, what is it?'

Leila shrugged again, impatiently. 'Honey, you hot in the saddle for that man, you don't want to hear anything I got to say.'

'That's not true.' Lucy took Leila's shoulders and swung her about, making the smaller woman's eyes meet her own. 'If you've got something to say, Leila, I want you to say it. We've been through too much together for you to refuse to speak your mind to me. Now, say it.'

Leila licked her lips. The lips worked as if trying to form words she didn't want to say.

'You ain't going to get mad at me?'

'Of course not.'

The lips worked again, and Leila looked away from Lucy. At last the words burst out: 'Well, all I can say is, it ain't right for a man like that to be courting you when all the time he's screwing hell out of the servants every night of the week!'

Lucy felt as if a pistol had gone off in her face.

After what seemed like an immense length of time, she heard herself saying, 'You don't . . . you don't know what you're talking about.'

'Oh, for God's sake!' Now, far from sullen, Leila seemed steamingly angry with her. She wrenched her shoulders from Lucy's grip. 'Miss Lucy, I am only telling you what every nigger in this house already knows!'

'I can't . . . can't believe . . .'

'You think I'm lying? Tell me if you think I'm a liar!'

'No. No, of course not.'

'Then listen to me! Will you listen to me?'

'Yes. Yes, I'll listen.'

''Cause what I'm telling you is true! It started when he was still living in this house. He weren't hardly back on his feet, that man, when he started spreading Zulie.'

'Zulie?'

'Zulie. Thought I heard a noise downstairs, and I went to find out what it was. Believe me, I found out.'

'And you didn't tell me.'

'Thought at first you knew. It was the night I found you walking about like you was upset.'

Lucy remembered the night. Paul had come to dinner that day, and that night . . . *Oh, God!* she thought, if she had actually gone downstairs that night . . . But maybe it would have been better if she had.

'No,' she said. 'I didn't know.'

'I figured that out later. By that time, Mr Ash had moved himself out to the guest house. I heard him telling you that, with him well again, it wasn't proper for him to be in the big house with you and no chaperone nor nothing. Hell, that wasn't the reason. He just didn't want you to catch him spreading Zulie.'

'And you know . . . you actually know . . .'

'Who don't know but you? Zulie, she don't hardly try to hide it no more. She's out there every night, regular as clockwork, except when she got the curse, and maybe even then. More than once I seen her go out there at night, and I seen her come back from there in the morning. Miss Lucy, fact is – *she was out there with him last night!*

Last night . . . after his proposal . . .

Leila shrugged. Her anger, if that was what it had been, was spent, and now she seemed sympathetic or even sorrowful. 'Lucy, honey, it ain't like I don't know most men want some fun before settling down with one woman. Hell, I even figure that gives me the right to do the same thing. But I do know I wouldn't want no man courting me

340

who was spending every night in bed with another woman. I wouldn't like that, Lucy-child, I wouldn't like that at all.'

No, Lucy thought, *of course not. Who would?* But she said nothing; there seemed nothing more to be said.

'And Mr Ash, he don't strike me as a man to give up his wenches when he gets married. He don't strike me as a man to give up much of anything at all. Course, maybe that's all right with you, but I don't think so. And my advice to you if you want him real bad is just – tear off a couple of pieces, and get your satisfaction, and tell him, "Big boy, be on your way!"

'But you got to make up your own mind.'

Leila left quickly. Lucy sank into a chair and stared out the window at the river.

Nothing more to be said.

The field hands could sleep as late as they wished on Sunday mornings, but Zag could not – not with some two dozen guests at Sabrehill and some nine or ten carriages and twice that many horses to be looked after. But he was grateful for the work. He was equally grateful that Binnie didn't appear for breakfast, and after wolfing down his food, he hurried back to the east service lane. There he busied himself making certain that every cushion on every carriage was spotless and that every shoe on every horse was sound. He did far more than was actually necessary, because work distracted him and kept unwanted thoughts out of his head. And he had thought too much during the night.

Of course, everyone knew what had happened. His woman had gone around giggling while another man played with her titties but had got scared when he started to spread her. And Zag had beaten the man up, and Cawly as well, and had kicked his wife's ass out. Orion and Paris and a few others tried to talk to Zag about it, but his snarls drove them away fast. Only Jebediah Hayes refused to be silenced.

'Now, why'd you have to break poor, dumb Cawly's jaw like that?' he asked, as they stood in the paddock.

''Cause he was aching for it.'

Jeb shook his head. 'You tend to overpay your debts, boy. And I do understand the provocation, but if you break up another hand the way you did Hayden, I'm going to make you *pay* for him, understand? I am going to make you *buy* me a new hand!'

Zag was surprised. 'I didn't hurt him so bad.'

'Oh, man!' Jeb made a gesture of dismissal. 'You just wrecked him, that's all. He's not going to be worth a damn for six weeks at least.'

Zag could hardly believe it, but if Jeb said it, it must be so. The overseer walked away, looking obscurely pleased.

Toward noon, Zag became hungry again and went to the big house kitchen. He ate more slowly this time, keeping a watch for Binnie, but she didn't appear. He told himself that that was exactly what he wanted.

On his way back to work he encountered Vidette. She did not look particularly friendly.

'You over being mad at Binnie, Zag?' she asked.

'Mind your own goddamn business, Vidette.'

'That poor girl, she cried the whole night through for you.'

'Not for me, honey.'

'Don't blame you for being mad, don't blame you for busting up Hayden and Cawly neither. But how long you aim to go on punishing Binnie?'

Zag wanted to get away from Vidette. 'Ain't punishing her. Done with her.'

'Aw, shit, Zag, what she do? She just a child, that one, ain't used to so much liquor and ain't been to a party like ours in her life. Sure, she done a dumb thing, getting drunk and letting Hayden climb all over her like that, but she *didn't* let him spread her, and she *do* love you – '

'Vidette, will you please stick a pig bladder in your big loud mouth?'

Vidette was silent for only a few seconds. 'Zag, I tell you something, I was sorry at first when you brung that little gal back from Charleston, 'cause we had some real good times. But you got a real mean streak in you, Zag, a real mean streak. So, bastard – go to hell!'

'I'm sorry you feel like that.'

'And I'm sorry I left something for you in your quarters! I'm real sorry I did!'

Anger flared. 'You don't go in my room without I say so!'

Something like the sound of a particularly rich fart emerged from Vidette's mouth, and she strode away.

Zag hurried to his room.

She was there, lying face down on his bed, and the sick feeling in his heart that he had been fighting returned in full force.

'I told you before, and I just told Vidette again, nobody don't come to this room except I give permission.'

She didn't look up at him. Her face was hidden by her arm and her hair. 'I just want to tell you . . .'

'Say it and git.'

'Just want to tell you . . .' She was crying, Zag realized. Had cried all night, Vidette had said, and was still crying. '. . . tell you I'm sorry.'

'All right, you said it.'

She kept her face hidden. 'I done such a awful thing to you, Zagreus.'

'Reckon I'll live.' He spoke quietly. There seemed to be no point in expressing either anger or grief.

Binnie shook her head. 'I don't mean just last night. I got you to bring me here – '

343

'That was my idea.'

'And I made promises to you, and I made you wait so long . . . even though you loved me and I love you.'

She paused, as if waiting his confirmation of their love, but he had nothing to offer her. He kept silent. He only wished she would stop crying.

'And then last night . . .' Her voice softened until he could barely hear her. 'Last night I hurt you . . . and made people laugh at you . . . and made it so you had to fight. And, Zagreus, I am so sorry I done that to you!'

Zag sighed. 'Well, you and me was supposed to stop getting along right about now, wasn't we? So that we could bust up and Miss Lucy could take you to Charleston and ship you north.'

'But, Zagreus, I don't *want* to go north. I don't want to leave Sabrehill ever.'

Zag considered that. He wasn't sure he could bear to have Binnie around, but neither was he sure he had the right to send her away. Damn swamp-rat bitch had had little enough in her life.

'Well, Binnie,' he said at last, 'reckon you don't have to leave on my account.'

'But you don't want me around here.'

'No, don't reckon I do.'

'So I ain't going to stay.' Binnie seemed at last to have her sobbing under control. 'But Zagreus . . .'

'Yes . . .'

'You ain't the only one I hurt,' she said passionately, and she raised her head so that he could see her tear-stained face and looked into his eyes. 'You ain't the only one I hurt, you got to know. All my life, almost since I can remember I had something I dreamed for. I wasn't always going to be no whore at The Roost. I told you how I was going away to a new place where I could love a good man who'd love me too and where I could have some respect

344

for myself. Well, I found that. I found it here at Sabrehill. And I – ' her voice broke, and she shook her head – 'And I threw it away!'

'Why, Binnie?' Zag asked dully. 'Why did you do it?'

Binnie sat up on the bed. She took a long, deep breath and expelled it shudderingly. 'Well, Zagreus, I could lie to you and say I was too drunk to know what I was doing. But I don't want to lie, don't ever want to lie to you. I was drunk, but I knew what I was doing, at least most of the time, and the way I tried to keep Hayden from spreading me shows I knew. Don't it?'

'Reckon it does.'

''Cause if I was too drunk to know, I would have just let him go ahead. So, hell. I knew.'

'Then why?'

She shook her head again. 'I don't know. Cause I'm dumb, I guess. And I got drunk. And I was scared.'

'Scared? Scared of what?'

'Oh . . . you and me . . . what we was going to do.'

Zag was baffled. 'But I thought you wanted . . .'

'I did. And I seen I couldn't hold you off no longer. But I was scared just the same.'

Bafflement turned to exasperation. 'Binnie, just what the hell was there to be scared about?'

She stared at him. 'I can't make you understand, can I, no matter how I try.' She shrugged and looked away. 'Well, maybe that ain't your fault. Maybe it's just 'cause you're a man.'

'Try again. I would truly like to understand.'

'Well . . . I told you how I could never figure out how Mrs Keegan *liked* it with men. Me, I never let myself feel *nothing* with a man. Kept my feelings to myself for when I was alone. 'Cause wasn't ever a man touched me that give me anything but pain.'

'Not ever?'

'Never. Until I met you, Zagreus. "She ain't good for nothing but spreading," Mr Keegan'd say, "go on, give it to her." Then when I tried to run away, they'd grab me and slap me around, all of them laughing like it was great fun, and they'd pull my dress up and maybe tear it off. Then maybe they'd make me do things to them that I don't want to tell you about, and that would go on till somebody decided to spread me. Maybe right there in front of everybody, some of them holding me down on a table while the others took turns. And they hurt me, Zagreus. I can't tell you how they hurt me. And all I could do was lie there and try not to scream, 'cause if I screamed, they hurt me all the more. It's a wonder I still got my teeth, I had to push them back tight in my mouth so many times.'

'Jesus Christ . . .'

Zag felt like a deaf man whose ears had suddenly popped open. And the whole mean ugly sound of an evil world was roaring into them. Binnie had told him her story before and had at least hinted at its horrors, and he had pitied her. He had even understood well enough to plead successfully her case to Miss Lucy. But, until now, he realized, he had heard far more clearly the sound of his own hopes, his own longings.

'It happened all the time,' Binnie went on, 'after that cook I told you about died. Oh, not every single night, but enough nights I sometimes thought I was going plumb crazy. Maybe I did go crazy now and then. I used to have the most awful dreams. And I'd wake up to find myself running about in the yard behind the inn, screaming at the top of my voice, and waving a big old hog-butchering knife. Trying to kill all the things that was after me.' She hesitated. 'I ain't had them dreams even once since I came to Sabrehill.'

'I'm glad.'

346

'I guess I didn't go crazy for good mostly 'cause I kept it in my head that one day I was going to get away from The Roost. And go so far they couldn't never drag me back. Took me a long time even to get such an idea. It was awful, the times when I couldn't believe in it.

'Then come that terrible night when I killed Mr Keegan. And you brought me here.'

'You was right to kill him, Binnie. You had the right.'

She didn't seem to hear him. 'Guess you know I didn't 'zactly cotton to being a nigger. And I know you hate being a slave. But, Zagreus, it turned out that Sabrehill was just about everything I ever longed for. And you were so good to me!'

Binnie started weeping again, but managed to control herself. 'You know something, Zagreus,' she said harshly, 'I coulda let you spread me anytime you wanted. Coulda let you stick it in and get it off while I closed my eyes and bit my lips to keep from crying. But I didn't want that. I didn't want that ever again.'

'I wouldn't want it either. I never done that to no gal.'

'But you know what I found out? I found out that Vidette and Rolanda don't flinch every time a man comes near them. They *like* men. They *like* to give pleasure and to take it. And I found out that Isa and Wayland ain't like Dora and Lacy Keegan. They *like* each other, Zagreus, and they *like* taking their pleasure together, and they do it with loving kindness. Zagreus, *it don't have to be like at The Roost!*'

'I know that, Binnie,' Zag said softly, 'I know that.'

'All I ever wanted was for us to be like Isa and Wayland.'

'So did I.'

'But, boy, was that an idea that took getting used to.'

'And yesterday . . .'

Binnie shrugged. 'Yesterday I thought I could. I'd

347

thought about it so long and talked to the other gals about it and fooled around with them. And you wanted it so bad.'

'I shouldn't pushed you like that.'

'You didn't push me. You was sweet as always. And I really *did* look forward to it.'

'But the more you looked forward, the more it worried you,' Zag said, trying to understand.

'I guess it sure did. Tried not to think about. Tried just to have a good time at the party.'

'And you drank.'

'Drank till *nothing* didn't bother me no more. And then . . .'

'And then? . . .'

Binnie was silent for a moment, and from her eyes, Zag knew she was looking sadly back.

'There was Hayden,' she said quietly, 'sharing his jug with me, and when he put his arm around me, it didn't hardly bother me at all. And he was joking with me and making me laugh. And when he started messing around with me . . . feeling me here and there, more all the time . . . I don't know, maybe I oughtn't tell you this.'

'Tell me, Binnie.'

'It scared me at first. But then I *liked* what he was doing. He made me feel good, and I wasn't scared at all, and I *wanted* that. I wanted to feel good and never feel scared or get hurt again.'

'But there at the end . . . he hurt you.'

'He sure did.' Bursting into tears again, Binnie fell back on the bed and rolled over to bury her face. 'And I spoiled everything, everything, everything!'

Zag slumped into a chair. He watched a chickadee on the window sill against the clear blue sky beyond.

They were due for some rain.

Somebody would be calling for his carriage and horses any minute now, wanting to leave.

348

What the hell was a man to do?

He was not so naïve as to think Binnie's tale-telling and her tears were completely artless. Any more than he thought it was by mere chance that her skirt was now so high he could damn near see up her ass. But in a man's world wasn't a woman entitled to use whatever tricks she could?

On the other hand, he didn't think her story was a lie or her tears were completely false. She was trying hard to be honest with him, or she wouldn't have said some of the things she had.

Zag went to the window facing the stable.

He had had such hopes for the two of them. And wouldn't a man be a damn fool to let a chance at happiness slip by simply out of pride? Hell, he didn't know.

Not a rain cloud in sight. Crop burning up.

'Orion!' he yelled. 'Paris! Hey, Orion!'

Paris came out of the blacksmith shop. 'Yeh?'

'Get Orion. Miss Lucy's guests be leaving anytime now, and you got to help them get off. Get Solon to help if you need.'

'Ain't you going to help?'

'No. I got me a big important job I got to do, and I don't want no interruptions.'

Zag left the window. He closed the trap door. He went to the bed where Binnie still lay sobbing and sat down beside her. He patted her shoulder.

'Anyway,' he said comfortingly, 'least you learned one thing from Hayden. You ain't scared no more.'

'Oh, yeh!' Her laugh was broken. 'That's me, Miss Scared-no-more. Leastwise not when I'm drunk. Sober, I don't know.'

'Well . . . in that case . . . don't you think we ought to find out?'

She raised her face slowly from the bed. She sat up, staring at him, hardly daring to think she understood his meaning.

"Cause I love you, Binnie,' he said.

She reached for him, then, and clung to him as if she might never let him go. He didn't care if she never did.

The moment Ash saw Lucy that morning he knew what her answer was going to be – not that he had had any real doubts. Her blue eyes sparkled, her manner was lively, and she found it impossible not to smile when she looked at him. Her hand fluttered through the air and landed on his lapel as lightly as a butterfly. 'Some of our guests may think they're staying for dinner,' she said as they stood together in the kitchen, 'but I'm being *very* helpful in getting them off early, because they all have *such* a long distance to travel!'

In other words, she was eager to be rid of her guests and to be alone with Ash. She was his, and they both knew it. He had known it the night before, when he had kissed her, and by God who would have guessed that the lady had such a short fuse? Kiss her twice and touch her breasts, and she was already halfway to bed.

He ate early in the kitchen and stayed out of Lucy's way. He had no wish to fall into conversation with any of the guests or do anything that might prolong their stay at Sabrehill. He spent a good part of the morning wandering about the west lane, through the gardens, and down to Sabre's Landing and back. He considered going back to his guest house and having his sport with Zulie, just to kill the time, but he decided against it. She had had plenty last night, and from now on he had to save some for Lucy. Zulie was just going to have to go on short rations until he had his bride-to-be well-bedded, married, and pregnant. But after that . . .

350

His first suspicion that something had gone wrong might have come while the guests were departing. Since the party had been for him, he had at least to make a farewell gesture, and he did so, shaking all the gentlemen's hands, complimenting the ladies, and seeing the carriages off. Lucy's eyes didn't seem quite the same, and her liveliness seemed forced. A time or two her voice broke, almost as if she were on the verge of tears. But he decided that she was merely nervous at the thought of being alone with him and of their meeting yet to come.

Orion – Ash thought that was his name – brought the last carriage. Lucy made her farewell to the gentleman and kissed the lady's cheek. Ash shook the gentleman's hand and helped the lady up to her seat. They watched while the carriage rounded the courtyard and went down the avenue of oaks toward the road. Ash turned to speak to Lucy and found that she was no longer beside him.

The moment had come.

No need to rush it. Ash stood in the courtyard a few more minutes and watched the carriage go through the open gate and turn onto the road. He waited still another minute before going slowly up the steps and through the open doorway into the passage. Leila was standing there, arms crossed over her chest, almost as if she were waiting for him.

'Where is Miss Lucy?' he asked.

'In the library.'

God damn, she had almost snapped the words.

'"In the Library, Mr Ash, sir,"' he corrected her, but gently. When he was in charge of Sabrehill, he would have to teach its niggers a few things.

Meanwhile, Leila merely stared at him with no particular friendliness, so he thought *To hell with it* and walked through the dining room into the library.

When Lucy turned to face him, she looked distraught.

351

Her face seemed pale, and her fingers were laced tightly together. He smiled at her, but she did not smile back. He went to her – 'Lucy . . . dear' – but she backed away from him and held up her hands as if to keep him away from her.

'Why, Lucy – '

She nervously licked her lips. 'Ash, last night . . . last night . . .'

'Last night, Lucy, was the most glorious night of my life thus far, and only with you will it ever be surpassed.'

'No . . . I mean – '

'I'm sorry if I got carried away and went too far. I had no right. But I do love you, dear Lucy, and the thought of continuing to exist without you – '

'Ash, you mustn't! No more proclamations!'

Ash tried to look kindly and sympathetic. The woman was obviously frightened by the strength of her own feelings.

'You know how I feel, Lucy. Nothing sweeter than this could possibly – '

'Oh, dear.' Lucy turned away from him and put a hand to her cheek. 'Why am I making such a fool of myself?'

'You could never make a fool of yourself, my dear. That is my prerogative – to make a fool of myself over you.'

Lucy seemed to consider that thought. Then, as abruptly as she had turned away from him, she turned back.

'Well, I can't let you do that, Ash.'

'Lucy – '

'Ash, you are in many ways a dear, kind man, and you are certainly a gallant.' Suddenly Lucy seemed to be quite in command of herself again. 'I cannot tell you how honored I am by your attentions. I not only like you more than I can say; in a way I even have a certain love for you, as one loves the memory of a childhood sweetheart.'

'Last night was not a memory of childhood, dear Lucy. Last night was a treasured moment – '

'Nevertheless, Ash – and I think it is best if I come right to the point – I find that I cannot possibly marry you.'

She said the words flatly and firmly in a clear, steady voice. There was no female nervousness, no girlish tremulo. There was, perhaps, even a hint of anger. Ash was dumbfounded. It was a little as if he had expected to meet a lover and instead had suddenly been confronted by a stranger with a pistol in hand.

'Lucy, I don't understand. If you want more time to think it over . . .'

'No, Ash, I have thought about the matter all I care or intend to. Again, I do thank you, and I am so honored. Never will I forget the honor you have done me.'

Like that. Flatly. As if the matter were finished and done with, now to be cast aside and forgotten.

The numbness was wearing off, and Ash felt the roar of building anger. His plans were being subverted again, his control of his destiny was being challenged. And he was damned if he was a man to be cast aside and forgotten. Not so easily, my lady.

'Never mind the honor,' he said, and he could speak as flatly as she. 'Why are you refusing me, Lucy?'

'On consideration, I merely think it's best – '

'Why do you think it is best?'

'Please, Ash – '

'If I have honored you so much, surely I am entitled to an honest answer.'

Now, Ash was pleased to see, her commanding air was beginning to fade away. 'Must we prolong this?'

'Only as long as you continue to be evasive. Last night I bared my most intimate feelings to you. That's not easy for a man. And, to your credit, so did you to me – or so it seemed. Hell, Lucy, we were within an ace of the bed, and you know it – '

'That is enough!'

'It is not enough. I love you, and you want me, and you damn well know it. Even this morning it was the same – ' He broke off for an instant as an obscure intuition was born. 'How did you "find" that you could not marry me?'

'Ash, I would like to part friends with you. I would like to think that we shall always be the best of friends.'

'And I, loving you, would like something infinitely better. Be so kind as to answer my question, Lucy.'

Her eyes, wide and unblinking, looked into his. She seemed to be considering her answer.

'Let us just say, my dear Ash, that I have some doubts as to your . . . love.'

'And what gave rise to these doubts?'

'I consider that to be a personal – '

'Good God, Lucy, don't I have the right to know? Last night we were practically lovers. Today am I to ride away without the slightest idea – '

'Oh, Ash, for God's sake, *don't be unintelligent!*' In an instant she was completely furious, shouting at him like a harridan. 'Or if you must be unintelligent, don't take *me* for a nincompoop! For God's sake, why can't I ever meet an intelligent man!'

He wanted to seize her, to shake her, but his obscure intuition had become clear in that moment, and he was groping for a way to handle the situation, a way to justify himself.

'All right,' she was saying, 'I admit it, I have been a fool since your arrival here! But I am a fool no longer!'

Ash closed his eyes for a moment. 'Lucy, will you listen to me?'

'Until now, I have never knowingly been rude to a guest in this house!'

354

'Thank you. Lucy, I have told you how I came to love you. I have loved you from the day I came here, and perhaps even from those boyhood days so long ago – '

'Please, Ash.'

'Listen to me. You're not one of these women made of ice. You must have *some* idea of how difficult it has been to live here so close to you, and not be able . . . even to touch. If it can be that way for a woman, how do you think it is for a man like me? And why do you think I insisted on moving out to the guest house? I do love you so much, Lucy, and if I had stayed in the house, so help me God, one night very soon I would have climbed those stairs. You *know* how we are when we're together, love.'

'I'm sorry, Ash, but I am not one of those who think that little black girls were put on this earth to protect the chastity of fine white ladies.'

'Nor am I. But neither am I a eunuch, for God's sake, and when an attractive wench literally throws herself at me, brings herself naked to my bed – '

'Spare me the details. It's enough to know that you bed her down every night.'

'Every night!' Ash feigned astonishment. 'Jesus, this is getting ridiculous. First, I'm a eunuch, and now I'm a stallion. My love, I hate to disillusion you, but even I, the magnificent Asher McCloud, known for his powers throughout the length and breadth of the land, might find *every* night just a little too much. A man does like a little time off for good behavior now and then, you know. Lucy, where in God's name did you get these fairy tales?'

He saw that he had at last shaken her. 'Isn't it enough,' she said hesitantly, 'that last night, immediately after proposing to me, you went to her – '

'I didn't go to her,' he said angrily, 'she came uninvited

to me. And if I did take her, which is none of your business, it was because you had put me in such an agony of need in this very room. A need that couldn't be denied, Lucy – a need for *you*, the woman I love!'

He had a sense, then, that the matter might hang in the balance. He had a feeling that Lucy might wish to be persuaded to his view. She looked into his eyes as if searching his soul.

'Lucy . . .'

But in the end, she turned away from him. She went to a window and looked out.

'I'm sorry,' she said.

'Marry me, Lucy. Marry me, and let me make you happy – '

'No, Ash. Again, I'm sorry.'

It was over. He saw that. She was no longer shaken, nor angry, nor in any way moved. She had made her decision. She was done with the matter.

But he was not. His impulse, his grinding need, was to beat this infuriating woman, to whip her half to death, to bring her screaming to her knees, and then to tear her house down around her. But he could not do that. In his mind he had already made Sabrehill his, and he meant to have it. In spite of her.

He had to find a way, he had to have time.

'And I can't tell you how sorry I am,' he said, striving to regain a gentle tone. 'Under the circumstances, I suppose you would prefer that I left Sabrehill, but – '

'As you wish, Ash. You will always be welcome here.'

'You're kind. As a matter of fact, I have some private business in Riverboro that I'd like to conclude. If you wouldn't mind my staying in the guest house for a few days – '

'By all means, stay as long as you like, and Ash . . .'

'Yes?'

Lucy turned from the window. 'If I've been tactless or unkind in any way, I'm sorry for that too.'

'Cousin Lucy, I can only say the same.'

'And now if you'll excuse me . . .'

'Of course.'

He left the house, trying to hide the burning anger that was behind his eyes, trying to hold down his long angry strides. By God, he thought as he looked about the courtyard, if the bitch thought he was going to give up all this, she had another think coming. He would never leave. Whether she liked it or not, he was Sabrehill's new master.

Still shaking with fury, he turned down the east lane. He would get a horse, he decided, and ride off his anger. Maybe ride into Riverboro and find Harpe. Tell him it was going to take a little longer. But not tell him too much.

Arriving at the stable, he found no one at work, and he shouted: 'Zagreus! . . . Zagreus, God damn it, where are you!'

There was no answer, not even the distant sound of a black voice.

'Zagreus! Hayden! God damn, come saddle me a horse! Orion! Move your black ass!'

Still no sound other than a horse moving in a stall. Ash felt sweat coming to his forehead. When he looked at his hands, they were shaking. *I am going to kill the first black bastard* –

'Zagreus!' Son-of-a-bitch was probably up in his room asleep. Ash crossed the lane and entered the coach house. 'Zagreus, will you get your lazy black ass – '

He broke off as he saw the girl coming down the stairs, and she froze as their eyes met.

He recognized her instantly. He didn't believe it, he couldn't believe it, but he knew it was true. Her skin was darker, but he knew those eyes, that face. He thought he even recognized the pin on her dress, a trinket he had forgotten to sell and had tossed to her.

And he thought he saw recognition in her eyes, too.

Bonnibelle.

7

Mr Quinn!

She stood perfectly still on the stairs, one bare foot on a step below the other. She felt as if those hard blue eyes that stared into hers were pinning her to the wall behind her. They paralyzed her.

Mr Quinn!

Only yesterday she had seen at a distance that stride that she knew so well. Only a moment ago she had heard that hated voice. But she couldn't believe it was him, she couldn't even *think* it was him. Not even God, who burned little babies in hell, could be so mean as to send Mr Quinn after her here.

She had been lying naked in Zagreus's arms when they had heard the call: 'Zagreus!'

'Oh, damn.' He had nuzzled her throat, his hand moving on the small of her back. 'Hope Orion or Paris is there.'

'Zagreus, God damn it, where are you!'

'Oh, well, guess I better – '

'No.' When Zagreus had attempted to sit up, she had pushed him back on the bed. 'I'll tell him you ain't here. Then I'll find Orion or somebody to help him, and I'll go get us something to eat. I am just plumb starved!'

Zagreus had laughed. 'You are just plumb angel.'

'Zagreus! Hayden! God damn . . .'

She had quickly pulled a dress over her head. She had opened the trap door and started down the stairs. At that moment it had seemed to her that she had gone beyond mere happiness. Every last thing that she and Zagreus wanted, they had. Every last dream, every last detail –

'Zagreus, will you get your lazy black ass – '

Mr Quinn!

He didn't look the same. This was a slim, dapper, well-tailored man, and she remembered someone more roughly dressed, heavier. She remembered a heavy black beard over a broad face, while this man was thin-faced and clean-shaven. But the eyes were the same. And the voice. And the stance. Surely this could only be Mr Quinn.

'Where's that damn Zagreus?' he asked.

How long had they been staring at each other? She didn't know. Now that he had spoken, she no longer saw recognition in his eyes, if, in fact, it had ever been there.

'Well, where the hell – '

'I don't know, sir.' She had to force herself to look away from the man, to speak, to continue down the stairs. 'Don't know where he is. Find him for you. Or find Orion –'

'Well, be quick about it, God damn it. I want my horse, and I want him now. Christ, what a lot of lazy niggers . . .'

She was fortunate. As she stepped out of the coach house, she saw that Orion was even then hurrying along the lane, having heard the call. 'Here come Orion. He help you.'

The white master – what did they call him? Mr McCloud? – crossed the lane to the stable, muttering to himself. Binnie felt that at any instant he might swing around toward her again in sudden recognition: '*I know you!*' She backed toward the stairs, then went up them, holding her breath until she was back in the room.

Zag saw at once that something was wrong, saw the strain on her face and the panic in her eyes.

'Binnie, honey, what . . . what . . .'

'It was him.'

She rushed to him, and he pulled her into his arms. Him? What do you mean, him?'

'Mr Quinn, Zagreus. Mr Quinn, right here at Sabrehill.'

Her voice was so small he could barely hear it. She seemed to be trying to hide in his arms.

'Binnie, honey, what you talking about?'

'That man down there.'

'That called for me? That was Mr McCloud. That was Zulie's Mr Ash.'

'No, Zagreus, no! I *know* Mr Quinn. I told you how him and Mr Harpe was about the meanest ever come to The Roost. What they done to me. How I heard the screaming in the night and they buried that man out behind the pig pen. Me watching from the dark kitchen, too scared to move. Zagreus, I ain't never going to forget Mr Quinn – I know him, *and he knows me!*'

'Honey child, this is crazy!'

'I know it is. It's like my nightmares was starting all over again.'

'He didn't say nothing to you, did he?'

'No, he – he just looked at me and asked where you was.'

'Well, then . . .'

'But I know it was him, I know it!'

Zag stroked her, soothed her. 'Well, honey, I'll tell you what. Nobody knows that man better than Zulie. Reckon by now not even Miss Lucy knows so much about him. So, soon as Mr Ash is gone, we find Zulie and ask her. We do that?'

She nodded against his shoulder.

'And everything going to be all right . . . all right . . .'

'Come on, Orion, move your ass!'

'Yes sir, Mr Ash, sir. Yes, sir.'

'Saddle my horse and be damn quick about it.'

'Yes, *sir.*'

But could it really have been Bonnibelle? She had just stood there on the stairs like any other slew-footed, sullen, lazy nigger, resentful of having her nap interrupted, no spark of recognition in her dumb, animal eyes.

But surely there *had* been a spark for just an instant!

If the wench were Bonnibelle, did Lucy know that she was harboring a fugitive? She must. And Ash knew by now that she was just soft-hearted enough to do such a damn fool thing. Hell, she'd even do it for a nigger.

One thing was certain: he could hardly question Lucy about the matter. 'Cousin Lucy, don't lie to me. I just recognized a wench from The Roost who's wanted for murder. Now, what the hell is she doing here? . . . How did I recognize her? Why, I happened to stop by The Roost a few times, and I heard about the murder of old Lacy Keegan. And furthermore, if you or anyone else questions the bitch, you'll find that she knows too goddamn much about me.'

But maybe it wasn't Bonnibelle, maybe it wasn't. After all, what kind of white trash would ever pretend to be a nigger?

He went into the stable, where Orion was saddling his horse. He tried to sound casual.

'Orion, who was the wench I just saw in the coach house? Don't think I've seen her before.'

'No, sir, you wouldn't seen her. That's Binnie, works over in the kitchen garden.'

'Binnie?'

'Zag's wife.'

'Lightest skinned nigger I've ever seen. Her folks look the same?'

'Don't rightly know, Mr Ash, sir. They don't live here. Binnie comes from Charleston.'

'Oh? She been here long?'

'Not so long, about a month, I reckon. She come about the same time as you, now I think about it.'

A month. Certainty grew. Ash wondered how many

362

questions he dared to ask. His mind felt fuzzy, and he wasn't sure he was thinking clearly. Too much was happening too fast, and anger and apprehension had dulled his wits.

'How did she get here, Orion?'

Orion laughed. 'Now, that there was funny, Mr Ash, sir. We all, we didn't even how she *was* here! Didn't *nobody* know! Then Saturday night party, there is Zag with his Binnie, and he tells it she come a whole night or two before with a coffle, and Miss Lucy buy her for him. And all the time he keeping her up there in his room in secret, having his pleasure with her, and nobody know!'

A story to cover the truth, Ash realized. A stupid, unbelievable story that would take in only a bunch of ignorant niggers. He was probably the first white man to hear it. The girl had arrived somehow, and Lucy had decided to hide her. Evidently with the help of Zagreus.

There could not now be the slightest doubt that the girl was Bonnibelle.

'Give me the goddamn horse, God damn you!'

'Why – why, yes sir, Mr Ash, sir!' The startled Orion leapt aside as Ash grabbed the horse's bridle, wheeled it about, and mounted.

If anger sometimes dulled the mind, it could also sharpen it again. And it could bring strength and determination. Sabrehill was his, he had already decided that, and as he rode through the courtyard toward the road, he was looking at his own domain. He would allow no widow's whim to take it from him. He would never lose it because of the chance arrival of a mere slut. He controlled, he made his own luck. He was the man who had murdered God and taken charge of his own destiny. He would take care of the white trash wench, he would take care of his widowed cousin, he would take care of everything.

A wind was rising, and distant thunder echoed his own anger.

He couldn't be stopped.

As soon as Mr Ash had disappeared down the lane, Zag took Binnie to see Zulie. They found her in her cabin out at the field quarters.

She thought Binnie was mad.

'That man is Miss Lucy's cousin from up in Virginia. He ain't nobody else. He's a gentleman, and he got a big plantation, even if the dirt ain't so good no more. He don't wear no beard, and he don't stay at no Roost and take his pleasure with the likes of you. He is Mr Asher McCloud and nobody else.'

'But I know him, I know them blue eyes!'

'Binnie, honey,' Zag said gently, 'lots white folks got blue eyes. Miss Lucy got blue eyes.'

'And I know his voice!'

'His voice don't sound no different than lots other white folks' voices,' Zulie said impatiently.

'And the way he walks. Even from way off –'

'Lots of people walk the same,' Zag said.

'Fact is, Binnie,' Zulie said, 'plenty white folks, you can't hardly tell them apart!'

'That's true, Binnie. You go to Charleston, walk down the street, you see lots of white folks all look the same. They ain't like us.'

Binnie shook her head in confusion. She wanted to believe them, Zag saw. She only wanted to be convinced.

'Binnie, honey, you just a little while ago told us you remember Mr Quinn heavier.'

'Yes, but he been sick. And he wears different clothes now, and his beard mighta made his face look wider.'

'His beard,' Zag said quickly. 'You say Mr Quinn got this big black heavy beard and mustache. Now, if he got

364

that, the truth is you don't know how he looks under it, Binnie. You got no idea, now, do you?'

'No, reckon not, not 'zactly.'

'The truth is Mr Ash just *reminds* you about Mr Quinn. Like you remind me about Cissie, when I first see you. Now, ain't that so?'

''Course it's so,' Zulie said.

Binnie's eyes moved uncertainly back and forth between Zag and Zulie. Finally she nodded.

'Reckon it could be.'

'Has to be,' Zulie said firmly. 'Binnie, Miss Lucy ain't going to have no Mr Quinn in her family. And there ain't no mistake who he is, 'cause she known him all her life. He was even here before, though Zag and me wasn't hardly more'n pickaninnies at the time. So she ain't wrong about him, you understand?'

Binnie nodded.

'And I ain't wrong about him. 'Cause I guess I seen more of Mr Ash than anybody here, even Miss Lucy, and my Mr Ash ain't nothing *like* the Mr Quinn you talk about. You believe me?'

Binnie nodded again

'You should. Now, just you stop being scared. You here at Sabrehill with Zagreus and me, and we going to take care of you.'

Binnie smiled, and Zag drew her into his arms.

'Zag,' Zulie said, 'take her home.'

'Thank you, Zulie,' Binnie said.

His arm still around her, holding her close, Zag took Binnie out of the cabin. Zulie watched from the doorway, smiling faintly and being glad for Zag, as the couple wandered slowly back toward the coach house.

Her smile faded. The wind was rising, and the oncoming clouds reminded her of the day that half-crazy Mr Buckridge had come by and said he'd free any nigger who got his daughter's killers for him. They also reminded her that it was that night that Zagreus had stopped at The Roost and Mr Keegan had been killed.

Maybe that was why she was frightened.

Once again they were in the grove near Riverboro. This time they dismounted and stood close together, holding their voices down as if even here they might be overheard.

'Ash, you have got to be out of your goddamn mind. You mean to tell me that your fine-lady cousin would hide away a good-for-nothing, murdering little whore? Why the hell would she do a thing like that?'

The man was maddening when he took that tone. 'I don't know, God damn it, I just know that she's there! And that we've got to get rid of her!' Ash remembered how yesterday he had considered killing Harpe. It was fortunate, of course, that he had not done so, but he wanted to now, he wanted to more than ever.

'How can you be sure it's her?'

'I told you, I saw her. And I asked a few questions. She arrived at Sabrehill at just about the right time.'

'If you had to ask questions, you couldn't have been too sure.'

'Well, I did ask, and I'm sure now!'

Harpe tugged at his blonde mustache and pondered the matter. 'I'm trying to see it all clear in my head. She come down the stairs, and you looked at each other. Did she recognize you?'

'I don't know. How could I tell? We just stood there and stared at each other. Why should she stare like that if I didn't look familiar?'

'Then she got a good look at you.'

'She got a damn good look. And she could realize at any time who I am.'

'Yeah,' Harpe said sceptically, 'but who'd ever believe her?'

The man was infuriating. Ash wondered how he had put up with him for so long. His hand was near his little pistol, and he kept thinking, *I can take him, I can take him*. But he needed Harpe. For just a little longer.

He forced himself to be patient. 'Harpe, you know we can't take any chances. Right now that bitch might be with my cousin. Saying something like "Miss Lucy, it just came to me who Mr Ash is. And there's something you ought to know." And right there, there's a suspicion. Why would the bitch say it if she didn't think it was true? And maybe could even be proved?'

'But she wouldn't do that,' Harpe said. 'First of all, I don't believe your Miss Lucy knows she's got Keegan's killer on her hands. And even if she does, neither of them is going to want you to bring it out public – '

'But they can put that killing on us!' Ash spelled it out. 'Harpe, if Lucy believes even half of what that girl can tell her, if she's even suspicious, she's going to want to know more. And that means sooner or later the law comes into it. And when the law starts asking questions, it's soon going to find a number of people who can identify us as two wild bastards called Quinn and Harpe who'll rape your wife and cut your throat for a dollar. And if the girl knows about the man we killed and buried – '

'Keegan killed him.'

'*We* killed him, and *we* buried him. If you don't believe it, ask the girl. And when she saw us kill Keegan, she got scared and ran like hell. Or maybe,' Ash added sarcastically, 'you think we can put it all on her.'

'No, of course not.'

'Christ, we should have killed them all that night. Keegan, Dora, the girl – all of them!'

'Yeah,' Harpe said drily, 'and then I suppose there

367

wouldn't be no law after Harpe and Quinn. Asher, you like to think you're the smartest son-of-a-bitch in the world, but sometimes you ain't, not by half.'

Ash felt himself flush. 'The important thing is, we have got to get rid of the girl, and do it as fast as possible.'

Harpe looked fretful. He walked away for a moment, kicking at weed clumps and scuffing the dirt. A steady breeze sent small clouds scutting across the sky, but the day remained hot, and Ash felt the sweat running down his body.

'You mean, I got to get rid of her,' Harpe said.

'I've got to keep in the clear, you know that.'

'And if I got to get rid of the girl, I reckon I got to get rid of her nigger stud, too. She's got any ideas in her head, he's the first one she's gonna tell them to.'

'Yes,' Ash agreed, 'you'd probably best kill the nigger. But the main thing is, I want that goddman girl dead.'

'And you expect me just to ride in there and find the girl and kill her.' .

'I don't know how you're going to do it. I just know there's got to be a way.'

Harpe scuffed more dirt and thought about it. 'Yeah,' he said after a moment. 'Yeah, there's a way.'

All right, he would get rid of the girl for Ash. He would get rid of the girl and her nigger stud, too. He could see the necessity, and he had no doubt that he could manage the task, but you had to know how to manage Ash. Hesitate, let him urge the necessary, let him think he was the one with all the brains. Then go ahead and do whatever had to be done.

'I wonder if there ain't a way we can use this Balbo Jeppson,' Harpe said, and Ash got the idea, and Harpe smiled to himself as he saw Ash begin to think that the idea was his 'own. He questioned Ash closely about Sabrehill, learning those facts that might prove useful, then sent him on his way. He himself rode to the Jeppson farm to pay a call.

He found Jeppson out behind his house directing several slaves in the repair of a shed. 'I usually give them Sundays off,' he said, 'but I keep them reminded that they'll work any damn time I say.'

'It's a kindness you're doing them, Mr Jeppson, sir. Nothing truer than the old saying that the devil finds mischief for idle hands.'

Jeppson appeared pleased by the sentiment. 'Anything I can do for you, Mr Burnwell, or is this here purely social?'

'Well, I wish I could say it was purely social, Mr Jeppson, but I got a problem, and I figure maybe you can help me with it. Maybe sort of advise me.'

'What kind of problem?'

'Nigger problem.'

Harpe saw that catch Jeppson's interest. Niggers were always a problem, and Jeppson considered himself a leading authority on them. He nodded. 'Maybe you better come into the house, Mr Burnwell, and have a drink and tell me about it.'

They went into the kitchen, which was part of the house, and Harpe found it to be barren and scrupulously clean; he imagined the whole house was that way. Jeppson poured carefully measured drinks, and they sat down at a barren table. Harpe offered pleasantries about what a nice place Jeppson had, and Jeppson said that it suited him and he was damned if he was going to waste his money on a damn mansion the way the goddamn gentry did. And what was more, he was making more money than plenty of those snotty sons-of-bitches, and they didn't know how to handle blacks if their lives depended on it. And now, what about Mr Burnwell's problem?

Harpe hunched forward in his chair and stared down at

369

his glass. 'Well, sir, part of the problem is that I'm still a stranger here, and I believe in foreigners minding their own goddamn business. So some people might say that this here nigger problem ain't my problem at all.'

'Generally speaking,' Jeppson said briskly, business-like, 'a nigger problem is every white man's problem. It's us against them.'

'Well, that's the way I see it too. But still I am a stranger. And if I see a problem – '

'If you see a problem, you got a duty to report it.'

'Yeah, but to who?'

'Why, to the white man who got it!'

'I ain't so sure about that.'

Jeppson bristled. His shaggy gray brows lowered, and his weathered face looked more craggy than ever. 'Now, see here, Mr Burnwell, you can't let a nigger get away with – '

'What if it's a white *lady* that got it? A fine white lady?'

Jeppson's breath went out of him slowly. He stared. 'You wouldn't by any chance mean Miss Lucy?'

Harpe waved him down. 'Now, now, let's go slow. All I mean is, I got my reason for coming to you instead of the owner of this nigger. Now, may I go on, sir?'

'Go on.'

'Now I got another question. I heard about free niggers that got everything a white man got, house, slaves, even heard of two or three that had a white wife. Guess there's no law in South Carolina against it – '

'No, sir!' Jeppson's fist pounded down on the table, and in an instant his face went violently red. 'No, sir, I don't give a damn about the law, I do not hold with that! Not under any circumstances, not even if the nigger is free! Not even if the woman is a – a goddamn wench, a whore, a slut – which she had got to be!'

'I sure go along with that.'

370

Jeppson sprang from his chair. He grabbed Harpe's glass and, his hands shaking, he poured two more drinks. Harpe saw him consciously trying to control himself.

'I tell you, Mr Burnwell, I blame the white woman one hell of a lot more than I do the black boy.'

'Well, so do I – '

'You know why? Because she is degrading the white race. The woman, who is supposed to control her feelings and uphold the race, is choosing to give in to them. She is turning her back on civilized men like you and me, and choosing to be an animal.'

'Yeah, and I guess that's just about the worst thing a woman can do.'

'Oh, no, Mr Burnwell! That's only half of it, and it ain't even the worse half!'

'Why, how do you figure?'

'Suppose that white woman gets a child by that black man? And she's going to, sooner or later. But it ain't like you or me was to get our relief with a nigger wench and she got knocked up. No, sir, that ain't nothing but another slave gets born. But a white woman gets herself knocked up by any black, free or not, her child is a *free nigger!*'

'Of course,' Harpe said, as if he were beginning to understand. 'That's exactly right.'

'It's just like she was turning against everything you and me believe in, Mr Burnwell. It's like she was turning our world over to the free niggers and the animals. And what's that if it ain't treason, Mr Burnwell?'

'I never heard a better word for it.'

'And what's the penalty for treason?'

Harpe smiled. 'Why, it's death, Mr Jeppson.'

Jeppson took a large swallow of whiskey, held his breath, and slowly exhaled it. He stared into the distance beyond the walls of the kitchen.

'I remember cases . . . I remember one a while back

. . . and it wasn't the only one like it. White woman. Was supposed to be respectable. It come out that she was spreading for a nigger. Know what happened to her?'

'I heard about a case or two where the woman was carried off . . .'

Jeppson nodded. 'They came and got her, all of them wearing masks, and carried her away. The story that got around later was that they all took turns with her. She wanted to act like a goddam animal, so she got treated like a goddam animal. It went on for hours. And when they were done – she was dead.'

'I'd say that was the right way.'

'Case I'm thinking about, they didn't even bother to bury her. Thought it might provide a leson. But I guess the animals and the birds got to her quicker than we – than anybody figured, 'cause they never found the body.'

'What about the nigger?'

Jeppson shrugged. 'Always geld them, of course. Knew one to be flayed and another burned. Even knew one to get away, but I don't recall no woman who was caught who got away. Mostly they got just like I said.'

'Dead.'

'When *we* took care of them.'

Jeppson didn't seem to notice his own admission. He sighed. Silence entered the room and stretched out. Jeppson poured another round of drinks, this time again measuring out the drams carefully.

'Well,' Harpe said, accepting his glass, 'it sure is a comfort to know that this problem of mine is going to be handled right.'

'If it's got anything to do with a white woman and a nigger, it going to be handled right.' Jeppson resumed his seat. 'And I think you had better tell me about it.'

'There really ain't a hell of a lot to tell. You know I

been looking around here, thought I'd find me some land. So this morning I rode out to that place, Sabrehill – '

'Sabrehill?' The interest in Jeppson's eyes sharpened.

'Yeah, I know Sunday morning ain't a good time, but I hadn't been out that way much, and I thought I'd look around. The gate off the road was open, so I just rode in, the way a man will, up between all them oaks, you know?'

'I know.'

'And I rode up to the courtyard – and, Mr Jeppson, I saw somebody I knew!'

Jeppson nodded slowly. 'You're going to tell me you saw a white gal.'

'Mighta figured you'd guess. Well, at first I figured I had to be mistaken. Must be a real light-skinned gal who looked like the gal I knew. But then I see that the gal is staring at me, and she looks real scared. And the next thing, she turns and scurries away, fast as hell, like she was trying to get away from me.'

'Figured you'd recognized her.'

'Must be. But Mr Jeppson – I got to be honest – I did *not* recognize her. I had no idea who that little gal might be. I was just goddam certain she was white and that I knew her from somewhere.'

'I'd take your word for it. Anytime.'

'So I got down off my horse. I called to a boy. 'O'Ryan, I think he said his name was. I asked, who was that light-skinned nigger gal who was standing there a minute ago. Why, that was Binnie, he says. Binnie, the wife of his brother, Zagreus.'

'Zagreus,' Jeppson muttered, smiling. 'Well, I'll be God damned. That goddamn worthless Zagreus . . .'

'You know him?'

'I'm what I call a nigger-watcher, Mr Burnwell. Zagreus is a troublesome nigger I promised something worse

373

than the whip, and now he's going to get it. But what about this Binnie?'

'Why, I never heard of no Binnie, Mr Jeppson.'

'A made-up name.'

'Maybe so. Anyway, I cannot help but think I know that gal from somewhere, and *she is white!* So I ask, when did she come here? And it seem she come here only about a month ago. Come here from Charleston.'

'A month ago.' Jeppson nodded. Harpe could almost see the machinery of his mind at work, ginning the cotton it was being fed.

'Mr Jeppson, I left then, right fast. And I been thinking about it all the rest of this day. Who is that gal? Where the hell could I have met her in Charleston? Somewhere I met her, but I have no idea – '

'Did you ever stop at an inn called The Roost?'

'In Charleston?'

'Between here and there.'

Harpe let his face go blank. Looked stunned.

'Oh, for Christ's sake,' he said.

'You been there?'

'I don't know how long ago. Year maybe? I stopped by for something to eat. There was this gal, I forgot her name –'

'They called her Bonnibelle.'

'Yeah, I think that was it. I remember I took her for a light-skin nigger 'cause she was so brazen with a real black nigger boy there. But when I said something about it, the master, old bald feller, he said, hell, she ain't no nigger, she's just hot for nigger cock. And I said, if she was my wench, I'd whip her ass off for that, and I'd kill her before I'd let her touch a black boy.' Harpe shook his head. 'I'll be God damned. Bonnibelle.'

Jeppson smiled. 'She killed the old bald feller. The master of the inn. The one you said that to.'

Harpe gave more of the stunned look, and Jeppson looked increasingly pleased.

'You mean to tell me that nigger-fucking wench killed a decent white man, and she's living there at that Sabrehill as some goddamn nigger's wife? When she ought to be goddamn dead by this time?'

Jeppson nodded, his grin steady, his eyes never leaving Harpe. Harpe thought he had never seen a happier looking man. Well, good for him.

'I thank you for your hospitality, Mr Jeppson,' Harpe said, hastily rising to his feet. 'If I'd known the whole story, I never would have bothered you.'

'Where you going?'

'Why, to the law.'

'But you don't have to do that!'

'Mr Jeppson, this makes everything different. This ain't just a case of a white wench bedding with a nigger, bad as that is. This is a case of murder. And I've got to get to the law just as quick as –'

Harpe moved toward the door, but Jeppson moved quicker, cutting him off.

'Why? So the law can let the wench off? So the law can let the nigger go?'

'But it wouldn't –'

'Maybe it would, maybe not. How can you be sure? You know the law belongs to the likes of the Devereaus and the Kimbroughs and that damn white whore out at Sabrehill. And they put more store on their niggers than they do on honest white men like you and me. You think that whore, Miss Lucy, ain't going to stand up for her Zagreus? And for Zagreus' white slut? Like as not, she knows all about the slut, and she got herself a paper proving it ain't Bonnibelle at all but a nigger she bought in Charleston. You go to the law, you ain't going to get no justice, Mr Burnwell.'

Harpe tried to look helpless. 'What you think I ought to do, then?'

Jeppson grinned and slapped his shoulder. 'You just leave it to me. Just give me a day or two – '

'Aw, no. Mr Jeppson, if that gal didn't recognize me, she sure as hell wondered who I was, same as I did her. And the minute she remembers, she's going to run for it, and maybe even before. She could be on the run from Sabrehill right now. I'll just have to go to the law and take a chance – '

'You're right, Mr Burnwell, we can't wait. We got to do it tonight. When it's good and dark. Soon as I can get some men together.'

'You mean we . . . do like you said?'

The answer was in Jeppson's eyes. 'I'd be mighty pleased if you went with us.'

Harpe smiled. 'Why, I'd be mighty pleased too.'

And Ash thought he knew how to handle people. Ash the boss, Ash the brains. Shit.

Ash the puppet.

The storm had passed by, the thunder was distant, and the rain now fell like a benediction, steady and gentle. As steady and gentle, Zag thought, as the loving he was now giving Binnie. The windows were open, and a cooling breath of air caressed their naked bodies, while outside the rain whispered ceaselessly, and Binnie, under him, in his arms, moaned as if to answer the rain.

I got everything, he thought, *everything I wanted*.

'What you say, Zagreus?'

'Nothing, honey child. I didn't say nothing, honey child.'

'Thought you said . . .'

'Maybe I said . . . I got my Binnie.'

'Oh, yes . . . you got me . . . oh, you surely do.'

She lifted herself harder against him, and her eyes narrowed, almost closed. Her face began to move from side to side and tighten with strain. In the lamplight, it's highlights and shadows shifted, and even in this moment he was struck again by the beauty she had for him.

'Oh, Zagreus . . .'

'Yes, my Binnie-child.'

'*Love me!*'

It was a command that could be answered in only one way, but it was not only her body that asked nor his that answered. He felt savage in his desire to protect her, to cherish her, to make her everlastingly happy. And now he loved her savagely, because he knew that that was what she wanted. Her knees rose higher, her feet spread wider. He raised himself to arms' length above her. Looking down at her, he saw the strain on her face grow as she whipped her head from side to side. He saw the rippling muscles of her torso, the wild quivering of her belly, and he thrust, plunged, struck with all his force, struck again and again . . .

. . . until, in a wild moment, it was over for her. She slowly subsided. Her storm had passed, and once again the gentle rain could be heard.

Her whisper: 'Oh, Zagreus, you so good to me.'

'Want always to be good to you.'

Then, eyes widening as she realized he was still with her, still in need: 'But didn't you . . .?'

'No.'

Disturbed: 'Honey, why not?'

'Saving it for you.'

Her laughter. 'So good. And when I think that I was afraid.'

Yes, she had been afraid – even that afternoon when she had come to him she had been afraid, though she had tried to hide it. The interlude with Hayden had meant nothing, had helped nothing. She winced when his hand moved over her while they embraced on the bed, and she hid her face against him as if to hide from the object of her fright. But he had been with frightened girls before; even Cissie had been frightened at first. And so he went slowly, doing no more than stroke her and nuzzle her at first, not even removing her dress until he sensed that she was ready. His own clothes were already off by then, and for a time he did nothing but lie beside her, his hand barely moving over her.

He wanted her. He wanted her so badly. But he was determined that he would lie with her like this a hundred times if necessary before taking her. He would do nothing against her wish, nothing that she did not truly desire.

'Binnie,' he whispered, 'don't have to do no more than this, if you don't want. Don't have to be today or tomorrow or any day that you don't want. We got all the time in the world, you and me.'

It was as if he had said magic words. She was still free to be afraid, and being free, the fear began to vanish. Her face had been turned from him, her eyes closed. Now the eyes opened, and she looked at him. Her hand drifted to his straining flesh and enclosed it. And suddenly he found her open and wet and hot.

The first time had been fierce. He had barely been able to hold himself back long enough to serve her, and afterwards he was afraid that she might be frightened again. But, no, she was happy – happy and triumphant, as she waited for the next time to begin.

'Oh, Zagreus, I can do it!'

''Course you can do it.'

'I can do it with you! . . .'

The second time he showed her that she need not wait so long for the next. When she had finished, she found

378

that he still held her fiercely pinned, still throbbed hard within her . . .

. . . even as now, while the rain whispered outside the windows . . . he, making it last, not only for his own pleasure, but because he wished her to know how fiercely he wanted to please her, wished somehow to tell her of how his love would endure.

And so they lay, still locked together, whispering love words, moving only to kiss with belly, breast, and lip, simmering gently, honeyfucking the minutes away until she signaled him with slight upward pressure and tightenings around his root, that she was ready once more.

I got everything, everything! he thought again. There would not be another day of his life without Binnie. If he were still a slave, together they had their own kind of freedom.

This time he couldn't last. Perhaps Binnie didn't want him to. As she started to come, she gave him such a wrench, such a twist, such a savage instant of love, that he had to join her storm. The lightning struck, blinding him, struck again, struck countless times. It seared and burned, and the torrents rushed, and he had to roar his joy.

That was the moment they chose to teach him.

He was a slave. He had nothing.

And he was about to die.

They had not even heard the horses coming. They were still clinging together, still in the last dying thrusts, when Zag dimly realized that boots were pounding up the stairs. The trap door was thrown open. It had not been barred, but it would not have mattered if it had been. Men – white men, masked – swarmed up into the room.

Binnie screamed.

And the horror began.

They clung together, still linked, as if clinging to their

379

lives. For Zag knew – every experience of his life told him – that this was the end. It was the end for him and quite likely for Binnie. They had been living in their own little world, and somehow the outside world had found out what they had forgotten – that he was black and she was white. These men might know, too, that Binnie was a fugitive, or they might not, but that hardly mattered. The only thing that mattered was that they had come here to kill.

They pulled Zag and Binnie from the bed. They tore them apart, Binnie still reaching for Zag and screaming. The sight of their hands on her naked body turned Zag's fear to fury and gave him the strength to throw his captors off, but they seized him again before he could reach Binnie, and they carried her through the trap door and down the stairs.

Him, they threw down the stairs.

He went headfirst, smashing, rolling, flailing into the darkness below. Steps jammed, scraped, pounded face, ribs, legs, filling him with pain. He had hardly landed when he felt a boot in his face, another in his belly.

'On your feet, nigger!'

Hands grabbed his upper arms and yanked him to his feet. More hands twisted his right arm behind him, raising it so high it threatened to slip out of the shoulder socket, and he was thrust out into the lane.

Ahead of him he saw Binnie on her back in the lane, being dragged over the cobblestones and through the mud by an arm and a leg. She cried out his name.

That in itself was enough to make him struggle. He twisted to the left, bent forward, twisted again, threw off a pair of hands. His right arm almost came free. But they knew how to handle a naked nigger – go for his legs, go for his feet. A boot cracked down on Zag's right toes, smashing them on the cobblestones; probably, like Jebediah Hayes, he would limp for the rest of his life.

But that might be only a matter of minutes.

They were being taken to the barn, he saw. One of their captors – he had no idea of how many there were – ran ahead, and by the time they dragged Binnie into the barn a lamp was burning. He heard the crack of a whip and her scream just before he himself was dragged into the barn.

'Now, we got to do this fast, Goddamn it, but we are going to do it right!'

Zag knew the voice. He could never have forgotten it. Nor could he have forgotten the heavy barrel-like body or the burning eyes behind the mask: '*One day you are going to pay for what you did, boy. You are going to pay, and you are going to pay worse than any whipping you might have got. Yes, sir, you are going to pay.*'

'No!' he cried out. '*No!*'

'Hear that, boys? The nigger says *no*. Show him the knife.'

There was just enough light in the barn to see, just enough to make the knife edge shine.

'Now you know what you're going to lose before you die. But what you lose, your woman is going to get – from every damn one of us!'

Wailing, Binnie tried to crawl away on the floor, and one of the men brought a whip down on her back. Another kicked her, sending her rolling over, and the whip came down again.

'Hear them screams, nigger? Going to be a lot more before we're through!'

The man with the knife moved closer, holding the blade high.

'Look at it, nigger . . . look at it . . .'

Zag moaned. He went limp in his captors' hands, his quaking legs barely supporting him. The masked men laughed, and he felt them relax for an instant.

That instant was all he needed. In one fast movement

he was free, and he ignored the pain in his right shoulder. He felt the pain in his right foot, but he used it as a source of power, used it to drive his right fist as he swung around. It was the same blow he had used on Cawly, and it had the same results. There was smashing of bone that could have been his hand but was not; the man was lifted from the floor and dropped to it, as inert as jelly.

Then there was the backhand smash, the same one he had used on Hayden, and a masked head turned grotesquely around: it was a blow that could break a man's neck.

Then there was the foot into the guts, the same hard driving blow that had rammed Cheney back against the wall: it sent a man gagging sickly halfway across the barn before he fell down.

'Get him! Get the nigger!'

Yes, he was free, but more were coming at him, and he knew he could not last for long. He could only hope that he might delay death until help came, might give Binnie and himself some small chance at survival. As a whip wrapped itself across his shoulders with a bite of fire, he grabbed it and slammed his fist into its owner's belly. The whip was his. And, turning, twisting, lashing out, he used it to clear space.

'Get the rope on him! Get him, get the rope. God damn it, *hang him up!*'

He was seized from behind, arms pinning his, and he threw the man off, but he was seized again. He heard Binnie's screams as a whip came down on her back, saw her try to run, saw a man grab her as she clawed at him, clawed down his mask: a grinning face with a long yellow mustache. Then he saw the noose dangling before his eyes.

They got the whip away from him. He tried to tear himself loose from the arms that bound him, but he was pulled backwards off balance. The man with the knife was coming at him, but he lashed out with both feet, and the man drew back.

Hemp scraped his face, tightened around his neck, the knot behind his right ear.

'*Hang him up!*'

The rope tugged at his neck, almost closed his throat. His arms were released, and he clawed at his throat. The knifer came at him again, and as he kicked to defend himself, he felt himself going up. His feet no longer touched the floor.

His throat closed altogether.

He was going higher, clawing at the rope, clawing at his throat. His lungs strained. As he kicked out, someone grabbed his leg and tugged at it, closing the noose even tighter, and he dimly heard someone say, *No, damn it, let the nigger strangle! Let him last a while!*

Higher . . . higher . . . his head pulled to one side . . . his lungs bursting . . . the knifer coming at him while he kicked . . . kicked . . .

Watch the nigger dance!

Jebediah was there, he saw from eyes that wanted to burst from his head . . . Jebediah, throwing men about, Jebediah lifting the knifer overhead and sending him crashing to the floor. Cheney was rushing into the barn like a maddened bull. But they were too late. Zag's lungs were screaming, his heart threatening to burst. He saw the flash of a pistol as a bullet pounded Jebediah back against a wall. Then Mr Ash was in the room, a pistol in each hand, and he shoved one out at the man with the yellow mustache and shot him through the head. But it was too late, too late. He couldn't hear, could barely see . . . Miss Lucy, pepperbox pistol in hand, firing, firing . . .

He was consumed by purple fire.

Jesus, Binnie it ain't right!

And this, he knew as the blackness came, was death.

383

Part Four

1

This was what she had feared.

She knew it had come even before she heard the first shot. She knew because the gods informed her. Even if they played with her, even if they occasionally punished her for overreaching, she was theirs, and they whispered into her ear.

She left her cabin and the light of the single candle that burned there, and ran out into the night. The rain fell steadily, turning the quarters into a swamp of mud. Then the shot cracked like a single snap of lightning, distantly, hollowly, and she screamed her younger brothers' names: 'Orion! Paris!' And ran, ran like hell, between the ranks of cabins, through the field quarters, toward the mansion's east service lane.

Toward Zagreus.

Passing the men's barrack, she shouted her brothers' names again. Every other hand in the quarters, every other servant, might be hiding in his bed, quailing as more shots rang out, but she had to get to Zagreus.

She ran along the path that led in the general direction of the big house outbuildings, her bare feet pounding, long legs stretching, every muscle straining, *willing* herself toward the coach house, *hurling* herself through the wet night. And then, as she got closer, she saw in spite of the rain that there was a light – a light in the big brick barn on the east lane. She left the path and ran toward it, hardly feeling the sharp pebbles and roots that cut her feet.

More shots exploded in the night. Horses whinnied. Dimly she saw that riders were galloping through the courtyard and down the oak-lined avenue to the main road. They were no more than the most shadowy ghosts passing between the trees.

She kept running. Never had the barn seemed so distant; in the night it seemed as if the harder she ran the more she remained in the same place, the kind of race one ran in a nightmare. Yet the light in the barn did grow brighter, and at last she was there.

Cheney was there, she saw, blood on his hands and shock on his face. Her own white lover was there, a pistol in each hand and his face grim. Miss Lucy was weeping as she bent over Mr Jeb, who lay bleeding on the floor.

'Jebediah, just lie still! I'll get help!'

And there was a black boy there, a naked black boy on the floor, lying in Paris's arms. Somehow Paris had arrived here before her, she realized with a kind of dull wonderment. He turned his grief-stricken face up to hers and said, 'Zulie, he's dead! Zagreus, he's dead!'

Even then, for a moment, she could not accept that this was Zagreus who lay in Paris's arms – not this shrunken, broken body laying in its own dying shits, this stinking corpse with the loosened rope still around its abraded neck, its eyes upturned under slitted lids, its purple tongue hanging out.

She might have screamed.

He was in her own arms; she had pulled him from those of Paris. Her mouth was over his, trying to give him the breath of life, trying to touch his soul with hers, trying to give him some vital spark even if she had to give up her own. Breathe, Zagreus. Live, Zagreus.

But if he breathed at all, she could not detect it; if he had a pulse, she could not find it.

Still, she had to try, she had to keep trying, because she could not admit that Zagreus was truly dead. This was her older brother, who had cared for her all her life, who had loved her.

She hardly heard the voices around her:

'Binnie . . . did they hurt Binnie, too?'

'. . . ain't around here, Miss Lucy.'

'Lucy, I'm afraid . . . afraid they carried her off.'

'Oh, dear God . . .'

Paris wept. 'Make him live, Zulie. Make him live.'

She tried. She would have given her own life for his, an even trade with Baron Samedi. But hard as she held her mouth to Zagreus's, as hard as she prayed, she still found no sign of breathing, no sign of life.

Someone touched her shoulder, and she looked up. Miss Lucy.

'. . . Zulie . . . so sorry . . . Mr Jeb . . . I think he's dying . . . can you help – '

'I got my own dead, God damn you!'

They left her alone after that. Momma Lucinda was there, helping to care for Mr Jeb, and Orion arrived, so shocked that Zulie had to hit him to bring him to his senses. Then she returned her work on Zagreus, never ceasing, until – she had to believe it, her doubt might have killed him – she thought she found, ever so slightly, a heartbeat.

'He going to be all right.'

'No,' Paris sobbed.

'Don't you say that!' She motioned to Orion. 'Take Zag to my house. You carry him, Orion, you the biggest of us now. Carry him gentle. We got to take care of him.'

They paid no attention to the others in the barn. Paris helped Orion to lift Zagreus into his arms. Orion led the way back through the dark toward the field quarters, carrying his older brother as if Zagreus were a baby. Zulie walked behind them, and Paris followed, weeping. The rain continued to fall gently and steadily as if nothing at all had happened.

The people of the quarters were at their doors now – they knew the raid, the lynching, whatever it had been, was over. Some rushed out of their houses to ask questions, but when they saw Zagreus in Orion's arms, they drew back in silence.

In Zulie's house, Orion gently lay Zagreus on the bed. While Paris lit more candles, Zulie again pressed her mouth to that of Zagreus, trying to give him her spirit.

'Zulie,' Orion said quietly, 'ain't nothing you can do. He's dead.'

'No.'

'He is, Zulie. We got to take care of poor Zag proper now. We got to – '

'No. He ain't dead, he ain't *going* to be dead.'

'But he is – '

'Then I bring him back. I bring him back to life.'

There was a shocked silence. Even the candles seemed to stop their flickering for a moment.

'Zulie,' Paris said in a voice of horror, 'you ain't going to make Zag no *zombie!*'

'Going to bring him back.'

'But you can't! You can't do that terrible thing to Zag! We got to bury him proper!'

'If he come back a zombie, I'll kill it and bury Zag myself. But I got to try, Paris, I got to try!'

'It ain't right, Zulie,' Orion said, 'you know it ain't right –'

'Orion, you and Paris just do like I tell you. You clean Zagreus up good now, and let me do what I got to do.'

And when that was done, when the right time came, she would work spells of vengeance as she never had before. Whoever had done this to her Zagreus would pay. There was an elm tree of which she knew, and her mother had taught her that through the elm she could petition Momma Brigitte. She would sprinkle the roots of the elm with flour and cornmeal. She would light candles on the roots and promise gifts. She would make Momma Brigitte, wife of Baron Samedi, understand that in return for vengeance she would offer any sacrifice.

Even human.

This rain was not like others. Usually the wind would come, whipping up the storm and bringing thunder and lightning, there would be a downpour for an hour or a night, and it would all be over, perhaps leaving floods behind. This storm had ended in a matter of minutes, leaving behind a steady rain that fell like ceaseless tears.

Lucy rested in the library. She had been up most of the night with Jebediah, but she knew she could not sleep.

She heard the passage door open. That would be Ash, she supposed. At least she hoped so. Perhaps he would bring news. She called to him, and he entered the library looking almost as weary as she felt.

'Anything?' she asked.

He shook his head. 'I asked at the tavern . . . at the church . . . ran across Major Kimbrough and Paul Devereau . . . talked to some farmers . . . If anyone knew anything, he wasn't saying.'

'I recognized Jeppson,' she said. 'Of course, I can't prove it was he, but I'd recognize him anywhere.'

'Well, they were all strangers to me, as far as I could tell. And I'm afraid we're just going to have to assume that, wherever they are, they have the girl with them.'

Lucy, feeling sickened, lay back on the sofa and closed her eyes. 'Ash, do you know what that means? It's not the first time Jeppson's friends have carried off a woman. And the word comes back about how they abuse her, and – and – Ash, sometimes they don't even find the body.'

'You mean . . .'

'I mean, if she's lucky she's dead by now.'

'Oh, Christ . . .'

Lucy opened her eyes to see Ash slump into a nearby chair. Yes, she thought, he too was weary. The strain of the long hours since the riders had appeared . . .

391

'Why did they do it?' she asked. 'Why, oh, why did they do it?'

'It's easy to guess. Rumor goes from one plantation quarters to another that you've got a girl so light-skinned that maybe she's really white. Jeppson hears, and he's out to get you. It's all he needs.'

'Oh, I suppose, but still . . .' Why the everlasting need for violence, for blood?

'Did you find out who that man was?' she asked. She meant the man he had killed.

He nodded. 'Stranger around here. Called himself Robert Burnwell. Fell in with Jeppson and his bunch evidently, and it was the unluckiest thing he ever did. Call me whatever rude name you please, Lucy, but I'm glad I killed the son-of-a-bitch.'

'Frankly – I cannot be sorry.'

They sat quietly, the only sound the constant rain. Ash rubbed tired eyes.

'How's Jebediah?' he asked.

'He has a chance. Momma Lucinda thinks he'll be all right.'

'You really care for that nigger, don't you?'

'He's not a nigger.'

'I'm sorry.'

'Jebediah is a good man. He's also an intelligent man. Someday he may even be a wise man.'

'If he's your friend, Lucy, then I'm his.'

Lucy managed a smile. She regretted sounding snippish.

'Zagreus,' Ash said. 'Have they buried him yet? I don't suppose in this rain – '

'I hear that Zulie has no intention of burying him. She plans to bring him back to life.'

'What?' Ash looked incredulous.

'Don't talk to anyone about it, Ash. She could get into very serious trouble. I'm just afraid she'll bring him back as a zombie – '

'As a zombie! Lucy, do you actually believe in such things?'

Tired though she was, Lucy forced herself to explain. 'Oh, not the way you think. My father's belief was that such creatures have never really died but have had their minds damaged in some way. It could happen because of voodoo drugs or because of some terrible experience, such as being hung. He told me he had seen zombies in New Orleans, and he had once seen a man who had been strangled and who later was no different from a zombie. He was like a – a human vegetable. It's not a fate I'd want for Zagreus.'

'I should think not.'

'Anyway, I doubt that she'll succeed.'

Ash stood up from his chair. He paced. He turned away from Lucy as if to avoid her eyes. She knew somehow that he was going to say something important, and she wasn't at all sure that she could cope with it.

'Lucy, I'm afraid this isn't the time to speak of certain things – '

'Then don't, Ash.'

When he turned to her, he looked hurt. 'But I must! I'll be leaving soon, and they must be said. Lucy, don't be unkind.'

She shrugged. 'Very well. What is it?'

'First of all, I want to apologize. I want to apologize for hurting you, for hurting both of us, for being a damn fool –'

'Please, Ash.'

'No, let me say it! I came here, a virtual stranger after all these years, and you took me into your home. You took me in sick, and you cured me.'

'Zulie cured you.'

'Zulie did a lot more than cure me – and I'm not putting blame on her. Hell, I'm not putting blame on anyone! Do you think she's the first wench I've had? Every friend I know has had his share before marriage, even if he never touched one afterwards. Do you really think that in that respect I'm so different from any other man you know?'

'No,' Lucy answered honestly. 'I don't suppose you are.'

'Thank you. Then I can't be too supremely villainous in your eyes.'

'Oh, I never thought you a villain, Ash.' She wondered if that were really true.

'If not a villain, then surely a fool. Because it took me so long to realize that I was in love with you, when I should have known from the first instant. But when I came out of the fever . . . and my need for a woman was so great, as it will be when a man's been ill . . . and Zulie literally crawled into my bed . . . I'm sorry to speak of this, Lucy, but I don't think I can altogether be blamed for what happened.'

'Perhaps not,' she said. 'Perhaps I reacted . . . a little too strongly . . . a little naïvely.' Was she really saying these words?

Ash dropped to one knee beside the sofa. 'Lucy, I am going to worry about you every day after I've left here. I am going to dream about you every night. Who is going to look after you when I'm gone? Oh, I admit that I was no great protection last night – but at least I killed one of those bastards, and I may have winged another.' He laughed. 'And I think you may have got one with that damn pepperbox of yours!' How did she happen to find her hand on his head, her fingers in that thick dark hair? 'And we did drive them off! There must have been at least seven or eight, but we did it. You and I and Jebediah and Cheney – and who knows how many more of your people might have been killed or carried off if it hadn't been for us?'

It was true, she supposed – they had, at the very least, put up a great fight.

'You were very brave last night,' she said.

'Brave! Jebediah and Cheney didn't even have weapons! And there you were, making that pepperbox spit fire! My God, what a woman!

'But what's going to happen to you after I'm gone? Who's going to be at your side, fighting your battles with you, doing his damnedest to protect you? When I think of your being alone . . . or just as bad – worse! – with another man . . .

'Lucy, I'm long past being a mere boy, and I've looked for the right woman for many years now. And to have found her at last and to have lost her . . . God, Lucy, if you only knew how I love you and want to marry you . . .'

How long did he talk to her like that, kneeling at her feet? How long did she sit there, weary, smiling faintly, her fingers moving through his dark hair?

Perhaps she had been a fool. Was it really so important that Ash had bedded an eager girl a few times? Had she ever expected to marry a man who had not? Wasn't she a little old to be acting like a romantic school girl?

And, whatever his faults, Ash certainly had his strengths as well. He was not unintelligent, he had a certain wit, a certain gallantry. He had virility, and he had ardor. And he was brave. He had fought for her, and he had killed for her. Yes, that savage, atavistic fact could not be ignored: he had killed for her.

And if Ash were a trifle calculating in his proposal, wouldn't she be just as much so in her acceptance?

Oh, Papa, she thought, conjuring up her father's memory, *I am so tired of being alone. I'm tired of fighting with my neighbors, I'm tired of the bloodshed and death that have come to Sabrehill in the last year. And you always said you raised me to be a real woman and a wife, and I do miss having a man in my bed.*

And so she found herself saying the words: 'Yes, Ash, dear. Yes, Ash, I'll marry you . . .'

* * *

A triumph.

He played the role to the hilt, even to laying his head in her lap while she stroked his hair. After a moment, he raised his head and leaned forward, and they kissed. Not a passionate kiss this time, just a gentle kiss, a comforting kiss, a fond and loving kiss. Then she informed him that she wished to go to her room to rest, and he helped her to her feet. He walked with her into the passage and stood at the foot of the stairs watching her go slowly up.

A triumph!

As he walked out into the courtyard and the rain, he had all he could do to keep from crowing aloud. He looked about and saw some niggers in the kitchen house and some more in the doorway of the butler's cottage. Hell, it was a world of niggers, niggers and pigmies, and one no better than the other. Only he was giant, only he was undefeatable.

Yesterday Lucy had turned him down flat. She had all but told him to go to hell. And Harpe had been worrying him. And then that damn sandhiller slut had turned up, a bitch who could ruin everything, if it weren't ruined already. And then he had known, *he had known*, that the whole damn world was conspiring against him and *they were going to take it all, all away from him, Sabrehill, the land, the niggers, everything – and there wasn't a goddam thing he could do about it!*

But he had done something about it. Immediately. As always, when all appeared lost, he had improvised brilliantly. He had got Harpe to bring Jeppson and his mob to kill the girl and her nigger stud, and he himself had done away with Harpe, thus eliminating all dangers and making himself the hero of the hour. A simple, elegant solution. With the result that everything he had worked and planned for was now going to be his.

He couldn't help it – he could hold back his laughter no longer. He raised his face into the rain and laughed,

laughed so damned hard that the niggers in the kitchen house stared out at him, but he couldn't stop. A giant had every right to laugh.

And hadn't he learned long ago that when you killed God, you became a god yourself?

Christ, he could do *anything!*

He lived.

At first he didn't think of himself as being alive. He knew himself only as a dark silence. But that darkness quickly became something purple, something like purple fire, and he began to know himself as pain. That was his only existence, and there was no way to turn himself back into darkness.

The pain grew. It grew brighter and harsher, and just as he thought it might extinguish itself by its own intensity, it began to divide. It was in his head, in his lungs – it was not himself but something he contained.

Then he knew that he was alive. Alive somehow and somewhere. Alive in the underworld, alive in some hell, alive on earth. At Sabrehill. Alive, somehow alive.

But it hurt so much . . .

He breathed.

Breathing hurt his throat and made his lungs ache, but he did it, he couldn't help doing it. He was alive!

He heard the thump of his heart – steady and hard, like a defiant fist clenching again and again.

He opened his eyes. He saw nothing but dim wavering lights against a field of darkness.

He spoke. The word was *Binnie*, but it came out only as a rasping sigh.

He felt Zulie's tears on his face and heard her voice: 'Oh, praise Jesus . . . oh, Danbhalah and Momma Erzulie . . . Mary, Mary, Aïda Wédo . . .'

She had worked steadily through the night and a day and

397

into the night again, chanting her spells, breathing life into him, wetting his tongue with medicines of foxglove and herbs. First there had been the heartbeat, weak but steadily growing stronger. And now, after a full day and night, there were the open eyes and the whisper.

'Oh, praise Jesus . . . Don't you worry about Binnie now, Zagreus. Everything going to be all right . . .'

She made him sip the broths that would bring strength. When he had finished, he closed his eyes again, and his breathing was slow and deep and regular. She sat and watched him for a time. Then, leaving the sacred candles burning, she crept into bed with him. Throwing a protective arm over him, she sighed one last prayer and joined him in sleep.

The next morning before Zag had awakened, Miss Lucy came visiting, driven out to the quarters by Paris. The mud left by the rain still hadn't dried up, but she was wearing an old dress, and she kicked off her shoes and climbed down from the carriage without waiting for help.

'How is he?'

'Sleeping, ma'am.'

'Paris says you think he'll be all right.'

'Soon to tell, but I think so.'

'Thank God. There are stories that you've brought him back as a zombie.'

Zulie shrugged indifferently. 'Like I say, soon to tell.'

Miss Lucy looked worried. 'That kind of talk mustn't spread. I mean, apparently there was talk that Binnie was white, and look what happened. You know how most people feel about voodoo, Zulie.'

Zulie shrugged again, not giving a shit if she'd forgotten her nigger manners. Right now she didn't gave a damn about anything but Zagreus.

'May I see him, Zulie?'

'Go right ahead.' *You own him, don't you? Go look at your property.*

Zulie half-expected Miss Lucy to tramp her mud over the clean floor rather than asking for a rag to wipe her feet, but Miss Lucy simply wiped them on the hem of her old dress. There were times, Zulie reflected, when Miss Lucy sure hell wasn't much of a lady.

Miss Lucy looked at Zagreus with what appeared to be genuine concern. She touched his forehead gently. Maybe he *was* something more to her than just a piece of property. Maybe. She had been good about Binnie, but, then, that had got her a free nigger, hadn't it?

'You don't have to do anything but care for Zagreus until he's better, Zulie. You know that, don't you?'

'Yes, ma'm.'

Miss Lucy gave Zagreus a last look and left his bedside. She was almost out the door before Zulie could force herself to ask the fearful question: 'Ma'm, anybody heard anything about . . . about Binnie?'

Miss Lucy shook her head, and her anguish, like her concern, appeared genuine. 'Nothing. I wish I could hold out some hope, Zulie, that they'll let her go . . . but I'm afraid we must face the fact that . . . we'll probably never see her again . . . alive. When those terrible people do these things . . .'

'Yes, ma'am.'

Miss Lucy left. When Zulie turned back to Zagreus, she saw that he was weeping. He had not been asleep after all, and he had heard.

That evening, Zulie found Binnie.

She had fed Zagreus and put him back to sleep. There was still more than an hour of good light left, so she went out to look for the big yellow five-petaled flowers that she used for certain of her medicines. They grew on the roots of trees, so she stayed near the woods, and before long she found herself not far from the cabin where she and Zagreus had hidden Binnie. The body lay out in the open among the weeds of a fallow field.

399

Zulie stared at it, some fifty feet away, not wanting to believe in it, wanting to think that the fading light was playing a trick on her. For a moment she couldn't breathe. She blinked her eyes and shook her head, but the illusion, if that was what it was, would not vanish. She wanted to turn and run, but she forced herself to walk slowly toward it.

The body lay face down, naked, filthy with dirt – so dirt-encrusted that it was a wonder that Zulie had seen it. As she got closer, she saw that one eye was open, staring. But, she realized, there were no animals near it, no birds . . . as if death had come very recently.

Fearfully, she knelt by the body.

When Binnie sat up, Zulie almost screamed. But then the girl was in her arms, weeping hysterically, her body racked and torn by sobs.

'Oh, Zulie, help me!'

'I will, Binnie, I will!'

'They going to kill me!' her voice was weak and broken, as if Binnie had wept for hours.

'Oh, no, ain't nobody – '

'I ran and I ran, and I didn't have nothing to fight them with, not even my old hog-butchering knife. And they was always behind me, laughing the way they do!'

'Binnie, ain't nobody going to hurt you.' Zulie held the girl tightly, trying to soothe her, though her own heart was pounding with shock.

'They chased me, Zulie, they chased me 'round and 'round The Roost. And they was going to bury me out behind the pig pen with that man they killed.'

'Honey, what you talking about? You talking about them men that carried you away?'

'Didn't carry me away' Binnie sobbed. 'I got out of the barn and ran in the dark.'

'You wasn't carried away? And here all this time we been thinking – '

'I ran in the dark. But then I heard Mr Quinn and Mr Harpe behind me, and they was laughing and yelling. "Going to kill you, Bonnibelle. Going to cut you up and bury you in the mud behind the pig pen. Going to kill you, Bonnibelle," they kept yelling, "going to kill you!" Oh, Zulie, I am so scared!'

'Nothing to be scared of. Zulie's here now.'

'But when they catch me – '

'Ain't nobody going to catch you. Ain't nobody chasing you. Why, everybody been thinking you was dead!'

Zulie rocked and stroked the girl. 'Binnie, you mean to tell me you been running around out here two days and nights, gone plumb out of your head?'

'They going to kill me,' Binnie insisted, 'like they killed Zagreus. Going to kill us both 'cause we know who they are. Going to kill – '

'Honey child! Binnie!' Zulie shook the girl gently. 'Zagreus ain't dead. Zagreus going to be fine!'

At last she seemed to have penetrated the girl's panic. Binnie's sobs gradually subsided and she drew back from Zulie's arms to look at her face. Her expression was incredulous.

'Zagreus ain't dead?'

'No, Binnie. I took him to my house, and I'm fixing him up good as new.'

'You lying to me.'

'Now, why would I do that?'

'They hung him. I saw – '

'You saw right. But Paris cut him down, and *I* brung him back! Gave him breath and made his heart beat. And,' Zulie added with a certain pride, 'how many conjure women you know can say *that?*'

Binnie shook her head slowly, as if trying to absorb the truth. Her tears had ceased to flow.

'Zagreus really ain't dead?'

'No, ma'am, and he ain't no zombie, neither. Tale is

401

going 'round the quarters that he ain't going to be nothing but a zombie, won't be able to talk nor nothing, but it ain't so. Give him a few days rest, and he'll be his old self.'

'No!' Binnie's eyes, as large and hollow as they had been in her first days at Sabrehill, suddenly became cunning. 'Let everybody think he's a zombie! Let them think he can't tell nothing he knows! That way Mr Quinn and Mr Harpe won't kill him!'

She must still be out of her head, Zulie thought. 'Binnie, honey, you know there ain't no Mr Quinn nor Harpe at Sabrehill – '

'But there is! I saw them!'

Yes. Still plumb crazy, and there was no point in arguing with her. 'I tell you what. You come with me back to the quarters, and we'll get you nice and clean – '

'But I can't go back there!' The panic returned to Binnie's eyes. 'I go back there, they kill me!'

'Please, Binnie – '

'I can't, I can't!'

Zulie considered. She could easily force Binnie to go to the quarters with her. She would have no trouble in handling her physically, especially now that Binnie was so weak. But she wasn't certain that that would be the wise thing to do. It might just drive her further out of her head. No, it would be better, Zulie decided, to go easily and slowly and to rely on persuasion.

She shrugged, feigning indifference. 'All right, ain't going to force you. But you sure a mess, Binnie. Going to have to clean you up somehow. Why don't I just take you to a stream, and while you start washing, I can get some soap and clothes and food for you. And then we can talk.'

The panic again faded from Binnie's eyes, and she smiled. She was agreeable. Zulie helped her to her feet and walked her, almost staggering, toward the stream. By the time they had reached it and found a good place for the girl to bathe, she seemed almost normal.

'I don't know what I'd done, you hadn't found me, Zulie.'

'Well, I did, so never mind.'

'I hardly even knowed I was naked till you come. All I could think about was Mr Quinn and Mr Harpe.' She giggled. 'Now I feel silly.'

'Don't you worry, ain't nobody going to see you. It's just like we was going swimming.'

Binnie stepped into the water. 'You know something, Zulie, you really did convince me that Mr Ash wasn't Mr Quinn. When Zagreus and me left your house the other day, I knew you just had to be right. They couldn't possibly be the same.'

'Why, course not.'

'But they are, though.'

The words caused an odd, numb feeling in Zulie's stomach; they weren't what she wanted to hear. And she remembered the strange fright she had felt as Zagreus and Binnie had left her house on the previous Sunday.

'Now, Binnie, honey, we ain't back to that!'

'You had me sure I was wrong. But when I saw Mr Harpe with those men that night then I knew I was right. Mr Ash and Mr Quinn was the same after all.'

'But they couldn't be!'

'They are, though. Zulie, if it was only Mr Ash, I could be dead wrong. But now I seen Mr Harpe as well. *Both* of them together in the barn.' Binnie shook her head. 'I been doing a lot of thinking out here, and it just don't make sense no more that Mr Ash ain't Mr Quinn. It had to been him that got Mr Harpe and them other men to come after Zagreus and me.'

'But Mr Ash fought to save you. He even shot a man. And how could you know your Mr Harpe when there wasn't much light and they all was wearing masks?'

'Oh, I knowed those eyes right off. And when I pulled down the mask and saw that long yellow mustache of his –'

'But that was the man Mr Ash killed.'

Binnie looked around at Zulie. She seemed to be pondering the matter, and after a moment, she nodded. 'Reckon he would do that. If he'd get Mr Harpe to kill me and Zag to shut us up, reckon he sure wouldn't mind killing Mr Harpe for the same reason. Wonder if one day he'll kill Dora Keegan just to be sure her mouth is shut for good, too. Wouldn't surprise me at all.'

Binnie looked as weak as a faded flower, and her voice was like dry leaves. But she sounded so reasonable, so sane, now. It was impossible to believe that she was still out of her head.

And suddenly Zulie knew that what she had said just possibly could be true. It could possibly be that Mr Ash was also somebody known as Mr Quinn.

She had to think about it. She didn't want to, but she had to.

'I'll go get you some clothes and some food,' she said. 'Don't go away from right here. I be back soon as I can.'

'And can you bring me a blanket? So's I have something to sleep on tonight?'

Zulie agreed to bring a blanket. She started back toward the quarters.

Yes, Mr Ash *could* be Mr Quinn. And if he were, he surely had a hand in Zagreus's hanging.

Zulie thought of the elm tree roots which only that day she had sprinkled with flour and cornmeal. She thought of the candles she had lit and the gifts she had promised to Momma Brigitte. She thought of the curses she had made and the sacrifices she had promised.

In return for vengeance.

When he awakened this time, the ache in his head was gone, and he was painfully hungry. He also felt extraordinarily weak, and he sensed that his voice was still a husky whisper. Aside from that, he was almost normal.

His first thought was of Binnie. Zulie had told him that she had been carried away. Had they heard anything, anything at all about her? Without her, living hardly seemed worthwhile, and they might just as well have left him hanging there.

The light and the sound from outside told him that the day was just getting under way. Orion and Paris came in, laughing, determinedly cheerful, trying to get a smile from him.

'All kinds things happening, Zag. Ain't that right, Paris?'

'Yeah, story going 'round that Miss Lucy going marry Mr Ash.'

'Ain't no story, Paris. Leila told me, so it *got* to be true.'

'I guess that burn old Zulie's ass!'

'Leila don't look none too happy neither. Mr Ash, reckon he been cheating on Miss Lucy with Zulie – '

'And on Zulie with Leila! *Haw!*'

Zag hardly heard what they said. He wanted to hear only about Binnie, but when he asked about her, they shook their heads – no, they had heard nothing – and moved on to other, less painful subjects.

Zulie arrived and shooed the younger brothers out. Zagreus needed his rest, she said, and in any case it was time for them to go to work. Zag noticed that her face was drawn and her eyes were puffy, as if she had spent a sleepless night.

'Glad you're awake,' she said, as she came to him and sat on the bed. 'Got news for you, good news.'

But she hardly looked as if it were good.

'What is it, Zulie? Is it Binnie – '

'She's alive.' Zag tried to sit up, but Zulie shoved him down again. 'She's alive, and she's all right. They didn't kill her or rape her or do nothing to her. She got away from them.'

All he could do was think stupidly, *Well, what's wrong,*

then? Because something had to be wrong. Such good news had to be impossible.

Zulie read his face. 'It's true, Zagreus. Binnie is all right. She ran out of the barn that night and they never found her.'

'Where is she now?'

'Out at that cabin where we first took her. I found her near there last evening. I'd told you, but you was asleep.'

'But why ain't she here, Zulie?'

'Oh, she was crazy out of her head for a day or two, and I think maybe she still is a little. Says for now I ain't to tell nobody but you she's all right. Says she going to stay out there till she can talk to you about what to do.'

Zag was confused. Binnie should be here, in triumph. Something was being held back.

'But why, Zulie? Why she do that?'

Zulie, anything but happy, avoided his eyes. ''Cause she's scared still. 'Cause she got this crazy notion again about Mr Ash being Mr Quinn. Or . . . Zag . . .'

'Yes?'

'Maybe it ain't so crazy.'

Zag absorbed the statement. If Zulie were beginning to believe . . .

He tried to sit up again, tried to push Zulie off of the bed. 'Zulie, I got to go to her!'

'No! She's all right out there. You rest a day or two, and then – '

'Get me my clothes.'

But when his feet were on the floor, he found himself to be even weaker than he had thought.

'Let me get you some breakfast,' Zulie said, 'and afterwards I'll go get your clothes, and we'll see how you feel.'

He agreed. But after breakfast, while waiting for his clothes, he fell into a profound sleep, and when he awakened in the late afternoon, his conversation with Zulie seemed dreamlike.

But he had to believe that Binnie was truly all right and out at the cabin waiting for him.

He got out of bed. Again he was ravenously hungry, and he found some dried meat and corn cakes which he washed down with warm water. He was still weak, but his weakness now seemed largely to be caused by his confinement to bed, and his legs stopped shaking as he moved about on them.

Zulie had fetched his clothes, and he dressed. Then after a very necessary side trip, he set out for the cabin.

She wasn't there.

The place looked undisturbed. The dust was thick, and the spiders crawled in every corner. The feeling returned that his conversation with Zulie that morning had been a dream. The news had been too good to be true. Binnie was gone, and he would never see her again . . .

'Zagreus!'

He turned from the cabin door and looked toward the woods. She was coming out from under the trees.

He didn't know what he had expected. She looked thin, and her eyes were big, but her hair was like black silk, and her face glowed. She was beautiful.

'Oh, Zagreus!'

He ran to her, gathered her up in his arms, lifted her off of her feet. His strength seemed to be coming back to him in great tides.

'Didn't think you'd come to me so soon, you darling,' she said, laughing. 'From what Zulie told me – '

'Couldn't nothing keep me away from you!'

She led him into the woods to a clearing where she had spread her blankets. Why should she sleep with those old spiders, she explained, when it was so much nicer to sleep out under the clear night sky. 'But you shoulda seen me this time yesterday! I was dirty and naked and still half out of my mind – '

'My poor baby!'

' – and I was so hungry I thought I'd die, and my head hurt so! But soon as Zulie come, I begun to feel better. And she made me clean up, and brought me food – brought me a big pot of soup, I don't know how she stole it!'

They fell onto the blankets, embraced, kissed, rolled about together; forgot Sabrehill and all of its people; celebrated being alive and being together again. He wanted almost at once to take her, wanted gently, tenderly, to make that affirmation of life and love, but he knew it was too soon. She was still too hurt and weak; she had been through too much.

And yet there came a moment when her eyes suddenly went hazy, and she reached for him.

'No,' he said.

'Yes.'

'Binnie, you don't have to – you ain't ready – '

'*Yes!*'

'But – '

She smiled.

And so for a timeless time they lay facing each other, still in their clothes, locked in their embrace. The forest around them was quiet, disturbed only by an occasional breeze. For long moments he might have thought she was asleep . . . but for a tremulous smile, a small flurry of movement, a happy sigh.

We really here, Zag thought. *We got each other.*

The affirmation was made.

Zag lay on his back, his clothes still open, the lowering sun warming his body and the breeze that rustled through the forest cooling it. Binnie sat beside him, running an old near-toothless comb through her hair. He was half asleep and almost mindless. Insofar as he thought at all, he thought he had never been happier, not even on the afternoon that he and Binnie had consummated their union.

But his mind, like the breeze, stirred, rising in little gusts: Mr Ash . . . Mr Jeppson . . . Zulie . . . Miss Lucy . . . And he found his eyes opening.

He watched Binnie for a time. Her eyes met his, and she smiled.

'Thought you were asleep.'

'Almost.'

'My, don't you look comfortable.' She ran a hand lightly up and down the front of his body, and he lay perfectly still, unwilling to interrupt the pleasure and the peace of the moment.

But he knew he had to say it: 'Binnie, we got to decide what to do.'

'I know.'

'You can't go on living out here in the woods forever. You got to come back in with me.'

Worry came into her eyes, and she stopped stroking him. 'Zag, Mr Jeppson and them others – they know they didn't kill me. Didn't hardly get a chance to do nothing to me but whip me a little. What you reckon they going to do about us now?'

'I don't know. Guess they know you supposed to be missing. Maybe they figure you run away.'

'But when they find out I didn't – '

'Miss Lucy ain't going to admit you ain't black. Like Jebediah said that night we first talked to her, she can always get papers to *prove* you're black. That'll get people around here after Mr Jeppson real good. Ain't nobody want him killing off their property.'

Binnie didn't look convinced that they were safe from Mr Jeppson, and Zag hardly blamed her. He didn't feel safe himself. But he wanted to look for the happier possibilities.

'And what about Mr Quinn?' Binnie asked. 'What's he going to do when he finds out that I'm still alive and you ain't no zombie? What's he going to do about us, Zagreus?'

Zag shook his head. 'Don't reckon it's me he cares about

so much as you. You the one we got to worry about, Binnie.'

'He been here a whole month now. If we could just keep me hidden till he goes away . . .'

Zag remembered the one piece of news he had failed to tell her. 'Don't look like he's going away. Leastwise, not for good. Him and Miss Lucy, they planning to get married.'

Binnie was instantly on her knees, her eyes bigger than ever. 'But they can't do that!'

'Going to.'

'They can't! Where you ever get such an idea?'

'Leila told Paris. And Leila would know, if anyone know at all.'

'But Miss Lucy wouldn't never marry that man, she knew what he was!'

'Reckon not.'

Binnie sat back again. She looked away from Zag, and her fingers interwove and twisted. She was coming to a decision, Zag knew, the only decision possible.

'Zagreus, we can't let that happen to Miss Lucy. Not after all she done for us.'

'What you figure to do?'

'Just going to have to go to Miss Lucy and tell her what I know about Mr Quinn.'

'How you going to make her believe you?'

'I'll make her believe somehow. I know Mr Quinn and Mr Harpe too good not to. And I got no reason to lie.'

Zag said what had to be said: 'Binnie, you got to realize, maybe you best just keep quiet. You talk about Mr Ash, he's going to talk about you. And maybe get us both hung.'

The fingers twisted together more violently. Then slowly they ceased to twist, and they separated.

'It ain't really what I want to do, Zagreus,' she said. 'Truth is, I just want to run and hide, like I been doing all my life. But I just can't do tnat now. Not and let something bad happen to Miss Lucy. Besides, I got a feeling that if I stop running now I might never have to again.' She smiled. 'Course, I won't do nothing you don't want me to, but I hope you'll tell me it's all right – and the right thing to do.'

What had happened to the terrified little gal he had carried away from The Roost, Zag wondered. Little Bonnibelle, so afraid for her life. She would never have dreamed of warning Miss Lucy. But life at Sabrehill had somehow changed Binnie, as had her loyalty to Miss Lucy and to himself.

'It's all right, Binnie,' he said, 'and the right thing to do.'

She put her hand back on his chest and began stroking him again. 'I don't think there's nothing to worry about, Zagreus. Least, I keep telling myself that. We just got to have trust in Miss Lucy. She helped us before, 'cause she got a good heart. Now we got to help her. And she ain't going to let nothing hurt us, she going to help us again.'

Binnie lay down, sliding into his arms, and began kissing him. 'Now, ain't that so, Zagreus?'

Zag hoped to God that was so.

2

When they started back in, the sun was just beginning to streak the western sky with crimsons and golds, while overhead it was still deep blue with strands of white. A peace seemed to have settled over the Sabrehill lands, a silence broken only by an occasional song bird or the distant cry of a field hand.

Zag carried Binnie's blankets and the few other things Zulie had brought to her; Binnie clung to Zag's arm. They traveled in a roundabout way, staying close to the woods and avoiding those hands who were still in the fields. They had considered waiting and coming in after dark, but had decided against it; Binnie was eager to get to Miss Lucy as soon as possible. Still, until they had seen Miss Lucy, it seemed wise to avoid spreading the word that Binnie was still alive.

They made it to the outlying end of the east service lane without difficulty, and Zag remembered how they had come this way five weeks ago. Had it really been such a short time? Now, as then, the lane appeared to be deserted, though Saul's roaring laughter could be heard coming all the way from the blacksmith's shop. Binnie giggled and got behind Zag, as if to hide.

They made it to the coach house without being seen. Not that it would have been such a calamity if they had been, Zag thought, but it was a good sign that things were working out so well.

Binnie led the way up the stairs and through the trap door. It seemed odd to think that this was the first time either of them had seen the room since they had been so brutally expelled from it. Zag, expecting to see reminders of that terrible night, felt sick as he stepped up through the trapdoor, but there was no sign of what had happened. The bed was smoothly made; the muddy boot prints had been washed from the floor. All was neat and in order. 'Thank you, Zulie,' Zag said aloud.

Binnie danced through the room. She turned and grinned at Zag. 'Welcome home. Welcome to the home of Zagreus and Albinia Sabrehill.'

No, there was no reminder of that night in this room. It was safe now, safer than it had ever been before. Binnie was right: their worry now was not for themselves but for Miss Lucy. Somehow they had to help her. But meanwhile . . .

He reached for Binnie. 'Come here, woman . . .'

A few minutes later there was a call from the stairs: 'Zag? Binnie?'

It was Zulie, and Zag told her to come on up. The moment her head appeared above the stairs, he saw that she looked even worse than she had that morning; in fact, she looked deathly ill. In a single day, she seemed to have aged twenty years. It wasn't only Miss Lucy who needed help, he realized; there was also Zulie.

'Soon's I saw you was gone,' she said, coming the rest of the way into the room. 'I know you gone out after her. You ought to rested another day.'

'I'm all right, Zulie,' he assured her. 'All was wrong with me was I got choked a little.'

'You got hung dead, and I brung you back!'

He found it a little hard to believe that he had really been dead, but who could say for sure? In any case, he might not have survived if it had not been for Zulie.

'You did,' he said gravely. 'And I thank you. I owe you forever.'

'So do I,' Binnie said. 'We both owe you, Zulie.'

'You don't owe me nothing. Somebody sure do, but it

413

ain't none of you. What I want to know is, what you aim to do now.'

'Tell Miss Lucy,' Zag said. He spoke gently and wished he didn't have to speak at all. He had some idea of what his sister was going through.

'Tell her about . . . Mr Ash?'

'This morning you said yourself that maybe Binnie's "crazy notion" ain't so crazy.'

'But might be she is wrong! She could be wrong!'

'I wish I was,' Binnie said. 'For all of us, I sure wish I was.'

Zulie's voice rose. 'And if she is wrong, you both going to be in deep trouble! Calling Mr Ash something like that. He ain't going to like that, Zag!'

'And if Binnie is right,' Zag said, speaking distinctly, 'and we don't tell Miss Lucy, we are *all* going to be in deep trouble. Zulie, we *got* to tell Miss Lucy, we *got* to. We got to do it right soon, sometime when Mr Ash ain't around, so's he won't be warned. We got to do it – '

'All right. Mr Ash ain't around right now. Went into town to talk to some people. Said he was going have supper with the preacher and talk about the wedding. Minute ago, Miss Lucy was in the office.'

Zag looked at Binnie. She nodded.

'Then we go there right now, Zulie.'

Zulie looked defeated. 'I go with you.'

Zag led the way back down the stairs. Out in the lane, Saul's laughter still boomed, and there was a clatter from the carpenter shop. It seemed astonishing to Zag that no one noticed Binnie and came charging toward her to see if it were really her. Across the courtyard, he saw as they emerged from the head of the lane, a small group – Vidette, Ettalee, Rameses – had gathered at the kitchen house door, but no one so much as looked around at them. Sabrehill was quiet and at peace.

Leila saw them.

414

She was coming out of the office doorway, headed for the big house. Her face went utterly blank as they approached her. She stood frozen for a few seconds, then went back into the office.

She was in the doorway when they got there.

'We want to see Miss Lucy,' Zag said.

'Yeah,' Leila said, 'I guess so.'

The sky was violent with crimson light as the sun sank lower, throwing its blinding rays through the office windows. Lucy sat at a battered old desk, listening to the girl's voice, which sounded so distant, so remote.

It's all too much for me, she thought; *a blow too many. I've gone numb, I can no longer feel . . .*

But, of course, what Albinia was saying could not possibly be true. By her own admission, the poor child had been out of her mind, or half out of it, since the lynch mob had come, and this was all a fantasy, a nightmare, a wild dream. Ash was Ash and nobody else, and perhaps there had never even been a Quinn.

But she knew there had been. She knew in spite of herself that every unbelievable word was true.

The girl was so certain:

'I *know* it's him. Miss Lucy, ma'am. There just ain't no way I could be wrong. I even got the money he give me, and a pin – Zagreus, we got to show Miss Lucy that pin – I *know* who give it to me. Miss Lucy, when a man done to you what he done to me, you don't forget him. You can put him out of your mind, but you can't never forget, no matter how hard you try. It's *him!*'

No, when a man did certain things to you, you didn't forget him. Lucy knew, from painful experience. Still, there were such things as lookalikes and coincidence.

'Albinia, you said yourself that at first you weren't certain.'

'I *didn't want* it to be him! I don't want it to be him even

415

now. I don't want to think it can possibly be. But when I saw Mr Harpe! Ma'am, I knew it had to be Mr Quinn. It had to be the two of them together, it couldn't be one and not the other.'

Yes, there was the matter of Mr Harpe. Albinia claimed to recognize not just one man but both. And she was right – if Ash were Quinn, he might very well prefer to have Mr Harpe dead.

As well as Albinia – or, rather, Bonnibelle. Yes, he would most certainly prefer to have Bonnibelle dead.

There was no solid evidence, and yet in an odd way it all hung together. Lucy didn't believe any of it, not a word of it – and yet she couldn't help believing.

No more, she thought. *Oh, please, no more of this.*

But the girl was still talking, talking on and on, repeating herself, pleading to be believed. Lucy hardly heard her. Increasingly, the light in the room was almost blinding, but she saw Zagreus's fingers clutching anxiously at Albinia's shoulder. Zulie looked sick, and Leila gazed steadily at Albinia with hard, angry eyes.

'. . . and when they got drunk, the things they bragged about! robbing travelers and looting plantations! We thought it was just talk at first, 'cause lots of men who come to The Roost like to talk rough and brag. But none of them was like Mr Harpe and Mr Quinn . . .'

Quinn. He had always preferred to be called that. Asher Quinlan McCloud. She had heard that thieves often took aliases similar to their real names, though she had never understood why. It struck her as a stupid thing to do. But perhaps there was a deep fear of losing one's real identity, of becoming lost in some godless limbo of crime.

'. . . and I remember the night they killed that man from Charleston. I heard the screaming . . . and later I watched in the dark while they buried him . . . and he's still there, ma'am, out there buried in the mud . . .'

Dear God, I can't take any more. The child is insane. I

416

shall tell Ash, and he will give the lie to it all, he will tell me what to do . . .

And all the time she was rapidly calculating, reviewing all the possibilities. How could she protect the girl? How could she protect Sabrehill? She could do little if her neighbors turned against her, therefore she must make them her allies. Put them on their honor as aristocrats and take them into her confidence – to a certain extent. Stay as close to the truth as possible in dealing with them, but if necessary, lie, and lie like hell.

What else? Get papers for Albinia, either as a slave or as a freed person of color? They might or might not be useful or necessary. In any case, Paul could be helpful with that.

The murder of Lacy Keegan? That was easy – if it had to come out, put it on Ash. He had killed the merchant at The Roost and God alone knew how many others. What was one more murder on his murderous head?

There were ways to handle this, damn it. A woman always had to find ways in this world.

'Leila,' she said, 'get Irish . . . Paris . . . somebody. I think we had best ask Mr Paul to come as quickly as possible. And after that, we may want to send for Mr Buckridge and Major Kimbrough too. We may need their help.'

There were ways . . .

But of course matters did not work out as smoothly as she had hoped; they seldom did. She had wanted to speak to Paul alone first, but evidently Mr Buckridge had been visiting him when Irish had arrived, for the two men came to Sabrehill together. Well, she thought, as she watched them approach, she would just have to find a way to speak to Paul alone later. Meanwhile, she would manage.

She met with them in the library. Leila escorted them in and left at once.

'Irish made it sound quite urgent, Lucy,' Paul said,

417

looking concerned, 'said you wanted to see me without delay.'

'Perhaps I shouldn't be here,' Mr Buckridge said. 'I'll just step outside – '

'No, no, I'm glad you came, Mr Buckridge.' It was best to give the appearance of complete candor. 'I had planned to talk with you anyway as soon as I had consulted with Paul. You see, one of my people has told me a most incredible story. I can hardly believe it, but I feel that as my closest friends and neighbors you should know about it. And please remember that I am speaking to you in the strictest confidence . . .'

She told no more than she had to, and she twisted the truth where it seemed advisable. Let them think, at least for now, that Albinia was a woman of color in her employ; don't confuse Mr Buckridge with the knowledge that she was white. Let Albinia be the frightened and fleeing witness to the murder of an innkeeper. She, Lucy, had innocently taken her in . . . She saw the sceptical light come into Paul's deep-set eyes, but he was wise enough to keep his questions for later.

'You're telling us,' Mr Buckridge said, 'that the man you thought was your cousin is an ordinary thief and murderer?'

'Oh, I have no doubt that he is my cousin. And I have every hope that Albinia is wrong about Asher. But until we know for certain that he's not this – this Mr Quinn, as he called himself – '

'Quinn,' Mr Buckridge said. 'I remember now. That big buck said, "Got it all, Mr Quinn." Quinn seemed to be the leader, and somehow I wasn't sure he was really a nigger.'

Lucy shook her head. 'With all respect, Mr Buckridge, you never once mentioned that name until you heard me say it. And neither you nor Royal recognized him – '

'Nevertheless, I'm prepared to swear on my honor that the man was called Quinn.'

'If you're right, sir,' Paul said, 'it may be that we've accounted for all three of them men who raided and burned your house.'

'I think we have,' Mr Buckridge agreed. 'We found one dead with my Abby. Mr Asher McCloud killed a man who was probably the second, even if he wasn't a nigger. And that leaves just Mr Quinn.'

'Quinlan,' Paul Devereau said. 'Asher Quinlan McCloud. Who preferred to be called Quinn.'

'It's all . . . all so . . . terribly circumstantial,' Lucy said faintly.

'Lucy, many a man has been hung on evidence considerably more circumstantial than this. But if we're wrong, Asher shouldn't find it difficult to clear himself. And if we're right, we may very well find other witnesses who'll place him at The Roost.'

'No need to wait for other witnesses,' Buckridge said. 'We'll know tonight. And if we're right . . .' He turned terrible eyes on Lucy, the eyes of some Old Testament prophet who sought vengeance in the name of the Lord. 'If we're right, he's mine, Miss Lucy. Mine!'

It was then that the numbness started to fade away and the pain began.

He thought of himself now as 'the master of Sabrehill.' There was no reason not to; he soon would be. The word would quickly spread that he was marrying Miss Lucy, and with Miss Lucy went the plantation. Of course, Paul Devereau would try to curtail his power there, but Devereau be damned. It seemed to Ash that the people in the streets of Riverboro that afternoon were already beginning to defer to him in a new way – not merely as a visiting gentleman but as a new power in the community.

Mr Asher McCloud, master of Sabrehill.

Not since that afternoon years before when he had met

Henry Brandon on a lonely riverbank had he had such a sense of power.

Now, if only he would hear some news of the girl, a guarantee that she was really dead. All he needed was a word or two, a snicker, a knowing glance. If there had been a place like The Roost nearby, one which he could have visited anonymously, he would have found out fast enough. But he was Mr McCloud now, and he had to be careful what he said and who he spoke to.

He ran across McClintock, the planter, in a tavern.

'You heard what happened at Sabrehill?'

'Yeah, terrible thing. But them trash, they hear a rumor that a wench is white and living with a nigger, it's just an excuse to go kill somebody.'

'Still haven't heard about anyone finding the wench.'

'You might never, Mr McCloud. You can just figure that you're out one dead nigger.

He was out one dead nigger. Not Miss Lucy; *he* was.

But he still didn't have the confirmation he was looking for.

It was the parson who gave it to him. Ash had gone to the parsonage to meet the man, with a view to the wedding and his future membership in the local church, and to have dinner with him.

'I can give you no hope, sir. Those sinners who would carry off a poor woman, white or Negro, in such a manner are very unlikely to release her alive. Off hand, I know of no case in which it has happened in this vicinity. Moreover, less than an hour ago I spoke to a patrolman who late this afternoon found some fresh bones. They were animal-gnawed and apparently human. Now, of course they may have belonged to some other poor stray soul who died on the road, or even to an animal. But . . .' The parson shrugged and left the matter to heaven. 'I happen to know that you will be hearing from the authorities shortly.'

It was finished, then. Bonnibelle was finished. The parson was saying something about the souls of niggers, and Ash nearly burst out laughing. In his own way, the man was just like Keegan – always looking back over his shoulder to see if God were watching.

The dinner was good, and the brandy that followed was better. The parson presented Ash with an excellent seegar, together with some current gossip. *The beginning of my new life*, Ash thought. The life of a rich and respected South Carolina planter. And if the parson were a bit of a bore, well, that was merely a penance for the sins of Ash's youth.

The sun was well down when he returned to Sabrehill, but he was conscious of *his* fields stretching out in the darkness on each side of the road. Yes, his fields, his stretch of the river, his mansion up ahead. He'd rid himself of the old place up in Virginia as soon as possible and move down here for good. To his plantation, his mistress, his newly-won riches.

The gate, as usual, was open, the gate house unoccupied. He turned off the through-road and started up the gentle rise that led to the courtyard and the mansion. Lights were burning in the mansion, and as he got closer, he saw that the courtyard, too, was lit up, as if there were guests. But he saw no horses, no carriages. It struck him as slightly odd but nothing more.

He turned into the east lane, and Paris was immediately before him. He dismounted.

'Take care of my horse, boy, and do it right.'

'Yes, sir, Mr Ash, sir. Yes, sir.'

Paris trotted off down the lane, and Ash walked toward the mansion. Cheney, the head driver – big scarred old bull of a man – wandered by, puffing on his pipe, and muttered his 'evening, sir.' Ash hadn't noticed him in the courtyard before.

The passage was open, light burning within. When Ash

421

entered, he found Leila standing there, arms crossed over her chest, as if she had been waiting for him. The little bitch still hadn't learned any manners. She nodded her head toward the door that led to the dining room and the library, and said, curtly, 'Miss Lucy is waiting for you . . . sir.'

So something was happening.

Ash shrugged. Whatever it was, he could handle it.

He heard Leila following him as he went through the dining room. When he entered the library, Paul Devereau and Owen Buckridge were already on their feet facing him, and he knew, as a wary bandit knows, that each had a pistol under his coat. He saw at once that Lucy had been weeping.

'Ashley, there is something we would like you to clear up. I'm sure it's just a misunderstanding, an odd set of circumstances – '

Even then he didn't really know. An odd numb feeling was creeping over him, a feeling of shock, yet he didn't really know.

He didn't really know until the girl walked in through the door on the other side of the room.

Everything seemed to be happening so slowly. The numb, shocked feeling was still growing, and Lucy was still saying the words: '. . . an odd set of circumstances – '

And there was the girl, with Zagreus standing behind her.

He had that familiar feeling of utter futility, the feeling that all of his life he had been toyed with by gods he would never begin to understand. All of his control was an illusion, had always been an illusion. He was the mouse that some great cat let run free – but only for the moment.

Now that he had everything he wanted – it was being snatched away from him.

And there was not a damn thing in the world that he could do about it.

No!

He might have screamed the syllable. He did not. He smiled. He dipped his hand into his pocket as casually as he might have done for a seegar. His smile stretched, but his anger was welling up and burning away his feeling of impotence.

They couldn't do this to him. Never. Not to Asher McCloud, not to Quinn. Not without paying.

Draw, you bastards!

The words were still dying on Lucy's lips, the girl was hardly into the room. Neither Devereau nor Buckridge had yet made a move toward a gun.

I can take them, I can take them!

They were reaching then, as they saw the little two-shot pistol appear, but it was too late. The gun was made for a much closer shot, but he could take them, even at this range.

He wasted time, moving the pistol from one target to the other and then back again: Devereau, Buckridge, Devereau. Yes, first Devereau and then Buckridge. Then, with them out of the way, he could do any damn thing he pleased. Burn Sabrehill if he wished.

No.

Not Devereau, not Buckridge.

The pistol barrels moved away from Devereau again and settled on the girl.

He saw her eyes widening with horror. Good. The damn little bitch. So she hadn't died yet. But she would. She had crossed him, she had cost him his winnings, and for that she had to pay. Cross Quinn – you pay.

He was in no hurry now. He was in complete control again. He even hesitated a fraction of a second to watch her eyes widen further and the horror in them grow.

Then he pulled the trigger.

After that, everything began happening fast again. He saw the bullet hit, saw it knock the girl back into the stable

423

boy's arms. Guns were coming out, but Ash saved his second bullet. He turned to find Leila behind him, a knife in her hand, but he brushed it aside and jammed his pistol into her belly so hard she fell gagging to the floor.

He was out the doorway, out through the dining room and into the passage. Cheney came charging through the door: now Ash knew what the driver had been doing in the courtyard. He would have preferred to save his shot, but there was no time. He pulled the trigger and sent Cheney reeling to one side of the door, then ran past him.

He had a choice: run for the guest house, where he had two loaded pistols, or run for the stable, where his horse was no doubt still saddled. There were two guns behind him, and a third coming toward the courtyard: Major Kimbrough, at a gallop, drawn by the shots.

Ash ran toward the east service lane and the stable.

He ran like hell. He saw Paris and the horse, shadows, still in the lane ahead of him: that little time had passed since his arrival that evening. He ran, and a ball burned over his right shoulder almost deafening him.

Paris ahead of him. Turning. Eyes big in the night, as big as the girl's. Cries behind him: 'Stop him! Boy, don't give him that horse!'

'No, sir, Mr Ash. No, sir, I can't – '

He still had the pistol in his hand, but it hardly occurred to him that that was what the boy feared. Wrapping his fist around it, he brought the weighted knuckles up into the boy's face and sent him sprawling.

Then he was on the horse.

'*Stop him!*'

He didn't make it three feet. He didn't even show his back to the bastards. He hadn't even turned the horse when a ball took its guts out, and it went down screaming.

He was lucky it didn't pin his leg. He leapt from the saddle just in time, and he threw himself down the lane as another shot crashed by him.

Darkness was ahead. Darkness and cover.

And he was running, running, running . . .

When the ball knocked Binnie back into his arms, it was as if it had gone through his own heart. There was a heavy blow and a moment of pain, and the world turned blood red, fading to black. As it cleared again, he found himself on his knees, still holding Binnie. Somewhere, distantly, a pistol exploded again.

He looked into Binnie's eyes. They were blank and staring, and for a moment he thought she was dead.

But she moaned.

Perhaps someone told him what to do, perhaps Zulie, who stood in the hallway. He didn't know. He knew only that he was standing again, standing and lifting Binnie in his arms, and carrying her through the hallway to the downstairs bed chamber.

Why did I tell her it was all right to go to Miss Lucy? he thought. *Why did I tell her it was the right thing to do? All I done was get her killed!*

Miss Lucy was in the room with them, he saw, her eyes wild and her fists pressed to her mouth as if to hold in screams. Leila was shaking her, slapping her, speaking harsh, angry words to her. Zag didn't know what she was saying and didn't care. The only thing that mattered was the girl in his arms. Leila snapped a few words at Zulie, and led Miss Lucy from the room.

'On the bed,' Zulie said. 'Put her on the bed.'

Zag laid Binnie down gently, carefully. The eyes were still staring, but now the lashes quivered.

'Zagreus . . . he . . . killed me . . . didn't he?' The voice was weak. She seemed hardly to have the strength to express her fear.

'No, Binnie. No, he didn't – '

'Always scared . . . one day he'd . . . kill me . . . bury me . . . like that man from Charleston . . . out in the mud . . .'

425

'No!'

Her eyes closed slowly. Her face beneath its sun-bronze was waxen. It seemed to Zag that he could see her breathing slowly come to a halt.

'Zulie, I think she dead!'

Zulie grabbed Binnie's forearm and desperately felt up and down her wrist. 'I don't know. Can't hardly feel nothing, but . . .'

'Help her!'

Zulie didn't look at him, perhaps didn't even hear him. She put Binnie's forearm down, and she seemed to be gazing beyond the girl to something else. The illness, the weariness, left her face. The face was still old, older than ever, but now it was bitter and angry.

'He done it,' she said. 'He done it to you. And he done it to her. Tried to kill you both. All the time, him pleasuring with me in his bed, and he brought them Jeppson people down on us and got my brother hung . . .'

'Make her live, Zulie. You brung me back – bring her back too.'

'I'll try.'

Zulie left the room for a moment, yelled for Irish, and told him what she wanted brought to her: hot water, clean rags, certain medicines of her own devising. She returned to the bed chamber and tore Binnie's dress open. The wound was so small it hardly looked deadly, but it seemed to Zag that the ball must be in Binnie's heart or close to it. He could hardly believe that she was still alive, but she *had* to be. Zulie had to *make* her alive.

'Least she ain't bleeding at her mouth. Ain't choking none on her blood. But I still can't find hardly no heart nor breathing . . .'

What for'd he have to do it?, Zag asked himself miserably. *Why? Why'd Mr Ash have to do such a thing?*

Because – what had it gained him? And therefore, why?

426

But the question was hardly necessary, because he knew the answer, the oh-so-obvious answer, at once.

Mr Ash was Mr Quinn.

'. . . *make me do things to them that I don't want to tell you about . . . and they hurt me, Zagreus. I can't tell you how they hurt me. And all I could do was lie there and try not to scream, 'cause if I screamed, they hurt me all the more –* '

And Mr Quinn had been the meanest of them all.

That was the reason. It was all the reason he had needed. He could have shot Mr Devereau and Mr Buckridge and thus made his escape more likely. But Binnie – no, Bonnibelle – Bonnibelle had been there. And Bonnibelle had brought him bad luck. So . . .

He had grinned as if to say: '*One last time, Bonnibelle!*'

And he had shot her.

Had moved that little pistol through the lamp light, brought it to bear on Binnie, and squeezed the trigger. And him all the time grinning. Still grinning while Binnie fell back into Zag's arms.

He got to pay.

'What?'

'I said, he got to pay.'

Zulie looked at him. Nodded.

'He got to pay for all of it, Zulie. *All* of it!'

For every last thing he had ever done to Binnie. For every single time he had laid a hand on her. He had to pay.

'Then, you make him pay, Zagreus.'

Zag moved closer to the bed. He leaned over Binnie and saw no sign of life.

'She dying, ain't she?'

Zulie nodded.

'You can't bring her back?'

'I try, Zagreus, I do everything I can!'

But that wasn't enough, not this time, not nearly. Yet

427

there had to be a way to save Binnie, and somehow Zag knew what it was.

'She ain't going to die,' he said. 'Somebody else going to die. Somebody else instead.' It was a vow. It was as if Zulie's gods had whispered to him, and he had struck a bargain with them. 'Somebody else, not her.'

That was the way to save Binnie: exact full payment, a life for a life. Zag knew it in his bones.

'You take care of her,' he said. 'I got to go now.'

'I come help you when I can.'

'You just take care of her.'

Zag went out into the passage. Lights still burned, but the house was as silent as if it were deserted. On the floor near the courtyard door, he found a smear of blood. Looking out the doorway, he saw activity in the kitchen house, and he hurried toward it.

There he found Cheney, shirtless, sitting on a chair while Momma Lucinda cleaned and bandaged his wound. That accounted for the second shot.

'He get you bad?' Zag asked.

'Shit, that little pea-shooter? Bounce off my ribs like nothing at all. Sure smart like hell, though. I recollect a time when a old wasp – '

'Where'd he go?'

'East. Headed east out the lane. One of them gentlemen shot his horse out from under him, but didn't stop him none. Major Kimbrough was with them and maybe Paris, and they all took out after him. I don't know about nobody else.'

Cheney wanted Zag to wait for him, but Zag didn't want to lose the time. Besides, he was afraid that Cheney might be hurt worse than he wished to admit.

He hurried to the coach house, hardly pausing to look at the dead horse that lay in the lane. He quickly found what he wanted: an old knife in a leather sheath, which he tied around his waist. Then, in the darkness of the lane, he stood quietly, listening. There was no one else in sight and hardly a sound; as usual when there was trouble, most people hid behind their closed doors.

Somewhere to the east an owl hooted.

Zag smiled. He was reasonably certain that it was Orion's hoot, meant to guide him. Mr Ash wouldn't know that.

He headed out the lane at a walk that soon turned into an easy lope. He didn't try to make time, didn't make any special effort to catch up with the others. He moved steadily, in an easy rhythm. If need be, he would run all night in this way.

He heard another hoot.

Paris.

Don't you worry, Binnie, honey, he thought, *you ain't going to die. Somebody else. Not you.*

They couldn't beat him.

That was the thing that he clung to, as other men clung to a belief in God. They couldn't beat him.

All right, it was true that his plans for Sabrehill were ruined, but that didn't mean that *he* was beaten. That had been a mere shake of the dice, and there was always a new shake, always new plans, new opportunities. He could still beat them all – and he had proved it! Taken by surprise by two armed men, he had at once put them under his gun. And then, when he could have taken them both out so easily, he had decided to take the girl instead. Just to show them that he could do it and still get away. Defying them! Giving them one more chance to take him.

But they couldn't. They'd never be able to do it.

Hell, they couldn't even knock him out of the saddle, a shot he himself would have found easy. He had landed on his feet, and then had come the running into darkness, Kimbrough on horseback behind him, and still he had got away. Once in the woods, he had been tempted to wait and take old bastard's horse away from him, but it hadn't worked out that way. Somehow he had never found a good opportunity, and anyway he had been too winded. And then Devereau and Buckridge had come on horseback, smashing about through the woods like a herd of elephants, and he had had to lie low. It had seemed like hours that he had listened to them shouting to each other and breaking through the thickets.

The odd thing was that apparently they hadn't had any niggers with them.

Well, they were gone now; they had given up for the night. They would be back after him in the morning, of course. The word would go out, carried on horseback, and every patroller, militiaman, and nigger field hand would have an eye peeled for him.

But they wouldn't see him.

There were 'outliers' who had escaped capture for years, whole maroon communities which had survived in the piney woods and the swamps, and anything a nigger could do, Asher McCloud could do better. As of now, he had permanently vanished from sight.

Not that he intended merely to vanish and survive, he thought, as he looked about, trying to get his bearings. Oh, no. The East was closed to him, of course. He had to leave Virginia and Carolina behind him for good, and no regrets. But there was still Alabama and Mississippi, there was still all of that territory opening up on the other side of the big river, and that was where his future lay – in the West.

That was the way he would head right now, he decided – west. Most likely they'd figure him to head downriver, make his way to Charleston, and get a boat. They wouldn't figure him to head for the sandhills like any nigger outlier. But he was a woodsman, able to travel fast and take care of himself out in the wild country where – he had discovered long ago – there was no god but yourself.

430

He looked for the stars, but the sky was black.

That was all right. He knew, generally, where he was, he knew the way he had come, and he could check his directions by touching the moss on the trunks of live oaks. His fingertips were the arrow of his compass.

To make better time, he left the woods, but skirted them, heading north. He could have followed the river in a westerly direction, but that would have led him too close to the plantation mansions with their dogs that barked in the night. He would stay far from dogs and people until dawn, and then . . .

He hadn't so much as a knife. He would find a weapon of some kind, and then food. Later he might want a horse. He had little money with him – he had left most of his money behind – but he didn't need much. By the time he did, he would have a weapon, and what was the price of a few dollars? A cut throat.

He paused, checked his bearings. Picking a tall tree, barely seen in the night sky, as a marker, he headed west.

He regretted nothing. All of his planning, his scheming, had failed to work out, ruined by mere chance, but still – no regrets. He was still young enough to make a new start in a new place under a new name, and –

Zulie!

The thought of her almost brought a cry from him, and he came to a stumbling halt. Yes, there was that one regret. He had lost everything – why, at least couldn't he have kept her? Just thinking about her was almost enough to make him turn around and go running back toward Sabrehill calling her name.

What had she done to him? He could almost believe in her voodoo love spells. Hell, he could almost believe that niggers and women had souls, even if he lacked one himself. And God knew, it wasn't simply that she had given him the best ride in bed he had ever had. When he was with her, he knew there was a better way to live; he

431

knew that a man and a woman could have something together that he had never before even dreamed of.

'Tell her you want to buy me. Make her sell me. I beg her, she ain't going to make me stay here. We can go to Charleston, find us a house . . .'

For Christ's sake, he thought, in sudden misery, it was true! If he had listened to her, if he had done what she wanted, he wouldn't be out here now, running for his life. He didn't need Sabrehill – he could have sold the place in Virginia and bought some land down here. Bought Zulie from Lucy. Lived with his woman, taken her to Charleston now and then to make her happy, hunted and fished and said the hell with the rest of the world. Other men did it, plenty of them, and he could have too.

But it was too late now. He had thrown all that away.

Somewhere an owl hooted, reminding him that he had to keep moving, but his feet were suddenly heavy. He had to force himself to keep going. Just a few more hours, he told himself, just until the hands started to appear in the fields. Then he would find a resting place. And after a rest, some stolen food, a weapon, perhaps a horse. He'd get away as easily as he had after raiding the Buckridge plantation.

But where was the tree he had picked as a marker?

It was gone now, somehow he had lost it, but that didn't matter. He was still sure of his directions, and he could always find them. He pressed on.

An owl hooted again.

Maybe, he thought, it wasn't too late. There was no need to think like a beaten man. He was getting away with a whole skin, so what was to keep him from sending for Zulie? There were ways to do it. In a matter of days, he would be far from here, and he would soon have money again. Enough money to get a message back to Zulie and to have an agent buy her. And she would come to him, too, because she didn't give a damn for anything in the world but him.

And he for anything but her, if he had only known it.

Christ, he thought, laughing aloud, he could probably go back to Sabrehill and steal her right now! Steal her and take her west with him. And wouldn't that give the bastards something to talk about for the next twenty years!

But that was thinking wildly, of course. He would have loved to do it, but right now he was better off on his own and –

An owl hooted, and another answered.

That was when he knew. And in the heat of the summer night he felt himself freeze.

He had thought there were no blacks out hunting for him. He had thought there were only Devereau, Buckridge, and Kimbrough. But there were others after him now. And they had found him.

There was another soft hoot. To his right. The first sound had been behind him. He plunged straight ahead.

In the brush ahead of him, something cracked.

He came to a halt again and listened. His heart pounded as if it might tear with the strain, and sweat poured stingingly into his eyes. He heard nothing; the night had never been more quiet.

He turned to his left and ran.

He heard them then – not a hooting in the night or the snap of a single twig, but a rushing pursuit to the left, the right, and behind him. There were at least three of them, perhaps more. Well, by God, he swore, it was going to take more. Even without a weapon, he wasn't going down without taking some niggers with him. They would find out . . .

He stopped, gasping for breath. His clothes were plastered to him with sweat, and he felt filthy with grime. He wanted to throw away the lightweight coat he was wearing, but that would make him more visible. The night still might aid him in making an escape.

He started to run again, but, hell, there was no point in letting them wear him down. They were with him, and he was not going to outrun them. When they wanted him, let them come get him – if they could. He kept walking, no longer certain of his direction, scuffing the ground with his boots to find a club or a rock.

It was as if they had been waiting for him.

He no longer heard them. He pushed by some brush and entered a small glade. The night was clearing, but he was halfway across the open space before he saw the dark figure on the other side, watching him.

He stood there, his mouth drying, feeling the strength of anger and desperation come to him.

Zagreus stepped forward. The moon slipped out from behind a cloud, and Ash saw his face clearly. He also saw the knife in the black's hand.

All right. He could take any black, even one with a knife. He would take the knife and slit that nigger's throat, and this time –

He heard them: they were behind him to his left and his right. He tried to turn, tried to beat his way free of them, but he was too slow. Paris had his left arm and was twisting it behind him, and Orion had his right, and suddenly his shoulders and his back were in agony.

The clearing was as bright as if it were daylight. Ash could see the whip mark over Zagreus's eyes and the rope-abrasion on his throat. He kept coming forward, slowly, cautiously, the knife raised, like an artist not yet sure where he will make his first mark.

'For Christ's sake,' Ash said, 'not like this! Give me a knife! Give me a chance!'

He fought the hands that held him. He twisted, turned, bucked – they, by God, would not do this to him. In spite of the pain, he got his left arm down and threw Paris off, kicking, swinging, wrenching free. Then he threw his fist at Orion, but Paris was on his arm again, dragging him down.

434

'*No!*'

No, they could not do this to him. No, he was Asher McCloud, and he could not be beaten. He could not be killed, not yet and not in this way. But Zagreus had seized his shirtfront and was raising the knife –

'Let him be.'

Zagreus, panting, leapt back from him. 'Zulie – '

'Let him be.'

She came out of the surrounding darkness into the brightness of the glade. Ash felt tears of relief pouring down his face. His arms were again twisted tightly behind him, and Zagreus still held his knife high, but that didn't matter. Zulie was here.

'Zulie . . .'

She interposed herself between him and Zagreus. He tried to smile at her, but she didn't smile back. He couldn't tell what the expression on her face meant – sorrow, compassion, hatred.

'Zulie, tell them to let me go. We'll go away together, you and me. I'll take you to New Orleans. You'll like it there, Zulie, better than Charleston. Just tell them, Zulie.'

His words might have been meaningless. 'You killed him,' she said. 'I know now. On account of you, they hung my Zagreus.

Ash stared. Laughed. 'But he isn't dead, Zulie! Look at him! He's as alive as you or me!'

'I brung him back, but you killed him. And likely killed his woman, too.'

'Please, Zulie!'

She shook her head. 'I made promises, I made vows. I put the flour and the cornmeal on the elm tree and burned the candles on its roots. And I made my prayers to Momma Brigitte.' She reached into the front of her dress, reached down toward her waist. 'For all that I got to pay now. And for what you done, you got to pay, too.'

435

'*Zulie!*'

And as he watched, she drew out the eight-inch blade, needle-thin and razor-sharp.

In the middle of the night, the screams began, rolling over the dreaming moonlit fields of Sabrehill to the great mansion overlooking the river. They came in tides and swells of sound, in moans and shrieks and dying wails.

I shouldn't have allowed it, Lucy thought, *I shouldn't have allowed it!* She rolled in her bed and tried to close her ears with her pillow. She braced herself until her jaw ached and tears came to her eyes, but nothing could protect her from those distant screams. *I should have told him no, they mustn't hurt him. I should have stopped it!*

'. . . told your Zagreus they could do anything they damn pleased to him, just so they caught him,' Mr Buckridge had said. 'That man killed my daughter. I take the responsibility . . .'

He was downstairs now, pacing up and down the passage. Paul was in the library, reading, or pretending to. Major Kimbrough had left.

I shouldn't have allowed it . . . didn't know it was going to be like this . . .

After a time, the screams ceased to be human. They rose and fell, great long animal calls, crescendos of pure pain turned into sound. Lucy ached with the effort of trying to force that sound back out of her ears, back out of her soul.

They mustn't . . . no more . . . no more . . .

After an hour she could no longer stand it. She threw herself out of her bed. Without even bothering to pull on a robe, she ran on bare feet from her room and halfway down the stairs into the passage. Mr Buckridge was standing down below in the middle of the passage, his arms across his chest, a seegar in his mouth.

'Mr Buckridge, you've got to stop it!'

Mr Buckridge raised his head. His eyes were feverishly bright and, she thought, happy.

'You say something, Miss Lucy?'

'You've got to stop what they're doing.'

'No. What they're doing is right.'

He's mad, she thought. *We've all gone quite mad.*

'Owen . . .' It was Paul, coming into the passage. His face, usually full, had taken on an almost gaunt look, and his voice was husky with strain. 'Owen, I've asked you, and I ask you again. Isn't this enough?'

'It'll never be enough. Not ever.'

'Well, I think it is, and I'm going out there. I'm going to put a stop – '

'No! This is my affair, Paul, and none of yours. Mine and those niggers'. More ours even than Miss Lucy's. And nobody's going to interfere. I'm putting my honor on that, Paul – my honor and my pistol. You understand?'

Paul nodded. He understood. He turned back toward the library.

'Miss Lucy,' Mr Buckridge said, 'I know this isn't easy for you. Even if he weren't your cousin, it wouldn't be easy. But I think it would be best if you just went back up to bed.'

Lucy said nothing. She didn't trust herself to speak. She thought of looking in on Leila, who was watching over Albinia, but she didn't want to go any further down into the passage, she didn't want to get any closer to Mr Buckridge. She didn't blame him, she didn't blame him for anything, but she wasn't sure that she ever again wanted to be in the same room with him.

She went slowly back up the stairs, closed her door behind her, and slid into bed.

The screaming began again.

A man was dying. Badly.

And I might have loved him, Lucy thought, as she fought her tears. *I really might have loved him.*

She remembered being fifteen and infatuated with a wildly handsome seventeen-year-old boy. She remembered the shooting matches and the horse races over muddy country roads. She remembered the parties, the dancing, the secret dreams of a kiss. And the gallantry, the élan, the gay laughter – the wild hopes for a bright future that would never have an end.

What happened to it all, Ash? Where did it go, all our dreams? What happened to us that we should come to this?

The screams stopped at dawn.

By some instinct, Lucy knew it was all over. Yet she lay stiff in her bed, fists clenched, every muscle aching, waiting, waiting, waiting for the next scream.

Please, Lord, no more. For he was only human, and so am I, and I shall never sleep again.

But it was over. And as the rising sun swept the morning mists from Sabrehill, Miss Lucy slept.

3

She was in the overseer's house with Zulie, looking after Jebediah, when Paul Devereau arrived that Sunday afternoon. Jebediah had very nearly died of his wound, but now, a week later, he seemed to be on the road to recovery. It was odd about Zulie, Lucy thought – that her hands could be so gentle and healing and yet do the cruel things they had done to Ash . . . and, at that, to the man who had been her lover. She found herself, if not actually frightened, somewhat in awe of the young black woman.

'Mr Paul coming,' Zulie said, looking out a window.

Lucy smiled at Jebediah, trying to show him more confidence than she felt. 'Now perhaps we'll know the worst. Wish us luck, Jebediah.'

'Good luck, Miss Lucy.'

She met Paul outside of the office. Her impulse was to cry out for information, but he looked so travel-strained and weary as he slipped down from the saddle that she restrained herself and called for a girl to bring damp towels and a cool pitcher of drinking water.

'One good thing will probably come out of all this, Lucy,' he said as he refreshed himself. 'For a while, at least, your neighbors will probably stop preaching to you about the need for a man at Sabrehill. You got them a man, one they all approved of, and look what happened. But don't think they are going to leave you alone forever.'

'We'll take one day at a time, Paul.'

When he had finished with the towels and the water, he still looked in danger of a heat stroke, and she took him into the mansion passage.

'And now,' she said, as they settled into chairs, 'tell me.'

'I've been doing a lot of hard riding and fast talking. And, while we're not out of the woods yet, we're pretty close to it.'

'Zulie and her brothers?'

'Oh, I was never really worried about them. When Owen Buckridge went out that morning and put two bullets into Ash's body, that settled any question that might have arisen. Your people were merely chasing Asher down for him.'

'Yes, but after what they did to Ash – '

'They did what they were told to do. And keep in mind, Lucy, what Ash and his friends had done to Abigail Buckridge. And, for that matter, to Zagreus's woman. Most people feel that Owen Buckridge had a certain justification in seeing to it that Ash didn't die easily.'

Never, Lucy thought, would she become accustomed to violence. Once she had thought herself hardened, but now she knew she never would be.

'Then you don't think Mr Buckridge will be indicted?'

'If he is, I don't think it'll ever come to trial.'

'And me? Surely most people won't agree that I did the right thing in harboring a suspected murderess.'

Paul shrugged. 'And what are you, Lucy,' he asked sardonically, 'but a lonely woman of great and gentle heart without a man at Sabrehill to guide you? And besides, you knew that Albinia didn't kill Keegan.'

'And how did I know that?'

'For the simple reason that Zagreus, one of your most trusted people, was with her all that night and vouched for her. And who else would have believed two mere Negro slaves? Against Dora Keegan, terrified by the evil Quinn and Harpe into protecting them? Anyway, their testimony against Ash wouldn't be acceptable in a court of law.'

'But Albinia isn't a Negress.'

'You are mistaken, my dear.' From a pocket Paul drew out a folded piece of paper, which he handed to Lucy.

'She is black. How else could I have purchased her on your behalf from Dora Keegan for five hundred dollars?'

Lucy looked at the paper, a receipt for five hundred dollars for the purchase of 'one mulatta Negro female.'

She began to understand. For Albinia's own safety, it was important that she be known as a harmless, frightened little black girl, and not as a white woman who would flee from a murder scene and go to live with a black man. Her very freedom lay in her supposed blackness and her slavery. It was an irony almost too sad to contemplate.

Paul must have seen Lucy's expression. 'It's not as bad as it seems. It just means that Albinia continues her masquerade.'

'Forever, Paul?'

'Not necessarily. In time she'll be forgotten by the people around here. Then you can send her north, if you like, just as you'd planned.'

Perhaps, Lucy thought. Perhaps.

'And what about Dora Keegan?' she asked. 'Is she apt to cause trouble?'

'Not at all. As I said, I rode hard and talked fast. I got to Dora first, and I am now her hero, her savior, her rescuer. Paying her five hundred dollars for the girl went a long way toward convincing her that Albinia really is black and that Quinn and Harpe, as she calls them, killed Keegan. I think she really believes it. After all, she never actually saw the girl do it, and apparently Quinn and Harpe had quarreled with Keegan a good deal. She now says she believes Albinia was frightened into running away and that she had nothing to do with Keegan's death. That will carry a lot of weight.'

'And that murdered man at The Roost that Albinia told us about?'

'He was there, all right. They dug him up. Dora was terrified when she realized that I knew about him, but I assured her that with me as her lawyer, she had little to worry about. She says now that she's been living in fear for her life ever since the first murder happened. Which is probably the truth. Once I had convinced her that Quinn and Harpe were both dead, it was easy to persuade her to call in the authorities, and that will be in her favor.'

'Then we are, as you say, almost out of the woods.'

'Almost.' Paul arose stiffly. 'Albinia will probably have to answer some questions. I'll come back in the morning and coach her.'

Lucy suggested that he stay for supper, but he was eager to get home and rest. 'By the way,' he said at the door, 'I had sketches of Asher and Robert Burnwell. I had no trouble at all in locating several people near The Roost who identified them as Quinn and Harpe. So if you had any last doubts in your mind . . .'

'Oh, I didn't,' Lucy said sadly. 'And I had proof, more or less, that Ash raided the Buckridge plantation.'

Paul looked surprised. 'Proof?'

'Do you remember the pin that Albinia kept wanting to show us? She said that Ash – Mr Quinn – had given it to her?'

'I remember.'

'I thought of it the next day and showed it to Mr Buckridge. He was hardly interested enough to look at it – he didn't need proof – but he said it belonged to Mrs Buckridge. Definitely.'

'I'm glad you told me. Anything that hurts Asher helps you and Albinia.'

'But, Paul, the thing that struck me was that we still hadn't seen the pin when we confronted Ash. We had really nothing concrete to go on. If Ash hadn't shot Albinia, he might have talked his way out of the situation – at least long enough to get away from here.'

'Lucy,' Paul said wearily, 'if Asher hadn't been an arrogant, mean-minded son-of-a-bitch, he would have shot Owen and me instead of the girl. He would have shot us and quite likely made his escape on horseback. But he was what he was, and he did what he did, and he wound up dying only a few hundred yards from this house after wandering about for half the night.' He shook his head. 'And he was a man who might have amounted to something. I remember telling you last fall that Sabrehill reminded me of an Elizabethan tragedy. Where Asher is concerned, I'd say it was more of a Greek tragedy.

'And now if you'll excuse me, Lucy . . .'

Paul left.

No, she thought as she watched him ride around the courtyard and down the avenue of oaks. *No, it's not a tragedy, either Elizabethan or Greek, for most of us. For most of us, Sabrehill is simply the place where we live. It's the place where we work and play and love, if we're lucky, and hate, if we're not. The place where we survive and perhaps dream of something better. And where one day we'll probably be buried.*

She would have to tell the others what Paul had said – first Jebediah and then Zagreus and Albinia. When she reached the overseer's house, she found that Zulie had left, and she was alone with him. She was just as glad. She and Jebediah always had a thousand things to talk about.

'I think, old friend,' she said as she sat down at his bedside, 'I think we are going to be all right.'

'Why, of course, Lucy-child,' Jebediah Hayes said, 'of course we're going to be all right.'

Would he ever forget that terrible night? Would he ever cease to dream of it? Even now he could feel the stickiness of the blood on his hands, he could feel it spurt against his face and his chest. The room over the coach house was quiet and clean and so distant from that night, and Miss Lucy's low musical voice was soft and reassuring, but Zag found it hard to take in what she was saying. Binnie, in bed, and Zulie, standing quietly by a window, seemed to be listening intently to Miss Lucy, but his own mind kept drifting away, kept drifting back . . .

'*Zulie!*'

He remembered Mr Ash's sharp cry, and then the look on his face – horror and disbelief – as Zulie took out her knife. Earlier the night had been dark, but once the moon was out, he could see every detail clearly.

'You can't! You won't! You love me, Zulie!'

'That don't count for nothing now. Zagreus, take his clothes off. All of them.'

Mr Ash struggled, but he had no chance of escaping. Once, when he almost tore loose, Zag hit him solidly in the stomach, doubling him over. There had been a time when he wouldn't have dared even to think of touching a white man, but now he took cold furious pleasure in what he was doing to Mr Ash. Hitting him. Ripping off his clothes with a knife. Humiliating him.

While Mr Ash sobbed: 'You can't, you can't, you can't!'

'Put him down on his back,' Zulie said, when he was naked.

They did as she ordered; everything was done to her orders. Paris knelt on Mr Ash's wrists, while Zag and Orion hung onto his legs, and Zulie went to work.

She worked on his head first, and for a time there wasn't much blood. Zag welcomed the first screams. He remembered Binnie's screams as she had been dragged naked toward the barn. He remembered her screams as they had fitted the noose around his neck and begun hoisting him up. He thought of her now, back at the big house, dying or perhaps dead. *Scream, you white bastard, scream!*

Mr Ash screamed.

He died at dawn.

There was a little mist on the land as the sun came up. Paris and Orion had long since departed, sickened by what they were doing, and Zag had been kept going only by thoughts of Binnie and by Zulie's goading, driving words: 'You know what he done. And tonight somebody got to die!' Now he and Zulie sat there for a few minutes, exhausted, knowing that there would be no more screams. When they saw Mr Buckridge coming through the trees, they got up and walked slowly away.

They heard the two pistol shots behind them.

They found a stream and washed away the blood, never looking at each other, never saying a word. Zag felt a kind of deep shame, such as he had never known before. He didn't know why he should feel it, he had only done what had seemed necessary at the time, but it was there.

When they arrived back at the big house, they found that Binnie was still alive. She opened her eyes and smiled at Zag.

Since then, there had been the dreams, which seemed never completely to leave him, even when he was awake. Dreams of that poor red rag of a body which had once been a man.

Zag looked around the room. Miss Lucy and Zulie had left, and he had hardly even noticed.

'Zagreus,' Binnie said.

'Yes, Binnie.'

'Come here.'

He went to the side of the bed.

'Sit down, Zagreus.'

He sat down, facing her, on the edge of the bed.

'I know what's troubling you,' she said.

'Ain't nothing troubling me, honey.'

'Oh, yes, there is. Zulie told me what you and her and your brothers done. What you done and why you done it.'

'Only what had to be done. Least, we thought so. Wouldn't have done nothing no different.'

'I know you wouldn't.' She reached up and stroked his head. 'Poor Zagreus. Never wanted to hurt nobody in his life. Never held no grudges, even when they put a scar on his face. Never wanted nothing but to make hisself some kind of a life. That's all. Ain't much to ask. Just some kind of a life. Ain't that right?'

'That's right, Binnie.'

'Well, you want to know something?'

'What's that?'

'I got anything to say about it, you going to have your life.'

Zag tried to smile.

'No, I mean it, Zagreus. Maybe we ain't got much compared to some folks, but we going to take what we got and make something grand out of it. Something truly grand.'

'Binnie, don't you realize that you are a slave now, the same as me? And you ain't even white no more, you're just another nigger?'

'No, I don't. Cause them words don't mean nothing to me no more. All I know is, you're my man, and I'm your woman, and I'm Albinia Sabrehill, which is the finest name a gal ever had. And I'm going to try to make it so you never have another unhappy day all the rest of your life.'

She was such a child, he thought, as he took her into his arms. After all she had been through, it was as if she had learned absolutely nothing.

But if that were true, why was he suddenly so happy?

You went on.

You went on because you were black and a slave, and that was all you could do. And maybe there would never be a Charleston, with a big house and fine clothes and servants and a carriage. Maybe you and your brothers would never be free from Sabrehill, but . . . somehow you went on.

And you dreamed. Most of the black people you knew lost their dreams, if they ever had any in the first place. But you kept yours. You had to, because if you didn't you

446

would die. That was the way you were made. You had to plan, you had to hope, because otherwise you might just as well throw a rope over the same stout beam where they had hung Zagreus and hang yourself in his place.

Some black folks did that.

Mr Ash, she thought. *Mr Ash is dead. Mr Ash is a dead dream.*

There was no Mr Ash, she thought, as she walked out into the lengthening shadows of the late afternoon. There was no Mr Ash, and there never had been. Because of some joke of the gods, she had loved him, but now she must put him out of her heart and mind as if he had never existed. There was no Mr Ash.

Then what did she have left?

She walked through the fields, a tall young woman with broad shoulders and long legs. Barefoot. A yellow kerchief around her small, neat head. She walked until she came to a very special tree. It was a gnarled old oak, its trunk so bent that one could almost walk up it as up an ascending path. She climbed the tree until she came to a spread of branches where she could sit as comfortably as if she had been in an armchair. This was her dreaming tree, and she had come here for as long as she could remember.

Mr Ash is dead, she thought as she settled into her place. *Ain't no Mr Ash. But Zagreus is all right, and he got his Binnie. So what is there for me?*

From her place in the tree, she could look far out across the fields. She could watch the sunset begin to glow pink in the west, and she could smell the faint breeze, rich with the scent of late-summer green.

Who going to take me to Charleston now? Who going to carry me away from Sabrehill? Send me a sign, Lord. Send me a sign, spirits. Who?

A gray-brown mourning dove fluttered down and landed on a branch of the tree. Then Zulie saw that there was a second one, and after a moment the pair flew off together.

Zulie smiled.

Was it possible?

She had never really believed that he existed. He was just a made-up story. Something to keep people happy and excited. No, it was not possible.

Still, a person needed a dream of some kind. A person could hardly live without one. So that would be hers.

She would make magic, cast spells.

'Come, Adaba,' she whispered, and the breeze carried her words away; who could tell where they might go? 'Come, Adaba. Come, oh, Brown Dove. Oh, come . . . come . . .'

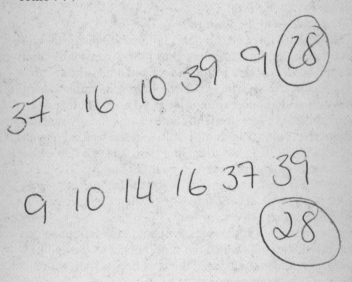